Out of the corner of ~~ing down the alley, lean~~
than anything that sma~~creature that was attacking me,~~ it started up with a frenzied snarling interspersed with rapid high-pitched barks, then sank its teeth into the creature's spindly back leg. The thing whipped around with dismaying speed, and the dog instantly released its grip and threw itself onto its back. The monster hesitated, then swiveled back toward me. The minute it did, the dog was at him again, snarling and growling like a crazed rottweiler. This time, though, the thing lunged for him, scary fast. But the dog was even faster. He was back up on his feet quick as thought, making a dash for the safety of a small crack where two of the buildings didn't quite come together.

The creature turned back toward me again, but the respite had given me a chance to take stock of things. I stepped forward, gathered some energy, used the unnatural cold and coupled it with the smell of garbage faintly hanging over the alley. Then I wove in the angle of the dog's head sticking out of the crack. I reached out and formed a fist.

"Freeze," I said, conversationally.

It stopped in midturn. Before it could shake itself free, I spun on my heel and faced away.

"Reverse," I said, then turned back to face it.

It started trembling, its outline wavering and dissolving into tiny droplets of color that swirled around aimlessly for a time. I let out a huge sigh and looked over toward the crack between buildings. The small dog edged out warily from his refuge.

"Louie," I said. "What took you so long?"

Praise for *Dog Days*

"Jazz, scotch, and dark magic. It's all waiting around every unfamiliar corner and at the end of every shadowed alley in a world that has both bark *and* bite. The supernatural lives, breathes, and slithers in a San Francisco where the dog days don't just get you down, they eat you alive."
            —Rob Thurman, author of *Nightlife* and *Moonshine*

. . . and for John Levitt's previous novels as J. R. Levitt

"A new guy on the block who is clearly a writer to watch. This is a fast-moving, compulsive read with an unforgettable climax. You're going to like this one a lot."
            —Stephen King

"Introduces an author of rare ability and a background that provides authentic details of police work . . . a rave-worthy mystery."
            —*Publishers Weekly*

"[*Carnivores* is] a fine novel that constantly surprises."
            —*Booklist*

DOG DAYS

JOHN LEVITT

ACE BOOKS, NEW YORK

THE BERKLEY PUBLISHING GROUP
Published by the Penguin Group
Penguin Group (USA) Inc.
375 Hudson Street, New York, New York 10014, USA
Penguin Group (Canada), 90 Eglinton Avenue East, Suite 700, Toronto, Ontario M4P 2Y3, Canada
(a division of Pearson Penguin Canada Inc.)
Penguin Books Ltd., 80 Strand, London WC2R 0RL, England
Penguin Group Ireland, 25 St. Stephen's Green, Dublin 2, Ireland (a division of Penguin Books Ltd.)
Penguin Group (Australia), 250 Camberwell Road, Camberwell, Victoria 3124, Australia
(a division of Pearson Australia Group Pty. Ltd.)
Penguin Books India Pvt. Ltd., 11 Community Centre, Panchsheel Park, New Delhi—110 017, India
Penguin Group (NZ), 67 Apollo Drive, Rosedale, North Shore 0632, New Zealand
(a division of Pearson New Zealand Ltd.)
Penguin Books (South Africa) (Pty.) Ltd., 24 Sturdee Avenue, Rosebank, Johannesburg 2196, South Africa

Penguin Books Ltd., Registered Offices: 80 Strand, London WC2R 0RL, England

This is a work of fiction. Names, characters, places, and incidents either are the product of the author's imagination or are used fictitiously, and any resemblance to actual persons, living or dead, business establishments, events, or locales is entirely coincidental. The publisher does not have any control over and does not assume any responsibility for author or third-party websites or their content.

DOG DAYS

An Ace Book / published by arrangement with the author

PRINTING HISTORY
Ace mass-market edition / November 2007

Copyright © 2007 by John Levitt.
Cover art by Don Sipley.
Cover design by Annette Fiore-DeFex.
Interior text design by Kristin del Rosario.

ISBN: 978-0-441-01553-5

ACE
Ace Books are published by The Berkley Publishing Group,
a division of Penguin Group (USA) Inc.,
375 Hudson Street, New York, New York 10014.
ACE and the "A" design are trademarks belonging to Penguin Group (USA) Inc.

PRINTED IN THE UNITED STATES OF AMERICA

10 9 8 7 6 5 4 3 2 1

ACKNOWLEDGMENTS

I'd like to especially thank my agent, Caitlin Blasdell, for her overall help and invaluable assistance with the manuscript, and of course, my wonderful editor at Ace, the ever-helpful Jessica Wade.

Thanks also to Alan Beatts, bookseller *extraordinaire* of Borderlands Books in San Francisco, for his unfailing support and sage advice.

ONE

WE'D JUST FINISHED UP THE LAST SET, AND IT WAS late. I was tired, so I didn't stay around long, just packed up my guitar and headed out. I had landed a sweet gig at Rainy Tuesdays with the Tommy Willis Quartet, courtesy of a bad flu bug that had knocked out Cal Simmons, Tommy's regular. The gig was booked through the weekend, and I could just leave my amp at the club, thank God. I didn't feel up to hauling it down the street or waiting for a ride to where my van was parked.

There weren't many late-nighters on the street by the time I left—even in San Francisco a lot of people have to get up for jobs in the morning. I had parked my van several blocks away over on Valencia, and I cut through Clarion Alley to save a few steps. Clarion is a narrow passageway that runs between Mission and Valencia, the site of a neighborhood arts project that's been ongoing the last few years. Brightly colored murals adorn the sides of buildings and enliven the fronts of wooden garage doors. Some are political in content and style, vaguely reminiscent of old Soviet Union revolutionary art. Some look like children's

drawings. Quite a few are done in comic book graphic design: a cartoon face angrily hovering over a toon town city,
cartoon bears frolicking in the grass, a wormlike elf, a
malevolent leprechaun. Along one long sky blue wall, stylized blackbirds plastered themselves in panicky flight.

I was halfway down the alley before I noticed how quiet
it had become. Too quiet, I thought, recalling every black-
and-white grade B movie I had ever seen on TV growing
up. It wasn't so much the silence as it was the *quality* of the
silence. Sharp, crystalline. Like high mountains on a winter's night when the stars are cold and bright and you can
hear a dog quietly barking five miles off. Definitely not
normal. Somebody was doing something and it didn't feel
friendly.

I stopped, set down my guitar case, and quietly backed
up against the side of a brick building. It was suddenly
cold, not that damp San Francisco cold, but clear and crisp,
like the silence. I took a couple of deep breaths and my
breath plumed out like steam. It's not easy to prepare for
an attack when you have absolutely no idea what form it
may take. All you can really do is relax, try to blank out
your mind, and wait. It's kind of a Zen warrior thing. If you
start wondering what's about to happen, start casting
around for possibilities and making plans, you're in trouble. Nothing will get you killed faster than preconception.

As I waited, the mural directly across from me caught
my eye. It was another cartoonish figure, a red spidery
creature with a ridiculous plump body and absurd tentacle
limbs, topped by an oversized head. The head was vaguely
wolflike, with sharklike cartoon teeth dripping cartoon
blood. It wasn't altogether clear whether the artist had intended the creature to be scary or funny. He probably
didn't even know himself, but in the faint glow of a distant
streetlight at 2:00 a.m., scary was definitely winning out.

But what concerned me most about it was its unusual
texture. The painted figure on the wall started to shimmer
like an oil slick gently moving on the surface of a pond. It
undulated in a rhythmic, pulsating fashion, becoming

clearer and more three-dimensional with every pulse. Finally it detached itself from the surface of the brick, wavered insubstantially for a moment, then coalesced into a solid, three-dimensional creature. Lifting up its head, it swayed slowly from side to side, sniffing the cold air. It was the size of a smallish tiger and although I could see right through it to the wall behind, it still looked concrete enough to tear off my head without any bother.

Actually, this was a pretty simple conjuration. Animating the inanimate is one of the basics in anyone's bag of tricks who possesses talent, although animating a two-dimensional painting was a neat wrinkle I hadn't seen before. If I'd had a minute or two to consider my options, I could have easily dealt with it. The problem was, I didn't have a minute or two. It scurried over toward me in ghastly silence, scuttling crablike on tentacle legs, quicker than I cared to see. The thing to do was quietly slip away, give myself enough time and space to regroup, and then efficiently take care of the problem. Unfortunately, I had cleverly backed myself against a brick wall. It wasn't about to let me leave and I wasn't quick enough to get around it without losing several important body parts.

Now, I'm good at inventing spells and manipulating my surroundings. Everyone has their strengths and weaknesses, and my strength is the ability to cast on the fly, so to speak. It's not that easy; you have to take into account all the variables—the time, the weather, the physical surroundings, emotions, sounds—everything. You bind them all together, weave them into a gestalt, draw on your reserves of energy, and try to come up with something that works. The foundation each time may be similar, but it's never exactly the same spell twice, because the situation is never exactly the same. It's a lot like jazz that way. And like jazz, it does require some talent to pull it off.

The stasis hanging over the alley was making it difficult, though. It didn't leave me much to work with. Whoever had set this in motion obviously knew me well enough to understand how I worked and the best way to deaden my particular abilities. I reached back and ran my fingers along the rough brick wall behind me, testing the texture. I noted the exact color of the thing rushing up sideways toward me. I felt the slight irregularities of the asphalt under my feet. Then I let out some potential and yanked at the blackbirds painted on the wall next to me, hoping at least to buy time with a diversion. They didn't look capable of doing much else. The birds shimmered briefly and then slid down the wall like refrigerator magnets that had lost their charge. They lay there flapping weakly until they all disintegrated into an oily sludge. Not one of my better efforts.

By this time the creature was right up on me, jaws gaping, two feet from my face. I muttered a couple of syllables, reached down as if I were opening a sliding window, and let out some more potential. The thing slammed into the shield I had managed to raise, barely twelve inches in front of me. It paused a moment, staring at me with huge yellow cartoon eyes, and exhaled noisily. I could see its breath misting in the frigid air, splashing against the invisible shield. I felt like one of the three little piggies, and not the one with the brick cottage. The shield started to dissolve like cellophane when a lit cigarette is pressed against it. I realized I was in over my head.

Out of the corner of my eye, I saw something the size of a large cat speeding down the alley, silent and purposeful. It was a small dog, lean and torpedo shaped, moving faster than anything that small has a right to. As it reached us, it started up with a frenzied snarling interspersed with rapid high-pitched barks, then sank its teeth into the spindly back leg of the creature. The thing whipped around with dismaying speed, and the dog instantly released its grip and threw itself onto its back, emitting a series of high-pitched squeals like a wounded piglet. The monster hesitated, then swiveled back toward me. The minute it did, the dog was at him again, snarling and growling like a crazed rottweiler. The creature turned again, and the dog repeated the exact same behavior, throwing itself down on its back in total submission, squealing piteously. This time though the thing lunged for him, scary fast, but the dog was even faster. He was back up on his feet quick as thought, making a dash for the safety of a small crack where two of the buildings didn't quite come together. The thing's teeth snapped together an inch or so behind a tail that was rapidly being curled between the dog's legs. It turned back toward me again, but the respite had given me a chance to take stock of things. Plus, the intrusion of the dog had given me a lot more to work with. I could see his head poking out from between the buildings, looking on with great interest. I stepped forward, gathered some energy, used the unnatural cold and coupled it with the smell of garbage faintly hanging over the alley. Then I wove in the angle of the dog's head sticking out of the crack. I reached out and formed a fist.

"Freeze," I said, conversationally.

It stopped in midturn. Before it could shake itself free, I spun on my heel and faced away.

"Reverse," I said, then turned back to face it.

It started trembling, its outline wavering and dissolving into tiny droplets of color that swirled around aimlessly for a time. The colored mist splattered against the building, blurred momentarily, and coalesced into the original cartoon, once again safely spread out on the building wall. I let out a huge sigh and looked over toward the crack between buildings. The small dog wormed his way out from the opening. He was black and tan, black with small tan marks over his eyes, a tan patch on his chest and muzzle, and tan paws. If you took a Doberman, left his ears and tail uncropped, shrunk him down to twelve pounds or so and thinned out his muzzle to a fine sharpness, you would have this dog. He edged out warily from his refuge and immediately sat up in a begging position, apparently waiting for a doggie treat.

"Louie," I said. "What took you so long?" I patted my front pockets. "Sorry. I forgot to bring the bacon." His ears drooped slightly. "You did good, though," I added, picking up my guitar case. "Let's go home."

He wagged his tail in acknowledgment and trotted off down the alley in front of me.

THE NEXT MORNING (TECHNICALLY 11:45 A.M. IS still morning) I was having my usual breakfast of black coffee. Breakfast is the most important meal of the day and coffee is the most important part of the meal. I just cut out the middleman. I live in a small in-law apartment in the Mission, a converted garage, really, but it has a small bed-room that I turned into a music studio, adequate kitchen, and a large space that doubles as a living and sleeping room. A small garden in the back provides some greenery in the midst of city concrete. The only problem is that the bed is near the open kitchen and I can never cook anything Indian or the bedsheets smell of curry for days.

Best of all, there is a narrow driveway I can park my van in. Parking in San Francisco, especially for an apartment dweller, is worth more than gold. Plus, it's relatively cheap and the landlord who lives upstairs is away two months out of three.

Blond wood paneling throughout gives it a homey feel, and the walls slope at different angles like a ship's cabin. When the wind blows in those San Francisco winter storms I can hear the upper part of the house creaking like a ship at sea. It is old, it is small, and it suits me fine. I had in-stalled a cat door in the back so Louie could come and go as he pleased. Considering the events of last night, it was just as well I had.

I cooked up a mess of bacon for Lou's breakfast. I can't imagine anything worse for a dog, but I owed him. Not that he's exactly a dog. Well, he is, but he isn't. I don't know just what he is; none of us do. All I knew was that if you had the talent and were very, very lucky, sometimes one would find you. Sometimes they turn up on the doorstep; sometimes they follow you home. I know one practitioner who stopped his car for a red light and one jumped in through the open passenger-side window.

Mostly they seem to be cats, which is probably where the idea of the witches' familiar comes from. Louie, being a dog, is kind of unusual. I've heard of ferrets and even a skunk, but I've never met one. Few are larger than a good-sized cat, which is the reason dogs are so atypical. It's too bad; Louie is great, but if he'd been the size of a full-grown Doberman life would have been a lot easier for both of us.

We call them Ifrits, after the Djinn of legend, but the truth is none of us know what they are or where the hell they come from. But they're not common. Most practitioners never find one. Maybe one in five, or even less, have the luck. It doesn't seem to matter how powerful you are, or how talented, or even whether you're a decent person or not. I'm sure Ifrits have their reasons as to who they hook up with, but what those reasons might be is anybody's guess. I was one of the lucky ones—about seven years ago, Louie strolled into a club where I was playing, looked at me, hopped up on the amplifier, curled his tail around his paws, and that was that.

They seem to live about as long as humans, which is convenient. They never switch practitioners. If someone with an Ifrit dies, you never see that Ifrit again. And on rare occasions, again for reasons we don't fathom, an Ifrit will simply up and leave. When they do, that's it. I've never heard of one ever turning up again. It's as traumatic for the practitioner as it would be to lose a child. Some never recover. It's not something I like to think about.

But the important thing, at least for those of us they hang with, is that they all possess a nearly infallible antenna for danger, coupled with a blinding loyalty that is mostly undeserved. Louie has an almost supernatural ability—I guess I should leave out the "almost"—to sense danger long before I even have a ghost of a clue.

Lou has other unexpected talents. I don't think most practitioners recognize the true potential of an Ifrit. They accept them as special—wonderful magical companions, certainly more than pets—and more loyal than the best friend you ever had. But I think Ifrits are more than that. Unless it's just Lou. He is different from other Ifrits. Take last night—he must have picked up on whatever was happening in the alley the minute I started walking down it. My apartment is at least two miles from the alley and he covered that distance in under five minutes. Usually all that he needs to do is to warn me of impending trouble. This time he'd actually had to do something about it. This morning, he looked smug. Of course, a dog eating bacon will always look smug, but today he definitely had an extra swagger.

There was one thing he couldn't help me with, though. What was that whole thing last night about? I'd been keeping a low profile the last few years, ever since I'd quit the enforcement squad. Five years had been enough. Even when I was working with them I'd never got into anything really heavy. More like, "Hey, don't do that again," than anything else. I had no enemies, at least no more than anyone else. Certainly not enough to account for last night. That wasn't someone trying to scare me or teach me a lesson. That was someone who wanted me dead.

I had no information to work with, so I put it out of my mind. The very thought of how much work and hassle it was going to take to figure it out made me tired. I didn't feel like going out, especially since the house of a practitioner is about as safe a place as he or she is going to find.

At about two the mailman shoved a bunch of letters through the mail slot by the side of the door. They scattered over the floor and when I picked them up, the only interesting thing was a postcard invitation to a party in North Beach from Pascal. As usual, he added a P.S., "Be there or be square." He thought it was funny. Pascal was well into his seventies, old enough so that not only did he not use e-mail, he didn't even like the telephone. He liked sending postcards. The only trouble was that half the time his invitations arrived after the party was over. It didn't really matter though; people always managed to get the word. This one was for tomorrow night. Ordinarily I would go, since there were always interesting people at his affairs, a nice mix of musicians, practitioners, Starbucks barristas, and politicos. And young women. Always women. But of course, I had a gig.

I spent the rest of the afternoon practicing scales, something I rarely do, but for once it was soothing. At nine I headed out to Rainy Tuesdays. I still had to make a living, and you can't bail on a gig just because of personal problems. Besides, I felt like playing. I briefly considered taking Louie along, but naturally they don't allow dogs in the club, and I could hardly explain that he wasn't *exactly* a dog.

Rainy Tuesdays is a new upscale club in the Mission that is trying to establish itself as a premier jazz spot. As a result, they pay some decent money, at least for San Francisco, and Tommy Willis had landed a regular weekend gig. Tommy knew he could count on me to replace Cal. That's one of the good things about jazz—if one of the band members flakes out, you don't have to cancel the gig—you just plug in a replacement and forge ahead. Of course, the better the group, the harder it is to find a player with the chops and talent to cut it.

Luckily for Tommy, I was good. In fact, I was better than Cal Simmons, his regular, and Tommy and I both knew it. But I do have two drawbacks—I don't like to practice and I get bored easily. The longest I'd ever played with one set of musicians was about six months, and there was a sense of mutual relief when I left.

I do make a great fill-in, though. I hate to brag (actually I don't) but there's a good reason I'm the first call for any jazz group in San Francisco that needs a guitar player to fill in. I know just about every standard by heart, sight read like a clarinet player, and can play most anything by ear after hearing it once. And as a result, I actually earn enough money from gigs to avoid having a day job.

Rainy Tuesdays is a nice space—small enough to connect with the crowd; big enough, hopefully, to survive fi-

nancially. It has a lot of small tables, a big curved bar with
a black leather rail at one end, and a killer sound system,
all wrapped up in an industrial retro look. A small stage
rests in the middle of the main room, lodged against the
back wall, raised maybe half a foot. There's room for close
on two hundred people and tonight it was half-full. They
say that jazz is making a comeback in San Francisco, but I
think the jury is still out on that one.

I got to the club about nine thirty and found a parking
spot a lot closer than I had the night before, half into a red
zone, but if I got a ticket so be it. I had no intention of
walking through the late-night streets after what had happened.

We were set up and ready to play by ten, about standard
for clubs these days. Apparently people who go out to hear
music don't have day jobs. Or maybe it's because nobody
sleeps much anymore. We got through the first set in fine
style. Tommy, who certainly is a monster on alto even if he
is a geek, had stretched out on "Giant Steps" and wowed
the crowd. That was great for him, but that's the problem
playing with a band where the leader is a horn player. All
of his showcase tunes, including his originals, are nightmares for a guitar player. Still, Tommy was the draw, a real
up-and-comer. The crowd certainly hadn't come because I
was on the bill, so I guess it was only fair that he play
whatever tunes made him sound the best.

After the set ended I wiped down my guitar and headed
toward the bar. I don't usually drink when I'm playing a serious gig—it helps you relax but it also tends to make your
playing sloppy. I picked up a Calistoga water and leaned
back against the leather rail, surveying the crowd. Most of
them were twentysomethings, younger than the usual jazz
crowd, which was nice. Maybe jazz really is making a
comeback. Several of them stopped by to compliment me
on my playing. Actually, I wasn't at my best that night what
with worrying and all, but I long ago learned to simply say,
"Thanks. Glad you enjoyed it."

When I first started playing out, there were times when

I knew I was playing like crap. When I got the "Gosh, loved your playing" speech, I had to bite my tongue to keep from saying back, "Really? I thought I sucked," or, "You don't know much about jazz, do you?" It finally came to me that those who had ears were simply being polite and I should probably do the same. And to those who didn't, well, a cynical response is just flat-out insulting.

Most of the jazz buffs drifted away and I was left chatting with Manny, the bass player, and idly scanning the room. On one wall hung the club logo: raindrops and a stylized umbrella done in blue neon tubing, very hip. Right underneath, at one of the small round tables, sat an attractive young woman. She was playing abstractedly with her hair, which was wavy dark with purple highlights, shoulder length. She wore no jewelry except for a thin silver band on the third finger of her right hand. I could see it as she fussed with her hair. Slim, medium height, dressed midway between casual and stylish in soft Levi's and a black top. An interesting face, not exactly beautiful, but close enough.

She was sitting alone, which is no easy feat for an attractive woman in a nightclub. Rainy Tuesdays, unlike a lot of clubs, is a place where most of the crowd actually comes to hear the music. But there are always those who are mainly there to try to hook up, who could care less who or what is playing, even with a cover charge and drinks at seven bucks a pop. I noticed one of those types easing his way toward her table. She looked up briefly and glanced at him, not hostile, but cold. I could feel the chill all the way across the room. The guy kind of stumbled, recovered, and made a smooth sideways escape, heading toward the bathrooms as if he had never had any other destination in mind. Manny had been watching along with me, and he glanced at me out of the corner of his eye.

"Wow," he said, lifting off heavy black-framed glasses and peering nearsightedly at me.

"Go ahead, you hit on her," I encouraged. "You don't really need those balls of yours anymore, do you?" He gave me a raspberry and wandered off in search of more agreeable company.

I picked up my bottle of water and headed over toward her table. When I had almost reached it, she looked up. Her eyes, a light gray, reflected a grave expression with just a hint of a smile behind them. There was no coldness there, no indeed. Instead, I glimpsed a warmth and spirit and depth that took my breath away. Nothing sexual, but something even more seductive, the feeling of instant rapport you sometimes get with another person, the feeling that here is someone you might actually be able to spend your life with, an instant connection of compassion and understanding. And underneath, right below the surface, a faint sensuality hovering, just waiting to be ignited into raging passion by precisely the right person. I stood there for a moment luxuriating in the feeling and then, regretfully, made a quick hand gesture and a sort of a cough. Her features blurred, and then there was nothing more than an attractive woman sitting at a table. I kissed her cheek, pulled up a chair and sat down across from her.

"Sherwood," I said. "Very nice, very nice indeed."

"I've been practicing," she said. "Remember, the last time I tried sending? You told me I could look forward to a promising career as a high priced hooker. I'm working on being a little more subtle."

"Very nice," I repeated. "Textured. Very three-dimensional. Of course, you've got a solid foundation to work with." She leaned back in her chair and regarded me warily.

"Was that a compliment or a dig?" she asked. "It's not always easy to tell with you, Mason."

"Just the facts, ma'am."

She laughed. "You know, if it didn't take so much energy to maintain the illusion, I might be able to keep a boyfriend for more than a few months."

"Speaking as a few months guy, that pretty much goes without saying for all of us."

"We lasted, what, almost a year?"

I nodded. "Probably a record for both of us."

We sat there for a while without saying anything. I wouldn't say that it was an entirely comfortable silence, but we hadn't parted on bad terms. It was just a little odd. I hadn't seen Sherwood for about a year now, and although she liked jazz well enough, I knew she hadn't come down to the club just to hear the music. I finally broke the silence.

"Not a coincidence, is it?" I said.

"What?"

"You showing up tonight."

She gave me a look, half-innocent, half-quizzical. "Something I should know about?"

I shrugged. "Is there something *I* should know about?" I countered.

She shook her head resignedly, a habit I remembered well. "My, but aren't we cryptic tonight?"

"Sorry," I said. "Somebody tried to kill me last night. It tends to make one a bit testy."

The look on her face told me a lot. There was concern there, but not surprise. So, her being here wasn't coincidence at all. Great, this was just what I needed. Something complicated. She reached across the table and placed her hand on top of mine.

"A mugger?" she asked hopefully.

I shook my head. "No such luck."

"What then?"

"I don't have the time to go into it right now," I said, "but it wasn't exactly run of the mill."

She nodded slowly. "Actually, that's why I came down here tonight. Not that I knew anything had happened to you, but there's been a lot of 'not run of the mill' going around lately. I know how you feel about Victor, but I think you might want to talk to him."

I looked at her without expression. "Couldn't I just opt for a trip to the dentist instead?"

"Come on, he's not that bad."

"Oh? Compared to who?"

Her face took on that familiar long-suffering expression

that I seem to elicit from a lot of people. "Why do you have to have such a thing about him?" she asked, tiredly.

I took a sip of my water, put my elbows on the table, and thought about it.

"Well, let me see. First of all, he's a control freak. He's a great believer in keeping the magical world in check so that it doesn't run roughshod over the rest of society, which is fine, but when he regards himself as the head honcho of—what did we call it?"

Sherwood chuckled. "The MBI—Magical Bureau of Investigation. But not within earshot of Victor."

"No, he doesn't have much of a sense of humor, does he?" Another strike against him. Victor holds firmly to the belief that life is a very, very serious matter, and everyone should act accordingly at all times.

"Well, maybe if you hadn't made that joke about Wilson . . ."

Sherwood was referring to a particularly ill-advised comment I'd once made about a practitioner who had accidentally turned himself inside out during a spell gone awry.

"How was I to know Wilson was a friend of his," I said, defensively. "But I don't like the way he pretends to be in charge, either. We all know Eli's really in charge. If it weren't for the fact that Victor is able to finance everything, since he has more money than God, Eli wouldn't put up with his airs for a moment."

"You're not the boss of me," Sherwood muttered just loud enough for me to hear. I didn't rise to the bait.

"I don't think that's entirely true," she continued. "Victor does make a great chief of staff, you know. And Eli may have the final say on things, but you'll notice he never uses it. I love him dearly, and he's brilliant, but he's not what you would call . . . grounded, is he now? Without Victor there wouldn't be any enforcement."

She was right. As usual. Eli is liable to go off into theoretical speculation at inappropriate times, like when someone is trying to kill him. He spends much of his free time working on what he calls his "special project." I don't know exactly what it is, but I would bet it has absolutely no practical application. So he needs someone like Victor. Technically, Eli is in charge, but much as I hate to admit it, the reality is that Victor runs things. That's one of the reasons we don't get along. I do have a problem with authority.

"Okay," I said. "Whatever. Does Victor have to refer to us as a 'strike force,' though?"

Our job had been to ensure that those practitioners without a moral compass of their own were still required to walk the straight and narrow. Mostly it was just stuff like reining in low-level talents who use their powers to run scams on the unsuspecting, but once in a while some truly dangerous situations come up.

And although I'd never admit it to Sherwood, in a lot of ways, I actually do respect Victor. Some remarkably unpleasant people roam the world, many of whom possess considerable reserves of talent. Some of them are even into what is commonly termed "black magic," although that's mostly for show, and dealing with those types takes a lot of balls, not to mention some major ability. Victor was born to the job. Somebody has to play cop and keep the bad guys in line, and better him than me.

"Anyway, most of it's your fault," I said.

Sherwood choked on her drink, though whether from indignation or laughter I couldn't tell.

"Of course it is," she said mildly. "But how so?"

"You two were close friends before Eli recruited me, remember? Then, after a while, when Victor's anal retentive side got to be too much even for you, things between you cooled off and he blamed me for the change."

"He does think you were a bad influence on me."

"Fair enough, since I think *he's* the bad influence."

Sherwood sat silently for a couple of seconds, staring down and idly stirring her drink, then looked up and said, "By the way, Vaughan was killed last week."

I sat up straight, not sure I was hearing right. "Vaughan? Vaughan Harris? Our Vaughan?"

She nodded, studying my face. I couldn't believe it. We hadn't been close, but Vaughan was the smartest, the quickest, and probably the most skilled of all the enforcers. This was not good at all.

"What happened?" I asked.

Sherwood shrugged and made a palms up, fingers spread gesture with her hands. "You really ought to talk with Victor about it. I've been away and don't know the entire story."

"He couldn't bother to come down in person?"

"He thought I might have better luck."

"Nobody ever said Victor was stupid."

Sherwood laughed, but without much humor. "Yeah. Well, Eli really wants you to come by, too."

"Oh," I said. That was a different matter.

I glanced over toward the bandstand and caught Tommy signaling impatiently with little hand gestures.

"I've got to play another hour or so," I told her. "Can you wait?"

She nodded. "Of course."

I stood up to leave and she reached out and put her hand on my arm. She paused, looked down for half a second, and when she looked up the shimmer was back, playing over her face.

"Loved your playing," she breathed adoringly.

"Yeah, you suck, too," I said, and ambled back to the stage.

Tommy started off with a slow blues, which gave me time to think. He gave me a couple of sideways glances to let me know he could tell I was just phoning it in, but I ignored him. You can't always be at the top of your game.

I'd met Sherwood some years back. She is a practitioner of course, working with Victor, and I had been brought in to join the team. I only lasted a couple of years before I finally got fed up with it and went back to playing music exclusively. It just wasn't me.

In the old days, anybody possessing talent whose actions exposed the magical community to scrutiny was summarily executed. Of course, that was a long time ago. Things are a lot looser in modern times, and a lot of ordinary people are aware that there are those among them who are not quite so ordinary. But they don't really *believe* it. It doesn't hurt that anyone who starts talking seriously about things like spells and magic is met with raised eyebrows and rolling eyes.

Most of us try to keep it quiet—not for any nefarious purpose, but just because it makes life easier to avoid all the attention that would follow. Besides, it does seem safest to keep things low-key. Nobody was really sure of what might happen if the existence of the talent were widely recognized, but centuries of secrecy was a heavy pull in the direction of not wanting to find out. And people like Victor do tend to be traditionalists.

Eli had talked me into joining up for reasons that were never very clear to me. He'd known me ever since I was a kid and surely must have understood I wasn't suited for the job. And Victor wasn't happy about it; he never completely trusted or even liked me much. He felt I had no respect for the old ways, which wasn't true, and felt I didn't have the proper dedication to the craft, which was. God knows how Sherwood felt about it. For all her vaunted compassion and concern for others, she keeps her own emotions very close to the vest.

Since Sherwood and I ended up working together, getting together was a natural progression. For a while it was great. We had instant rapport—much like what she had projected toward me earlier—except that it was real. Or at least I thought it was. With matters of the heart it's not always easy to tell.

We made an attractive couple, even turning heads sometimes when we went out. Sherwood's warmth and vibrance make her seem even more attractive than she already is. Myself, I'm a shade over six feet, in shape, with dark shaggy hair, an angular face, and a brooding intensity I carefully cultivated as a teenager and now find difficult to shake. An arcane tattoo depicting two intertwined briars makes a circle midway on my right forearm, adding to the mystique. When people ask its significance, I tell them offhandedly that it has none—like so many others before me, I got drunk when I turned eighteen and stumbled into the nearest tattoo parlor. Truth is, it means a lot. But besides myself, only Eli knows why I got it, and when, and where.

But after a while, basic differences started wedging Sherwood and me apart. She ended up functioning as the voice of my conscience, which naturally I didn't much care for. Not that she ever said anything, or even that she put out disapproving vibes. It was more that she had to be so goddamned *good* all the time. I used to hope she would lose her temper over something petty, just once, but it never happened. Maybe she waited until I wasn't around to flip out. Anyway, it got so I couldn't even say or do anything the least bit unpleasant when she was around, because I would immediately see how it looked through her eyes and feel horribly self-conscious. And that's just no way to live.

For her part, she felt that I was wasting my potential, in more ways than one. She fervently believed that somewhere inside me was a wonderful human being struggling to get out. I knew better. But it must have been a sore trial for her to be around me all the time, watching me flail through life. So, we ended up with a mutual parting of the ways. We remained friends though, and from time to time I really missed her. I'm sure the fact that despite her good girl persona she was incredible in bed had nothing to do with it.

Thoughts of Sherwood and bed led to other thoughts, and before I knew it Tommy was no longer glancing over at me; he was flat-out glaring. I'd been cruising along, casually comping, not noticing it was eight bars past where I was supposed to take my solo. I pulled myself together and redeemed myself over the next few tunes. We closed out the set with one of my originals, "Samba Du Jour," and I headed back to the bar to get a scotch rocks this time. I had a feeling I was going to need it.

I carried my drink back to Sherwood's table a bit warily. I didn't care for the direction our discussion had taken. I pulled out the chair opposite Sherwood and sat down again. She looked up and said accusingly, "You played a D9 chord instead of the major seventh at the end of that last tune. Wrong chord. I thought you never make mistakes."

I shook my head tolerantly. "First of all, it's my tune. So I can play any chord I want. Second, stop trying to show off your ears. Tommy is the one who made the mistake; he played a C instead of a C sharp. I was just covering for him."

She frowned. "You're lying through your teeth."

"Am not."

"Are too. I recorded the entire set."

"Did not."

"Did too." We stared at each other straight-faced for about ten seconds, then gave it up.

"It *is* good to see you," I said, meaning it. "It's been way too long. It shouldn't take a bunch of bad shit to get us together."

She sighed. "I know. I've just been so busy. A lot of weirdness has been going on. You know?"

"I can see that. Which brings us back to why you're here, I suppose."

She sighed again. "I'm afraid so. The thing is, a lot's been happening that we don't understand, and figuring weird stuff out was always one of your strong points. We could really use the help." She put a hand up to stop me as I opened my mouth. "I know, I know. You're not cut out for our kind of work. You're not even sure it's worth doing. Etc., etc. We've been down that road before, I know."

"But?"

"But this is different."

"Different how?"

"Well, you said somebody just tried to kill you, for one thing."

"Good point," I conceded.

"And Vaughan isn't the only one who's been attacked."

"Anyone else been killed?"

She shook her head. "Not so far. I still can't believe it happened."

I was having trouble getting my head around it myself. Vaughan was one of those guys who never make mistakes. Then I remembered how close I had come myself last night. Anyone can be taken out with a surprise attack if it's quick enough and manages to catch them off guard. The world's greatest marksman can walk unsuspectingly past a doorway and have some teenage gangbanger pop out and bust a cap in his head. Still, I had the feeling that involving myself with Victor again wasn't going to make things any safer for me.

"I don't know how much help I could be," I said, waffling.

A look of exasperation flitted across her face. "You'd be a lot of help, Mason. You know that. Stop selling yourself short." It was an old argument.

I realized it was the second time this evening she had used my name. We all tend not to do that, except Victor when he's pissed. It used to be considered very bad manners among practitioners, almost insulting, to address another by name unless you knew them well. It was just custom, since that stuff about the knowledge of true names giving power over another is fantasy, and younger practitioners tend to ignore it. But her use of my name again at this point was a subtle reminder of what our relationship used to be. Not really playing fair, but then, I'd done the same thing to her earlier.

Sherwood was wrong, though. It wasn't that I sold myself short. I simply possess very high standards, and unfortunately find myself unable to meet them. She leaned across the table and took my hand again. Definitely not playing fair.

"Please," she said. "Just come down and talk to Victor. Half an hour." She played her trump card. "Eli will be there, too. How long has it been since you've seen him?" I slumped down in my chair and gave up.

"Okay," I said.

"Tomorrow morning?"

"How about afternoon? At the 'Institute'?" I said sarcastically, putting the word in quotes.

"Don't be snide."

"Okay." I apologized. "At Victor's, then. Two o'clock."

I packed up my gear, got my check, and headed home. I offered Sherwood a ride, but she wisely declined. My van is pretty reliable, an old, clunky, green GMC, but it needs tires and struts and a lot of other things before it could really be called a safe method of transport. I said I make a living playing music. I didn't say it was a good living.

I was careful when I left Rainy Tuesdays, more aware than usual, but not that concerned. The attack that had been launched on me the night before had taken a lot of thought and energy, and I didn't think anything else would happen so soon after. Besides, what could happen in the five minutes it would take me to drive home? Okay, I admit it. That was a stupid question.

TWO

A LIGHT RAIN WAS FALLING WHEN I LEFT THE CLUB, not an unusual occurrence for a December evening in San Francisco. The smell of rain on pavement brought with it a wave of unfocused nostalgia: childhood memories and adolescent angst, all mixed up with reflections of past girl-friends, missed opportunities, and a hopeless longing for simpler times. The sense of smell drags up emotions like no other sense can. They say it's because smell is centered in the oldest part of the brain, the part we still share with the scaly reptiles we once were. All I knew was that life was getting too goddamned complicated and it didn't look like it was going to improve much anytime soon.

I hadn't felt like this since I was a teenager. Back then I felt as isolated and confused and alone as only an adoles-cent can. All of my emotions and most of my actions were colored by the belief I was somehow different. True, most teenagers feel that way, but it turns out I really *was* different. My mother had a touch of the talent, as did my father, but she wanted no part of such things and turned a blind eye to anything that suggested I was similarly blessed. Or in her mind, cursed. Something had happened when she was younger that turned her against all aspects of talent. My father disagreed. Looking back, I can now see the source of their many arguments. I knew the fights were about me, but I didn't know why, or what I'd done wrong.

If it hadn't been for Eli, I don't know what would have become of me. He was coaching a youth football program. My mother insisted that I get involved in sports, over the objections of my father. Talk about role reversals. I think she believed that once I'd experienced the joy of knocking other kids off their feet, my interest in other things would wane.

Eli of course had no problem recognizing what I was, or at least what I would become. He took me under his wing and introduced me to a world I had never imagined could exist. Then he taught me, with infinite patience, everything he could about the art. I still remember the first time I managed a conjuration of sorts, on a rainy night like this one, when I managed to turn all the streetlights in front of my home a deep chartreuse. Not all that impressive, perhaps, but for me it ranked up there with that other first time we all remember.

I walked the half block to where my van was parked and ran a quick psychic check to make sure no unpleasant surprises were waiting for me inside. I set my guitar in back and walked around to the driver's side, dropping my keys in a puddle and stooping to retrieve them. I straightened up and opened the driver's door, yawning. When I saw the object sitting on the front seat I automatically recoiled. It was a cheap child's doll, oversized and naked, holding out two chubby arms. In one of its hands it held out what appeared to be a small slice of rancid watermelon. I didn't want to look more carefully to find out what it might actually be. In the other, a curled parchment roll secured with a black ribbon was proffered. The doll's eyes were rolled back in its head in an appalling parody of death, and something red and sticky was smeared over it. I stared at the doll with mixed bafflement and revulsion. This made no sense at all.

It bore no relation to any charm I'd ever seen or heard of. Then I heard the words of Eli, my old mentor and the smartest man I know, echoing in my head. One of his many, many, lectures about attack and defense.

"Misdirection, son. That's the secret. Just like stage magic. Not everything has to do with power and talent, you see. Start clucking like a chicken, and when they stop to see what the hell is wrong with you, knock 'em upside the head with a two-by-four. Sometimes magic alone just won't cut it."

Ah, yes. Misdirection. I whirled around just in time to see the singularity floating softly down to envelop me. Everything went black for a moment, then the world lurched back into view like a television that has been turned off and back on. There I was, still standing outside my van on a rainy night. I looked around cautiously, although it was a little late for caution. No one in sight. I stood there foolishly, rain dripping off the end of my nose, every sense alert. Nothing. Nothing wasn't necessarily a good thing, though. I could hear the wind and the splash of rain on the street, but that was all. No traffic. No pedestrians. The usual background noises that are always present in a city, even late at night, were missing. So. I didn't know exactly where I was, but it wasn't the San Francisco I was used to.

I didn't know much about singularities. I never was that interested in the purely theoretical aspects of things. What little I could remember came from a late-night dinner at the Café Arguello with Eli one evening.

"They usually only diverge in subtle ways," he'd said. "They don't depart too much from reality—our reality, that is. Can't, that would take too much power. You might not even realize you were stuck in one at first. As to what they truly are, that I can't tell you. Some say they're portals to an alternate universe. Some say they're constructs, totally artificial. One of my colleagues, Georgio, even maintains that they're nothing more than an unusually powerful form

of mental illusion, although he admits there are a lot of
things that leaves unexplained."

"And you think?" I'd asked.

"I really don't know. All of the above if I had to guess.
I'd know a lot more about them if I'd ever been in one,
but that's not something I'm eager to experience. The
chances of getting out and back home are apparently not
the greatest."

"But it can be done?"

"Oh, yes. It's not easy, but what seems to work . . ."

He'd trailed off as the waiter interrupted us to ask about
dessert, and by the time we got our choices straight the
conversation had veered onto a different tack. It's amazing
how such seemingly trivial things, things that seem so in-
significant at the time, can come back to haunt you. Damn.
Trapped for eternity by an overly solicitous waiter.

I climbed behind the wheel, threw the doll onto the
floor with distaste and sat gazing out at the rain-soaked
street. Finally I decided to drive home. If my home was
still there. There wasn't much else I could think of to do.
The streets were ominous, dark and eerie. Empty, empty,
empty. Not a person, not a car in sight. Oh, there were cars
parked along the curb, just no cars on the streets. If all the
people had just disappeared, then why weren't there abandoned cars in the middle of the road? Oh, right, it wasn't
really as if everyone had vanished. It was just that I was
now in a different world, one that possibly wasn't even
real.

I turned onto Valencia, which stretched away as far as I
could see. Empty, empty, empty. I ought to be taking notes
for Eli, I thought. He'd be fascinated, spinning out theories
as to exactly how this sort of thing operated. It would keep
him happy for weeks. That assumed I was ever going to
see him again.

I pulled up outside my place and parked in the driveway. Just habit—I could have left my van in the middle of
the street for all it mattered. I unlocked the front door,
walked in, and flipped on the lights. They worked, which

didn't surprise me since all the streetlights and traffic signals had been operating normally on the way home. I called out to Louie with a faint irrational hope that somehow he had been sent along with me, but there was only silence. I turned on the TV and got nothing but snow. I'd kind of hoped for a late-night movie, not impossible, considering.

The first order of business was clear. There was a question that needed answering, though I had a feeling I wasn't going to like the answer. I paced around the house, avoiding thinking, putting off doing anything. Finally I made myself stop, grabbed a couple of sheets of newspaper that were stacked on the windowsill, crumpled them up, and placed them in a pile on the floor. I glanced around me, although I knew my surroundings well enough that I didn't really need to, gathered enough power to set the floor underneath on fire as well as the intended paper, shot out my hand, palm down, and tried one of the simplest conjurations I know. The newspaper remained perfectly intact, resting forlornly on the floor without so much as a scorch mark to show for my efforts. Okay, talent didn't operate here. I hadn't really expected it to; that would have made it all too simple.

Disappointment set in, even though I hadn't been counting on anything. I suddenly felt unutterably weary. Clearly, I don't handle stress very well. I just wanted to lie down and sleep until everything was back to normal. Although with a million thoughts running through my mind it didn't seem likely I was going to be able to sleep. I stretched out on my bed anyway and closed my eyes. Those million thoughts were really only variations on one theme: what the hell am I going to do? I had a feeling there was an obvious answer, something to do with different ways of looking at the world, maybe something Eli had said that I'd paid no attention to at the time. The thought kept eluding me, almost surfacing and at the last moment sinking back into the subconscious. For no particular reason I started thinking about Sherwood and then there were birds singing outside the window and it was morning.

I lay there for a while, listening, not thinking at all. Eventually I got up, visited the bathroom, and made some coffee. I opened the freezer and took the last of the Jamaica Blue Mountain that I had been hoarding, given to me last summer as a gift. I ground the beans and waited for the coffeemaker to do its thing. If ever I deserved a superior cup of coffee, it was today. Besides, I was curious. If I was living in a construct, would the Blue Mountain still have that unbelievable velvety smooth taste? It did. What that proved, if anything, was not clear but I savored it nonetheless. I took a long shower, put on a clean black sweatshirt and Levi's, and figured I was about as ready to face this brave new world as I was ever going to be.

Outside was a ghost town, devoid of people. And cats. And dogs. Only the birds seemed to be in fine form, chortling and squawking as if there was no tomorrow. Which, I reminded myself, there might well not be. I leaned against my van, trying to come up with an idea or a place to go. This singularity couldn't extend forever. If it did, that would mean I'd been transported to an entire other world, and that wasn't possible. So if I could get out toward the edge of it, where the reality was thinner, maybe I could find a way back. I thought for a while longer and finally settled on Ocean Beach. Why not? At least it was a sunny day for a change.

I headed up Guerrero Street to 280, got off at John Daly, then across to Skyline. Empty, empty, empty. I did the U-turn and pulled into Fort Funston where the cliffs plunge down to meet Ocean Beach, parked, and strolled out onto the observation deck that sits on the edge of the bluff. Most days there you can watch the hang gliders swooping back and forth like ancient pterodactyls searching for quarry. Today the sky was abandoned except for the birds who had reclaimed the skies.

Fort Funston is the place where dog owners in San Francisco take their dogs to run off leash. There is a three-

mile or so loop that winds along the cliffs, down to the
beach, and back up onto the cliffs again. Technically it's
not an off leash area, but you'd never know it. On any
sunny weekend afternoon you can easily count three or
four hundred dogs running loose: pugs and Pomeranians,
Labs and goldens, rottweilers and Dobies, along with the
most amazing collection of crossbreeds and just plain
mutts. Some were as goofy as could be, doggie clowns,
some sedately dignified with slowly wagging tails, some
flat-out hysterical. But they always seemed to be having a
grand old time—in all the years I'd been going out there,
I'd never seen a serious fight. A few quicksnarl disagreements from time to time, but that was about it.

I come here with Lou on occasion. He seems to enjoy
playing dog once in a while, and it gives me the chance to
stretch my legs and clear my head. You almost need a dog
to come out here, though. If you are just innocently taking
a stroll with no dog accompanying you, people tend to
view you with suspicion, much as they might a childless
middle-aged man sitting near a school watching children
play. I wouldn't be surprised if someday a special pass for
the dogless was required.

I dangled my legs over the edge of the platform and
watched the waves breaking on the sand far below. The sky
was a steel gray with the sun angling planes of light into
different layers. It edged out from the usual sea mist and
highlighted the occasional wave crest with gold trim. I
could see as I looked toward the horizon that the sea started
to go fuzzy, looking more like dirty felt than water. Sure
enough, the singularity thinned out there, though what
might lie beyond was a metaphysical question that I didn't
have time for at the moment. But if I could get out there,
possibly I could find a way through and back home.

Too far to swim, though. The wind was chilly but fresh,
smelling of salt and fish and a hundred other things. If I
didn't turn around I could imagine what the coast must
have been like a couple of hundred years ago before the
cities were built and civilization put its ineradicable stamp

on the shore. Despite the mess I was in, I felt oddly at peace. I remembered an old quote I'd once read, D. H. Lawrence or somebody, ". . . a world empty of people, just uninterrupted grass, and a hare sitting up." It was an appealing thought, but this wasn't exactly a world—more like a fold in a blanket, I expect.

I idly watched the shorebirds, thoughts drifting. There seemed a lot more of them than usual, a whole lot more. Little sanderlings scooting back and forth, timing the waves, always just out of reach of the foam. Some bigger birds, maybe godwits or curlews; sea ducks bobbing and diving, and of course the raucous gulls, screaming and chattering as they fought one another for some prime morsel of food. And through it all, the sound of the surf, hissing and booming, timeless and hypnotic.

I must have sat there at least an hour looking out over the ocean and the distant horizon before I got an idea. It wasn't particularly brilliant. I needed a boat. And I knew just where I could find one. On the way to Fort Funston I'd passed Lake Merced, a small man-made lake where people fish and boat. A boathouse stands on the east end, not too far from where I now sat. I'd often seen rowers practicing there in racing sculls, mostly large six- or eight-man boats, but a few of the single sculls as well. Those single sculls are fiberglass, light enough for me to wrestle one single-handedly into my van. I could drive right onto the beach farther down, launch the boat, and skim across the ocean waves to the very edge of the singularity. I hauled myself to my feet and took one last look at the ocean stretched out in front of me, but when I turned to leave, a slight problem reared its head. Literally.

Twenty feet away from me sat three very large dogs, watching. I had thought there weren't any dogs in this place. On second look, they weren't dogs at all. Unless I was very mistaken, I was looking at three full-grown wolves. And not any cartoon wolves either, constructs that I could defeat by using talent. Not that I had any talent to use here. These were real, solid, living, breathing carnivores.

I froze until my heart rate returned to something more manageable. Intellectually, I know that wolves are much maligned, that they seldom if ever attack humans and, unless you happen to be a deer or a rabbit, are somewhat benevolent predators. What I hadn't known is that wolves instantly instill an atavistic fear far beyond the power of intellect to rationalize. For the first time in my life, I truly understood the meaning of the word "prey."

I tried to look behind me without turning my head, an operation which was not particularly successful. From what I could remember, I had no more than five feet of leeway before the cliff plunged steeply down for a hundred and fifty feet or so. Not much to work with.

The wolves were still sitting quietly. In front sat what I assumed was the alpha male, just ahead of the other two. His tongue was lolling out like that of an overgrown puppy. His left ear was partially missing, giving him a raffish look, but aside from that he looked sleek and healthy and well fed. I wasn't sure if that was good or bad. Now that I'd had a chance to study him, he didn't look that dangerous after all. Maybe I can bluff him, I thought. I took one step forward, slow yet confidant. The big male snapped to attention, tongue snapping back into his mouth, and suddenly he looked twice as big and very dangerous indeed. Okay, time for plan B.

I slowly eased my head to the right, trying to see if there was anything usable as a weapon, while at the same time watching the wolves out of the corner of my eye. No such luck. I turned my head to the left and repeated the maneuver. On the ground, a few feet away, lay a large branch blown there from nearby trees by the wind. It wasn't much of a weapon, but it was better than the alternative, the alternative being nothing at all. I stood there, indecisive, and then gave a mental shrug. I had to do something, and there's no time like the present. Darting to one side, I snatched up the limb and charged toward the wolves,

screaming like a madman. I'm nothing if not subtle. The
three of them nearly fell over their feet, looking positively
comical in their eagerness to get away. They didn't go far
though, stopping about fifteen feet away and sitting back
down again. The two in the back turned to each other and
exchanged a momentary glance as if to say, "What the hell
was that?" then turned back toward me, staring compos-
edly. It was such a human gesture that it made me think
twice. I know very little about the behavior of wolves, but
this struck me as unnatural. Not that I should have expected anything else.

It almost seemed like they wanted something from me.
I hesitated, then slowly lowered myself down until I was
sitting cross-legged on the ground. I kept myself ready to
spring up at a moment's notice in case it turned out they
were simply masking eagerness for an early dinner. The
big male padded slowly sideways, head down, watching
me out of the corner of his eye. I couldn't figure out why
he would be cautious of me until I realized it was the other
way round. He was being careful not to spook me.

He reached a patch of ground, stopped, and then started
digging vigorously. He stopped, glanced over at me, then
resumed digging. As soon as he'd created a shallow trench,
he stopped digging and did the same sideways walk back
to his original position. He flopped down on his stomach
and stared at me, tongue lolling.

I wasn't sure what he wanted. I was used to trying to explain things to Lou, so nonverbal canine communication
wasn't new to me, but this time I was the one who couldn't
seem to catch on. Then I got it. I was supposed to look at
whatever it was he'd dug up.

I got cautiously to my feet. The wolf didn't move. I
eased over to where he'd been digging. As I approached
the spot, small bones from some unfortunate creature he'd
unearthed crunched under my feet. A tiny glint in the sand
caught my attention and I bent down to see what it was. It
might have been a piece of glass, only it was a deep red

color. Whatever it was flickered brightly as the sun hit it from different angles whenever I moved my head.

I brushed sand and bones away, realizing that what I had thought was tiny was just the edge of a larger object, about the size of a marble and just as round. I picked it up and held it up to the sky, letting the sunlight stream through it.

I don't know much about precious stones, but I did know I'd never seen anything like this before. It was smooth and round, deep red like a ruby, but as the sunlight passed through, other colors were gradually revealed, greens and blues and even an inky black. Yes, I know black isn't a color, but this black was. I stared intently, now seeing swirls of blue and purple that roiled around hypnotically in the center of the stone, constantly expanding and contracting. It took some effort to finally break eye contact and slip it into my pocket. I had momentarily forgotten about the wolves, which should give you a faint idea of how hypnotic the stone was.

The big male had meanwhile silently come up behind me, and when I turned he was only a few feet away. He opened his mouth wide, showing some truly impressive teeth, and I panicked. Before I could do anything stupid, he sat down, threw his head back, and let loose with a powerful howl, oddly familiar from countless movies and TV shows. Immediately, the second wolf added his voice, a minor third above. Fellow musicians. The third chimed in a semitone apart, giving the chorus an odd twist that sent a chill through me. Hearing it in a movie is not the same as hearing it for real from five feet away. Abruptly, they stopped, and sat looking at me again. After about ten seconds they started in again, only to stop as abruptly as before. Again, they stared at me. They repeated this odd behavior a third and then a fourth time, each time staring at me a little longer. Wolves don't possess human expressions, but I could swear the big male was looking frustrated. He jumped to his feet, almost causing me to topple over as I backed up frantically. He stood there and uttered what could only be described as an impatient bark. I didn't even know that wolves could bark. Then again, I no longer thought that these were truly wolves.

He lifted his muzzle to the sky and howled once again. It gave me a weird idea. I filled my lungs and joined in with him, tentatively at first, then with more confidence as the other two added their voices. They looked at me approvingly, or at least that's how I interpreted it. I followed their lead, weaving my own motif through the dense texture of their howls. Thank God for the voice lessons I had taken during an aborted attempt to become a singer. The thing that most worried me was that I might disappoint them and embarrass myself. Once a performer, always a performer.

I must have been doing okay, since this time they didn't stop. Our voices blended together into a bizarre wolf/human hybrid song. As I hit one especially long and quavering note, I noticed the ground start to glimmer. I closed my eyes and threw myself into it wholeheartedly. The sound enveloped and surrounded me, like Buddhist chanting where breath and sound and body all merge into one. It was the same feeling I've gotten once or twice when I'm playing at my absolute best, but a hundred times stronger. I don't know how long it went on—in that state, time doesn't have much meaning. I was swept away by the music, if music it was, totally enraptured, transported out of time and space. A small part of my mind noted that phenomenon, since being transported away was exactly what I wanted, but I let that thought slip out of my consciousness as quickly as the flicking silver tail of a fish disappearing in deep water. The concreteness of thought is always the death of magic, however you want to define it.

I became aware of a fifth voice adding to the chorus, high-pitched and sharp. It would have seemed out of place had I not been in a space where such a concept did not exist. I knew that sound. I focused on it and as it grew stronger and more insistent, the music of the wolves faded to a muted drone. Along with it came a rhythmic pounding, intrusive and unpleasant. Finally the noise became so distracting that it broke my trance state. My eyes flew open and I found myself sitting cross-legged on my bed at home, howling at the top of my lungs. Beside me, on the floor, sat a small black-and-tan dog cheerfully keeping me company with a series of high-pitched howls of his own. The pounding resolved into the sound of a fist on the front door, along with some muffled curses.

I staggered to the door and opened it to find my next-door neighbor Gary, usually a tolerant sort, looking not so tolerant. He was so mad he could hardly speak.

"For Christ's sake, it's three in the fuckin' morning! What is wrong with you?"

I apologized the best I could, assured him of prospective quiet, closed the door, and staggered back to the bed. Louie hopped up and looked at me worriedly. He made a whining noise in the back of his throat, the noise he makes when he wishes he could speak, or when he sees a squirrel up a tree out of reach. He'd had something to do with my return, but what that was, I hadn't a clue and I doubted if I ever would.

"It's good to be home," I told him. At the sound of my voice he relaxed, as if he hadn't really been sure it was me until I spoke. I looked at the clock on the bedside table. Three in the morning. But what day? I turned on the TV and flipped over to the Weather Channel. They always run a scroll with the time and date on the bottom of the screen. Sunday, December 04, 3:00 a.m. So the day I had spent out by the ocean hadn't happened. Or somehow I'd been returned to the moment I'd left. Or something. I'd let Eli figure it out.

An odd idea struck me, and I crossed the room and pulled open my bureau drawer. My black sweatshirt was sitting in the drawer, sloppily folded, as well as on my back. Cool. I was ahead of the game. I'd got an extra sweatshirt and a pair of Levi's out of the experience. So it hadn't all been for nothing.

On the other hand, my guitar wasn't in the house. And my van wasn't in the driveway. I wondered if it was out at

Fort Funston or still parked by Rainy Tuesdays. I was pretty sure it was still by the club, given the way things had unfolded. Which meant it was still poking into a red zone. Which meant if I left it there until morning, not only would it get a ticket, it would probably get hooked by the city. Which meant two hundred dollars for the towing and an additional two hundred a minute for storage, or something like that. If you have an older car and it gets towed, you might as well just buy another. It would probably be cheaper. Not everything about San Francisco is great.

Also, that meant my guitar was still in the van and I couldn't leave a valuable instrument there overnight. It wouldn't last two hours, not in the heart of the Mission. And besides being worth a lot of money, it was my guitar. It had taken me years to find just the right model, and after that, just the right instrument, a 1950s blond Gibson Bird-land with a clean, mellow tone and action smooth as but-ter, even with heavy-gauge strings. There aren't many around anymore. Besides Lou, that guitar was about the only thing I cared about these days. There wasn't any choice; even with everything I'd been through, I was still going to have to get the van.

I looked out the front window. Still raining, drops splash-ing on the empty driveway. I could call a cab, but I had no money. I briefly considered calling Sherwood, but couldn't bring myself to bother her. Not to mention all those questions. It was only about a half hour's walk anyway.

I desperately wanted a cigarette. I could feel the cool and soothing smoke filling my lungs, calming my nerves. Un-fortunately, I'd quit smoking years ago. I'd quit smoking dope, too, for different reasons, but I never missed it the way I did tobacco. Devil weed it surely is. I sighed, slipped on my old semiwaterproof leather jacket and a battered slouch hat, opened the door, and walked out into the night.

"Come on, Lou," I said. I wasn't about to walk back through those streets without him. He looked out at the rain and looked back at me as if I had suddenly grown an extra head. "Yes, I know," I said, trying to placate him, "but I've got no choice."

He made some obscure dog noises and stepped through the door out into the rain, where he ostentatiously began shaking himself before he even had a chance to get wet. Then he started trotting down the street without a backward look, martyrdom evident in every line of his body.

"Hey," I told him. "I don't like it any better than you do."

I walked until I reached Valencia and turned onto it, a slightly safer option than walking down Mission Street, although at three in the morning walking anywhere through the Mission is never entirely comfortable. I'd only gone a couple of blocks when I noticed three Latinos, early twenties, walking toward me about a block away. They were wearing 49ers jackets and red headbands. Gangbangers. *Norteños.* They were walking silently, never a good sign. I suddenly felt extremely white. Louie started growling softly. His sense of danger is not confined to the supernatural.

"I see them," I muttered. As they approached they split apart, two on one side of the sidewalk, one on the other, so I'd have to pass between them. Very subtle. I felt a sudden surge of rage. I'd had enough for one day, and here was something I could vent my anger on and still feel justified. Someone needed to pay for my bad day, and these were the perfect candidates. They were about to be very, very sorry.

A second later I had myself back under control. I couldn't go around blasting lowlifes just because I'd had a bad day, whether they deserved it or not. There were better ways to deal with them.

"Lou," I said. "Want to have some fun?" He wagged his tail and uttered a short bark. As the three approached, the one on the left reached under his jacket. Lou looked back at me and I nodded. He charged toward the three, doing his usual snarling and barking, stopping about five feet away. They all took one automatic step backward, and then started laughing.

"Eh, *perrito*," said one, amusedly. "What you gonna do, dog?"

I crossed my arms and started chanting, repeating non-sense syllables under my breath. With illusions it's the rhythms that count, not the actual words you speak. Slowly, Louie seemed to grow larger. First, up to the size of a beagle, then a Border collie, then a German shepherd, until finally he was the size of a full-grown Irish wolfhound. I twisted my fingers and foaming saliva started dripping off his now imposing canines. For a moment I thought I'd gone too far. They weren't running; they were standing paralyzed with fear. I hoped they weren't going to stroke out. I uncrossed my arms and Louie shrunk down to his normal size, like a balloon rapidly deflating.

"Gentlemen," I said, nodding to them as we walked by. They didn't make a sound. I continued down Valencia without a backward glance, feeling a lot more cheerful. What I had done to them was not the kind of thing they were likely to tell anyone about; and even if they did, they would be greeted with shouts of derisive laughter.

Ten minutes later, I was standing next to my van. I momentarily panicked when I couldn't locate my car keys. If I had left them at home I think it would have pushed me over the edge. I finally fished them out of the bottom of a pocket, opened the passenger door to let Louie jump in, grabbed the now pathetic doll from the floor, threw it in the gutter, and drove home uneventfully for once.

Safe at home, I collapsed onto the bed. I needed sleep. Tomorrow I would be seeing Eli and Victor, and I had a feeling it might take a lot longer than the promised half an hour.

THREE

BY THE TIME I WOKE UP IT WAS PAST NOON, AND the rain still was coming down. Gray light leaked through the front window and it was chilly in the house, if not downright cold. California, for some reason, has never embraced the concept of central heating. I sat up and swung my feet onto the floor. Louie unburrowed his head from out of the covers where he usually slept. He may be an exceptional creature but he still gets cold and miserable whenever the temperature drops below fifty.

I fed him some breakfast, not bacon this time, and drank my usual multiple cups of coffee. We headed out along the Great Highway toward Victor's house. Now when I say house, it hardly conveys the true nature of the place. Victor lives in a huge Victorian near Taraval with a stunning view of the ocean from the upper stories. There are three of them—stories, that is—with balconies on the two upper levels and twin squared-off gables on top which give the whole thing the appearance of a fort, which in many ways it is. I wondered at first how Victor had found such a place, since it was the only house in the area that even remotely resembled a Victorian. Eli told me in confidence that Victor had actually built it less than ten years ago, razing the original home and using plans modified from a house he had once owned in London. It must be nice to have money.

I pulled into his driveway and parked next to his silver BMW M5. That car is one of the few things Victor is passionate about, besides battling evildoers. It's not flashy; Victor would never own anything ostentatious or vulgar. If you don't know any better it appears to be a relatively sedate sedan. But in truth, it can do one-seventy, outperform about anything but a Ferrari, and costs double what I make in a year.

The contrast between my old van and his high-performance car always amuses me, just as it always irks him. He thinks my battered van is nothing but an affectation, refusing to believe it's simply the only vehicle I can afford that will handle all the jobs I need it to do. His other car was the brand-new Lincoln Navigator parked at the far end of the driveway. No old and battered vans for Victor.

I looked critically at the house, hoping to spot some flaw, but it was still pristine. Victor had painted it a creamy pale yellow with white trim and he keeps it immaculate, or at least he hires people who do that. He certainly has enough money, obtained from God knows where. That's another thing about him that annoys me. Not that he has money, more power to him, but that he's so dismissive and contemptuous of those who don't and are trying to remedy the situation. "Money is nothing but a tool," he's fond of saying. "It's just not that important." Sure, when you've got it.

Lou jumped out onto the driveway and we went in through the big front door. It was never locked; it didn't need to be. Not only was this Victor's home, it was also the central location for his little band of warriors. As a result, a lot of care has gone into its protection.

As I've said, I'm good with spells. But the protection around this house was on an entirely different level. My spells are like my jazz playing: I take what's around me

and improvise on the spot. Like jazz, it takes a lot of dedication and work to reach the level where you can just let it
flow naturally. It's a very useful skill. It's hard to catch me
off guard—although considering events of the last couple
of days you'd never know it—since I don't have to rely on
preset spells or protections to defend myself.

But the warding around this house was far more advanced than anything I could manage. If what I do is something like jazz, then this warding would be closer to a
classical composition, a symphony or concerto. It was layered and textured, balanced and complex. When you're
working to create a safe haven, using static spells, you can
take infinite pains—if you have the time and inclination. A
lot of very skilled people had worked on that house. The
warding could be broken, of course, most anything can, but
it would take more than a few uninterrupted days for even
the strongest practitioner. And that would be about as
likely as someone getting a few undisturbed days to drill
unnoticed through the back wall of the White House.

The house looks normal on a mundane level, but to psychic eyes the warding around Victor's house is easily per-
ceptible. The best analogy I can think of is that of sight, but
there is also something of touch there, as well as a few
other things that don't translate at all.

Lines of force are woven around the perimeter, a lattice-
like grid in grays and blacks, powerful and forbidding,
crackling with power. Filling in the spaces of the grid is a
diffuse swirl of something that I don't understand at all,
glowing with a color that doesn't exist. It isn't anything
you'd want to fool with, any more than you'd climb up a
transmission tower to play with the high-tension wires in
the power grid.

Certainly there are more secure places, but not that
many and not in this country. The most famous is in Italy,
a modest villa which was warded by Giuseppe Moldini
back in the seventeenth century. Moldini is to enchantment
as Bach is to music. His warding of this villa is a composition of such beauty and complexity that it transcends

practicality and becomes high art. In the three hundred plus years since he lived, no one has figured out how to dismantle it and I doubt if anyone ever will. These days that degree of talent and skill just doesn't exist.

Still, the protection around Victor's beach shack serves its purpose well enough. I walked down the hallway and up the stairs to the second floor where Victor had his study. Or library. Or den. With Victor, it could never be just a room. I knocked on the closed door to be polite, since he was well aware I was standing right outside. His familiar bass voice rumbled, "Come."

Victor was comfortably ensconced behind his desk, a blond maple antique with carved scrollwork legs which provided the only light touch in the room. He looked good. Well, he always looked good; it was one of the things that was important to him.

Sherwood hadn't yet put in an appearance, but standing by one of the tall windows was someone I was very glad to see. Eli. He turned away from the window and approached me, face beaming. He ignored my outstretched hand and enveloped me in a bear hug, almost lifting me off the ground. It wasn't hard for him to do since at six feet four and close on two-sixty there aren't many people he doesn't dwarf. Eli had been an offensive lineman in college. He hated football; it was just his ticket to an education. Now he was a full history professor at USF and, being a proud African-American, naturally had specialized in European history, specifically the late Middle Ages. He wore absurdly tiny wire-rim glasses, his hair was beginning to recede and his slightly scraggly beard was beginning to gray, but he was still an imposing figure.

"How you been, boy?" he asked, thumping me on the back. "I hear you've been getting yourself in some trouble."

"Not my fault," I said.

He smiled. "With you, it never is, is it?"

"How's the project coming?" I asked, half-teasing.

Eli was always working on his pet project, but he never would tell me what it was. I pretended it was going to make us all rich, when in reality it was more likely to be academically brilliant and totally impractical.

Louie ran up and put his paws on Eli's knee. He studiously ignored Victor seated at the desk, but Eli was one of his all-time favorite people. Of course, Victor doesn't care much for Louie either, so it's not like it bothered him. He got up from behind the desk and offered a perfunctory hand.

"Mason. Would you care for some coffee?" he asked.

Always the perfect host. Victor would have made a great villain in a James Bond movie. He did have his own espresso machine, however.

"Cappuccino?" I asked hopefully.

"Don't be a nuisance. Coffee."

"Black," I said resignedly.

"Eli?"

"Black will be fine."

As Victor fussed with the coffee, I took a moment to look around. It had been awhile since I'd been in this room, but it was exactly the same as I remembered. Victor isn't much for change. Once he gets something the way he likes it, that's the end of it. He's either totally comfortable with himself or extremely rigid, depending on how you view such things. The room isn't one I would care to live in myself but it does have a certain something.

It's been decorated by someone with impeccable taste perhaps too fond of PBS English period dramas and Sherlock Holmes movies. Massive overstuffed chairs are scattered throughout at seeming random. Oil paintings in heavy frames hang on dark mahogany walls, and an ornate sideboard dominates. All that's needed to make it perfect would be Victor with a briar pipe. Unfortunately, like me, he had given up tobacco some years back.

The only jarring note in the room is a large freestanding safe which is set against one wall. I often had wondered why Victor needed it, considering all the other protections in the house, but I wasn't about to ask him. Not that he would have told me.

   Two things save the room: tall, broad windows that let
in massive amounts of light, and against the far wall, a
huge working fireplace. Ocean fog drifted past the windows, making the warmth and cheer of the blazing fire ir-
resistible. Louie trotted over toward the fire intending to
curl up on the hearth, but the favored spot was already occupied by a large, fawn-colored Persian cat. Sort of. I
wasn't the only one with a helper. Victor had Maggie.
   Usually Ifrits get along very well, seeing as there aren't
that many of them, but Lou didn't care much for Maggie
and never had. He knew better than to growl at her; after
all, we were in her home. He stalked stiffly to the end of
the hearth, as far away from her as he could get and still
have the benefit of the fire. The feeling was mutual. Maggie turned her head and hissed at him.
   "Children, children," said Victor reprovingly, putting
down the coffee and walking over to make sure they both
behaved. He bent down to pick up Maggie, ignoring Lou.
Appropriate, though petty.
   "Sherwood spoke of an attack," he said, turning his
head to look at me over his shoulder. As usual, getting
right down to business. "Details, please." He acted as if I
had never left, like I was working for him, a magical jun-
ior G-man reporting back. I caught Eli with the hint of a
smile on his face.
   I related the story of the thing in the alley, leaving out a
few details that didn't show me in the best light. Eli was
concerned, listening carefully, pulling thoughtfully on his
scraggly beard and peering at me through those absurd little glasses he affects. Even Victor listened without inter-
ruption, less impatient than usual. Then I moved on to the
singularity and the world empty of people. This totally fascinated Eli, especially the part about the mechanism of my
return. I jokingly mentioned the unexpected addition to my
wardrobe.
   "Have you still got the clothes?" he demanded.
   "Sure. I'm still wearing the Levi's."
   Victor did his quizzical eyebrow trick at the idea of

wearing the same pair of pants two days in a row. He can be such a charmer.

"Good God," said Eli. "How dumb can you be? Have you learned nothing from me after all these years?"

"Well . . ."

"Think, Mason. Think! You're walking around here with an object from another dimension clinging to your butt. Why not just put some talisman you found there in your pocket and carry a sign reading, 'Please, please, take me back.'"

"Well . . ."

"No, not 'well.' Not well at all. Those Levi's are still connected to where they came from. A small boy could push you back there without looking up from his video game."

"Children don't exhibit talent until puberty," put in Victor. My God, maybe he had acquired a sense of humor after all. More likely he was just trying to set the record straight.

Eli's concern was making me nervous. If he was worried about the Levi's, what would he say when I pulled out the jewel I'd brought back? Talisman in my pocket was uncannily close to the truth. It wasn't like he didn't know what he was talking about. Although Eli possesses only a moderate talent at best, he makes up for it with vast intellect. A major authority on the principles and history of the Art, he devised a good many of the spells that ward this very house, although he had to get someone else to implement them. Eli was a composer, not a player, but as a composer he's a genius.

"I'll get rid of them as soon as I get home," I promised, putting off mentioning the jewel.

"You will not. Take them off. Now."

"Not in my house," muttered Victor, shuddering. Okay. It was official. He did possess a rudimentary droll sensibility.

"Don't worry," I reassured Eli, "I'll take care of it. I'll burn them when I get home, promise. The sweatshirt, too." Eli started to get into it again, but I was saved by an unexpected distraction. The door to one of the back rooms opened, and a young man came out, stopped when he saw us, and grinned nervously. Aha. Victor had a new boyfriend.

"Sorry, Victor," he said, apologetically. "I was just going out. I didn't realize we had company."

He wasn't the usual Victor type, which is mostly generic surfer dude. Victor averages about one a month, and I don't think any of them have a clue as to who he really is or what he really does. This guy had dark unruly hair and a glimmer of intelligence in his eyes.

I carefully kept my face expressionless. I was afraid if I so much as cracked a smile, Victor would turn him into a toad on the spot. This guy had unwittingly crossed the unspoken Victor line. It wasn't that Victor gave a rat's ass what we thought, although he was a *very* private person. But the young man had said he didn't realize "we" had company. Victor has never been a "we" in his life, and I doubted he was about to start now. I waited for the explosion but he fooled me.

"It's still raining," he said mildly. "Take a coat."

The guy gave Eli and me an all-purpose wave of acknowledgment and slipped out the front door. Victor stared at me, daring me to make some sarcastic comment, but I maintained my innocent demeanor. After he'd stared me down for an appropriate length of time, he put Maggie back down on the hearth and disappeared into the back of the house.

"Wait here," he ordered. "I've got something to show you."

Eli joined me as I crossed over to the front window and looked out. Down below, the young guy was standing in the rain, hatless, dark hair plastered down over his ears.

"How long has this one been flavor of the week?" I asked.

"Danny? A couple of months. But this is different." He lowered his voice, speaking with an uncharacteristic glee. "Victor's in love."

He stretched out the word love in a way that would have been mocking if it were anyone but Eli saying it.

"Victor?" I scoffed. "Give me a break."

Eli nudged me to shut up as Victor came back into the room and stood by the window with us. He gazed out to see what we were looking at just as Danny glanced up and caught our eye. I snuck a quick peek at Victor. He had a half smile and a faraway expression that told the whole story. I shifted my gaze down to the figure standing in the rain, and just for a moment, I could see him through Victor's eyes. Metaphorically, of course, not the way I can with Lou.

As Victor appeared in the window, Danny's whole face lit up. Hunched over against the wind, he wrapped his arms one around the other and stared up at us. His dark hair was matted down by the rain, his thin face turned up toward us with an expression of hunger and longing that had little to do with sex.

I have to admit I've never truly understood how a man can be in love with another man. Attracted, sure, why not, but with the kind of emotion that brings either wild joy or abject despair? I don't get it. Sure, I do intellectually, but not really, not in the heart, not where it counts. For that matter, I barely get how women can fall in love with men. We're not that great. Maybe Victor's not the only one lacking the empathy gene.

Oh, in case it's not clear, Victor revels in being a gay stereotype. Small, neat, and dapper, he sports close-cut hair and one of those beards that consist of nothing but lines. A line down the jawbone, a line outlining the chin and lips, a line from the lower lip to the middle of the chin. All precise, all perfect. Expensive understated clothes. Today, a simple beige cashmere sweater that cost probably eight hundred dollars.

Prissy. Bitchy. The perfect gay neighbor on a bad sit-com. But just as Eli is the smartest man I know, Victor is perhaps the most dangerous. Tremendous talent coupled with an unshakable conviction that his way is not only the right way, it is the only way. A gay Vince Lombardi, minus the empathy. Incorruptible. Loyal. The tenacity of a hungry weasel, and about the same compassion. Not very likable, but I would do a lot of backtracking to avoid having him as an enemy.

Victor sat back down at his desk and held up a velvet pouch.

"Is that what I'm supposed to look at?" I asked. He nodded briefly.

"Well?"

"In a minute," he said. "I want to wait for Sherwood. Meanwhile, we can talk."

"I'm really just here to listen," I said.

"And listen you shall. There's more going on here than you know." We were interrupted by a quick knock on the door. "Ah, here she is now," he said, as Sherwood opened the door and stuck her head through. She saw me and fluttered a quick wave as Victor motioned her in. She settled into one of the armchairs.

"Sorry I'm late," she said. "What have I missed?"

I briefly went over things again to bring her up to speed. Victor waited impatiently, finally breaking in. "The question now is—" He was interrupted by a sudden scrabbling from the direction of the fireplace followed by a growl, a hiss, and a sharp yelp.

"Hey!" I yelled. "Cut it out."

Maggie had her back arched and Louie was facing her, teeth bared, with two crimson streaks running across his nose. Victor walked over to the fireplace and picked Maggie up again. He leaned against the mantel, now looking more like a James Bond villain than ever with a Persian cat draped over his arm.

"Really, Mason," he said. "If you can't keep your companion under control you shouldn't bring him with you."

I started to point out that the only blood visible was on Louie's nose, but thought better of it. You don't win a lot of arguments with Victor. Eli stepped in as he usually does.

"No harm done," he said. "Just a little disagreement." He smoothly changed the subject. "You see, Mason, this is the problem. In the past few months, there's been a growing feeling of something not quite right in the city. There's someone out there who's causing problems, testing their power."

"In what way?"

"At first, mostly stupid things. More like mean-spirited practical jokes than anything else, but clearly designed to test power limits."

"Such as?"

"Like Belinda Williams coming home from work one evening to find her cat frozen stiff on the living room floor."

"Not—"

"No, not an Ifrit, just a pet. But still pretty awful for her. Remember Monica Warren?"

"Sure. Kind of a flake. Flaming red hair."

"Not anymore. She woke up one morning and her hair had turned jet black. How about Chuck Paris?"

I thought for a moment and shook my head. "Don't think I know him."

"Low-level practitioner. He has a small apartment in the Marina. Works for us from time to time, minor stuff. Well, he was out of town for a few weeks, and when he got back, everything in his apartment was gone. And I mean everything. Furniture, television, clothes, books, canned goods, letters, you name it. Even his shower curtain was missing. The soap from the soap dish. Everything. And no sign of an intruder. He did have some basic wards in place."

"I think I read about that in the paper," I said. "I didn't know he was a practitioner. I just thought it was a little odd."

Victor set Maggie back down on the floor and walked back over to his desk. "Always right on top of things," he commented.

Eli continued, ignoring him. "It *was* odd. In fact, so odd that Vaughan decided to look into it. He said he had a feeling about it. A week later, he told us that he was on to something but he didn't want to talk about it until he was sure."

"*Unless* he was sure," Victor corrected.

"Yes. Anyway, a week later Vaughan was dead."

"What happened?" I asked, trying to imagine what sort of freakish apparition would be too much for even Vaughan to cope with.

Eli paused, thinking. "Apparently, it was a hit-and-run driver. No witnesses. A pickup truck was found a few blocks away with blood traces on the bumper and a shattered windshield. Stolen, the night before in Oakland."

"Quite a coincidence."

"You could say that. I went over to Chestnut Street to take a look. From the psychic imprint I'd say it happened about four in the morning. But here's the interesting thing. I found a pile of recently burnt-out fireworks in an alley half a block from the impact site. Do you see?"

"No." Then I thought for a moment. "Oh, I do see," I said, and I did. Misdirection. Vaughan walking across the street, every sense aware for magical avenues of harm. Fireworks going off in the alley, a startling distraction. A pickup truck speeding down the street. A mundane death. "Yes, I do see," I said again.

Sherwood had been quiet up to now, feet curled up in one of the big armchairs, watching me intently. Louie had gone over and curled up beside her. He had never much approved when we split up.

"I've looked everywhere I could think of this last week," she said, "trying to get a handle on this. Nobody seems to know anything, but there's a real feeling out there that someone's up to something."

"Well, that's certainly helpful."

"Yes, I know."

"But the question now," said Eli, pushing his glasses down on the bridge of his nose, "is how these attacks on you figure in."

"Maybe the attacks aren't connected," I said, weakly.

From the other side of the room Victor uttered a most un-Victor-like snort. "Puh-leez," he said.

"Get fucked," I said automatically, then remembered

Victor's long memory and penchant for taking offense and getting even. "Sorry," I apologized. "I mean, thank you for your contribution, Victor." Sometimes I can't help myself either.

Eli stepped in again. "I think we can take it as a given that they are. The interesting thing is that the second attempt wasn't necessarily meant to kill you. I think it was meant to neutralize you. So maybe it's not so much that anyone wishes you harm as it is they want you out of the way."

"Why?" I asked. "I'm not involved in anything."

"That is the question. But I'd be extra careful if I were you. Keep Lou here close at all times."

"I always do." I noticed that Victor was looking bored again. "Hey," I said brightly, "I've got an idea. Maybe a trip to Mexico is in order. That way, whoever's got it in for me is satisfied, and I get a vacation. Mexico in December sounds mighty inviting right about now."

"Mason," Sherwood said warningly.

I put my hands up in surrender. "Okay, okay. Just kidding. But I'm not sure what it is you expect me to do. If you guys can't find anything out . . ."

Eli folded his hands together in his best professorial manner. "Okay, tell me," he said, "what is Victor's greatest strength?"

I resisted the temptation to give one of several caustic responses that immediately sprang to mind.

"Power," I replied. "Power and tenacity." Like a crazed wolverine, I added silently.

"Very good. And Sherwood?"

That was easy. "Empathy. And intuition. She knows when something or someone isn't right. And maybe even more important, her ability to cover her true emotions. She could keep a secret from even the strongest practitioner and her masking would go completely unnoticed. So she can't be read and she can't be fooled."

"And yet, she dated you," Victor murmured, just loud

enough to be heard. I instantly regretted having stifled my wolverine remark.

"And yourself?" Eli continued.

"My winning personality?"

"Be serious, please."

I thought about it. "I honestly don't know," I finally admitted. "That's what I've been trying to tell you. I don't know how much help I can be. I've got some skills, but so do a lot of people."

"It's your talent for improvisation. I don't think you realize how rare that is. It's part of the same thing that makes you a good musician. You have an instinctive understanding of relationships that others have to study for years to comprehend. The problem is, you're lazy."

He got no argument from me there. He turned to Sherwood.

"You know jazz. What's the most difficult thing most beginning players face, theory-wise?"

She considered it. "Lots of things, I guess. It depends on the student. Maybe the relationship between chords and scales, what to play when and where."

"Chords and scales are the same thing," I said automatically. "A chord is just a fragment of a particular scale."

"And when did you learn that?"

"It's not something you have to learn," I said. "It just is."

"Exactly," said Eli, obviously pleased. "You never had to learn it. It's just there for you. Most musicians struggle to learn concepts that are instantly obvious to you. It's the same with your talent. You use what's around you to get the results you want. You never had to learn the relationships that allow the flow of power. You just see them."

"And that's bad because?"

"Because, given your natural gifts, you could have been an amazing practitioner, one of the greats, if you had worked at it."

"That never really interested me," I said.

"Or, you could have been a truly great musician, instead of a talented sideman."

That one really hurt. Especially because I knew it was true. Eli saw that and hurried on.

"Be that as it may, it has an unintended side effect which is useful, quite serendipitous."

"And that is?" I said, still smarting from the criticism. Eli was one of the few people whose opinion meant something to me.

"People are comfortable around you. Nontalented people. Most of us are so layered with spells, protections, and various magical objects that we put out something that makes ordinaries feel uncomfortable. They don't know what it is, but they feel it. We have to shield most of the time when we're in the regular world if we don't want to make others ill at ease. But you have no magical aura hanging around you. Why do you think you have so many nontalented friends? You project nothing. You don't need to; if you have to use your talent you just reach out and it's there for you."

"And people talk to you," put in Sherwood. "They trust you."

"Those who don't know you," added Victor.

Eli gave him a look, like a long-suffering father dealing with perpetually unruly kids. Even Victor felt a little abashed, I could tell.

"If I remember correctly, Mason, you used to have a lot of acquaintances who were less than ideal citizens."

"Still do," I said, glancing over at Victor.

"Excellent." Eli beamed, deliberately taking my statement at face value. "Talk to them. I'm sure they run into stuff we never even hear about. We certainly aren't getting anywhere. Find out anything you can. We're not expecting an answer or a name, just a lead. Anything out of the ordinary, anything that would make someone sit up and think, Well, that's pretty strange, before they go about their business."

I nodded. "That shouldn't be too difficult."

"And be careful, Mason," Sherwood added. "I seem to

remember you hanging out with a fairly harsh crowd when we first met."

"Most of them are pretty good people," I protested. "Some of them, anyway." I thought carefully. "Well, a few of them." I thought again. "Yeah, okay. I'll be careful."

I got to my feet, but Victor held up a hand holding the velvet pouch he had brought out. "Wait," he said. He walked back over, carefully unzipped the pouch and shook the contents out onto the polished surface of this desk. "Take a look at these."

"Something connected to all this?"

"Quite probably."

Two jewels spilled out of the pouch. One was slightly larger than the other, large enough to sit comfortably on a nickel. They were different from the jewel I had found in the singularity, clear, like diamonds, but they were also the same. Like two breeds of dogs are different, but they're still both dogs. Maybe Victor had thought to surprise me with them; if so, I had a bigger surprise waiting for him.

"Killer," I said. "How much did those set you back?" Since Victor considers me a boorish Philistine I try to be deliberately crass as often as possible just to bait him. Childish, I know, but I can't help it. He brings out the worst in me.

"He didn't buy them," said Eli. "They were found on Vaughan's body. Examine them."

I picked up the larger of the two stones and randomly rolled it around on the palm of my hand. The stone caught the light and reflected it back, throwing off planes of glittering brightness shot through with hard, metallic colors. It held the same fascination as the one I'd found, swirls of color changing constantly, catching the eye and refusing to let go. It reminded me of something that I couldn't quite put my finger on. It seemed obscurely important that I figure out what that was, and the longer I looked, the more important it became. Victor coughed loudly in my ear, making me jump, and the spell was broken.

"Pretty, isn't it?" he said.

"What the hell is it?" I asked.

Victor smirked, pleased to have shaken me. "Take a closer look."

"In a minute," I said. I pulled my own stone out and laid it down on his desk. "Look familiar?"

This time it was Victor who looked shook up. He picked it up and glanced at it briefly before handing it to Eli. "Where did you get that?" he asked.

Eli was regarding the stone warily. I expected him to go off again about the danger of returning with foreign objects, but he didn't. Maybe the danger only applied to things I was wearing.

"The singularity," Eli said. "Obviously."

"The wolves showed me where it was," I said.

"Why would they do that?"

"I have no idea. I was hoping you could tell me."

"I have no idea either. But I can see that these jewels aren't just an interesting sideline. They've got to be at the crux of things. I would guess they're the reason Vaughan was killed."

"My jewel and the one from Vaughan are almost identical," I pointed out. "So there's got to be a connection."

"Clearly."

"Have you examined them?"

"I have."

"And?"

"Look for yourself," Victor put in. "Use your talent. Assuming, of course, you have any."

"All right," I said. "But give me a minute. I need to get a feel for it first."

Of course I was lying. What I needed was a few moments to get my head together. Before, I had been looking at the stones themselves, not their essence. I'm not very good at magical examination; it's not my strong point. I knew that. Victor knew that. But I wasn't going to admit it. I sent out a probe and got nothing. I pumped energy into it to make it react. Usually that's not a smart thing to do with an unknown object, but I felt safe with Eli watching. Nothing. I tried a couple more tricks, but it just sat there, impervious to my efforts. Frustrated, I looked at Eli and shrugged.

Lou had been edging over to see what the fuss was about and I held out my hand to show him. He froze, staring at it with the canine equivalent of disbelief, then the hackles on his neck stood up and he took three backward steps. He glanced up at me and walked over to the other side of the room, as far away as he could get.

"That's what I thought," said Eli, taking it out of my palm and handing it back to Victor. "Maggie puffed up to twice normal size when she saw it. And don't be discouraged by your lack of success. No one else has been able to figure out what they are either. I don't understand how the same type of gems, if that's what they are, turned up in both your singularity and on Vaughan's body. But it's no coincidence."

"And one more thing," said Victor. "You think diamonds are expensive? If I took these two stones to Harry Winston's, I could trade them straight across for everything else in the store."

"You should leave that stone you brought back with me," Eli added. "It's not a good idea to be carrying it around, considering where it came from."

"Fine," I said. "But can I borrow one of these, then? If I'm going to find out where they came from I'm going to need one to show around. Besides, I've always wanted to possess riches."

"Sure," said Victor sarcastically. "Take them both. Just stuff them in your pocket like you did yours. Don't worry—if you lose them, there's plenty more where they came from."

"You know, Victor, it might not be a bad idea to give him one," Eli said thoughtfully. "I'm sure Mason will be careful, and he just might find something out." He fixed me with his special warning stare. "You *will* be careful with it, won't you, Mason?"

"When am I never not careful?"

Eli let that pass. Victor was about to add something

when his phone rang. When he answered, he listened for a while, then responded with short acknowledgments and a final question of where, before hanging up.

"Life goes on," he said to Eli. "We need to do a run."

Doing a run meant investigating a report of magical wrongdoing, anything from serious bad behavior to petty theft. I was ready to leave, but Eli stopped me.

"Want to come along?" he asked. "For old times' sake?"

"Sure," I said. "Why not? Something heavy, I assume."

Victor gave what passes for a smile with him. "Hardly. A report of a kid over in the Tenderloin casting petty spells on enemies for money."

"Sherwood? What about you?" Eli asked.

"No, I've got things. But you boys have fun."

Victor looked at his watch. "We need to get over there quickly. Mason. We'll take your car."

I found it hard to believe Victor would condescend to ride in my old van, but then remembered we were going to the Tenderloin. Victor wouldn't take one of his own precious vehicles to that section of town. Even magical protection was no guarantee a homeless person wouldn't piss all over the tires.

On the way over, I concentrated on driving while Victor and Eli gossiped about their counterparts in other cities. Each major city, and some rural areas as well, has a counterpart to Eli. Or Victor. There's no true organization in practitioner society; no one is ever "appointed." Victor and others like him assume the responsibility on their own, primarily because they can. Not many practitioners can carry it off, and even fewer want to. The ones who take charge do it primarily out of a sense of noblesse oblige. If not me, then who, Victor often pointed out. If he hadn't been a practitioner Victor would have ended up in politics. It wasn't altogether selfless, though. He enjoyed the power trip way too much to ever give it up.

"So, what happened with Alejandro?" Eli asked, referring to Victor's counterpart in L.A.

"There was a mini coup. You remember Ricardo?"

"Of course."

"Well, he apparently felt himself far more capable of running things than Alejandro, so he announced that from now on, he would be in charge."

"How delightful of him. And what did Alejandro do?"

"What do you think? Told him, 'Great, good luck,' and went off for his first vacation in five years."

I'd met Alejandro a couple of times and didn't care for him; he made Victor seem like the model of kindness and tact. A particular type of person tends to gravitate toward power positions, and most of them push my buttons. But I could still appreciate his cleverness in defusing the situation.

"How long did Ricardo last?" I asked.

"Longer than I thought he would," said Victor. "Almost a month. By then he was begging Alejandro to come back and take charge again."

I believed it. The only thing I could think of worse than working for Victor would be to have the job myself.

I found an open parking space on Eddy Street near Van Ness and edged the van in. Victor slipped a quarter in the meter and put a freeze spell on it so it wouldn't run out. For someone with such a rigid sense of ethics, you'd think he wouldn't be using talent to scam a little time, but he claimed it was only because he was working.

"You wouldn't expect a cop to put money into a meter on a police call, would you?" he said. "On my own time, I pay." He probably did.

Victor took a moment to cast a delicate sheen over himself and Eli—nothing you could put your finger on—but they both now looked like they belonged in the neighborhood. Not street people, not junkies; it was more subtle than that. They were now just people who fit in. I hate to admit it, but the man is good. He started to do the same for me, then dismissed the idea.

"You'll do just fine," he said.

We walked the half block down to the KFC on the cor-

ner of Polk Street. Lou stayed by my heels, acting the part
of a well-trained dog. Victor told us to wait, crossed over,
and approached a man waiting outside the restaurant. I was
impressed; I hadn't thought Victor would ever be able to
cultivate street-level informants without me. He spent a
few minutes speaking with the guy, a middle-aged man of
indeterminate race and few teeth, handed him some folded
bills, then rejoined us.

   "Okay," he said. "Here's the deal. There's a young girl
living at the Eddy Hotel who claims that for twenty bucks
she can get revenge on anyone you want by putting a curse
on them. Nothing spectacular, just enough to screw up
their lives a little. She seems to have had some success,
enough so that people take her seriously at least. Somebody had a beef with a liquor store owner, and the girl is
going to take care of it for him. Right now she's sitting inside the restaurant eating chicken wings, but she'll be on
the move as soon as she's finished."

   This situation was unusual, but not rare. It's a necessary
part of the job. Occasionally, young kids with true talent
are blithely walking around unaware of practitioner society. It wasn't that Victor was concerned with petty curses,
any more than the cops would spend time and effort track-
ing down a simple shoplifter. But if the girl was really able
to do what she claimed, it meant she had some untrained
ability. If so, she'd need to be taken off the streets and
paired up with a mentor, someone who could keep an eye
on her and show her the ropes. Otherwise, she might eventually grow strong enough to cause real trouble. And, depending on circumstance, that might lead to a mundane
investigation that could cause trouble for us all.

   Eli had established a group home for just such individuals, a combination home for troubled teens and school to
develop talent. Sherwood spent a lot of her time working
with the kids there. Her empathy and kindness makes her
perfect for the job; the girls idolize her as a role model and
the boys, naturally enough, fall all over themselves to gain
her approval. All the boys have a crush on her and a few of

the girls as well, but she never has a problem with any of them. She makes it clear what the boundaries are, and no one who knows her ever dreams of crossing them. That includes me.

We waited for the girl to come out, standing a couple of doors down from the corner. A few doors farther down from where we stood, an older street person swerved off the sidewalk and, with no self-consciousness, dropped his pants, squatted down between two parked cars, and made a large deposit in the street next to the curb. I'd forgotten the special charm of the Tenderloin. Lou wrinkled his nose and looked up at me with disdain.

"Right," I said. "Like you've never taken a dump in the street."

The door to the KFC opened. "That's her," Victor said.

She was your typical gutter rat: no more than seventeen, spiked hair, nose ring, a motorcycle jacket and oh-so-cool demeanor. Her hair was red and green with black roots, springing up over a pale face covered with pimples and sores either from untreated acne or drug abuse. She was carrying a skateboard under one arm, and a small backpack completed the street uniform. We were going to have trouble following her if she got on the skateboard, but she kept it tucked it under her arm as she strolled toward us.

We moved unhurriedly away, keeping about a half block ahead of her. When she passed the spot where the homeless guy had squatted, she paused. Grabbing a couple of pieces of cardboard from the gutter, she maneuvered the man's deposit on top of the first cardboard section, using the other to scrape the stuff onto it. A paper bag that had blown up against a car wheel provided a handy container. She transferred the mess, and holding the bag carefully away from her body, continued down the street. Odd, certainly, but not magical.

Halfway down the block, she stopped in front of a liquor store, then turned back and began to walk in the other direction. We trailed behind, weaving through pedestrian traffic. The girl stopped a couple of times as if unsure where she was going, took a few tentative steps each time, then strode along, never looking back. She reminded me of something, but I couldn't put my finger on it until Lou brushed up against my leg. That was it; she was like Lou on the trail of a scent.

Eventually she cut through an alley and stopped next to a gray Toyota parked in a red zone. She quickly scanned the surrounding area, but didn't appear concerned about being seen. In the Tenderloin, people mostly ignore anything not directly affecting them.

The first thing she did was to carefully shake out the human waste onto the street next to the driver's door. Next, she opened the backpack, pulled out a squirt bottle, and walked around the car, trying each door. The left rear door had been left unlocked, so she opened it, unlocked the driver's door, reached in, and popped the hood release. Finally, she walked to the front, raised the hood, looked into the engine compartment for a second, and then sprayed something inside with the squirt bottle. From where we were standing I couldn't see exactly what she was doing, but wetting down the distributer was a good bet. She closed the hood and put the bottle back in her pack. After walking a ways farther on, she crossed over to the other side of the alley and hunkered down on her skateboard to watch and wait.

"Seen enough?" I asked. This run was a bust. The girl was clever, no doubt. She'd come up with a convincing scam to showcase her supposed powers, but she was no practitioner.

"Let's wait awhile," said Eli.

In no more than fifteen minutes, a well-dressed Middle Eastern gentleman appeared, stepping carefully over the accumulated filth of the alley. Our girl straightened up against the wall, showing interest, so it looked like this might be her target. The man walked directly to the car, stepping squarely on the pile of crap that had been left by the driver's door. He cursed loudly and spent the next five minutes trying to scrape the residue off his shoe.

He finally got most of it, climbed into the driver's seat, and put his key in the ignition. The engine turned over strongly but wouldn't catch. After a fruitless couple of minutes, he opened the hood and peered inside hopefully, the way people do when they have no idea what they're looking for. He got back in the car and tried again, without success. When he got out again he slammed the car door hard enough to make the car rock and pulled a cell out of his pocket. He leaned against the car and spoke loudly into it for a while. Across the alley, the girl sprang to her feet, flipped her board over, and pushed off down the street. I couldn't be sure, but I thought she was smiling.

"Well, that was fun," I said. "Can we go now?" I noticed both Victor and Eli looking at me with tolerant amuse-ment. I was used to it from Victor, but not Eli. "What?" I said.

Victor got that condescending look on his face. "You have been out of the game for a while, haven't you, Mason?" He motioned toward Eli. "You want to explain it to him?"

Eli nodded. "You have lost a step, Mason. Think about what you just saw. This girl finds the fresh ahh . . . deposit, right as she comes out of the restaurant. A piece of card-board and a paper bag are conveniently available where she needs them. When she finds the car, she puts the stuff down in plain sight, but guess what—our victim, who has been walking carefully down the alley through a minefield of dog poop, somehow doesn't notice until he steps right in it. And then, further luck! The door to the car has been un-characteristically left unlocked. Who, I ask you, forgets to lock his car in this neighborhood?"

"And if you knew anything about cars, you'd know that simply spraying water on the distributer won't keep it from starting," Victor added. "Oh, it's *possible*, but you have to take off the cap and spray inside the distributer if you want to be sure it has any effect."

I *was* out of practice. I'd just accepted a whole string of "coincidences" without examining them for a minute. If I was going to be doing any investigating on my own I'd have to start paying closer attention.

"So she is using talent, then?"

"Of course. She just doesn't realize it. We'll have to get her into the Home. She shouldn't be allowed to run around loose much longer. Sherwood will take her on, I'm sure. Hopefully this girl will turn out to be a worthy lost soul and not just an obnoxious street kid with talent."

"You didn't mention the most interesting part," Victor said.

"How did she find the cat," I said, finally getting it.

"Exactly."

"You think she could be a Finder?"

"She could well be. Or, she could have scoped out the location beforehand. We'll have to wait and see."

A Finder is a practitioner with a minor but rare talent. A Finder can locate anything, any person, any object. It has nothing to do with power or depth of talent; the ability is more along the lines of an idiot savant. Lou can do something similar, but with more restrictions. It's a useful talent to possess.

We wandered back to my van and spent the drive back speculating about the source of the gems, but without any further information it wasn't very productive, so conversation wound down after a while. I dropped them both off at Victor's, then headed back to my place. About halfway home I realized I never did get any coffee.

FOUR

I STOPPED ON MY WAY HOME TO GET A VEGGIE
burrito at La Taqueria on Mission. When I got home I
shared with Lou, who wasn't happy about the lack of beef,
but since he'd pretty much eat anything I didn't worry.

I did some hard thinking about who would be my best
source of information. Rafael Ramirez was the obvious
choice. Music was one of his many talents, but he had others less respectable. As an occasional fence, he knew as
much about precious stones as did most jewelers. He might
not be able to tell me what my stone was, since it wasn't a
normal gem, but might well know if there were any more
like it floating around.

But I hadn't seen him in a year, and considering his
lifestyle, it was about fifty-fifty whether he was even still
among the living. It might be difficult to track him down.
Usually I relied on Lou to locate people for me but he
couldn't help me this time. He has to know a person or at
least have met them before he can locate them, and he'd
never run across Rafael.

I spent the early part of the evening hitting various bars,

mostly in the Mission, trying to get a line on him. The
Make Out Room. Elixir. Galia. I even drifted up to Jerry's
in Bernal Heights, a place I hadn't frequented for a spell.
Jerry's clientele is sketchy at best, one bare step up from
street people, but a lot of odd people drift through there
and you can pick up some interesting info from time to
time. But no one had seen Rafael in a couple of months and
no one was much interested in talking about him anyway.
Apparently Rafael had burned a lot of bridges in the last
year or so.

I knocked off the search early and decided to make a
quick stop at Pascal's party. If I left his place by nine-thirty
I could still make it to the last night of the gig on time.
There were always a few practitioners at his parties, ones
that didn't move in the same circles as Victor or Eli.
Maybe I could pick up something there.

I took Lou with me. He loves parties. He runs his cute
dog routine and snarfs up enough tidbits of cheese, pâté,
and whatever else he can beg to feed himself for a week.
Shameless is not the half of it.

Pascal lives on Stockton, just down from Washington
Square Park. Finding a legit parking space in North Beach
big enough for a van would involve magic far beyond my
capabilities, something along the line of restructuring the
universe. But I did have a trick. Right where Columbus
crosses Greenwich a fire hydrant guards a prime spot near
the corner. I parked next to the hydrant and then spent
some time weaving an illusion which made the hydrant appear to be a nondescript electrical junction box. Usually I
don't like to use talent the same day I'm playing a gig. It
uses some of the same reserves, and makes me feel like
I've already played a set even before I start. But making
one thing look like another is a lot less taxing than a spell
which causes people not to notice it in the first place. The
tricky part is providing a comfort level so that no one will
question the substitution. If I just left the illusion unprotected, the first traffic cop who knew the neighborhood
would stop to see what the hell had happened to the hy-

drant he knew was there yesterday. And it wasn't an illusion that could stand up to much scrutiny.

I watched the people passing by and picked out the ones who obviously lived in the neighborhood, reaching out and taking a bit of familiarity from each one. Then I layered each piece of comfortableness into the illusion until it felt like something which had always been on that corner, familiar and unremarkable. Satisfied, I walked down the sidewalk toward Pascal's.

The giant edifice of St. Peter and St. Paul's Church loomed over me as I strolled along, spires and turrets layered on top of each other like wedding cake tiers. Over the front entrance, resting in niches, sit four large sculptures: a lion, an angel, and two ferocious winged creatures. I regarded them warily, remembering the alley, but they remained reassuringly immobile.

The entrance to Pascal's flat is a five-feet-tall grillwork gate that accesses a tunnel, burrowing under the streetside building. You have to stoop to walk through it, and water pipes and tangled electrical conduits hang festively from the ceiling. It wasn't a problem for Pascal, who barely clears five feet, if that, but most others have to use a shuffling crouch to pass through. The tunnel opens onto an interior courtyard, enclosed by three-story buildings, each with a wooden porch and stairs leading down to the courtyard. Lines filled with clothes in various states of dryness crisscross overhead. Jazz and rock and salsa echo off the sides of the buildings. It's like being transported back to the fifties, when all of North Beach was like that, a bohemian casualness that's all but disappeared. Or so I've been told.

Pascal's flat is on the top floor of the largest building. He owns not only the flat but also the entire building, and most of the surrounding ones as well. And a few more around the city. As a young man he had arrived in San Francisco with money—some say from drugs, some say smuggling—from points unknown, and had bought up as many buildings on the cheap as he could. Now he's a very rich man. He speaks French, Spanish, and Arabic, and English with a slight, indefinable accent. For all I know he speaks another ten or twenty languages as well, and nobody is sure what his mother tongue might be. He never talks about anything before his arrival in San Francisco. There's definitely a story there.

There were already a lot of people at the party, even though it was early, and someone I didn't know let me in. I threw my jacket in a small front room with a bunch of others, stuffing it in a far back corner where I could locate it later. It's scuffed up more than the usual ubiquitous black leather jacket of the San Francisco yuppie/hipster scene, but it was still fair game. Go to any party these days, throw your leather jacket in the bedroom among twenty or so others, and your chances of retrieving it are fifty-fifty at best. I know people who have gone through four jackets in a year—if theirs are gone, they simply take one that looks close. And there's always the chance of things coming full circle at some other party and them eventually ending up with their original jacket.

I could hear voices proclaiming, "ooh, how cute," so I knew Lou was already working the room. I chatted with a few people I knew, catching up, not asking questions, just trying to get a feel for anything off-kilter. As far as I could tell, nothing. Everyone was relaxed, mellow, having a good time. Maybe we were all just being paranoid. Then I saw Sandra.

She was leaning against the back wall of the main room, quietly observing. That wasn't her style; she was the original party girl, the walking equivalent of three shots of Jack Daniel's. I'd known her a long time and we'd come close a couple of times but never actually hooked up. She wasn't much of a practitioner; she was more a painter and preferred her art to her practice. I could relate.

She looked unwell, sick. Always thin, she now seemed positively emaciated. I might have suspected crystal, maybe even smack, but I happened to know Sandra had never touched so much as an aspirin in her entire life. I moved over beside her, and disturbingly, she didn't even notice.

"Hey," I said, gently pushing on her shoulder. She turned her head.

"Oh, hey, Mason. S'up?"

"Not much. Just hanging out." She nodded.

"What you been up to?" I asked.

"Oh, stuff," she said vaguely. This was not the Sandra I knew.

"You okay? You don't look so good."

"Yeah. No, I'm fine. A little down lately, that's all. I thought maybe a party would cheer me up."

Sandra was one of the few practitioners with an Ifrit. There were those who thought it wasn't fair, since she barely used the little talent she had, but there's no figuring Ifrits. Sandra's Ifrit was Moxie, a scruffy little brown terrier type who was the smartest Ifrit I'd ever met, though if Lou overhead me say that he'd probably pee in my shoes. Not that Lou isn't smart; he is. They all are. He's smart enough to understand most of what I say—maybe not the exact words, but certainly the sense of them. He can open doors if he's strong enough, twisting the knob in his mouth. On the other hand, he'll eat a pound of bacon if he can get it, throw up, and do it again an hour later. Certain things he never seems to learn. You just have to remember he is a dog, or a reasonable facsimile. He isn't like a dumb human; he's brilliant, but still a dog. Sort of. But he wasn't as smart as Moxie.

"So, where's Moxie?" I asked.

Sandra stared straight ahead and answered in a listless voice. "She's gone."

"She's gone? What do you mean, gone? Where did she go?"

Sandra shrugged, almost imperceptibly. "I don't know."

I waited for a fuller explanation but none was forthcoming. She went back to staring out across the room. I didn't like this at all. I slipped away, and again, she paid no attention. I stood across the room for a while, watching her. Lou came over from across the room and ran over to greet her, but before he reached her he stopped, stared, and then slunk quietly away, tail curled between his legs. Again, not good.

I was going to have to check her out on the psychic plane. That was something I didn't like doing; it took a lot of energy and always left me weak and disoriented afterward. It's not as simple as shifting your perspective, the way you might when examining the warding on a house. Exploring auras is more subtle and involving. It's almost like merging with the other person, and doing it without their knowledge and permission, even with the best intentions, is a terrible invasion. Like a doctor, who without asking, decides to check you for a hernia in the middle of the dance floor. But there was something very wrong with Sandra, and in the state she was in I didn't think it would even register I was doing anything.

I called Lou over to stand watch. Whenever you check auras you're no longer totally in your body. I needed his help to deflect anyone coming up to chat, not to mention how vulnerable I was going to be to anyone with bad intentions.

"Sandra," I told him. "She's not well." He didn't make any sign, but he clearly got it. "Guard. I'm going to check on her."

I slid my back down the wall until I was sitting on the floor. Lou sat in front of me, and I dismantled my ego and drifted into a dream state, though not that drifty, unfocused state we usually call dreamlike. More a chaotic swirl of emotionally charged dark confusion. Some practitioners can function perfectly well in that state, but I don't have the training or experience. I always feel like someone on acid for the first time.

It's hard to focus in that condition, or sometimes to even remember why you're there. As a result, I usually just observe and then try to make sense of what I've seen when I come back. I drifted through the room, watching the auras of the party guests with their shifting planes of color shot through with bright sparks, similar but endlessly different. The few practitioners present were easily identifiable. Practitioner auras are different in a way that's hard to put a finger on, but you know one when you see it. One caught my attention momentarily—a practitioner, but subtly wrong. Not just different, but wrong. I'd have to remember to check it out.

I glanced down at Lou for reassurance. Ifrits have their own auras, different from people, but nothing like animals. I could see energy flowing smoothly from Lou's aura to mine, stabilizing me, something I'd never noticed before.

I'd almost forgotten about Sandra by the time she came into my awareness. Her aura was swirling chaotically, almost flinging itself away, but that wasn't the worst thing. Right in the middle was a huge black scar, as if something had been torn away. Like a heart scan showing a massive MI, or an MRI of a brain invaded by a monstrous tumor. I'd never seen anything like it. Was this what happened when an Ifrit abandoned a practitioner? The sight was so horrible, so disturbing, that it broke my trance and shocked me back into my normal consciousness.

I got shakily to my feet, feeling sick to my stomach. I always did after visiting the psychic realm, but this was worse. Sandra glanced over toward me with blank eyes. I felt I should do something, but had no idea what. I was thoroughly spooked, and slipped quietly away.

Obviously something major had happened to her. The question was, had Moxie left because of what had happened to Sandra, or was the psychic scarring a result of the abandonment? I selfishly hoped it was the former. We all want to believe there must be a reason if an Ifrit leaves, that it must somehow be the fault of the practitioner. That way we can say, well it's sad, of course, but it won't happen to *me*.

After taking a few minutes to calm down, I started looking around for the practitioner with the unusual aura. I found him lounging against a tiled counter in the spacious kitchen, sipping a glass of red and talking animatedly with two very young women. I recognized him immediately, though I'd never had much to do with him. I'd always figured him for one of those low-level wannabes who spend a lot of time hanging out with nontalented people, trying to impress them with practitioner mystique. Especially women. His main claim to fame was that he, too, had an Ifrit, supposedly a raven of all things. Again, go figure.

He looked pretty much the way I remembered him; small and wiry, no more than five-four, constantly vibrating with suppressed intensity. Wound much too tight for my taste. The wrinkle lines that crackled around his eyes could have been from laughter, but I was betting it was more from too much clenching of teeth. Close-cut curly hair, starting to go gray. A straight nose and freakishly tiny ears.

A sense of power hung around him, very different than the last time I had seen him. He looked up as I came in, giving a friendly smile and wave, holding up one finger as if trying to remember who I was, politely giving me a chance to name myself.

"Mason," I said, offering a hand.

"Of course. Christoph." He glanced around. "Nice party, isn't it? Where do you know Pascal from?"

"Oh, around," I said, vaguely.

Lou poked his head in, having finally figured out that the kitchen would be a likely source for all things edible. Sometimes I wonder just how smart he really is. Christoph noticed him and gave me an appraising look. Apparently I had gone up a notch in his estimation, having shown up with an Ifrit, although I'm not sure why. As I said, a connection with an Ifrit hasn't much to do with the worth of the practitioner.

I wondered where his raven was, although I wasn't gauche enough to ask. Having an Ifrit who could fly could be very useful, I guess, but it might be problematical at a mixed party.

I didn't bother to introduce Lou. I felt an instant distaste for the man. Maybe it was from the aura I had seen swirling around him. I've learned to trust that gut feeling—

sometimes it proves wrong, but not often. I knew I should pump him for information, but I could barely stand to be in his presence.

Christoph continued chattering on, oblivious to my short noncommittal responses. Maybe he was the type who could hardly conceive that not everyone found him to be fascinating. The two young women by his side clearly did.

Sandra wandered into the kitchen, still wearing her vacant expression, barely acknowledging us. Out of the corner of my eye, I noticed a quick smile flit over Christoph's face. It wasn't a smile of amusement, which would have been bad enough, but more the smirk of someone who thinks they know something you don't. There was something definitely off. I stopped ignoring his conversation and focused in with renewed interest like I was supposed to.

"So, what have you been up to lately?" I asked heartily. He eyed me cautiously before deciding I was just making conversation.

"Oh, I've got some irons in the fire," he said. "Right now I'm concentrating on how to make some money." He gave a self-deprecating laugh. "I get tired of being poor. I mean, what's the sense of having talent if you can't use it to better yourself?"

"Sure," I replied, "but that kind of thing is kind of frowned upon, isn't it?"

"You mean like with Eli and Victor and that bunch?" He gave me a calculating look. "I seem to remember you hanging out with that crew, no?"

"Well, that was awhile ago," I said, shrugging. "I don't see a whole lot of them anymore."

Christoph took that in, then decided he wasn't about to embrace me as his new best friend and confidant on the basis of one sentence.

"Oh, I wouldn't do anything unethical," he assured me. He gave me another look, this one sharper. "But you can't tell me you've never sat down and dreamed about ways to cash in on your abilities. Unless you especially enjoy your romantic life of poverty?"

He had me there. But how did he know my money situation unless he'd been keeping tabs on me? Interesting.

"Who hasn't," I said, lightly. "What about you? Have you come up with anything clever?" I was clumsily fishing. I've never been good at the whole "get the bad guy to tell you his secrets" thing. Christoph laughed, genuinely amused.

"Well, no. Not yet. But one can always hope."

I had enough sense to realize that pushing it wasn't going to get me anywhere, not to mention I had no idea if there was anywhere to get. Christoph might be a bad guy, but he might just as easily be nothing more than an obnoxious boor. I was about to be late for my gig anyway, so I made excuses, pulled Lou away from a group of intoxicated partyers who seemed to be betting on how many canapés he could eat without getting sick, said good-bye to Pascal, avoided Sandra, and five minutes later was back on the street.

It was misting out, that almost-rain so typical of San Francisco. I'd only gone a couple of blocks down from Stockton, passing by a blind alley, when I heard noise. A confused muttering of voices, then a couple of louder yet indistinct shouts, then, a woman's scream. I looked over and saw two stocky men pulling a woman toward a dark corner. One of the men had hold of her arm and the other had his hand either on the back of her neck or in her hair. She wasn't giving up easily though; besides screaming she was striking out with her free arm, and doing some damage.

I started running toward them. I may not exactly be a knight in shining armor, but I wasn't about to let a woman be hauled off the street and raped right in front of me. I'd run about ten steps when instinct cut out and actual thought cut in. What were the chances of a street attack happening just as I was walking by, especially now? I stopped abruptly, and as I did, the figures struggling down the alley faded away like so many wisps of smoke. Perfect.

The alley dead-ended in front of me about thirty yards farther down. I turned around and could barely make out the street I'd just left, obscured by a flickering blue neon curtain blocking my retreat. This could prove interesting. You'd think I would have learned by now not to blindly rush into a dark alley. It looked like Darwinian evolutionary theory was about to be upheld yet again, since I was clearly too stupid to live.

Lou looked up at me with disgust. The illusion hadn't fooled him, of course, but when I'd sprinted off down the alley there wasn't much he could do but follow.

The pavement under my feet began to bubble and roil. Small blisters appeared on the surface, and as each popped it expelled an unpleasant sluglike creature about the size and shape of a hot dog. Gray skin, rough and wrinkled, covered them. From one end, two projections sprouted like antennae or snail horns, but other than that they were featureless, eyeless but not necessarily blind. A viscous slime dripped off them which gave off an acrid, unpleasant odor clearly distinguishable from the normal back alley smells of rotting fruit, old coffee grounds, and dog crap.

They looked more unpleasant than dangerous, but I wasn't betting on it. It seemed unlikely anyone would go to all this effort in an attempt to make me feel nauseous. As more and more of them emerged, Lou started hopping around as if the ground was hot, trying to avoid coming in contact with them. A larger than usual specimen surfaced directly in front of me, sprouting up like some mutant fungus, and I took a step backward to avoid it.

Unfortunately there were several more of them behind me, and as I stepped back I trod on top of one. It spurted open like a bratwurst that had been left in the sun too long, splattering over my shoes and pant legs. A revolting stench filled the air. Immediately, the tops of my shoes started to smoke and ragged holes appeared on them as if someone had poured sulphuric acid on my feet. I felt a quick burning as the slime made it through my socks and started in on my feet.

I ripped off the shoes and socks, which left me standing barefoot on the cold, damp bricks. Being barefoot wasn't the ideal condition to deal with these things, but more than that, I now felt irrationally vulnerable, like having to fight naked. The pavement was at full boil, slugs proliferating like popcorn in a kettle. Avoiding them wasn't going to be an option much longer; the alley would be knee-deep in the things in a matter of minutes. I noticed that my abandoned shoes were not only dissolving under the slime, but were being rapidly shredded as well. Apparently the slugs also possessed rows of razor-sharp teeth.

Part of me cooly appreciated the cleverness of the trap—a vicious monster can be fought, a powerful spell countered, but this was going to be trickier. It was too late to set up a protective circle; there would be as many inside as out. I could immobilize some of them, but not enough of them to matter. I could block the effects of the acid for a while, but eventually sheer numbers and sharp teeth would overwhelm my defenses.

I looked around for escape, something to wall off the things, or even better, something to climb up onto. Nothing. Except . . . on the back side of one of the buildings was an old-fashioned fire escape, one with a wide barred landing on each floor and iron grid stairs connecting the landings. If I could get up there, I'd be safe. The final flight of stairs, the one that would reach the ground, had a counterweight system with a latch that kept it secure up against the last landing. From above, it would swing down gently when unlatched, swinging back up when you stepped off onto the ground. From below, it was snuggled safely out of reach, preventing access from the street.

Talent isn't very good at dealing with inanimate objects. It's a lot better affecting energies and living organisms. Objects aren't my strong suit anyway, and there was no way I could trip an iron latch twelve feet over my head and swing the iron stairs down. I might, given enough time, figure out a way to accomplish it, but of course you never do have enough time. That's the whole point. Lou was meanwhile eyeing me, as if studying the possibility of scrambling up to the relative safety of my shoulders.

"Forget it," I snarled, annoyed at his selfishness. "I've got a better idea." I pointed up toward the fire escape. "Up there. Get the latch." He looked up to where I was pointing and then looked back skeptically at me. I didn't have time to explain.

I picked him up and gauged the distance carefully. I wasn't going to have a second chance to get it right. He caught on and stiffened his muscles to make it easier to cast him through the air. If I could toss him up on that first landing, he could trip the catch and the stair would swing down for me to climb. If I missed, the fall would probably break his neck, and even if it didn't the slugs would finish him off soon enough.

"On three," I said, swinging him back and forth like I was tossing a heavy rock across a stream. He flew through the air, all four legs bicycling in an attempt to keep his balance, like an Olympic long jumper. He hit the front railing bars, and for a sickening moment I thought he wasn't going to make it, but he hooked one paw through the bars and scrabbled his way onto the landing.

He ran over to the latch holding the stairs, cocked his head, and stared at it with blank puzzlement. Oh, great. I had forgotten he wasn't mechanically inclined. I couldn't see the mechanism from where I stood down below, so he was on his own. I wanted to yell at him to hurry up, but realized that wasn't going to help the situation.

By this time I was dancing around, trying to avoid another exploding sausage debacle. Unfortunately, the dancing had the effect of energizing the slugs, who immediately started writhing around, uttering excited metallic, hissing, chittering sounds. Then I heard a bark. A light bulb had finally gone off in Lou's head and he reached down with his muzzle, twisted something I couldn't see and pulled back. He was having trouble, even though his jaws are twice as strong as you would expect from a dog that size. I finally heard a clunk as the lever released. Naturally, the stair, instead of swinging down, remained sedately in place.

Weight. It needed weight to make it move. "Run along the stair!" I shouted, motioning frantically, all the while continuing my Savion Glover impersonation. He dutifully jumped up onto the horizontal stair and deliberately walked out toward the far end. He didn't weigh much, but it was enough. As he approached the final rung at the end, the stairway gracefully levered down and presented itself. As soon as it touched down I bounded up the stairs to the safety of the platform above, with the stairway swinging up behind me.

I looked down at the now seething mass of slime-covered slugs with fascination tempered by disgust. Whoever had conjured up this mess had some power, no doubt about that. I focused in on the flickering blue curtain still blocking the entrance to the alley. I could tell it hadn't been constructed with much care; it hadn't needed to be since it was intended only to keep me penned up long enough for the slugs to do their job.

Even so, it would have taken quite a while to dismantle it, but I didn't need to. I searched through it until I found a flaw in the energy flow, then diverted it enough to form a pocket right in the middle large enough to squeeze through. With some of the diverted energy I fashioned a protective layer around my feet and lower legs, picked up Lou, and stepped back on the stair. It swung smoothly down, depositing me right in the middle of the now almost knee-deep sea of wriggling slime.

I walked carefully toward the curtain opening, shuffling my feet along the pavement in a vain attempt to avoid squashing any more of the creatures. They popped and squirted under my feet, covering the ground with a greasy slime that made for some wildly uncertain footing. I fought down the impulse to run, forcing myself to walk slowly and deliberately, trusting that the protection around my feet would hold until I got out of the alley. I didn't want to lose my balance and end up sprawled face-first.

I pushed through the curtain not a moment too soon, as my energy shield frayed and dissolved off my feet. As soon as I did, the curtain collapsed behind me and the alley pavement started bubbling in reverse, sucking down slugs like a giant pool of quicksand. Two minutes later, not a trace of anything remained.

Still barefoot, I hobbled back to my van. I just had time before the gig to stop by my house and pick up my guitar and a pair of shoes. As I drove back crosstown I had a lot to think about. I didn't like the vibes I'd got from Christoph. Was his presence there and the following attack just coincidence? What about his aura, and his reaction to Sandra? And why did he seem so much more powerful than I remembered? Power, like athletic ability, is mostly inborn and doesn't vary much. And why these attacks on me? Much as I hate to admit it, I'm not anything special. But one thing was for sure: I'd had enough and someone was going to pay. After all, that was my only good pair of shoes.

FIVE

NEXT MORNING I WAS UP EARLY DESPITE GETTING
in late. The gig hadn't gone well, which was no surprise
considering my condition. Tommy just might be thinking
twice before he hires me for another gig. I drank several
cups of coffee, then called Eli to tell him about the events
of the previous night. He was concerned, of course.

"This is getting serious," he said. "Maybe you should
stay closer to home. Or at least not go out alone."

"I don't," I said. "I've got Lou with me. Besides, what
am I supposed to do, call you every time I've got a gig?
And if I don't go out, how do I find out what's going on?"

"Still, you need to be careful."

I couldn't argue with that. I spent the rest of the morning puttering around and trying to think of another good
source for some info. After last night, finding out exactly
what was going on had become a high priority. Since
Rafael had gone underground, I needed to come up with a
second choice, and after some thought, I settled on Deuce.
Deuce was a guy with the unlikely name of Jackson Jackson, so naturally everyone called him Deuce. He'd moved

up a few years ago from L.A., where he'd been running a scam of some sort until Alejandro suggested he might want to relocate. Handsome, smooth, articulate, always dressed in the latest fashion of cool, he could have been anything he wanted. But he was cursed with the possession of some minor talent, and accordingly spent most his time figuring how to use it to scam his way through life without attracting too much unwelcome attention.

He'd once conned me into showing him how to perform a simple transfer illusion, how to make his driver's licence appear to be that of someone else, hoping to avoid an outstanding warrant when he retrieved a car from the city impound lot. The next thing I knew he was using his newfound ability to change the faces on playing cards and running a three-card monte game down on Market Street.

The funny thing was, I'd seen con artists doing the same thing better without a smidgen of talent, just using their natural skills. Still, he made out okay, and anyway he was one of those people who'd rather spend two hours working a scam than one hour on actual work, even if the work made him twice the money. Being a natural con artist he tended to make a lot of friends, so he ended up knowing something about almost everyone and everything, at least as far as his little corner of the world was concerned. I hadn't seen him for a while either, but I guessed Louie could track him down him without too much trouble.

Lou was outside taking care of some dog business of his own, but I had warned him to be back before it got too late. He breezed in about noon and I sat him down.

"We need to find someone," I told him. "Do you remember Deuce?"

He looked puzzled, but I couldn't tell if he didn't remember who Deuce was or if he just didn't understand what I was saying. Sometimes I forget I can't just talk to him like I would another person. I got some cards out of a desk drawer, two aces and a queen, and played an impromptu set of three-card monte. Louie watched intently.

"Find?" I asked. "Can you find him? Deuce?"

He uttered an abrupt bark of comprehension. Okay, so we were on. I didn't feel like wrestling with downtown traffic, so I got out my backpack and leather jacket and headed off toward the Twenty-fourth Street Mission BART station, Lou trotting along beside me. When we got there I opened up the backpack and he jumped in. The pack has a fine mesh netting along the top half that he can look through, and of course I never fasten the top flap. Being small does have its advantages; if he were a full-sized dog I could never have sneaked him on BART. Being unnoticed is probably a more efficient survival skill than being ferocious anyway. Of course I could have just masked him, but it takes energy and concentration to carry that off for extended periods.

I got off at Powell Street and rode up the long escalator to street level where I let Louie out of the backpack. No one looked twice. If a dog in a backpack is the strangest thing you see on a typical San Francisco street you're walking around with your eyes closed. It certainly couldn't compete with the guy tap dancing on a wooden platform, shirt off, one pant leg rolled up. He was thin but muscular, with no more body fat than a low-fat latte. Down the street from him was a black guy in a cowboy hat singing songs in French with the voice of an angel.

It had stopped raining by then but it was still cold and gusty. Louie stood on the corner, shivering slightly, nose quivering in the wind. He looked liked he was casting for a scent, but that just wasn't possible. There are tens of thousands of people streaming through the downtown area at any given time. But he was casting for *something*, because after a minute or so he gave a sharp bark and trotted off east down Market Street, glancing over his shoulder to make sure I was following. When we reached Fourth Street he stood indecisive for a few minutes, then continued on down Market. Just before we reached the Four Seasons Hotel, I noticed a small crowd gathered in a plaza between buildings. I strolled over to the edge of the crowd and there was Deuce, crouched on the sidewalk, shuffling his cards and talking up a mark. In front of him was a soft black cloth that he was using for the card layout, secured against the wind by some fist-sized rocks on the corners.

The mark was almost a carbon copy of Deuce, except larger and louder and blacker. A tall, good-looking guy, except where Deuce played it understated and hip, this guy was flashy and crude. Shaved head and diamond stud in his left ear, but too large. Flashy watch. An expensive suede jacket, but the sleeve was pushed up on the left arm so you wouldn't miss the watch. His girlfriend, a young Asian woman with long black hair, was pulling at him, trying to get him to leave but he was having none of it. Apparently he was down quite a bit and wasn't about to let some chump on the street get up on him. Deuce was keeping up a running line of patter as he moved the cards from hand to hand, all the while eyes darting left and right, keeping an eye out for cops.

"It's easy, just follow the little lady, anybody can do it, it's as simple as can be, watch where she goes, put your money down and win yourself a little cash, watch her now, watch her now."

His hands were moving fast but it didn't look that hard to tell where the queen was. The hands stopped and the guy pointed at the card in the middle. Deuce flipped it over and revealed the queen. He flashed a rueful grin.

"Sharp eye, sharp eye, got me that time, my man," he said.

The mark put down a twenty and Deuce shuffled the cards again. This time, the mark lost, then won, then lost a couple more times. This went on for a while and the guy won a few, but lost more. He was clearly down more than a few bucks overall and was beginning to get pissed. He threw down a fifty, raising the stakes, and guessed wrong again. Deuce scooped up the fifty and the three cards all in one motion.

"Damn!" the mark said.

"Got to keep a close eye, got to keep your eye on the lady."

"One more," the guy said, ignoring his girlfriend, who was still tugging on his arm.

"One more, last time. How about some real money? Win yourself some real money, buy your lady something nice. How about it?"

The guy knew he was being taken but he couldn't figure out exactly how it was being done. You could see he was still convinced he could beat the game.

"How much we talking?" he asked.

"Two hundred dollars, lay it down, win it all back and then some. One chance. One chance only."

The guy hesitated, not wanting to lose any more money but not wanting to back down, either. He knew he could beat this con. Deuce started to roll up the cloth, and the guy took the plunge. He reached in his pants pocket, pulled out a money clip flush with bills, and peeled off five new hundred dollar bills.

"How about five?" he said, making it a challenge.

Deuce smoothed back out the cloth, pulled out five hundred dollars of his own, and stuck both stakes under one of the rocks to keep them from blowing away.

"We have a player, ladies and gents, we have a *man* here," he said.

This time his hands moved quite a bit faster but always smooth and under control. All the while, he kept up his patter. "Watch the lady, watch the lady, she moves and she grooves, she spins and she wins."

The small crowd leaned in for a better look. The guy was watching with a look of ferocious concentration. Of course, with Deuce's other type of talent, he didn't stand a chance. When Deuce stopped, the guy unhesitatingly leaned over and put his hand on the end card to his left. Before Deuce could move, he flipped it over himself. Ace of spades. Deuce flipped over the other two cards, showing the queen on the opposite end, lifted up the rock, and pocketed the money. He put the cards away, rolled up the cloth, and was up and walking down the street in a matter of seconds. By the time the guy could make up his mind whether or not to do something about it, Deuce was halfway down the block. The guy stood there not really knowing what to do. Finally he grabbed his girlfriend's arm and roughly pulled her away as if the whole thing had been her fault. The crowd drifted away, several of them shaking their heads in admiration. They certainly had got their money's worth. And Deuce certainly had improved his performance skills. It was like watching a formerly lame musician suddenly rip off a killer solo.

I followed slowly in his direction. This was clearly not the place to stop him for a chat, and with Louie following there was no way I could lose him. We strolled down Market to Third, turned south, crossed Mission, and finally turned off onto Minna, a small alley that runs parallel to Mission. Louie stopped outside a café called Mirabelle's and sat down on the sidewalk. I took off the backpack and he hopped in. It was too chilly to leave him outside and I thought I might be a while. I put a small masking on him so he would seem to be a sweater unless you looked closely.

There weren't many people in the café, just a bunch of small round wooden tables awaiting the coming after-work crowd. Deuce was sitting alone at a back table enjoying a latte with a big basket of thick-cut fries sitting in front of him. I pulled out the chair opposite him and helped myself to a seat, putting the backpack with Louie in it on the spare chair. He looked up over the menu and a big smile spread over his face. Either he was genuinely glad to see me or his acting skills had improved along with the three-card monte.

"Well I'll be damned!" he said. "Mason! What brings you out on this cold December day?"

I smiled back. It was hard not to like Deuce, even if he was a scammer. I suppose that's a good con man's stock in trade.

"I felt a compulsion to watch some three-card monte," I said. "You've improved."

His smile broadened. If he felt uncomfortable in any

way it didn't show. "I have, haven't I? Did you see the show down on Market?"

I nodded. "I was dazzled. But one thing puzzles me. I was waiting for the power surge on that last blow-off, but I didn't feel a thing. How did you pull that off? You're not good enough to shield like that even if you tried."

His smile grew even broader, if that were possible. "I don't use my talent when I'm playing anymore. It's all good old-fashioned sleight of hand. Let me tell you, it took a whole lot of work to master it."

"I believe it, but why bother?"

"Well, for one thing, it keeps people like—what's that guy's name?"

"Victor?"

"Yeah, Victor. It keeps people like Victor off my back. And secondly—" He broke off, looking embarrassed for the first time. "Well, to be honest, if I use my talent it feels too much like I'm cheating people."

"But you are. What's the difference how you do it?"

He seemed a bit annoyed. "Jesus, Mason, I thought you of all people would get it. It's not the same. Not the same at all. People *expect* me to cheat; they just think they're smart enough to catch me or beat me anyway. But they don't expect me to *cheat*."

Actually, it made a sort of sense the way he explained it. Louie poked his head out of the backpack, having noticed the tempting smell of fries wafting toward him. He stretched his neck forward and delicately lifted one out of the basket.

"I see you've still got Lou," Deuce said.

"Can't seem to get rid of him."

Lou looked over at Deuce and gave him a brief noncommittal tail wag. Friendly, but with reservations. Sort of the way I felt. He ducked back into the backpack as a waitress came over. I ordered a cappuccino and we chatted for a while, checking up on mutual acquaintances before I got into the reason I had looked him up. Or rather, tracked him down. Deuce was very keyed in on what I was talking about.

"Oh, yeah, absolutely," he said. "You can feel it." He adopted a phony British accent. "An evil, malign influence, pervading the very air we breathe. Seriously, man," he said, dropping the accent, "something's not right in this town. I've been thinking of heading up to Portland, or maybe back to L.A."

"L.A.?"

"Well, maybe not L.A. Not for a while, anyway."

"Any idea what's been going on?"

He shook his head. "Not really. Though I did hear about some freak who's found a way to accumulate a bunch of power and is in the process of becoming one serious motherfucker. Trying to become some sort of superpractitioner, I guess."

"Come, on," I said. "Even you know that's not possible. Talent's an inborn trait. You can certainly maximize your potential with practice, but you can't acquire power. Any more than a normal person could 'acquire' the ability of a Michael Jordan."

"Don't I know it," Deuce said ruefully. "Still, that's what I hear. Who knows? Maybe some dude has figured out a way to pull it off."

"Any talk of who it might be?"

Deuce shook his head. I reached in my pocket and pulled out the gemstone I'd borrowed from Victor, placing it carefully on the table in front of him. Lou wrinkled his nose and curled a lip when he saw it.

"Ever seen anything like this before?" I asked.

Deuce reached out a hand to pick it up but I intercepted him, grabbing hold of his wrist. Letting a con man with talent handle a priceless stone wouldn't be the smartest of moves, and Victor would kill me if I lost that stone.

"Don't touch," I cautioned. "Just look."

Deuce laughed, not offended in the least. Then he focused in on the stone and stopped laughing. He stared at it for a full minute, then shook his whole body as if throwing off a spell.

"Wow," he said. "And here I was thinking it was all bull-shit."

"So you have heard something, then?"

His eyes kept returning to the stone, so I picked it up and returned it to my pocket. It's not that I didn't trust him. Well, yes, of course it was.

"Stories," he said, nodding. "I've heard some stories. A new kind of precious stone. Some new type of diamond that's magically enhanced, but permanent. Supposedly, if you manage to get your hands on one, you can buy an island and retire." He absently handed over a now cold french fry to Lou and looked at me enviously. "You got yourself an island picked out yet?"

"The stone's not mine," I told him. "Any idea at all where they come from?"

"Not a clue. Until two minutes ago, I thought it was just another bogus pipe dream. You know, like an urban legend?" He stared down at the table where the stone had been. "Hey," he said, as a sudden thought struck him, "why not ask Rafael? If anyone would know, that's the dude."

"I'd love to. Can't find him. Nobody's seen him for months."

"You didn't hear?"

"Hear what?"

"He got busted. Not dope this time, something heavy. Kidnapping, I hear."

"Kidnapping?"

"Yeah, kidnapping and rape."

I shook my head. "Rafael? Hardly. He may get out of control sometimes, but there's no way."

"Tell that to the cops. That's what they popped him on."

"When was this?"

"A couple of months ago. They're holding him down at the Hall of Justice. I think his bail is like, a jillion dollars."

SIX

SO IT WAS THE GOOD NEWS/BAD NEWS THING. I'D managed to locate Rafael, but talking with him was going to be difficult. But not impossible. I stopped by an Office Max and picked up a plastic I.D. holder with a metal clip and a blank card, a marker, and a loose leaf binder with some sheets of paper. It was still only early afternoon so I walked down to Sixth Street and then across to Bryant.

The Hall of Justice is a large gray building that takes up the entire block between Sixth and Seventh on Bryant. The main floor holds the various courts, the parking violations office, and the like. The upper floors house the jail complex. I know quite a bit about the place from previous incidents that I won't go into.

Most of the inmates are in for short-term misdemeanors, simple assaults and petty thefts and the like, but the jail also houses serious felons awaiting trial before being shipped out to state prison. They are stashed away up on the seventh floor, along with inmates pending appeal and long-term residents. That's where Rafael would be.

Sherwood once worked at the jail as a volunteer for the

California Service League. Always doing good. Once a week she taught anger management classes to some of the more irritable residents. I remember she'd had a jail clearance I.D. with her picture on the front and the words JAIL CLEARANCE in big letters on the back, along with some other writing. The Service League, among other things, provides volunteer GED tutoring for those inmates wanting to get their high school diplomas. A lot of them are considered either escape risks or too dangerous to attend classes, but they still get to learn, with one-on-one help in a locked interview room.

I didn't feel like waiting for regular visiting hours, which are only once a week anyway, so I decided to pass myself off as a GED tutor. With the black marker, I printed JAIL CLEARANCE in large letters on the blank card that came with the plastic holder, and slipped the card through the plastic so it could be read through the back. In the front I put my driver's licence. It didn't fit very well, but that didn't matter.

I held it between my hands and made some sounds. It took three tries before it looked appropriately blurry. I'm not very good at this sort of illusion. Making one thing look like something else is fairly easy, but this called for more subtlety. The trick was to fashion it so that whoever looked at the card would see whatever they expected to see. As long as the basic form was similar it could pass for anything.

Now, if I just handed it out cold, all anyone would see was a blur. But if I gave it to a jailer and said it was a clearance card, that's exactly what they would see—a jail I.D. in perfect detail. There are plenty of practitioners who wouldn't have to go through all this, who could create an illusion out of thin air, but I'm not that good.

Telling Louie to find somewhere warm to wait, I put the loose-leaf binder under my arm and walked up the steps into the building. I passed through the metal detector with no problem, drawing a blank-eyed stare from the bored cop manning the post. Clipping the makeshift I.D. to the collar of my jacket, I waited at the elevators next to the snack shop, the ones that go directly to the jail floors. A sheriff's deputy in his tan uniform gave me a friendly nod as we got on the car together. I punched the button for the seventh floor and he got off at three.

The elevator on seven opens into a compact steel mesh cage with a door controlled by an electronic buzzer on one end. Once through that, you enter the jail proper through a reinforced steel door, also electronically operated. The doors work in sequence; if one is open the other won't function until it closes. The guard on duty sits by a console behind a narrow bulletproof window that looks out onto the cage, kind of like what you see in bank teller windows in high crime areas. A sign with large letters warns about contraband. No weapons. No drugs. No cell phones. It didn't say anything about magical gems so I figured I was okay. I approached the window and pointed to my mythical I.D., flipping it over so the no-nonsense black woman sitting there could see the "jail clearance" stamp.

"GED tutoring," I told her confidently. She gave it a cursory glance and, apparently satisfied, buzzed me through the door. The second door buzzed as soon as the first swung shut.

Immediately through the door is a large guard room and a long hallway stretching past it left and right. Another steel mesh door on the right leads to the felony cell blocks. I walked over and stood in front of it, acting as if I knew what I was doing. The guard suddenly shouted, "Hey!" at me and I turned around casually. No problem. That's what my outward demeanor projected. Inside was another story.

"You forgot to sign in," she said, gesturing at a large logbook by the door that I had overlooked.

"Sorry," I apologized, walking the few steps back to the station. The book had a place for name, agency, time in, time out, and inmate visited. From the scrawled entries above it didn't look like anyone took it too seriously, so I scribbled something illegible on the page. The guard looked at me with a spark of curiosity.

"You new here?"

I shook my head. "I've been doing it awhile. Been out at San Bruno mostly."

"Nasty place," she commented.

"That it is," I agreed.

I walked back to the mesh door and this time she buzzed me through. A row of tiny interview rooms lined one side of the corridor, a couple of them occupied with inmates talking to what were obviously attorneys. At the end of the corridor was another guard station. Right behind it a broad yellow line striped the floor and a sign on the wall warned unauthorized people not to cross. The guard at the station, a clean-cut white guy, glanced incuriously up from his magazine as I approached.

"Yeah," he said.

"GED tutoring."

"Who do you need?"

"Ramirez."

"First name?"

"Rafael."

He picked up a master list, flipped over a few pages and ran his finger down the line of names, muttering, "Ramirez, Ramirez." He stopped his finger and said, "Ramirez, Rafael, A-8." He picked up a walkie next to him and said, " 'A' block, send down Ramirez." A voice came back asking him what for. He turned to me.

"GED," I reminded him.

"GED," he said into the radio. He motioned to the interview rooms. "Take any one that's empty. He'll be out in a minute."

"Thanks," I said, choosing the one farthest away from the station. Inside was a table bolted to the floor and two yellow molded plastic chairs, scuffed and dirty. I sat down, leaving the door open, and about two minutes later, another guard arrived with Rafael in tow. He was wearing the usual orange jumpsuit and when he saw me he walked in and sat down without changing expression. The guard closed the door and locked it behind him. We looked across the table at one another.

Rafael and I go back a long way. We'd played together in a salsa band called Ritmo Caliente back in the day, and he'd been wild even then. He started out as a part-time criminal and turned it into a full-time job. When his criminal activities started interfering with his musical ones he quit playing music entirely, got heavy into crystal, and started carrying a gun. Whenever he was doing speed he got mean, although he was always cool with me. Still, people who hung with him always seemed to end up getting shot or stabbed or something. Self-preservation has always been an overriding concern of mine so after a while I stopped hanging out with him.

He himself had no talent, but a cousin of his did, and he had told Rafael a lot more about the life than he should have before finally going on to die of an OD. Rafael figured out early on that I had some of the talent, though no idea of how much, and I never enlightened him. He brought it up a few times but I always deflected his questions. He was way too unstable to be a confidant. Still, he was fascinated by the whole scene and heard more of practitioner gossip than I ever did. I was hoping that even in jail he might have heard something useful.

"Mason," he said. "When they told me there was a GED tutor waiting for me, I knew something was up. It's been what, a year?"

"Close enough. How long you been in here?"

"About three months. My case keeps getting postponed. You come to get me out?"

"Sorry, I don't have that kind of money," I said. "What kind of mess have you got yourself into, anyway?"

"Hey, this time it's totally bogus. A bullshit beef."

I looked at him skeptically. "Oh? A frame-up, right?"

Rafael laughed "Well, no," he admitted. "Not exactly. What happened was this: I'd been dealing crystal for a while, making a shitload of cash. Business was good, I was just rolling in money, you dig? So, one weekend I get an o.z. at my crib and I decide to party. Now, you remember I always liked hookers. I mean that's my thing, right?"

"Right."

"Yeah, so I call up this hooker I party with sometimes, real high-class, you know, but real nasty, too? She comes over and we're down with it doin' blow and partying and shit, and she's having such a good time she doesn't want to leave. So I figure, great, why not, and she stays there all weekend getting fucked up and stuff.

"So when she finally decides to split, it's like Monday or something by then, and I notice that most of my stash is missing. Okay, I tell her, you're not going anywhere until I get my stash back, in fact you can give it up right now or strip down right here in front of me and she says 'fuck you' and so I have to slap her around a little and finally I get my stash which she's got stuffed down you know where and I'm so pissed by then that I just kick her out on the street buck naked."

"Which she doesn't care much for."

"Right. And what I don't know is that her pimp has been looking for her all weekend and she's afraid he's going to beat on her and all for flaking on him so she tells him I wouldn't let her leave or call and that I raped her and stuff. Hell, we didn't even have sex, just blowjobs, you know? Anyway he decides to call the police. A pimp! Calling the fucking cops! Can you believe that?

"So then the cops show up and she's got all these bruises and shit 'cause her pimp beats on her anyway for lying to him but she says it was me, so they pull me out of my crib and arrest me and shit for kidnapping and rape 'cause she said I kept her prisoner, and then they were going to drop the charges 'cause they don't really believe her but it turns out that there's a prostitutes' union, can you believe *that*, and there are all these hookers and stuff down at the courtroom protesting and so the DA decides to go ahead and prosecute after all. Is that fucked up or what?"

"Hey," I said, trying not to laugh. I mean, he could do some serious time over this. "What do you expect? This is San Francisco."

Everybody in jail has a story, and all the stories are self-serving, but this one did have a certain ring of truth.

"You got a lawyer?" I asked.

"The best. She better be. I already paid her five thousand dollars." He sat there quiet for a moment, then laughed and punched my shoulder. "Anyway, what's up with you, man? What you doin' here?"

I dug the stone out of my pocket and placed it on the table between us. Rafael looked at it without expression.

"What can you tell me about this?" I asked.

He picked it up and hefted it a couple of times, trying to get a feel for the weight. Then he put it up to his eye. He kept it there for a long time. Then he lowered his hand and hefted it a couple more times before closing his hand into a fist. He looked across the table at me and his usual easygoing expression had vanished, replaced by that mean, suspicious, hard demeanor that I'd only seen when he was doing meth. That Rafael was a dangerous guy.

"Where did you get this?" he said, more an accusation than a question. I became painfully aware that we were sharing a small room with a locked steel door.

"Dude. Chill. It came off a dead man." He continued staring at me for a full thirty seconds, then, gradually, his expression lost its hard edge and the old Rafael was back.

"Sorry," he said. "Actually seeing it was a trip. I thought for a moment you were fucking with me."

"So you've seen it before."

He shook his head. "Actually, no. But I spent two months trying to get hold of it."

"If you never saw it before, how do you know it's what you were looking for? And what is it, anyway?" Rafael gave me the same unbelieving look I get from Lou when I'm having steamed vegetables for dinner.

"Jesus, Mason, have you looked at it? You think there's more than one of those things in the world?" Actually there were at least three, but I didn't want to complicate matters. "And you want to know what is it?" he continued. "Damned if I know." His suspicious look made a brief reappearance. "It seems you'd know a lot more about it than I would, anyway. I mean, look at it. Is it my kind of thing, or yours?"

Rafael might not have any talent himself, but he'd been

around people who do most of his life. He could recognize a magical object even if he didn't know what it was.

"What do you mean, you spent two months trying to get hold of it?" I asked. He leaned back as much as the molded plastic chair would allow.

"Well, here's the deal. I heard about this special jewel . . ."

"How?"

He flashed a sly grin. "You know me. I got contacts. Anyway, it was supposed to be something special, worth a shitload of cash. I heard a hundred grand." He held up his fist, still holding the gem. "Maybe more. Now that I've seen it, much more. There's nothing else like it, right? The only problem was, the guy who had it was one of you guys."

"A practitioner?"

"Yeah, right. A practitioner. Well, I didn't want to mess with him, but I found out where he lived, and I figured I could wait until he was gone, slip in the house, find it, and he'd never know what happened to it."

"You were going to rip off a practitioner? Bad idea, Rafe. Bad idea."

"Yeah, no shit. Anyway, I scoped out the place for a while and finally got up the nerve to go in, so I pry open this window and climb through. At first everything was cool, nothing scary, just a bunch of empty rooms and stuff, but then something happened. There was this mirror on one of the walls, and when I walked by, my reflection got stuck. I mean, like I was just frozen there inside the mirror, you dig?"

I did. It was an image capture spell, flashy but not that difficult. A security camera would have done just as good a job.

"It totally freaked me out. I could barely make myself go upstairs."

"Wait a minute," I said. "There's something here you're not telling me. I know you like money, everyone does. But not that much. It's not like you're ever even broke. You knew what you were getting into, breaking into a practitioner's house. It's not worth it. Why didn't you get the hell out of there?"

Rafael nodded. "Yeah, you're right. The thing is, I also heard that this jewel could do things. That it was special. Like, if I had it I could be just like you guys."

Now it made more sense. Rafael had always been jealous of those with talent. Talent was the one thing he'd always wanted, more than money, more than sex, and he'd risk his life for a chance to acquire some. He started rubbing his forehead abstractedly.

"So then I go upstairs. There are like, three rooms, and so I go in the first one and it's mostly empty, and there's a door leading out on the other side. So I go through that, but then somehow I'm back downstairs where I started.

"Now I'm really scared. I figure, screw the jewel, it's time to get out of here, so I climb back out the window, only that doesn't work either. I'm on the other side of the house, but I'm still inside. Weird, you know? So then I tried the front door. Same thing. I tried a bunch of other stuff. But I couldn't get out."

"Well, you got out somehow," I said. "You're here."

"Yeah. Which is just great, you know? Anyway, I ended up sitting on the floor, just waiting. It must have been a couple of hours. Then I heard a key unlocking the front door, and it opened partway, stopped, and then swung all the way open. I don't think I ever was so scared in my life."

"Who was it?"

"That's the thing. I don't know. That's the last thing I remember. The next thing I know I'm walking down the street about a block from my crib."

A memory wipe. I should have known getting information wasn't going to be that easy.

"Do you remember where the house was?" I asked. He shook his head.

"Not a clue. I don't even remember who the guy was who lived there. And I don't want to. I think maybe I'm lucky it wasn't worse."

He was right about that. Memory wipes on ordinaries are highly discouraged, since one occasional side effect can be the complete destruction of higher brain function. So. Dead end on this line of inquiry.

Rafael's bust had come a week later—suspiciously timely. One thing for sure—the idea of a pimp calling the cops for help was ridiculous. Unless he'd been encouraged to. The result being that Rafael stayed out of commission for an extended period, with no more chance to go poking around places he shouldn't. A setup seemed likely, but I didn't mention anything about that possibility. It wouldn't do him any good and he had enough to worry about.

Rafael was getting fidgety and his fist was still closed tightly around the jewel. I held out my hand.

"I need that stone back, Rafe."

He hesitated, holding his breath. I could see him weighing the possibilities, running through scenarios that would end up with him keeping the stone. He couldn't go anywhere, but he could swallow it, for example, and where would that leave me? I could just see explaining to Victor that I hadn't exactly lost the stone, it was just that someone had eaten it.

I used some potential and let a quick illusion flit over my face, just to remind him I could be dangerous as well. A stereotypical devil mask, complete with flickering tongue, sharp teeth and rudimentary horns. It was a momentary glimmer, not lasting long enough for him to be sure what he'd seen, but long enough.

"Hand it over, Rafe," I said.

He let out his breath and dropped it into my hand. "Just a thought," he said. "Probably better I don't have it anyway. It's trouble, isn't it?"

"Looks that way."

"Oh, well. Sorry I couldn't be more help. Hey, you looking for the four one one on anything else?"

I ran down the attacks on me for him. In his own weird way Rafael's not a bad guy, and I knew he'd help me out—if it didn't cost him anything. I told him I was looking for any leads at all, anything else weird he might have noticed in the last year, anything unusual.

"I hear you," he said when I was done. "You know, right

before I got busted, there was some funny shit going down. You checked out The Challenges?"

"The what?"

"The Challenges, man. You not hip to that?"

"Not really."

Rafael looked at me with something like pity. "You don't know shit about stuff, do you?"

"Not really," I said.

"Okay, listen. On the first Tuesday of every month, just before it gets dark, some of the heavy hitters gather for what they call The Challenges. You know those big fields in Golden Gate Park where they play soccer and there's that big track that goes all around?"

"The Polo Fields?"

"Yeah, that's the place. It happens over there, on the east end."

"And what is it they do there?"

"Just what it sounds like, dude. They challenge each other. I guess."

"Over what?"

"Shit, I don't know."

"You never checked it out?"

"Well, that's the thing. I tried once. I went over there, but you know, as soon as I got close I started worrying about what might happen to me if I were caught, not being one of you and all. So I turned around and started back to my crib, only halfway there I started thinking I was being a pussy and there was no reason anything would happen and then when I got close I started thinking again of all the things that could happen to me. I mean, I didn't want to get turned into a skunk or something, you dig? So I gave it up and went back home again."

"And when you got home you couldn't understand why you got so freaked, right?"

"Exactly. I don't know how they do it, but I could tell I wasn't supposed to be there."

It made sense. Not exactly an aversion spell, but along the same lines. If it was cold, you would decide to come back another day when it was warmer. If you were hungry, you'd suddenly really need to get something to eat. If you were fearful, the place would seem truly dangerous. In any case, you would never get close enough to find out what was going on there.

Rafael glanced over through the small window set up high on the door and waved at another inmate being led down the hall in shackles.

"Julian. He got written up for fighting. They screwed up and put him in a cell with one of the *Sureños*. What the hell did they expect?" He turned back to face me. "The thing is, the dudes who go to these challenges are some heavy players, and they're not too nice, I hear."

"How long has this been going on?" I asked.

"I'm not sure, maybe a year. So, what do you think? Is that any help?"

"Could be," I said, getting up. "Worth checking out, anyway. Thanks, Rafe. Listen, is there anything I can do for you? Besides walking you out of here," I added hastily. "I don't have those kind of skills."

"That's okay. I'll be out of here soon anyway. There's no way they can hang this on me, not with the lawyer I got." He smiled ruefully. "You know," he said, "there's been so many things I *have* done where I never got caught, maybe this is just karma catching up to me."

"You believe that?"

"No, not really, but you got to be philosophical in here."

I pressed the buzzer to summon the guard. "You done?" he asked, unlocking the door.

"Yeah," I said. "I think he's learned all he can."

I went through the entry process in reverse order—through the first door, sign out the log, second door, cage door, down the elevator. But when I reached the lobby, the elevator door opened and showed me the basement instead. I pressed the lobby button but the elevator stubbornly stayed put, the door mindlessly opening and closing. It wasn't until I'd left the elevator, found the stairs, walked up a flight and found myself back in the basement that it dawned on me that it might be more than a simple elevator malfunction. It was the same type of loop that had trapped Rafael so effectively. Interesting. But I wasn't Rafael.

I climbed up the stairs again, slowly this time, sending out small probes to check for a discontinuity. If it was there I couldn't find it, and when I pushed open the fire door on the landing it just opened back into the basement again. I was more annoyed than worried. This type of spatial loop isn't that hard to set up, although it does take some power. But it's not that hard to get out of either. Usually, I relied on Lou to deal with this sort of thing; Ifrits have little trouble wriggling through spatial holes. Of course, Lou wasn't with me. I'd left him outside.

The elevator was in the middle of a bland, featureless hallway that stretched out equally in both directions. It could have been the basement of any office building anywhere in the world. I picked left at random, walked down the hall and around the corner, and ended up where I'd started. I tried the right-hand side next, just to be sure, and this time the corridor continued on. About fifty feet farther along it dead-ended, but another corridor branched off at a forty-five-degree angle. I didn't like that. A large bureaucratic structure doesn't usually have corridors shooting off at odd angles. I was being guided in that direction, which is always a good reason not to go that way.

At the far end of the angled corridor I thought I saw something move, something low to the ground, but it might have just been nerves. Even farther back something glittered briefly, like a tiny Fourth of July sparkler. Or a magical gemstone. I briefly thought about investigating, and if I'd had Lou with me I just might have, but I decided not to go looking for trouble until I at least had some idea of what kind of trouble it might be.

I walked back to the elevator and contemplated. Since it was no longer the "real" elevator, it couldn't take me where I wanted to go. But I had something else that wasn't "real," my I.D. card, still clipped to my collar. Easy enough. I got into the elevator, took off the card, placed it on the floor, and hooked it into the energy flow of the elevator. Then I sucked up the blurry lines, returning the card to its original blank Office Max incarnation. Sweet as could be, the reverse on the card carried the elevator along with it, and the small shiver of dislocation told me I had the original back. I punched the lobby button and a minute later was walking out of the building.

Something more to think about. That incident wasn't a serious attack; it was merely designed to keep me out of the way for a while, although I'll bet I'd escaped a lot quicker than was bargained for. But out of the way of what? Again, not enough information.

Louie of course was nowhere in sight, so I sat on the low cement wall that runs along the side of the building and passed the time with a black gentleman who walked up to me and introduced himself as Spaceman.

He wore a motorcycle helmet plastered with stickers, hockey shin guards and knee pads on the outside of his pants, a leather jacket similar to mine except for the bicycle reflectors stuck onto it and the keys and cymbals hanging from the lapels. He displayed mirrored sunglasses, a nose ring from which dangled heavy iron crosses, black gloves and spiked bracelets around his wrists. In his belt he had stuck a large ray gun from *Star Wars* or something. Even by San Francisco standards he deserved a second look.

He sat down next to me, jangling like a set of wind chimes.

"Yo," he said.

"Yo," I agreed. He was silent for a few seconds.

"You a Raiders fan?"

I shook my head. "Niners."

"Niners? How can you be a Niners fan?"

"I live here. What choice do I have?"

"Raiders. Raiders, man. The Niners are a bunch of pussies. They're . . ."

He trailed off as words seemed to fail him concerning the shortcomings of my chosen team. We talked Raiders and Niners for a while until he veered off into politics. His speech was high-pitched, rambling, and disjointed, but despite that he was able to make a surprising amount of sense. Eventually, Lou showed up to rescue me, licking his lips. If ever a dog existed that could survive on the streets, it was him. Lou sat down and stared at Spaceman. Spaceman stared back.

"He yours?" he asked.

"In a manner of speaking."

Lou didn't seem his usual self. He was acting twitchy, turning his head every few seconds to check over his shoulder, restlessly standing on one paw, then another. Or maybe I was projecting. Maybe he was just getting cold and bored and wanted to go home. Spaceman continued his staring awhile longer and abruptly got up off the wall. He walked away, but after five steps he stopped and looked back over his shoulder.

"You be careful now," he said, in a completely different voice. "I can see it hanging on you. The black man is not your friend." He continued down the sidewalk and quickly turned the next corner. I looked down at Louie.

"What was that about?" I asked.

Lou sat impatiently, not interested. We walked over to Mission to catch the bus and I slipped him into the backpack again. On the bus ride home I couldn't get Spaceman out of my thoughts. He was obviously nuts, but he did have a quality to him beyond that, almost like an oracle of sorts. Did he mean a particular black man or black people in general? Or somebody dressed in black? And why can't oracles ever be more direct? Would it kill them to be specific? When you come right down to it, advising someone to "be careful" just isn't all that useful.

SEVEN

FIRST THING NEXT MORNING I CALLED ELI, BUT HE wasn't home. Probably teaching a class out at USF. I left him a message and he called back later that afternoon.

"Mason," he said. "Anything new? Any more trouble?"

"Nothing worth talking about. I do have a question, though."

"What's on your mind?"

"Have you ever heard of something called 'The Challenges'?"

"I have," he said.

"What's the deal with it?"

"The Challenges? Well, it's a game of sorts. Nowadays, at least. It wasn't always."

"Have you ever bothered to check it out?"

"Yes, but it hasn't been active for a long time. Why?"

"Well, apparently it's still going on and some very heavy hitters are involved in it these days."

"Interesting. Very interesting."

"You think it's worth looking into?"

There was a brief silence. "Definitely. I'm surprised I haven't heard about this before."

"I hear it can be difficult to attend uninvited."

Eli chuckled. "Yes," he said, "it always has been. Where is it being held these days?"

"Golden Gate Park. First Tuesday of each month. At dusk."

"Ah. You realize today is the first Tuesday in December? Perhaps we should attend the coming session."

"We?"

"Absolutely. I'll need your help. You have a lot of ability, Mason, and even some common sense, although you don't have the background or training to totally comprehend sociological complexities."

"The black man is not my friend," I muttered under my breath.

"What?"

"I said, thanks for the kind words."

"Don't pout. You know I'm right."

"Yeah, I suppose I do," I said. "But shouldn't you be taking Victor instead?" I wasn't that eager to go. I thought it would be more productive for me to look for that practitioner's house Rafael had broken into.

"Victor's in L.A. for a couple of days. Trouble with Ricardo again."

"Oh. Okay then. So, can you tell me exactly what it is that goes on there?"

Eli cleared his throat. "Well," he said, "it's pretty much what it sounds like. A challenge. A duel, if you will, utilizing talent."

"Are there rules?"

"Oh, definitely. The challenged party sets up a situation which the challenger must overcome, or a problem he or she must solve. If they do, they win. If they don't, they lose. Pretty simple, actually."

"And when did all this start?"

"A long time ago. It's a very old tradition. Once it was a socially accepted method of settling disputes. Back then it was dangerous, with losers often losing their lives as well as the contest."

"And now?"

"Well, over the years, the practice gradually fell out of favor. Then, about thirty years ago, during a period of constant disputes among practitioners, it made a comeback. It served much the same function, but this time it wasn't so lethal. The winner still acquired a certain amount of power from the loser, but it no longer proved fatal."

"I thought talent was an inborn trait. You can't acquire magical power that way. Or can you?"

"Well, yes and no. You can acquire power, but not a lot."

"Why not? If you kept fighting duels, the more times you won, the more power you would accumulate, right? And the more power you accumulated, the easier it would be to win, and so on and so on, until eventually you'd become all-powerful. Am I right?"

"No, not exactly," Eli said. "First of all, you can't gain a practitioner's power unless there's an agreement in place—a legitimate contest. So you would need a lot of contests. If you were to attack someone randomly, ignoring the formal rules of contest, no transfer of power could take place. Second, you don't gain all of a practitioner's power even if you do win the contest, just a portion of it. Third, there's a built-in check against the scenario you suggest. Are you familiar with chess rankings?"

"Vaguely."

"Well, in chess, when a stronger player defeats a weaker, he gains ranking points. However, the greater the disparity in strength, the fewer points he acquires. If the disparity between the two is large enough, say a grandmaster who defeats some patzer, no points are gained at all.

"Now if their rankings are equal, one goes up a little and the other goes down a little. If they should play again, the now stronger player gains fewer points and the weaker loses less."

"And if a very weak player defeats a much stronger one?"

"He gains a significant boost. The stronger loses a significant amount. It's the same in power duels."

"I see. So you can't gain unlimited power just by knocking off weaker opponents one by one."

"Precisely. Things even out in the long run, and once you establish your personal level of skill, whether in chess or in talent, you tend to remain close to that level."

I thought about that for a minute. "Then what's the point?"

"Some people just like the rush. Talent junkies. And remember, long ago when it was serious, there were no rematches. That's one of the reasons practitioners kept the extent of their power a closely guarded secret. You had to have good reason to challenge someone if you weren't sure what level of expertise you might be facing. Even today, you know that asking about the extent of another's talent is gauche, like asking someone how much money they make.

"During the last revival safeguards were instituted," Eli continued. "And it was quite the rage for a few years, but after several practitioners ended up severely damaged despite the precautions, it fell out of favor again. Practitioners went back to more mundane ways of resolving differences."

"Except, apparently they haven't."

"Apparently. And that's interesting, because there always is a reason why things come back into vogue."

I didn't share Eli's view that all trends are grounded in rationality, but I let it pass.

"And what would that reason be?"

"I have no idea. That's why I think it's time for a bit of fieldwork. Meet me about four and we'll see what we can find out. Be sure to bring Louie with you."

Like I needed him to tell me that. "Okay," I said. "I'll pick you up in a couple of hours."

· · ·

ELI LIVES OVER IN THE RICHMOND, NOT FAR FROM Golden Gate Park. He was waiting on the sidewalk outside his flat when I pulled up, and by four, we were driving through the park. I cut across and turned left onto John F. Kennedy Drive, parking near the horse stables. It was only a five-minute walk from there to the Polo Fields. It was still light when we got there, but dusk was fast approaching.

Gathered in the northeast corner were perhaps forty or fifty people, aimlessly milling around. They were too far away to see exactly what was going on. When we still were fairly far off, I had a thought. If we were to just walk up to the group and there really was something bad taking place, either we'd end up in trouble ourselves or they'd simply wait until we left to resume whatever it was they were up to. It might be a good idea to observe cautiously at first, keeping a reasonable distance away. I turned to Eli, but before I could explain my reasoning he turned to me and said, "You know, maybe just walking right up in the middle of this isn't the best way to go about it."

I opened my mouth to agree but got distracted by Lou pulling on the leg of my pants and growling softly. The distraction cleared my head. Eli and I stared at each other with sudden realization.

"Damn, they're good," I said.

"Indeed they are," he agreed. "Even forewarned didn't help. No wonder no one ever disturbs them."

"Any ideas?" I asked.

"Well, probably we should go back to the van to come up with a counter for this. I'm not thinking too clearly so close to the—" He broke off with a curse, something he hardly ever does. "Damn it! I can't even tell if that idea is mine or not."

Lou was entirely unaffected. He came up behind Eli and started nipping at his ankles. Eli jumped away with an agility that belied his bulk. "Hey, stop it!" he said.

"I think there's our answer," I said, pointing at Lou.

"We need a sheepdog. Look, you're already two steps closer than you were a moment ago."

"It's not very dignified," he protested.

"Come on," I said, and started walking toward the group again.

Every time a new excuse to turn around popped into my head and I tried to stop, Louie was behind me snapping at my heels. When we unaccountably found ourselves veering to one side, Louie steered us back on track, doing a stellar imitation of a Border collie herding a couple of recalcitrant sheep. About a hundred yards from the group, he eased off and, job done, scampered ahead toward some bushes at the edge of the clearing. We walked on with no further problem.

"I guess if you get this far you're supposed to be here," I observed.

As we got closer I recognized several people I knew, which was no surprise, but there were a lot more that I didn't, and that was unusual.

"You know any of these people?" I asked.

Eli nodded. "A lot of them. I haven't seen most of them for some time, though."

As we got up to the edge of the crowd, a middle-aged woman in a tan business suit approached us. She looked like a younger version of Miss Marple, with glasses, a benign expression, and wisps of graying hair escaping from a somewhat untidy bun.

"Eli!" she exclaimed. "Why, you're the last person I'd expect to see here." She glanced casually at me but I got the feeling she'd registered everything she wanted to know about me in that one quick look.

"Sascha. Good to see you," said Eli. He didn't introduce me.

She smiled fleetingly. "Have you come to see Christoph? There's this woman from San Diego who traveled up for a challenge. She's supposed to be truly amazing, really hot stuff."

So Christoph was involved in this. Well, well.

"I thought it might prove interesting," Eli said blandly, acting as if he knew exactly what she was talking about.

"Well, to tell the truth, I kind of hope he'll get taken down a peg or two. He's becoming a bit insufferable lately, if you know what I mean."

"I know the type."

She chuckled. "Yes, I'll bet you do. How's Victor, anyway?"

"Oh, he's fine. Doesn't much approve of this sort of thing, you know."

"Yes, I know. And yourself?"

"You know me. I'm interested in all sorts of things."

She looked over at me for the first time. "I don't think I know you," she said. "Come to try your luck?"

"I don't think so," I said. "Maybe another time."

"Well, good luck if you do."

She twirled her fingers at Eli and rejoined the larger group. Several of them glanced over at us with curiosity. I felt like the new kid on the first day of school. Eli was standing calmly, observing, but his hands were busy clenching and unclenching into fists. He was not happy.

"Problem?" I asked.

"This is a travesty," he said. "This isn't about resolving differences or settling disputes. This isn't serious. This is entertainment. This is like the Roman arena. This is a *game* to them, for God's sake."

I didn't say anything. It didn't seem like such a big deal to me, but Eli has a great respect for tradition and history. It was a big deal to him.

The subdued muttering of the crowd took on a note of pleased anticipation as a man detached himself from the gathering. His longish hair was white, but it must have been dyed, since he was young, no more than twenty-five. He was nattily dressed in black jeans, a black silk shirt, and so help me, a black cape.

"Give me a break," I whispered. Eli made a shushing motion with his hands.

"Okay, everyone," the man said. "Today we've got

something special, so we're going to dispense with the pre-
liminaries. You all know Christoph?" There was a murmur
of assent from the group.

"You know that freak?" I asked, whispering again. Eli
made the same shushing motion.

The white-haired guy set up two folding chairs facing
each other. He turned back to the crowd with a flourish.

"Our challenger," he announced.

A woman made her way out of the crowd. Thirty-five,
maybe forty, zaftig with waist-length straight brown hair
and sparkly rings on every finger. An ankle-length color-
fully patterned dress draped her ample body, leaving only
her bare feet uncovered. Since the temperature was rapidly
dropping, I thought she might at least have considered san-
dals. She was exactly who you'd expect to find behind the
sales counter if you entered a store that sold incense and
tarot cards. Sascha reappeared by Eli's elbow.

"Don't be fooled by that New Age hippie look," she
warned. "This woman is one very tough cookie. And she'll
need to be. Christoph doesn't like to lose."

The guy with the white hair showed her to one of the
folding chairs, where she sat down and waited comfortably. He then paused theatrically, and throwing his arms up
in the air, shouted, "I bring you . . . CHRISTOPH!"

I half expected pyrotechnics and a smoke machine,
maybe with "We Are the Champions" playing in the background, but Christoph simply walked out of the crowd and
took his place in the remaining chair. He was wearing a
wool poncholike garment striped in grays and blacks, and
he nodded formally at the woman in the opposite chair as
he sat down. Power crackled around him; he'd been partially shielding at Pascal's party. I was annoyed with myself. I should have seen through it. White-hair walked over
and addressed them both.

"Christoph, you are the challenged party. You choose
the field of play." Christoph nodded. White-hair faced the
woman.

"Moira," he said, "you must either escape or overcome." She nodded, never taking her eyes off the man sitting across from her.

"Are you both ready?" Two slight nods. "Then begin."

The crowd became still. For some thirty seconds nothing seemed to happen. I wondered if there were some kind of mental struggle going on between them, intense and unseen. If so, it wasn't providing much in the way of entertainment. I noticed the fog was beginning to close in and realized it wasn't the usual San Francisco winter mist. It was a dark murk, paradoxically glowing with inner light as if a car with its high beams on squatted in the center. It settled down over the entire area of the Polo Fields, and as the outside world was cut off, the tendrils of vapor divided and started forming shapes, leisurely at first, more rapidly as the process continued. Slowly a picture emerged, a forest of fantastic plants and giant trees, all in a spectral monochrome. Then, gradually, color emerged, infinite shadings of green shot through with red and yellow flowers, then purple birds and huge butterflies, then a yellow tropical sun too bright to look at beating down on the jungle, and finally the sound of birds calling, insects buzzing, and a myriad of noises too obscure to identify.

Christoph leaned back in his chair, not relaxing, but clearly well pleased with himself. He had a right to be. I had never before seen an illusion so complex, not counting the singularity I'd been in, which wasn't precisely an illusion. This was not the same Christoph I'd met a couple of years ago. Eli might pooh-pooh the idea of anyone gaining huge amounts of power to boost their natural talent, but he'd acquired something from somewhere. An appreciative murmur ran through the crowd. Sascha took me by the arm.

"Pretty remarkable, don't you think?" she said, keeping her voice low. I was too impressed to come up with my usual flip response.

The woman in the chair bowed her head, tented her fingers so that the tips of them touched her chin, and exhaled noisily. She momentarily went out of focus until an astral body separated itself from her and rose to its feet. It wavered and then snapped into focus, looking as real and substantial as the original woman.

"Doppelgänger," explained Eli, unnecessarily. "In the old days she would have gone in there herself. If she got out alive, she won. If not . . ."

His voice trailed off as the double walked toward the edge of the rainforest. A path opened up invitingly before her and as she hesitated, the white-haired emcee moved up to where the original Moira still sat and laid his hand on her shoulder. The man nearest him took hold of his other hand, and a woman next to the man took his. The whole group crowded closer together, arms linking up until it looked like a peace rally or a sixties love-in. Eli and I got caught up in it, with Sascha between us. She put her arm around my waist, but couldn't manage to get the other around Eli's bulk and was forced to settle for linking her arm through his. People on both sides of us grabbed our free arms. I felt distinctly uncomfortable.

The point of all this became immediately apparent. There was a temporary dislocation before I found myself looking at the entrance to the jungle through Moira's eyes, or at least through the eyes of her doppelgänger. And it wasn't limited to just vision. I could also feel the oppressive heat, smell the rotting vegetation, hear the rustling of unknown creatures hidden in the tangle of luxurious foliage. Except for having no control over voluntary movement, it was no different than being there myself.

I/she/we took a step forward onto the path that reached out into the forest. It ran straight for about fifty yards and then curved off toward the left. Moira started down the path with a confidence I certainly wouldn't have possessed. Maybe she was more used to this sort of thing than I was. At the point where the path curved, a large spotted jungle cat stepped out from behind concealing bushes. It appeared to be a cross between a jaguar and a leopard, stocky yet agile and lithe. It looked back down the path with huge unblinking golden eyes before stepping back around the curve and out of sight.

"Christoph," Eli said, speaking quietly in my ear.

Moira moved down the path, all of us moving with her. It was a weird overlay; I could hear the noises of the jungle and, at the same time, low-voiced comments from people around me in the crowd. About halfway to the curve, the path began to close off behind her, greenery rippling in waves as it boiled up and choked off any avenue of retreat. Directly ahead, a series of vines started rapidly growing out from the side of the path, giant green snakes writhing and twisting. She chuckled easily, obviously not intimidated. With her right arm she reached inside a pocket hidden somewhere in the voluminous dress and pulled out what felt like gritty sand. With the other she described a circle in the air as she threw the sand onto the path, at the same time uttering a single word.

"Wither," she hissed with such malevolence that it made me slightly sick to my stomach. Or her stomach. I was still having trouble getting a handle on the dual perception thing. The vines curled up and did just that, rotting away with fast-forward videotape speed. She turned and extended her hands at right angles to the path.

"Wither," she hissed again, with even more venom. The forest melted away in front of her, lush green plants turning yellow, then brown, then crumbling away like wisps of memory. Trees were left standing, but stripped bare of leaves, limbs jutting out stark and sere like oak trees in the dead of winter. She walked through the suddenly bleak terrain, territory which turned barren in front of her with every step, as if she were ushering in ahead of her a plague of biblical proportions.

My attention was distracted by an gentle tugging on my pants leg. Caught up in the drama of the contest, I ignored it. The tugging became more urgent, so I wrenched my consciousness back to a mundane level and glanced down to see what the problem was. Lou, of course. He saw he'd caught my attention, raised one paw, and stiffened into a

parody of a bird dog spotting a quail. I followed his sight
line and saw Christoph sitting motionless on his chair. His
hands were folded in his lap, covering something. Something bright and glowing, light shifting like a tiny aurora
borealis. Or a jewel of swirling colors.

As soon as Lou saw I'd noticed, he scurried off again. I
relaxed my focus and allowed myself to be drawn back
into the construct. I hadn't missed too much of the action.
Moira was now walking through the path of destruction up
a small rise. At this rate it wouldn't be long before she
sliced her way out of the jungle, but Christoph didn't come
by his reputation for nothing.

She crested the rise, and on the other side was a wide
lake, stinking and muddy under the tropical sky. Since it
blocked her progress, she started walking parallel to the
shore, but the lake moved right along with her, transform-
ing the green jungle into a muddy swamp.

Frowning, Moira walked up to the lake's edge and
stared across the water. Jesus, I thought, she may be powerful but she's not very bright. Maybe she didn't watch
enough television. Anyone who has ever seen nature shows
on cable knows what happens when you walk up to the
water's edge in the tropical jungle. Besides, although she
obviously could see whatever I could, she didn't seem to
notice the faint ripples ruffling the muddy water ten feet
from shore.

The only thing that saved her was her serendipitous decision to retreat from the water's edge mere seconds before
the water erupted. A twelve-foot crocodile launched itself
out of the lake and onto the bank, moving incredibly fast
for something that huge and massive. The other part of my
senses heard several muffled shrieks from the watching
crowd, all of whom of course were experiencing it just as
I was. Moira threw herself backward as it lunged toward
her, roaring like some berserk prehistoric monster. She
scrabbled frantically in one of her pockets, just managing
to come up with a lump of clay which she threw right into
the gaping jaws. The minute it made contact, it expanded

like a deploying airbag. The beast choked and twisted on the ground, the thrashing tail almost doing the job the jaws had failed at. The crocodile lost all interest in Moira and slithered back off the bank to the safety of the water, still trying to disgorge gunk from a mouth suddenly full of clay.

Without a second glance, Moira walked a few more paces away from the lake and stared out over the water. Reaching into yet another pocket, she pulled out a scrap of material, a handful of toothpicks, and a silver dollar. Moira had come prepared, I'll say that for her. She shook her head, obviously dissatisfied, and reached up to run her fingers through her hair. She looked down at her fingers, something evidently catching her eye. All I saw was fingers covered with rings. She wrenched one of the rings off and held it up to the sky. It was a large crystal, too large to be a diamond, but nothing like our problematic gems. Cubic zirconium? That just seemed wrong. Whatever it was, Moira was pleased with it. She began humming a tune that was almost familiar, but not quite, drawing out and holding the pitch at the end of each phrase. The crystal began vibrating, charged with energy. It rapidly heated up and when it reached the stage where it became almost too uncomfortable to hold, she intoned, "As above, so below, like calls to like," and tossed it into the lake. A bit too New Age for me, but the results were impressive. I could hear an immediate hissing sound and the place where the crystal sunk boiled up in a frantic rush. The turmoil expanded rapidly from that point, until the entire lake was seething.

When I was a youngster, I once tried to make fudge from scratch. Unfortunately I got distracted and cooked it way, way too long. As long as the syrup was still hot it seemed fine, dark and liquid and creamy. But as it cooled, it reached some critical point of temperature and suddenly expanded with that same hissing noise until the entire pot was filled with a rock-hard brown confection. It couldn't have taken more than five seconds for the whole thing to go from liquid to solid. And what a solid. It was so hard you could barely chip it out with a chisel, and I had to throw the pot away, fudge and all.

This was the exact same thing on an immense scale. Within seconds the entire lake had solidified into one solid mass, foamy and uneven, just like a giant batch of ruined fudge. Moira gave a grunt of triumph and stepped out onto the frozen surface. She started off at a good clip but slowed down significantly before she was halfway across. The energy she had expended up to this point was taking its toll. Still, the edge of the forest was now visible straight ahead, just past a series of rocky outcroppings that started a few yards from the opposite shore.

Moira reached the shore, moving slowly. I didn't think she had enough stamina left to overcome another obstacle, but I wouldn't have bet against her either. As Sascha had said, she was tough. She avoided a path that led through a series of large boulders, choosing instead to walk directly up the slight grade toward the edge of the illusion. She passed by a particularly large outcropping of granite, moving warily. As she rounded the bulk of it, a figure appeared in front of her. It was a perfect copy of Moira, or rather a copy of a copy, a "tripleganger" if you will. Both she and her twin stood motionless, and then her twin slowly reached up behind her own neck and undid the clasp holding the back of her dress. She smiled and started disrobing. How embarrassing for Moira, I thought, naked with an entire crowd of strangers looking on. Then I got it. It was the signature ploy. I automatically tried to spin around, forgetting that I was nothing more than a passenger along for the ride. I had the advantage of having seen this sort of thing before; I wondered if Moira would figure it out before it was too late.

The sound of small rocks falling from the outcropping above finally alerted her, but not in time. Maybe she was slowed a fraction by her weariness. In any case, she had only made half a turn when the big cat landed on her shoulders, crashing down from the rock above like an avenging angel. Or demon. She screamed, as did almost everyone in the crowd, and then the strong jaws and sharp teeth were clamping down on her neck. I could smell the rank cat odor and the fetid breath. I could feel the sharp teeth tearing through soft flesh. The spurting of blood from torn arteries came as a shock, but by that time I couldn't breathe; the jaws had clamped down on the throat in the typical predator's killing bite. Color seemed to leach out of my field of vision and a deathlike lassitude overcame me as the blood was diverted away from the brain and onto the ground. Just before losing consciousness I could swear I heard the heavy cat chuckle deep in its throat.

I came to with a huge shock of dislocation, the way you sometimes wake from a disturbing nightmare late at night. I was standing in the field clutching the hand of the person next to me in a death grip, who was returning the favor. We let go simultaneously, both embarrassed. Eli peered over at me, looking shook up himself. Moira had fallen from her chair and was lying on the ground. For a moment I thought she was dead, but she sat up shakily and Christoph stood up and offered her his hand. You could see that she didn't want to take it, but in the end decided that acting gracious was the way to play it. She looked pale and washed out, as if she'd been up for three nights without sleep. Christoph, on the other hand, looked positively vital, glowing with health and energy. I guessed that the transfer of power from loser to winner occurred the moment her double had died.

Christoph left Moira standing there and strolled over to the edge of the crowd. He immediately became involved in a discussion about something, presumably tactics, with a young black guy who was wearing a watch cap. He looked vaguely familiar but I couldn't place him.

"You know that guy?" I asked Eli, pointing over in his direction.

"I know him," he replied.

"And?"

"No one you'd want to know. A dark path practitioner. Very influential in some circles."

I laughed. "Really. I mean, no one does that stuff anymore, do they?"

Eli favored me with a tolerant smile. "Don't knock it if you haven't tried it."

"Whatever," I said, dismissing it. "I think I'll have a word with Christoph before we leave."

I walked over to join them just as the black guy he'd been talking to slipped away into the crowd. Christoph saw me coming and broke out into a smile. But this wasn't the friendly smile he had offered at Pascal's party. It was a mocking, self-satisfied smirk.

"Well, I'll be damned," he said. "Never thought I'd see you here. Come to try your luck in the game of life?"

"Not my kind of thing," I said. "Is that what it's called?"

His expression grew smirkier, if that's a word. "Well, it's what *I* call it. The losers call it getting their asses kicked." He was bubbling over with jollity and good cheer. If I hadn't seen the contest I would have assumed he was high. Maybe he was, in a way.

"You really ought to try it sometime," he continued. "I've heard you're quite a talent in your own right. It would be interesting to see what you're made of."

"I mostly try to stay out of fights," I told him.

"Smart man. But that's not always possible, is it?"

Again, was he just being obnoxious, or was he baiting me with double entendre remarks and hidden meanings? Somebody on the other side of the crowd beckoned him over.

"Sorry," he said. "My adoring public calls. I'm sure I'll be seeing you around, though. You be careful, now, you hear?" He bounced away, throwing me a glance over his shoulder as he left. Was that his attempt at a friendly good-bye or some cryptic warning? I decided it didn't matter. Either way, he was an asshole.

I located Louie sitting off by the bushes beside a large gray tabby, so there was at least one other Ifrit here. They sat side by side, watching. Not for the first time I wondered what Ifrits thought about all things practitioner. Back at the edge of the crowd, Eli disengaged from Sascha and came over to collect me.

"I think we've seen enough," he said. "We'd best be going."

That was fine with me. I needed time to digest what I had just seen, and even more time to recover. It's not every day that your throat gets crushed by a powerful carnivore. I jerked my head to let Louie know we were leaving and fell into step beside Eli. We walked in silence back to the van. Driving back to his house, I had so many questions I barely knew where to start. But as soon as I opened my mouth, Eli put his hand up like a traffic cop. He's a great one for gestures.

"Tomorrow," he said. "I've got a lot of thinking to do. Just drop me off and I'll call you tomorrow when I've gone over things in my head."

I shrugged. Five minutes later, I was dropping him off outside his flat, neither one of us having said a word. Fifteen minutes after that, I was pulling into my driveway at home. Louie looked over at me and yawned.

"Yeah," I said. "Another boring day. A piece of cake. Just a walk in the park."

EIGHT

I MET ELI FOR COFFEE THE NEXT DAY OVER AT Muddy's, a coffee shop on Valencia and Twenty-third that's within walking distance of my flat. It was a beautiful day for once, sunny and hovering close to sixty degrees, glorious after the December rains. I left Lou outside by the café door and he settled down after looking reproachfully at me. He knew perfectly well there was good stuff to eat inside.

Once inside I decided to avoid the macho black coffee and indulge in a latte instead. The café was filled with the usual mix of Mission denizens: yuppies with laptops, working guys on a coffee break, young hipsters, faux bohemians. By the time Eli arrived, I was on my second cup. He got a latte of his own and sat down at my table.

"I'm pretty sure I saw Christoph with one of those jewels last night," I said as he took his first sip.

He rolled the coffee around in his mouth, not answering, a singularly obnoxious habit. He gave the impression that he was deeply considering the flavor of the roasted beans, when I was pretty sure he couldn't tell one type of coffee from another. Finally he swallowed and cleared his throat.

"When?"

"In the middle of the duel. Lou pointed it out. Christoph was covering up something in his lap and it was glowing." Another sip of coffee gave him time to consider.

"You know, I might be a bit out of my depth here," he said.

I took a sip of coffee myself. "Amazing. I don't think I've ever heard you say that before."

"I say it all the time. Just not out loud."

"So, you have no idea what this Challenges thing was all about?"

"No, it's more that I don't understand the point of it. It's clearly about gaining power, but why? As far as I know, you can't make the transfer permanent. Unless somehow one of those jewels . . ."

"What about Christoph?" I asked, changing the subject. "Have you found out anything more about him?"

He gave me a sour smile. "I did some research earlier this morning. Guess who just bought a new house?"

"Uhh, could it be . . . Christoph?"

"And guess where said house is located?"

I waited patiently.

"Try Sea Cliff."

Sea Cliff. Real estate isn't one of my areas of expertise, but houses there run in the low millions. The shabby ones.

"I didn't know he had that kind of money."

"He didn't. Apparently he now does."

"Those gems, you think?"

Eli shrugged. "It wouldn't take a whole lot of them to make you rich. Maybe it's not about power. Maybe it's about money."

"Or maybe both. Any ideas yet on where they come from?"

"No."

"So now what?"

He took a large gulp of cooled off latte. "Well, I think

we'll take a ride down to Half Moon Bay. I know a man there who just might be able to help. He runs a small café, nothing fancy, just coffee and sandwiches. On weekends he plays jazz with some of the locals, just for fun, mostly."

"Anyone I know?"

"You might. He used to be an enforcer."

"Wait a minute," I said. "You don't mean Geoffrey, do you? The guy who retired? Used to be Victor's idol?"

"That's him."

"He was always studying and practicing, trying to be some sort of superwizard, right? When I was a teenager we used to call him Gandalf."

Eli nodded. "You always did have a lot of the brat in you."

"Well, as I remember it, the guy was a little off. He was supposed to be this all-powerful individual, and then one day he goes off the deep end and just withdraws from everything. Stops being a practitioner, anyway. He started playing piano or something, right? After a while he just sort of faded away."

"So there was something wrong with him because he preferred playing the piano to working with Victor?" Eli asked mildly. "I realize the piano's not anything serious, like the guitar, but . . ."

"That's not what I mean, and you know it. He was totally gung ho on the whole enforcer thing, so when he quit suddenly it was peculiar, that's all. Like if Victor suddenly decided to throw it all in and become a potter or a surfer or something."

"Stranger things have happened."

I snorted. "Stranger than Victor on a surfboard? I don't think so."

Eli took another sip of coffee and did the rolling around in his mouth routine again.

"Anyway," he continued, "Geoffrey didn't exactly quit for no reason." He paused again. "Have you ever heard of the Transcendents?"

"You have got to be kidding."

"Humor me."

"Well," I said, "aren't they supposedly practitioners who have reached a form of ultimate enlightenment, like a yogi reaching Samahdi. Then they renounce everything magical and go around with a begging bowl, or—"

"Or open a café perhaps."

"You can't be serious."

Eli sighed theatrically. "So young, yet so open-minded."

"Oh, come on. I mean, really."

"Let me put it this way. If the most powerful and knowledgeable person you know reaches the pinnacle of accomplishment, then turns around and walks away from it all, what would you think? That they were mentally unbalanced, or that maybe they knew something you didn't?"

"I see your point. But I might still vote for unbalanced."

"Yes, you would. But let me run a theory by you. It's not just mine; a lot of people over the years have come up with similar ideas. Throughout history, extremely powerful men and women have always existed, the elite of practitioners. And a small number, at the height of their powers, have simply given it all up and retired to the simple life. As far as I can ascertain, for the rest of their lives, none of them ever again so much as cast a spell to keep bread fresh."

"By inability or by choice?"

"No one knows for sure. None of them spoke about it much and when they did it was like listening to Zen koans."

"But I'm sure you have an opinion."

"How well you know me." Eli geared up into professor mode. "Okay, here's the idea: What happens to these people is analogous to the Yogi you mentioned, but with a crucial difference. The practice of magic is basically the manipulation of reality by the use of talent. How that is best accomplished has long been a matter of conjecture. Some use complex rituals, some learn arcane focusing disciplines, some employ objects of power—the list of various methods is almost infinite. And they all work, though some more effectively than others. There is no one way, as long as the path you choose is one that can access power. The reason that black magicians can be so powerful is not anything supernatural, it's that the symbols and practices they use are fraught with emotional significance, and they use that emotion to focus their power."

"Graveyard dirt has more resonance than dryer lint."

"Precisely. And whether we create our own source of power or simply tap into some vast underlying reserve is another matter for conjecture. But one thing is clear—the more powerful the practitioner, the less the need for reliance on power objects, complex spells, or theoretical magical systems. You actually do something similar yourself, which is quite impressive considering your lack of training and dedication."

Eli is the master of the left-handed compliment.

"Current theory," he continued, "holds that whenever a practitioner reaches a critical level of knowledge and power, all those devices we usually rely on become mere props, irrelevant and even distracting. The ability to directly affect reality then takes no more effort than does a fish swimming through water. Magic becomes no different than eating or sleeping or singing."

"But apparently no one ever actually gets to that place," I pointed out. "I'm pretty sure I would have heard about them if they had."

Eli smiled. "Well, there is a catch," he admitted.

"Isn't there always."

"Oh, yes. By the time you reach the level where you are able to directly manipulate reality, by definition you've also reached a stage where you're no longer concerned with such things. Once you understand that the square peg goes into the square hole and the round peg goes into the round hole, there's not much point in actually doing it."

"There is if it results in world peace."

"It doesn't seem to work that way. Direct action isn't an

option. Read *Autobiography of a Yogi* by Yogananda if you want to understand why."

"So you open a café instead and drink coffee all day?"

"That's one possibility."

I was still skeptical. "You know, I was a teenager when Geoffrey was around and don't remember him that well, but he never struck me as an uncommonly spiritual type."

"Oh, he wasn't. But that's not necessary. Are you up on your French Symbolist poets?"

I peered at him suspiciously. With Eli, it was sometimes hard to tell when he was putting me on. He saw the expression on my face and hurried on.

"Baudelaire and his circle. They believed that the way to salvation was equally accessible through both the highest path and the lowest. Since in his day—and in ours, for that matter—sainthood is quite difficult to achieve, it makes more sense to seek enlightenment through following the path of sin and degradation. It's the great circle—when you get all the way down it's identical to all the way up. Each path leads to the same destination."

"I see," I said. "So if you diligently practice black magic, complete with human sacrifice and demon summoning, eventually you achieve enough spiritual enlightenment to, say, open a café next to Mother Teresa."

"Cynically stated, but theoretically, yes."

"I don't buy it."

Eli shrugged. "Well, it's only a theory."

We sat there for a while drinking coffee in silence. Finally I asked, "So, do you think that Geoffrey could tell us anything useful?"

Eli scratched at his beard. "Oh there's no doubt of that. The study of magical objects was a speciality of his. If anyone could tell us what those stones are, it's him. I also expect he could tell us about everything else going on, if only he would. But he's become odd over the years, even for a Transcendent. It's difficult to get him interested in current problems and even more difficult to get him to answer any questions. Even when he does, he tends to be cryptic."

"On purpose?"

"I don't think so, but it's hard to tell."

"So why do you think he'll be interested enough to help us?"

Eli smiled. "I think we have a hook. You remember I told you that the Challenges started up again about thirty years ago? Who do you think was behind that revival?"

WE TOOK ELI'S CAR DOWN TO HALF MOON BAY. Since he's too large to fit comfortably in a compact he had bought himself a silver Volvo 900 S. "Safest car money can buy," he would say, extolling its virtues at length to anyone who would listen and to a lot who wouldn't. On the way down I tried to get him to tell me more about Geoffrey, but all he would say was wait and see.

So we chatted about inconsequential things, because as tight as Eli and I have become, he stays mostly closed off about his private life. He doesn't clam up; he diverts questions he doesn't want to answer until you find yourself discussing the role salt plays in modern culture without knowing how you've got there. I knew he had been married a long time ago, before he took me under his wing. His wife had died young, but I didn't know any details and he never talked about her. I'd met a few women he'd dated, none of them practitioners, but they seemed to always drift away before I could get to know them. Someday, I hoped, he'd finally start to open up, but that day looked far, far away.

The day was pleasant enough to roll down the windows, so Lou spent the ride with his head stuck outside, nose quivering. It's hard to remember sometimes that he isn't really a dog. We wound along Highway 1 with seaside vistas suitable for postcards on the right and occasional fish-oriented towns popping up every few miles. We passed by Mavericks, the big wave-surfing mecca for northern California, and pulled into Half Moon Bay a short time later.

Half Moon is maybe fifteen thousand people or so,

pretty much divided equally between locals who live off the tourist trade and locals who just live there. Every fall they hold the event which has put them on the map: The Half Moon Bay Pumpkin Festival. I'd heard the festival mentioned all my life, but I didn't really have much of an idea what it was all about, except that it obviously had something to do with pumpkins.

Geoffrey's café was in the middle of town, which meant it was on one of the three or four streets that make up the "downtown area." It was a comfortable looking place with a few tables out front under a faded wooden sign that identified it as "Lucinda's." It was the type of sign that looked like it had been there for a while, probably outlasting the original Lucinda, whoever she might have been, by a good many years. There was a parking space right in front of the café, one of the advantages of small town living. Eli pulled in, turned off the engine, and gestured broadly.

"Here we are," he said.

Right on cue, the café door opened and a man emerged, a slight figure holding a cup of something. He stood in the doorway, blinking fretfully at the sun. After a minute, he moved over to a table by the sidewalk, sat down, crossed his legs, pulled out a pack of cigarettes, lit one up, and inhaled a long drag, satisfaction evident.

"Geoffrey," Eli informed me.

"A spiritually evolved master who smokes cigarettes?" I asked.

"What can I say?"

"Oh, I'm not putting it down," I said. "I rather like the idea."

I examined the man sitting at the table. I never would have recognized him. Of course I hadn't seen him since I was a kid, but my memories were of a strong and vibrant man, intense, a little scary even. This man was slender, almost frail, and although I knew he must be getting on in years it was still hard to judge his age. His ginger hair wisped in the afternoon breeze, and as he took a delicate sip from his cup I could barely make out a faint bristle of reddish mustache nestling on his upper lip. He was wearing a short-sleeved preppie yellow shirt, like those with the little alligators on them, but without the alligator. He took another drag on his cigarette, holding it gently, almost effeminately, although I didn't get any gay vibe. He had that asexual quality that certain people seem to possess, a Dalai Lama kind of persona. Maybe he really was one of the enlightened ones, although I don't recall the Dalai Lama smoking Marlboros.

Louie had been looking at the sitting figure with a fixed stare, and now he gave a slight whine. Most unusual. He jumped out the window, ran over to the table, barked twice, and rolled over on his back in the classic submissive dog position. I'd never seen him do that before for anyone.

Geoffrey looked down at him and smiled happily. It changed his whole face. He projected such joy and delight, such warmth, such down-to-earth goodness that it temporarily silenced the cynic who perpetually resides in me. Whatever else this guy was or was not, he was no fraud.

"An Ifrit!" he exclaimed. He made some sounds that sounded like a language consisting of barking and growling. Louie jumped up onto the table and started licking his face.

"Just an ordinary retiree," Eli said smugly.

I was feeling a bit jealous. "Are we going to talk with him or not?" I asked, curtly.

Eli gave me a knowing smile and got out of the driver's side. I got out of my side and joined him, and together we walked up to the table. Geoffrey looked up and spotted us.

"Eli!" he said, the smile returning to his face. "How nice to see you. Can I get you some coffee?" He gestured toward Louie. "Not with you, is he?" Then he glanced at me. "Oh, of course." He scrunched up his eyes and nose like someone who needs glasses but won't wear them. "Ahhh . . . Mason, isn't it? I know, I'm being impolite to name you. Kind of a silly convention, don't you think? Sit down, sit down." His eyes twinkled. I mean they really did, flickering in a way I hadn't seen before. I found myself breaking out in a grin. We sat down and Lou immediately jumped off the table and into my lap. I suddenly felt better. Geoffrey turned his attention to me.

"I remember you," he said. "You were kind of spoiled as a kid, but with great talent." He peered at me again in that shortsighted way. "Oh, my. You're a musician! And very good, too. Hey, my group's playing at the café this Saturday. You want to sit in? It would be a trip for everyone. We're not in your league, of course, but we do have fun."

About that time I started buying into it. Either there was something extraordinary about this guy or Eli was setting me up for the most extended practical joke ever devised. And that sort of thing isn't his type of humor.

"Not in my league? Why aren't you?" I said. I didn't elaborate.

"An excellent question," he replied. "I ask myself the same thing every day." He chuckled. "The simple answer is for the same reason I'm not Barry Bonds. Also, it wouldn't be . . . appropriate."

I digested that. Eli saw the conversation going off on a tangent and interrupted. We had business here.

"How about that coffee?" he said. "Coffee would be great."

"Just water for me," I added. "I've had my quota of coffee for the day."

"Tea, then? No? Right, I'll be back in a jiff."

Geoffrey went back into the café. Eli turned to me. "Yes, I know," I said before he could speak. "Focus. Let you do the talking."

When Geoffrey came back with the drinks, he and Eli did small talk for a couple of minutes. Geoffrey seemed particularly interested in one of Eli's historical theories about farming in Europe during the Middle Ages. I waited until it seemed like the topic was going to expand into other parts of the world and then started making phony coughing noises. Eli gave a start, and quickly deflected the conversation back to business.

"Geoffrey," he said, "I hate to change subjects so abruptly, but I've got a problem that's beyond me, and I'm hoping you can help."

Geoffrey's face sort of collapsed into itself, like that of a child whose ice cream scoop has just toppled off the cone onto the floor.

"You know I would love to help you," he said, "but if you'll look back on our history you may recall that I never seem to be as much help as you hope I'll be."

Eli nodded, agreeing. "Be that as it may, I'd still like to get your input on this."

Geoffrey took a final puff on his cigarette, stubbed it out on the bottom of his shoe, and placed the butt carefully on the side of the table. Being California, there are of course no ashtrays anywhere in the state.

"Okay," he said. "Shoot."

Eli cradled his coffee cup in huge hands. He presented a concise outline of everything we knew, along with several guesses. The strange occurrences, the attacks on me, the precious stones, the Challenges with Christoph the ringmaster, etc. Geoffrey perked up at that, wanting every detail.

I thought it was an admirable presentation, but then again, Eli was used to lecturing. Except for the part about the Challenges, Geoffrey spent the entire time ignoring Eli and playing with Louie. He would raise his hand; Lou would raise a paw. He would scratch his nose; Lou would scratch an ear. At one point Geoffrey made a hand gesture almost too subtle for me to catch and Lou gave him a disgusted look, hopped down, and curled up under an adjacent table. At one point Eli got a bit exasperated.

"Geoffrey, are you paying attention?" he demanded.

Geoffrey looked up, abashed. "Oh, yes, yes. Just multitasking."

Eli continued on, and by the time he got to the end, Geoffrey was leaning back in his chair with his eyes closed. We all sat in silence for a while. I hoped Geoffrey hadn't fallen asleep. Finally he stretched and opened his eyes.

"Quite a tale," he said.

I waited for him to add something. When he didn't, I said, "Any thoughts?"

"Sorry," he said. "I was just mulling it over. I don't keep up much on things anymore, but I am aware of Christoph. A very sad fellow." He paused again and thought for a minute. "Also a very nasty piece of work."

"Yes, but what's going on?" I asked.

"Well," said Geoffrey, "I think it all comes back to Christoph. Clearly he's trying to gain power—in fact has gained it, quite a bit of it. He's made these Challenges a game, a competition. Why? The jewel, I would think. Perhaps he's found a way to use it to suck dry the other contestants, like some sort of psychic vampire, and make the power transfer hold. If he focuses their power through the jewel, he could change the energy into a form that would be permanent.

"I'll bet if you were to look up the ones he's defeated recently, you won't find many of them around anymore. If they are, they won't be of much use to themselves or anyone else. It wouldn't be immediately apparent, but after he's done they're nothing but walking, burned-out husks.

"If he continues, eventually he'll amass enough power to do just about anything he wants. If he thought he could get away with it, I wouldn't be surprised to see him challenging practitioners to actual duels, lethal ones."

"Why do that?" I asked.

"Because that way he could gain all their power, not just a piece of it. It wouldn't gain him anything to just kill practitioners, of course, it has to be a voluntary contest for a power transfer."

"So I understand," I said.

Eli interrupted. "Wait a minute. Isn't that counterproductive? I mean, when you attain a certain level of power, regardless of how you got there, don't you . . ." He trailed off.

Geoffrey laughed. "Reach Buddhahood? Like me? That's a great theory, Eli my friend."

"Still," Eli said stubbornly, "something happens after you reach that level."

Geoffrey reached into his shirt pocket and retrieved another cigarette. He pulled out a vintage silver Zippo lighter and lit it, taking a long pull before answering.

"Well, yes, of course. But what happens to your psyche depends somewhat on how you go about it." He pointed at me. "You're too young to remember the LSD craze of the sixties. A lot of people just wanted·to get high, but there were plenty who saw it as a means to enlightenment without all that boring work and study and fasting. Instant Nirvana."

"That seems to have worked out well for them," I said.

"Of course it didn't. But they were able to experience an analogous state that was very much like what true mystics experience. It didn't lead anywhere because they hadn't changed as individuals, unlike those who achieved that state through a more disciplined path. But although the place they reached·wasn't identical, there is some overlapping—I wouldn't discount it totally.

"What Christoph wants to do, I suspect, is something similar. He wants to reach that critical point where all things become possible, or perhaps he has something specific in mind. And if he's able to gain that strength not through study and experience, but by completely artificial means, he then will be able to remain the same individual he's always been—and that's precisely what he wants. Same Christoph, but now with truly frightening power—like an impulsive teenager with a flamethrower."

"That doesn't sound so good for the rest of us," Eli said.

"No, probably not."

"What about Vaughan?" I asked. "His death seemed distinctly unmagical. And why would Christoph kill him, anyway? He can't be gaining power by simply running down practitioners. Can he?"

"The gems," Eli said. "Vaughan found out about the gems."

"But why go to all that trouble? I mean with the hit-and-run and all."

"A magical killing would have us investigating every avenue. But if it could be passed off as something unfortunate and mundane, maybe it would slip under the radar."

Geoffrey was listening with mild interest. Eli pointed to him. "Show Geoffrey what we're talking about."

I pulled out the stone and handed it over. Geoffrey held it up to the sky, letting light stream through, casting color in every direction.

"Nasty," he commented, not the reaction I expected.

"Ever seen anything like it?" I asked.

He looked vaguely puzzled. "I don't believe I have."

"Whatever it is, with all Christoph's newfound power, could he simply have created it, or at least transformed it from something else?"

"No, he couldn't have created anything like this from scratch," Geoffrey said. "That would be far beyond him. But it's certainly possible he's transformed it from something else. Maybe from another precious stone, although I don't think that's it."

"Any thoughts at all about what it might be?"

Geoffrey handed the stone back to me with obvious distaste, wiping his fingers off on his shirt as if there were something slimy on them.

"I have heard about something like this. But I never put much credence in the stories. No practitioner would go to those lengths or stoop so low."

"What do you mean?" I asked.

"It's not important. Just stories. I can tell you one thing: this jewel is extraordinarily unpleasant. Creepy, actually. Can't you feel that?"

I couldn't. I guess I wasn't an evolved soul. But I might have been more skeptical if Lou hadn't clearly felt the same way about it. I put the stone back in my pocket, waiting for Geoffrey to continue, but it didn't look like he was going to open up any further. He stared off into space again until Eli noisily slurped coffee to get his attention.

"Geoffrey," he said, "I know you're no longer a practitioner, but could you at least use your abilities to examine that stone and tell us what it is?"

"Well, 'could' is a very tricky word," Geoffrey said.

I started to get a little pissed off. "Not really," I said. "It's a simple word and a simple question. Do you have the ability to find out what it is or don't you?"

"I'm sorry," he said. "But I don't use talent anymore."

"But could you?"

He looked at me with the expression of someone who is trying to explain to a dog why he has to go to the vet. I was beginning not to like him quite so much.

"I hate using analogies," he said. "It makes people think they understand what you're saying when in reality they are further away than if you just say nothing. But against my better judgment, I'll try one. If you got bored tomorrow, could you immobilize Louie here and torture him to death?"

"I *could*, but I wouldn't. But I have the *ability* to do to so."

"Really. So is it possible that you will indeed do that tomorrow?"

"No, of course not. I would never do that. But I *could*."

"So it's both possible and not possible at the same time, then?"

"Those are just word games," I said.

"Not at all. Exactly what the word 'possible' means is the crux of the matter. That's why I told you I hate analogies. I'm just trying to explain to you that I can't answer your question in any way that would be meaningful to you. I'm truly sorry."

I gave up, but I did have one final question. "Well, what about this? If it is Christoph behind all of this, why would he try to kill me? According to you guys, he wouldn't get any power out of it unless I agreed to a duel, which I'm not about to do. And it's not like I've ever done anything to him. I barely knew he existed before last week."

"Oh, that seems clear. He wants you out of the way."

"Well, duh, but why?"

Geoffrey gave me a serene and infuriating smile. "I'm sorry, but I just can't tell you that."

"Oh? Why can't you? Let me guess, the word 'can't' has infinite meanings, am I right?"

"Why, no," said Geoffrey mildly, "it's a fairly clear concept. I just mean that I don't know."

ON THE WAY BACK, ELI TRIED TO CONVINCE ME that we were lucky. "I've never seen Geoffrey that direct before," he told me. "He must be extremely interested, at least as much as he can be."

I was still annoyed by Geoffrey's attitude. Okay, now it was clear Christoph was up to no good. And it involved the gems. And he was dangerous. And powerful. But we still had no idea what the gems were, where he got them, or why he wanted me out of the way.

By the time we got back to the city, we had run out of things to say. The beautiful afternoon had clouded over, and water was starting to drip from the sky. Eli dropped me off at my place, gave me a melancholy salute, and drove off. I picked up my mail from the mailbox, unlocked the front door, stepped inside, and found an unpleasant surprise awaiting me. In the middle of the room, lounging in my only easy chair, sat Christoph.

NINE

FINDING AN INTRUDER SITTING IN YOUR LIVING room is bad enough for an ordinary person. For a practitioner it's a disaster. First of all, it means that your personal warning system has gone dead. But if my own system was deficient, Lou's should have been operating at peak efficiency. That's what he was best at, after all. I would have bet large sums of money that no one could have been sitting inside without him being aware of it. Second, and worse, it meant that someone had been able to circumvent all my protective spells and wards—not an easy task, especially since Eli had helped me with setting them up.

Overcoming the protection around my house in the few hours I had been gone shouldn't have been possible. It wouldn't be enough for my uninvited guest to just be strong; he either needed intimate knowledge about the place, which wasn't likely, or failing that, he needed to be incredibly strong, orders of magnitude stronger than I was. And as far as I knew, there wasn't anyone, even Christoph, with that kind of power. Obviously I was mistaken.

He was wearing a black silk shirt open at the collar and

black jeans, just like the white-haired emcee at the challenges, minus the cape. I wondered if it were some sort of informal uniform. He lounged insolently in my chair, the effect somewhat spoiled by the fact that it's difficult for anybody under five feet five inches to insolently lounge. Despite the lounging, he still looked like he was wound way tight. Louie started up with a low, constant growl, rumbling softly and comfortingly next to me. I hung my jacket up on the hook behind the front door and turned around as if finding Christoph sitting there was the most natural thing in the world.

"Make yourself at home," I said, flatly, without a trace of sarcasm.

"I already have," he replied. "Nice little place you've got here."

The rumbling from Louie grew louder.

"You might want to quiet him down," said Christoph. "It's not a polite way to treat a guest and he's starting to annoy me."

Entering a fellow practitioner's house uninvited is almost unthinkable. Breaking in and uttering implicit threats is totally beyond the pale and Christoph knew it. He was sending a clear message—he no longer needed to observe any conventions, or even to be civil. He was that strong, stronger even than at the Challenges. I noticed he still had layered protective spells around himself, though, ones that could surely handle anything I could throw at him. He wasn't as sure of himself as he pretended.

And it's not like he was invincible. You can be martial arts champion of the world and still have a lot of trouble against two merely competent fighters. And despite what you see in the movies, your chances against three skilled opponents is essentially nil. Christoph knew I had allies, people like Victor and Eli who would come after him if anything unfortunate were to happen to me. As with previous attacks he'd want to be circumspect, if only to preserve deniability. Which meant that whatever the reason for the visit, it wasn't necessarily lethal. That's what strict logic told me. I wish I was a bigger fan of logic.

"You're in my chair," I said.

"Very observant of you."

I wasn't sure enough about the value of my logic to push the issue. "What is it you want, Christoph?" I asked, temporizing.

He smiled his tight little smile. "Oh, I thought we might have a little talk," he said. "You should be flattered. Usually I send one of my more interesting . . . acquaintances. But I understand you've run into some problems of late. Squirmy problems. Trips to interesting places. Things like that."

"You could say so. Any idea of why that might be?"

"Hard to say. Maybe someone doesn't care for you."

I was feeling slightly more comfortable. People who want to carry on conversations usually don't want to kill you, at least not until they're finished. I walked over to the fridge and got myself a beer which I didn't really want. I didn't offer him one. That was the point, of course.

"Isn't this the place where you explain your plan for world domination and make me an offer I can't refuse?" I said. I was only partly joking.

He seemed annoyed. Again, the point.

"Being flippant doesn't suit you, Mason," he said. He obviously knew less about me than he thought. "But yes, I am offering you an opportunity. I don't often do that. You should pay attention."

"I'm all ears," I said.

He looked around at my apartment. "Do you really enjoy living like this? Wouldn't you like to have money— I mean real money, like your friend Victor?"

"Money's nice," I agreed.

"And power. Power to get anything you want. Any woman you want, for that matter."

I was beginning to understand. This wasn't about esoteric philosophy or practitioner politics. It was about the same things that drive the mundane world: power, sex, and money. Christoph was silent for a moment, trying to gauge my response. I didn't think he'd really come here to offer

me a deal. He had no reason to. But he wanted something.
I threw him a curve.

"Those gems. Like the one you used at the Challenges.
Are they part of this deal?"

He laughed, a high-pitched giggle that made him even
scarier. "You noticed that, did you?" he said. "I thought
you might have." He reached down somewhere in his shirt
and brought out a row of stones hanging from a silver
chain like a necklace.

His fingers brushed over the stones in a repetitive
rolling motion, and the expression on his face subtly
shifted to an almost sexual lust. I had thought it was all
about greed, but there was something else going on here. I
guessed that the stones were affecting him in ways he
didn't even understand. Whatever he had done to get them,
he'd surely made a devil's bargain. He held the stones out
toward me.

"These could be yours. You have no idea what it takes
to obtain them. I hate to make deals, but you've turned out
to be harder to get rid of than I expected."

"Speaking of which, what's the deal with that?" I said.
"What did I ever do to you?"

"Do? Nothing. It just that your presence is, well, incon-
venient. Nothing personal, you're just in the way."

"I'll bite. In the way of what?"

"Ahh, that would be telling, now, wouldn't it?"

"Well, this is a lot of fun," I said, "but do you have a
point?"

"Of course. Why do you think I'm here? I have a proposition for you."

This was better than I'd hoped for, a golden opportunity
handed to me on a silver platter, to mix metallic metaphors.
Whatever the proposal, all I needed to do was play along,
maybe acting somewhat resistant at first, than reluctantly
bowing to superior logic, or power, or whatever. Even a
few minutes of groveling might be in order. Christoph was
the cocksure type who would buy anything if you were ob-
sequious enough. Then, when I found out what I needed to

know, I'd hook up with Eli, Victor, and whoever else we could get and take care of the problem. It wouldn't matter how strong Christoph was if we put together enough force to overwhelm him. I'm not a big fan of the one-on-one confrontation if you can avoid it.

Then, as things often do, it all turned to shit. Louie, never the most patient of creatures, decided he'd had enough of conversation. He started growling again, stalking stiff legged toward Christoph, forgetting he was only as large as a medium-sized rabbit.

Christoph raised his hand and pointed at Lou. "I thought I told you to keep that dog quiet," he said.

Wow. A double insult. Giving me orders in my own house *and* referring to Lou as a dog. For someone with an Ifrit of his own, he seemed contemptuous of them. I took a deep breath. I needed to apologize for Louie and smooth it over. I could do it. Until I found out what I needed to, passive non-confrontation was the mature and intelligent way to go.

"Don't tell me what the fuck to do," I said. Like the scorpion on the back of the frog, I just couldn't help myself.

Christoph gave me an angry stare. He raised his hand and pointed at Louie again. I didn't know what he intended; a practitioner attacking an Ifrit is unheard of, but it rapidly became academic. Louie saw what he perceived as a threatening hand being raised and instantly launched himself with the single-minded desire to sink his teeth into it. Christoph uttered a short guttural noise, clenched his fist, and Lou gave a most undoglike sigh and slumped to the floor as if every bone in his body had suddenly been removed.

If I had taken a moment to think, I'm not sure what I would have done, but I didn't. Somewhere in the back of my mind I must have been aware of the fact that no magical assault would do me any good. Christoph at present was just too powerful. But I did have my talent for improvising with materials at hand. What followed was sheer reaction. Before Christoph could focus his attention on me, I had reached over and snatched up the cherry maple softball bat that rested next to the front door. Those Saturday after-

noon softball games I used to play in Dolores Park were finally going to pay off. I whirled and swung in one motion,
trying to hit a line drive past the third baseman. Christoph
was raising his hand in my direction when the bat hit him
across the mouth. If he hadn't been protected, that would
have been the end of it right there. His jaw would have dissolved in a mass of splintered bone and teeth, and it would
have taken him a year to recover, if he ever did.

But of course, he wasn't that vulnerable. His warding
spells were geared toward attacks from magical energy, but
there is always some crossover protection. Still, some of
the force got through. I'm a fairly strong guy, and I hit him
hard enough to numb his mouth, making it difficult for him
to pronounce words. I smashed down on his wrist, making
it impossible for him to gesture. Then I started in on his
head. It was like hitting someone wearing a football helmet; the blows bounced off, but they still shook him. If I
could hit him enough times he would end up with a con-
cussion and lose consciousness, protective spells or not.
He managed to stagger to his feet, but by that time I'd
clubbed him ten or eleven times and he was beginning to
go glassy-eyed. I caught him one in the throat, and he gave
a cough. I moved to the side and hit him on the base of his
skull. He stumbled forward and seemed about to go down
when suddenly there was a slight pop and he vanished.

I'd never seen anyone who could do that before, but
right now I wasn't interested. I dropped the bat and
crouched down beside Louie, who was lying motionless on
his left side. I picked him up, and he dangled limply in that
disturbingly boneless way that usually signifies the ab-
sence of life. I ran my hands along his side and cleared my
mind, reaching out, seeking that spark of life. Nothing. I
tried to relax further, not easy to do with surges of adrenaline still racing through my body, and reached out again.
There it was. Faint, shadowy, but definitely present. I stood
up and noticed my hands were shaking, whether from
stress or relief I couldn't tell. I tried to think of a healing
spell, but came up blank. I may be good at improvisational

magic, but when it comes to specifics, especially in the subtleties of the healing arts, I suck. It takes a lot more skill to repair a knife wound than it does to inflict one.

There was one thing I could do. I curled Louie up, grabbed the clock off my bedside table, scrabbled around in a couple of bureau drawers until I found an old tube of super glue, and added a rubber band to stretch it out. I muttered a few words, wishing I'd paid more attention to all the things Eli had tried to teach me over the years, ran my hands up one side of Louie's body and down the other, and laid a stasis spell over him. He turned rigid, like a little porcelain dog covered with fur. It wasn't very good, but it would last a couple of hours until I could get help.

I rang Eli's number but only got voice mail. I left a message saying it was urgent, then called Victor. He picked up immediately.

"Louie's hurt," I said. "I put a stasis on him but I need help."

"Get him over here," said Victor. "Is it bad?"

"Bad enough."

"Bring him here," Victor repeated, and hung up.

I placed Louie in my backpack, easing him in gently. I knew it wasn't true, but it felt like if I dropped him he would shatter. There was a moment of panic when the van, usually so reliable, refused to start. I forced myself to wait a full minute, in case I'd flooded it, and it finally kicked over. Driving over to the beach house, I traveled fast, but not crazy fast. The last thing I needed would be to be pulled over by the cops and have to waste time dealing with that situation. Louie would be fine until we got to Victor's, as long as the stasis lasted. For maybe the first time ever I felt reassured by the knowledge that Victor was in truth a far more skilled practitioner than I was.

Fifteen minutes later, I was laying him down on the rug in Victor's study. Danny the boyfriend sat quietly in a chair in the corner, staying out of the way but looking interested. Maggie drifted over on silent feet and gently reached out a paw, touching Lou on his muzzle. Victor shooed her away.

"Not now, Maggie. Let me see what we've got."

He lowered himself cross-legged on the rug and opened up a satchel of black leather, like an old-fashioned doctor's bag. He took out a crystal, several wooden dowels, a mirror, and several other objects not immediately identifiable. He arranged them in patterns, then rearranged them, then breathed on Louie's face, all the while muttering to himself. Danny started looking puzzled. I guess Victor hadn't revealed much about his real life to him yet. After about ten minutes, Victor sighed and got to his feet. He had a worried look on his face.

"I don't think I can do anything," he said. "This is beyond my skill."

I felt the blood rush out of my head. I had assumed that Victor would be able to handle it. For all the snide things I had to say about him, the truth was that I had always counted on him at crunch time. He saw my face turn pale.

"Hold on, Mason," he said testily. "I said *I* can't deal with it. I didn't say nobody could. I *might* be able to pull it off, but he's so far gone that if I screwed it up there wouldn't be enough time to try again. I'm afraid what we need here is a specialist."

The blood started returning to my face. "Who do you know?" I asked.

"I assume you want someone good?"

I didn't say anything, just stood there staring.

"Right. Well, there's a woman who lives around Soda Springs, up near Donner Summit. Her name is Campbell, and she's one of the best. She's technically not a practitioner; doesn't seem to care much about such things. She calls herself a healer. Practices Wicca, of all things."

"I don't care if she prays to a sheep in the sky as long as she can help."

"Well, if anyone can, she's the one. You'll have to go up to see her, though. She's a lot stronger on her home turf." He broke off and put his hand on my shoulder, a very uncharacteristic gesture for him. "Don't worry, Mason. I've seen her do some very impressive work." He glanced down at Louie's still form on the rug. "We're not rid of him quite yet. I'll give her a call and let her know you're coming."

After he made the call, Victor came back and replaced my stasis spell with one of his own, one that would last longer. It also got rid of the frozen stiffness mine had caused. He didn't say a word about my obviously inferior effort. He also made sure I knew how to remove it so the woman would be able to work on Lou.

"Be careful," he cautioned. "He's probably got no more than half an hour at most after you take it off. Make sure everything is ready to go before you do." He gave me a map he had printed up on his computer, marked with a circle representing her house. "It's pretty easy to find," he reassured me. "You shouldn't have any problem." That phrase was not one of my favorites, from bitter experience, but I let it pass.

Victor gazed out the window. It was growing dark and the rain was really starting to come down. He sighed, looked at me, shook his head, and reached into his pocket.

"Here," he said, handing me a car key. "Take the Navigator. It's all-wheel drive and it's bound to be snowing up there. That van of yours will never make it. Oh, and you'll need a coat." He went over to a closet and pulled out a North Face ski parka as if he'd had it waiting there for just such an opportunity.

I thanked him abstractedly and scooped up Lou. He went back into the backpack and since he was no longer stiff as concrete I curled him up as if he were sound asleep. Victor walked back over to where Danny was sitting and rested one hand lightly on his shoulder He was going to have some 'splainin' to do.

Downstairs, I fumbled with the keys to the Navigator until Victor came down and showed me how to work the keyless entry. I was on the road five minutes later. It wasn't until then that I realized he hadn't even asked me what exactly had happened. People can sometimes surprise you.

I headed across the Bay Bridge and out I-80 toward Reno. In good weather, it takes about three hours or less to Donner Summit, but with the rain coming down it was going to take longer. After you pass Sacramento the highway starts gaining elevation, and the rain grew colder. Then it started turning to sleet. Then it started turning into snow. The wind picked up until I could barely see the road. Every so often snowplows would come rumbling by, but there was no way they could keep ahead of the accumulation.

The Soda Springs exit is almost at the Donner Summit, and a foot of snow covered the road by the time I reached it. The Navigator plowed through as if it were a dusting of sand, barely even sliding, while cars with chains were clunking along hesitantly. I thought of all the times I'd cursed the drivers of SUVs and blessed the fact I now had one.

I headed down Donner Lake Road, then Soda Springs Road. I was supposed to turn off somewhere along the way, but now that I was off the main road, the snow was even deeper. The flakes were coming down horizontally, slamming into the windshield, and even with low beams the snow reflected and swirled until I could no longer see farther than the end of the car hood. Eventually I turned off the headlights and drove with only the parking lights on. I still couldn't see the road, but at least I had some idea of where it was. I stopped and turned on the interior lights to check the map Victor had printed out for me. I should be right on top of where the turnoff was supposed to be. I turned off the dome light and started inching along, and sure enough, about a hundred yards farther along the road, there was a smooth patch veering off to the side that could only be a road.

The wheels of the Navigator spun out as I cautiously made the turn but I kept momentum going and made it without getting stuck. I didn't have time to congratulate myself though because almost immediately after, the road disappeared into a snowdrift deep enough to high center even the Navigator's ample clearance. After a few futile attempts to rock it out, I got out to assess the situation. I pulled on the North Face parka Victor had lent me, mentally blessing him again. He may have had no psychic powers, but his Boy Scout be-prepared philosophy was almost as good.

As soon as I got out, I could see what I had done. The

road curved off to the left, and I hadn't. Not being able to
see anything, I had simply driven straight off the road into
a snowbank. The car wasn't going to be moving again anytime soon.

I climbed back in and considered my options. I could sit
there and try to periodically run the engine to keep warm
until the snow let up. Of course, if that took more than a
few hours, which seemed extremely likely, the stasis spell
on Louie would wear off and he would die. Or, I could start
trudging off on foot, but if I got lost in the blizzard, which
also seemed likely, we would both die. Or, I could call for
help on my cell phone, except I didn't have one. Never had
seen the need for one. Victor had one, of course, and I'm
sure it was always fully charged, but he had neglected to
lend it to me. Most unhelpful of him.

The Navigator did have a state-of-the-art GPS system,
however, which let me know exactly where I was. I pulled
out the map Victor had given me again and correlated the
position on the GPS screen with the map. It looked like I
was close to the house where this Campbell woman lived,
but I couldn't tell how close. I was in pretty good shape,
and although I had no gloves and my shoes weren't the
ideal footwear for stumbling around in the snow, I should
be able to make it.

I checked on Louie, who was still curled up in the backpack as if he hadn't a care in the world, struggled the pack
onto my back over the bulky parka, flipped up the hood to
protect my head, climbed out of the car, and started off on
foot.

You'd think I could have just put a warming spell over
myself and avoided all the hassles of uncooperative ele-
ments. And indeed I could have, except for the fact that
maintaining a warming spell in blizzard conditions would
take about the same amount of energy as keeping warm by
running through deep snow. After five minutes, I would
have been too exhausted to move. As Eli often reminded
me, magic is a tool, not a panacea. I did compromise and
put a slight spell on my hands, just enough to keep them

from freezing, because I needed them free to maintain my balance while slipping and sliding through the snow.

For a while, everything was fine. I kept to what I assumed was the road, which at least seemed to be headed in the right direction. The wind whipped the snow into my face, occasionally coming at me almost level. I had to squint to protect my eyes, which made it even harder to see where I was going. It was hard at times even to breathe without getting fine snow crystals into my throat and lungs, making me cough. It was the mountain equivalent of a desert sandstorm. At least I didn't have to worry about dying of thirst.

The combination of uncertain footing and strong winds knocked me off my feet several times. One of those times, I must have gotten turned around, because I began to notice the occasional tree popping up, which seemed unlikely if I had managed to stay on the road. Still, I was fairly confident I was headed in the right direction. At least, I was until the trees started getting thicker and I plunged into a couple of drifts up to my hips. I had to waste even more precious energy putting a protective spell on my feet before they froze solid and stranded me in the middle of nowhere. I could feel the energy leaching out of me faster than was safe.

It dawned on me that I was well and truly lost. I was on my way to being the guy you read about in the paper, the guy who leaves his car and wanders off into a raging blizzard, the guy who ends up being found a few days later frozen in the snow. Or, if it's a particularly hard winter, being found by hikers sometime in late spring. The regret you feel for this poor fellow is always tempered just a bit by the thought, "What the hell was he thinking? Stay with the car, bozo."

The trees cut the force of the wind, but to compensate, they made it so I could be walking in circles for all I knew. The smart thing to do would be to build a snow cave in the shelter of a couple of the trees, start a fire, and hunker down. It's not that hard to survive a storm if you have warm clothing, means of making a fire, and you don't lose your head. Unfortunately, Louie wouldn't be so lucky.

I tried to think of a locating spell I could use to guide

me in the right direction while I still had the energy to pull it off. For about the thousandth time in the last few days, I wished I'd been more diligent in my studies. There were a lot of magical things I could do, but none of them were going to help me much in this situation.

I slipped off the backpack and sank down with my back to a spruce tree. The wind circled around the tree and the snow swirled in eddies around me. My eyelashes were thick with ice crystal, and the clean smell of the snow mingled with the sharp cold smell of spruce and pine. It was beautiful, and dangerous, with snow piling up between the tree trunks and the wind alternately sighing and shrieking through the upper branches of the trees.

I don't think I'd ever felt so discouraged and helpless. I thrust my hands deep into the pockets of my parka, trying for a little extra warmth, and felt a crumpled up piece of paper with numbed fingers. It was Victor's map. I had jammed it into my coat pocket before I started out. It was too dark to read it, and at this point it was useless anyway. What I really needed was one of those handheld GPS systems from Sharper Image, all high-tech and glowing. At least that would have enabled me to get to a town.

Glowing. A germ of an idea wormed its way into my consciousness. How about a map that glowed? How about a map that glowed in real time with my position and my destination? How about a nice, low-tech, magical GPS of my own devising? I smoothed out the paper, trying to keep it shielded from the wind and snow. I concentrated on centering myself, seeing myself as the focus of the universe. Many of my friends would say that wasn't too difficult for me. Clear tang of evergreen. Taste of snow crystals. Wind rushing through the trees. Louie, curled up in the backpack, silently dreaming away. Cold seeping into my bones. I took a deep breath and blew across the paper, not a cold exhalation, but warm like when you huff on your hands to warm them.

The map started glowing with a faint phosphorescence, sparking like the tropical sea when you trail your hand in the water off a boat at night. A small glowing figure was off to one side, and a larger one pulsed up toward the top of the map. I held the map up close to my face and saw that the larger spot was a tiny house. Damn. I was better than I thought. I had been hoping for nothing more than blurry points of light.

One thing I could see was that I was farther away from the house than when I had left the car. I had been veering off at a forty-five-degree angle, heading toward God knows where. Charged with new energy, I picked up the pack, oriented myself, and struck out in what I hoped was the right direction. I still couldn't see much of anything, but the moving figure on the map kept me going. I had to detour a couple of times around what appeared to be deadfalls, although it was hard to tell under the covering of snow. Eventually the trees thinned out and I assumed I was back on the road again, although by that time there was nothing but smooth unbroken whiteness. I checked the map and saw that the little figure and the little house were now almost touching, but I still could see nothing. Then, during a momentary lull in the gusts of wind, I saw a glimmer of light off to my left. I summoned up my last reserves of energy and plodded up an incline toward the light source. Suddenly, a shape loomed out of the snow, resolving itself into a small cabin no more than fifty feet from where I stood. There was a white glow in one of the front windows as if someone had hung out a Coleman lantern, and what looked like flickering candlelight farther in. It made sense; in a storm such as this the power was probably out all through the region.

I staggered the last few steps to the front door and pounded on it with numb hands. It flew open as if someone had been waiting there for me and a blast of blessed warmth rolled through the open doorway. Framed with the glow of candlelight stood a woman who reached toward me like a welcoming angel.

"You must be Mason," she said.

TEN

FOR A MOMENT I THOUGHT I'D ENCOUNTERED A
supernatural being. A spill of blond hair backlit by flickering candlelight created an aura around her head, projecting
the illusion of a metaphysical apparition. Then the warmth
pouring out through the open door melted the frost from
my eyelashes and the figure morphed back into that of an
ordinary woman. She stepped aside and as I half staggered
into the house she closed the door behind me.

The cabin was one large room. The source of the gratifying warmth was immediately apparent; in one corner of
the room stood a cast-iron potbelly stove, except that it was
square instead of potbellied. Close by was a futon on a
raised platform, and next to it sat a low wooden bench with
amber bottles of various sizes, cobalt blue glass jars, crystals, dishes of vegetable matter, and sundry other things. I
guessed they were all the stock in trade of a Wiccan healer.

Near the stove, on the floor, lay a piece of patterned fabric that looked like a prayer rug. I walked over to it,
shrugged out of the backpack, opened it, and lifted Lou cautiously out. His body was cold. I pointed down at the rug.

"Is here okay?"

She nodded, and I placed him carefully down, shrugging off my coat and taking off the warming spell on my hands and feet to save some energy. She walked over to us and knelt beside the still form.

"I'm Campbell," she said, running her hands along his body. "I can't believe you made it here. Where's your car?"

"It's a ways," I said. "I had to hike the last mile or so."

She glanced briefly out the front window, where the snow was battering harder than ever. "How in the world did you find the place in this storm?" she asked, continuing her examination.

"I had a map."

She had her head down on his belly, listening intently. I don't think she heard my answer. She lifted his head, examined his ears, ran her fingers down his spine, acting for all the world like a judge at a dog show. I started to wonder if Victor's faith might have been misplaced. Finally she straightened up and moved over closer to the stove. She stood there silently regarding me until I finally broke the silence.

"Well?" I asked.

"It's hard for me to tell much yet," she replied. She hesitated, started to say something, then stopped.

"What?" I prompted.

She stood there without replying. She no longer seemed like an angel, at least not like the traditional image that we grow up with. But she burned brightly with health and boundless energy, with the animation that makes even an ordinary woman seem especially attractive. And she was anything but ordinary. A wide mouth, strong nose, and weather-streaked blond hair. Or maybe that was just a look. What do I know? She wore a faded red sweatshirt and jeans, but even so, I could see she was strong and firm underneath, like an athlete. A silver chain holding a smooth green stone hung around her neck, and she reached up and pushed her hair away from where it had fallen over her face.

"Well," she finally said, "usually when someone is ill or injured, I can focus in on the problem." A small frown ap-

peared on her face. "Doing something useful about it is another matter, but I'll usually have a good idea what's
wrong. But something's blocking me here. Since Victor
sent you here, I'm going to assume you know what I'm
talking about. Most people just think I'm a New Age flake
when I mention things like that."

. I nodded. "I do understand," I said.

"The other thing is maybe more important. I need all the
information I can get to be able to help. And to put it
bluntly, that's not exactly a dog, is it? What is it, and what
are we dealing with?"

I mentally apologized to Victor for doubting his judgment. This woman definitely was no flake.

"He's an Ifrit," I said. "A sort of semimagical creature, I
guess, but I can't tell you exactly what he is because I don't
know. No one does. But, I think, he's also very much a dog.
If you just consider him in that way it should work out."

She nodded without comment. "And the blocking energy?"

"It's a stasis spell. As long as it's in effect, his condition
won't deteriorate. I wanted to wait until you were ready
before I removed it. I don't think he has that much time."

Campbell slowly walked over to the bench containing
all the bottles and jars. She started sorting through them,
picking out some and discarding others.

"I understand the logic," she said, "but unfortunately I
won't know what I'll need until I can get a look at what his
problem is. He seems to be injured, but at the same time he
seems to be ill. What did happen, anyway?"

"We had a disagreement with someone and it turned violent. He got caught by a power surge, or a spell, or a psychic
blast. It doesn't matter what you call it, because none of
those things are anything more than labels. If I knew what
the mechanism of it was, I could have fixed him myself."

"Wrong word," she chided. "You fix cars. Living things
are healed."

I didn't say anything. I wasn't in the mood for hair splitting, and I certainly wasn't about to alienate someone who

might be Lou's only hope. Something must have shown on my face, though, because she apologized a second later.

"Sorry," she said. "Now is obviously not the time for grammar lessons. I tend to say things like that when I'm worried."

She reached under the bench and pulled out a small cast iron pot sitting on three stubby legs. It couldn't have held more than a pint. She set it up next to Louie, lit a can of Sterno, and placed it under the pot.

"Witch's cauldron," she said, smiling to show she wasn't serious. Or at least, not completely. She started rummaging around in the glass containers again. "I can at least set up the basics, things I'll need whatever the specifics turn out to be." She picked up a bunch of small earthen bowls and started placing herbs into them, a different herb in each bowl. "Spearmint leaf," she murmured. "Always good for clarity." Another pinch of something went into another bowl. "Hyssop. Burdock root. Eucalyptus. Maybe some angelica? Couldn't hurt." A long pause. "Hawthorne berries. That should do it."

I started having doubts again. Magical energy, as far as I knew, was not affected by twigs and berries. She turned and gave me an appraising look. Whatever else her abilities, this woman was adept at reading body language.

"You don't have to believe any of this is necessary," she said. "If it makes you more comfortable, just think of it as metaphor. It may well be just that, but one thing I do know is that I can't work without my tools."

I realized she was right. It was no different than my needing a folded piece of paper before I could work a locating spell. She was simply a practitioner from a different tradition, a folk tradition, even if she didn't view herself that way.

She crossed over to the small kitchen area on the opposite wall of the cabin. She turned on the sink tap and ran her fingers under the stream of water. I thought she was just cleansing her hand, but she crossed back and flicked water off her fingers onto the heated iron brazier. The drops sizzled and popped with a satisfying crackle.

"Hot enough," she said.

She picked up the small earthenware bowls filled with herbs and put them down next to the pot. Then she lowered herself down next to Louie, sitting cross-legged, and looked up at me.

"Okay," she said." I guess I'm as ready as I'm going to be."

I walked over to Louie and bent down over him. I didn't feel very confident, but there was no point in worrying now. As was usual of late, there weren't a whole lot of options. I placed my hand just over him, less than an inch away, utilized the technique Victor had supplied, and took up the energy surrounding him. Campbell immediately bent over him and ran through the routine she had done when I first arrived. When she was done, she straightened up, and I didn't like the look on her face.

"This is going to be more complicated than I thought," she said. "And you were right; we don't have much time."

"What's the problem?" I asked.

"Do you know anything about computers?"

I didn't see the relevance, but as she said, we didn't have much time so I simply said, "Not much."

"Well, let's just say that his problem is in a place I can't access, so I'm going to have to move it to somewhere where I can. But there is one good thing. His problem is artificial, not organic, so if I can bring him back he'll be fine. It will be like nothing ever happened."

While she was talking, she headed back to her herb collection. She opened an amber jar. "Lavender, valerian root." She reached under the bench and came out with a sandalwood box. "And something stronger."

Campbell threw a touch of the lavender and valerian into the brazier. They started smoldering together, and a thick, syrupy odor filled the room. The fragrance of lavender combined with another scent both pungent and almost offensive. I assumed that was the valerian root. The wood-burning stove was already pumping out enough heat to make the room feel close, and the heavy scent started making me sleepy in spite of myself. Then she opened the sandalwood box and added a hefty dollop of a dark treacly paste. A perfume I was somewhat familiar with immediately crept into the room, creamy and distinctive. Campbell looked over at me.

"Opium," she confirmed. "I have to shift what's left of him out of the space he's in and into a natural coma before I can bring him out of it. That is, if you can consider a drug- and spell-induced coma natural. It is dangerous, though. There's so little life force left in him that the opium might be the last straw that pushes him over the edge." She suddenly looked unsure of herself. "I'm sorry. I don't know any other way to go about it."

I didn't say anything, giving tacit agreement. She picked Louie up and cradled him in her lap. The fumes from the brazier grew thicker, cloying and heavy. Without the slightest trace of self-consciousness she started singing in a low, pleasant voice, a lullaby I had never heard:

> *Slumber my darling*
> *I'll wrap thee up warm*
> *And pray that the angels*
> *Will shield thee from harm . . .*

Her voice trailed off until there was only an inaudible whisper of song echoing in my head. She gave me a quick smile. "Stephen Foster," she said.

I thought I noticed a slight change in Lou. Although he hadn't so much as twitched, he now appeared more asleep than dead. Campbell laid him back down on the rug and sprang to her feet. She quickly seized a metal cover and put it over the brazier, cutting off the fumes. She grabbed a couple of pot holders on the refrigerator where they hung from their magnets and dumped the contents of the pot into the sink. Then she started trying to scrub out the gummy residue, burning her arm in the process as it brushed against the side of the pot. She pronounced a couple of choice words that are not to be found in most healing rituals.

"Good enough," she pronounced, and set it back on the floor. "I knew I should have bought that extra pot, though." She gestured at me. "Get a chunk of wood ember out of the stove and put it in the cauldron. Quickly, he's barely hanging on."

As she spoke, she picked up a muslin bag and started emptying out wood shavings onto the floor, selecting the ones she wanted using criteria I couldn't even guess at, except that they were all paper thin.

I opened the door of the stove and looked around vacantly for some tongs. My mind was still fogged from the remaining scent in the room. Campbell gestured impatiently at the wood bin next to the stove and there they were. I thrust them into the stove, found a nice glowing ember about half the size of my fist, carried it over, and placed it in the brazier. Meanwhile, Campbell had sat back down next to Louie and was holding him again.

"When I tell you, sprinkle the shavings over the ember," she instructed.

She sat up straight and began to chant. I've done some chanting in my time in order to enable spells, but this was a different sort of thing. Witchy, I thought. She spoke in a clear, matter-of-fact tone:

> The way is deep, the way is cold
> Still, your story's yet untold
> Renounce sleep, embrace desire
> Let it blossom into fire.

She looked over at me and inclined her head toward the brazier. I threw a handful of shavings onto the ember and they immediately caught, sending up a flare of scented fire. At the same moment I felt a flash of energy come off her.

"Now the herbs," she said.

I sprinkled them into the flame and another cloud of smoke poured up, but this time it was sharp and astringent. Just a whiff of it cleared my head.

"If you pray, now's the time to do so," she said.

She leaned over the brazier and inhaled a good-sized lungful of smoke. I could see her chest heaving, trying not to cough it out and lose it. It reminded me of a teenage girl with her first joint. Then she leaned over and, holding Louie's muzzle, clapped her mouth over his nose and blew the smoke in. Kind of a cross between CPR and super-charging a friend.

I thought I saw him twitch, and then, just as I was sure I had imagined it, he let out a tremendous sneeze. Almost instantaneously he scrambled out of her lap and went into a sneezing fit, one after another. When he finally stopped, he looked around wildly and then focused his gaze on me.

"Welcome back," I said.

TEN MINUTES LATER, LOUIE WAS SOUND ASLEEP, curled up on a cushion by the stove. Campbell told me not to worry. "It's exactly what he needs," she said. I watched the steady rise and fall of his rib cage, so different from the boneless coma he had been in, and was reassured.

"I don't know how to thank you," I told her. We were sitting at her kitchen table, drinking some odd sort of tea she had brewed.

"Not a problem," she said. "Although a small contribution to defray expenses is always welcome."

I reached into my pocket and pulled out my wallet. I emptied it out on the table. Sixty-three dollars and some change was all I had. I pushed it over toward her, saying, "I can send you an additional check as soon as I get home."

"Ah, yes, the check is in the mail," she said, smiling to make sure I knew she was joking. She reached over and picked out two twenties. "This should cover it. The only expensive thing was the opium, and I only used a pinch."

"Are you sure?"

"Well, you can owe me a favor. I have a feeling you might be a useful person to know. Be warned, though. I'm one of those people who may actually turn up on your doorstep one day."

"Consider me warned."

We sat for a while drinking tea, listening to the storm raging outside, gusts of wind intermittently slamming into the side of the house.

"I ought to call Victor," I said. "Let him know how it turned out."

"Can't. Phone's dead," she said, drawing her finger across her throat.

"You have a cell?"

"Nope. You?"

"I keep meaning to get one," I said.

"Me, too."

We both digested this brilliant exchange. "Where do you know Victor from, anyway?" she asked.

"We kind of move in the same circles." I wasn't sure how much to say or how much she knew about him.

"You're a practitioner, then," she said. That answered that question.

"I guess so. I like to think of myself more as a musician, though."

"Classical?"

I shook my head. "Jazz, mostly. Guitar."

"That's great. You make a living at it?"

"If you want to call it that."

"You must be good, then. All the jazz musicians I know spend more on their equipment then they take in from gigs."

I waved a hand toward the snow falling outside the window. "I wouldn't think there's much call for jazz in the middle of nowhere."

She laughed pleasantly. "It isn't really the middle of nowhere. On a summer's day it's actually quite civilized around here. And there's a lot of gigs in Tahoe and Reno. They just don't pay a whole lot of money."

"Welcome to my world."

We sipped tea silently for a few minutes. "What about you?" I asked. "How do you know Victor?"

"My ex-boyfriend and his ex-boyfriend are the same person."

"Ouch."

"No, it was fine. He was a great guy—he just wasn't very clear about his sexuality. It got to be too much drama for me, so we agreed to go our separate ways."

"And then he hooked up with Victor?"

"I'm afraid so." She giggled: "After that, he wasn't very clear about anything. Now he's thinking of going to seminary school."

"Did he know Victor was a practitioner?"

She shook her head. "He was completely clueless about it. He was pretty much clueless about most things. He thought I was totally nuts, with my healing spells and such. God knows what he thought Victor was about. He was sweet, but a bit lacking in the brains department." Her face took on an abstracted expression. "Not lacking in others, though." She sat quietly for a minute, then gave herself a little shake. "Afterward, I ended up moving to this area. New Age healing is very big around here, and I do some massage work and stuff like that. I make enough to get by, and it allows me to indulge in my two passions."

"Which are?"

"Telemark skiing and photography."

"In that order?"

"Unfortunately, yes. Which is probably why I'm not the creative soul I always thought I would be, although since I mostly do wildlife photography the two complement each other fairly well." She gestured at a framed photo hanging on one wall. "That's one of mine."

I walked over to look at it. It was a close-up of a wildcat, or maybe a lynx, sitting perched in the branches of a snow-covered tree. There was snow falling and he looked extremely unhappy about it.

"Look closely," Campbell called out.

I did, and after a moment noticed three porcupine quills sticking out of his muzzle next to his nose. "Poor kitty," I commented. "Did you heal him?"

She snorted. "Yeah, right. He would have torn my arm off."

I sat back down at the table. "Very cool," I said.

"Thank you. It gives me an excuse to get out and ski. I can pretend I'm working on my creative soul."

"And what about Wicca?" I asked.

"Wicca's not something I take completely seriously. Oh, the healing part I do, but the rest of it? Like I said earlier, it's just a metaphor that enables me to project whatever healing powers I might have. The rituals work just fine, but making Wicca the focus of life just isn't me. I'm afraid the local Wiccan community considers me something of a renegade." She turned and peered out the window. "Look. The wind is dying down."

It was indeed. The snow was still falling, harder than before if anything, but now it was drifting in a postcard winter wonderland fashion. There was barely enough light to see the drifts and mounds that showed where bushes and hollows were covered with snow. Campbell pulled over a couch and set it next to the window, motioning to me to take a seat. We sat together in silence and watched the falling snow. After a while she reached over and started playing with the hair at the back of my neck.

"Do you have a girlfriend?" she asked.

I gave her the raised eyebrow look. "Not at present. Idle curiosity?"

"Not entirely. I love it up here, but I do feel isolated sometimes. It's not every day that a handsome stranger turns up at my doorstep seeking assistance."

"Handsome, you say?"

"Well, passable, at least. After a couple of months of winter, one's standards do tend to lower a bit."

"Stop, you're embarrassing me."

She continued to play with my hair. I moved a bit closer to show her that the attention was not unwelcome.

"Of course, I do have *some* standards," she said.

"Such as?"

"Living. Breathing. The ability to speak in complete sentences, although I'm flexible on that one."

"Huh?"

"Good enough."

We sat in companionable silence for a while. It's not often you find someone you can do that with unless you know them very well, and even then it's rare. I pulled her over to rest in the crook of my arm and we sat awhile longer. She turned her head and looked directly at me.

"So, what do you think?" she asked.

At least I had enough of the social graces not to ask, "Think about what?" There's a fine line between using humor to flirt and being totally obnoxious.

"I think it probably would be very nice," I said. "As long as . . ."

"As long as I realize we're talking a one-time thing, right?" she interrupted.

"Maybe two times."

"Promises, promises. If men could only deliver." She smiled at me and stood up. "The fact is, you're an attractive man. And after that healing I did, I'm drained. The best way to replenish one's energy, as every good pagan knows, is through sex. Not to mention I haven't had sex in three months. She held out her hand. "Come, on," she said. "Time for bed."

I wasn't used to such a direct approach. I seem to be drawn more to the shy ones, the delicate type that has to be coaxed into it. That way, of course, if it isn't any good they can hardly be blamed for the ensuing fiasco. This was a lot easier. So far.

I followed her over to the futon by the stove. It was warm and cozy, and with the candles finally guttering down, the light was dim and romantic without any planning or effort.

"You know," I said, "I didn't exactly come prepared."

"I'm a healer, remember?" she said, pulling me down onto the mattress. "With certain abilities. I don't get pregnant unless I want to. And I don't get diseases. Ever. One of the perks of the great Wiccan tradition."

I made one of the better decisions of my life and kept my mouth shut for once. Or at least I didn't use it to pro-

nounce any more words. We started kissing, softly at first,
then with increasing urgency. Campbell slipped her sweatshirt over her head and eased out of her jeans. She wasn't
wearing anything underneath. All that cross-country skiing
hadn't gone to waste either. I could see long muscles rippling under her skin, and nice skin it was. I started strip-
ping down, suddenly feeling adolescent and fumbling,
while she watched me. Nervousness reared its ugly head.
Maybe I was one of those stereotypical men after all,
strangely fearful of confident, strong women. I finally got
rid of the last of my clothes and she reached up and pulled
me down on top of her. She began to gently stroke my
body, and the mere touch of her hands made me instantly
hard, as hard as I'd ever been in my life.

"I have other talents besides healing," she whispered in
my ear. "It's related, you know."

My heart was pounding too hard to want to discuss it
with her. I returned the favor, running my hands up and
down the length of her, and when I eventually slid my hand
between her legs, she was wet. She shuddered, opening her
legs slightly.

Well, I'm not going to go into further details. A full description of the next hour or so would be very much like
the sex itself—fascinating if you are the one taking part,
but repetitive and monotonous if you just have to sit and
listen. All I have to say is yes, she did have talents. The
ending was apparently as satisfying for her as it was for
me, unless she was a terrific actress, and she didn't strike
me as the type who would put on a show just to soothe my
ego. Besides, I could see her skin glow. Apparently she
wasn't kidding when she said that sex replenished her energies. We lay there without speaking, until she leaned
over and kissed me lightly on the cheek.

"You did good," she said. Then she turned over with her
back to me, pulled a comforter over both of us, and snuggled her way into the curve of my body, spooning us. In
less than a minute, she was asleep. I lay there awhile
longer, luxuriating in the uncommon experience of having

a naked female body pressed sleeping next to mine. All things considered, the day had turned out not so badly after all. I thought about getting up to extinguish the rest of the candles but I didn't think about it very hard. As I drifted off, I remembered having said something about doing it twice, and felt extremely grateful I didn't have to live up to my brag.

The next thing I knew, there was sun in my eyes. The storm had ended and there was brilliant sunshine streaming through the front windows. The woodstove was still giving off a little spark of warmth, but the room had grown cold. I could hear the refrigerator humming, so the power had been restored sometime during the night. There was a small warm furry lump wedged against my legs, which meant Louie was back to normal.

Campbell had appropriated most of the comforter during the night and I tried surreptitiously to ease a little of it back in my direction. Her eyes jumped open almost immediately and widened in what I could only characterize as horror.

"My God!" she cried. "How drunk was I?"

Not for the first time in my life, I was at a loss for words. Then she laughed. "Sorry," she said. "I couldn't resist. I wish you could have seen the look on your face."

"Very amusing," I said, not amused at all.

"I'm sorry, that wasn't funny," she said, trying to stifle her laughter. She grabbed me and pulled me close, wrapping the comforter around us both. Lou made a small noise of protest at being disturbed.

"Brrr," she shivered. "Woodstoves are great, but they don't have thermostats."

"Allow me," I said, a bit formally. I was still being slightly pissy about being made fun of before my morning coffee. I slid out from under the cover, opened the stove door, and quickly threw a few logs in from the pile on the floor. Then I set them ablaze with a hand gesture and some gathered sunlight. As soon as the logs were burning nicely

I jumped back under the comforter. Campbell looked at me with new respect.

"Wow," she said, this time wide-eyed for real. "Now there's a talent I could use."

"My pleasure," I said smugly.

Louie poked his head out from under the comforter at the end of the bed, tested the temperature, and dove back under. We all stayed in bed until the stove had warmed the room, which didn't take long. Campbell leaned over to one side and came up with a blue terrycloth robe. She put it on and bounced up, heading to the kitchen portion of the room.

"Coffee?" she inquired.

"Do you have to ask?"

She busied herself with beans and a grinder. I watched her through half-closed eyes, almost slipping back into sleep. Finally, the smell of coffee brewing and the call of nature forced me out of the bed. I hurriedly threw on my clothes, and when I came out of the bathroom she had poured me a large mug of steaming black coffee. She headed to the bathroom and pointed toward the end of the table.

"Sugar's over there, milk's in the fridge."

When she came back, Lou had assumed his begging position, nose twitching, looking hopefully around. Campbell regarded him skeptically. "Are you positive he's a magical creature?" she asked.

"Semi, remember?" I said.

"Hmm. Well, I don't know what I can give him to eat. I don't have any meat in the house."

"He's pretty flexible. Anything but twigs and tofu and celery."

This time I was the one favored with a dubious look. I gave her my best innocent, bland smile.

"Don't tease," she said. "One thing you should know, I can dish it out but I can't take it." She glanced up at the cupboard next to the sink. "I could make pancakes."

Louie immediately started jumping up in the air, barking hysterically, losing all pretense of dignity.

"Pancakes are his favorite," I explained.

"Oh."

The telephone was working again, so I called Victor while Campbell stirred up eggs, flour, milk, and some chopped apples into a batter. It took a while because he had a lot of questions about Christoph, ones I couldn't answer. By the time I was done filling him in, the smell of pancakes was wafting through the room. Lou had quieted down, but now was positively drooling. She shoveled three large cakes onto a chipped plate and asked, not serious, "Does he get butter and maple syrup?"

"Just a tad," I said.

She hesitated until she was sure I wasn't joking, put a pat of butter and a dollop of syrup on top, and set the plate on the floor. Lou walked over delicately, sat up, and put one paw on her knee.

"His way of thanking you," I explained.

"Good manners is always an attractive quality in a dog," she said.

Lou reverted back to his canine persona and started gobbling the pancakes fast enough so that he choked a couple of times. Campbell and I ate at a more measured pace, interspersing bites with conversation. Eventually the discussion turned to exactly what had happened to Lou the previous day, and what we were up against with Christoph. It felt strange talking about it with an outsider, but she wasn't exactly a civilian herself when you came right down to it.

She sat quietly, elbow on the table, chin in hand. I realized that I liked her a lot. I kept talking, telling the story of the singularity and the rescue by wolves, mostly because I enjoyed watching her sitting there. But I also thought she might have some insight into what had happened there. I certainly didn't.

Campbell listened soberly. When I was finished, she said, "My grandmother used to tell a story very similar, although in her version the person never made it back home. So I don't know how she could have known what happened, but she was an amazing woman, not Wiccan, but far stronger in craft than I will ever be. One thing that's clear is that the wolf is your totem."

"My totem?"

"Your guardian spirit. An archetype. Some people have them and some people don't. It has nothing to do with who might deserve it and who might not. There doesn't seem to be any reason why some people are blessed—it hardly seems fair, but that's apparently just the way it is."

Sort of like Ifrits and practitioners, I thought. "And have you got one?" I asked.

"No," she said, looking suddenly so sad I was sorry I had asked.

"So, this wolf totem protects me?" I tried hard to keep the skepticism out of my voice, but I don't think I succeeded very well. "Then why haven't I ever run into them before? I'm sure I would have remembered."

"Mock if you wish, but my grandmother knew a lot, and she took it for granted that there were such things."

"But she wasn't Wiccan?"

"She was a Catholic. As was my mother."

"What happened to you?"

"It's a long story. In any case, a totem only appears when it's needed. Have you ever had a magical attack on your life before?"

I hadn't. You'd think the life of a magical practitioner would be full of excitement and danger, but it wasn't. Apart from music, I led a relatively placid existence.

"And what, pray tell, would be your alternative explanation for why a pack of wolves would suddenly appear and help to transport you back home?" she added.

She had me there. "Perhaps I'm a werewolf," I said, teasingly.

She grabbed my hand with enough force to make me wince, turned it over, and stared into the palm.

"No, you're not," she said, exhaling with relief. "After last night, I couldn't have handled that."

I looked at her closely. I couldn't tell if she was putting me on or if she really thought there were such things. Then again, I wasn't so sure myself anymore. This last week had shaken a lot of my cherished rationality.

"Hold on a second," she said, getting up from the table. She walked over to a wooden trunk on the other side of the room, rummaged around in it for a while, and came up with a small, tarnished silver box. She brought it back to the table, opened it, removed a small object, and set it on the table.

"My grandmother gave me this," she said. "Her mother gave it to her, and she was supposed to give it to my mother, but she gave it to me instead. She said I had the greater need."

I examined the object closely. It seemed to be made of ivory and wood, the wood black and polished, the ivory yellow with age. It was a figurine no larger than a pack of gum and appeared to be a man with the head of a wolf, or maybe a wolf with a deformed body. The wolf motif again.

"This is very old," I said. Campbell nodded. "And kind of creepy." She nodded again.

"My grandmother said it was a talisman of protection, the only real talisman she had ever possessed."

"What is it supposed to do?" I asked.

"I have no idea. My grandmother said I would know what to do with it if the time ever came."

I turned the figurine over in my hand and sent out a cautious probe. I was careful—one of the few rules I abide by is to never mess with things I know nothing about. Something about it was unsettling, but I couldn't tell just what that was. What seemed to be a smooth skin covered it, so that my probe just slid off. It was like trying to grasp an egg yolk out of a bowl without breaking it or having it slip away. Whatever it was, I had no desire to break it open to find out.

"Interesting," I said.

"It's yours. This is what I'm supposed to do with it."

I shook my head. "I really appreciate the thought," I said, "but it's not my type of thing."

Campbell leaned over and took my hand. "Mason, listen to me. There are things I sometimes know. I don't know what the mechanism is, but there are some things that I just know. You're meant to have this figure. I don't know why, I don't know how, but I do know it's protection for you. Take it."

"It's from your grandmother. It's clearly valuable. I wouldn't feel right about it."

She took a deep breath. "You owe me," she said. "Remember? Well, here's your chance to pay your debt. Take it. If nothing else, it will give me some peace of mind." Her voice broke a little. "Do you honestly think I sleep with just anyone who turns up at my door? Take the goddamned thing."

"You mean goddess-damned, don't you?" I said, trying to lighten the tone. It didn't work. "Okay, okay. Thank you."

What else could I do? I slipped it into my pocket as we sat there in an awkward silence. The sun streamed through the window and fell across the table. She looked at me and smiled.

"You don't know nearly as much as you think you do," she said.

"Believe me, I'm aware of that."

I stood up and stretched. Campbell took the hint. "I suppose it is getting to be about that time," she said.

"I'm afraid so. I'd like to get home before dark, and right now, I don't even know where my car is."

She stood up, still holding onto my hand, and pulled me toward the front door. We stepped out on the porch, and it was a beautiful day. The temperature had risen into the high thirties, and an unbroken blanket of new snow glistened over everything in sight. The air was crisp and fresh. I could hear the sound of a snowplow working a few miles off. Campbell pointed down the gentle pitch of the hill which led to her cabin. No more than a hundred yards away, at the bottom of the slope, I could see a Navigator-sized lump with a car aerial sticking up through the snow.

"Fuck!" I said. "I wandered around for two hours last night trying to find your place when I was practically on your doorstep."

"Count your blessings," she said. "People have died up here within sight of their own houses. Mountain country in winter is not forgiving."

As we stood there, a snowplow churned by on the road below the house, throwing plumes of snow ten feet in the air. Several streamers landed on my already buried car.

"Great," I said. "I was hoping for an extra half hour of shoveling."

I packed up Louie in the backpack again—the snow was melting fast but it was still deep enough to be over his head. My shoes were finally dry, but since they wouldn't stay that way long, I borrowed a pair of Sorels that apparently had belonged to Campbell's ex. They didn't really fit, but they were better than what I had. After she produced a shovel from the back of the cabin, I was ready to take off.

"Just leave the shovel sticking up in the snow," she said. "I'll get it later."

"You're staying put? A true lady always walks her gentleman caller to his car," I pointed out.

"So I've heard. Tell you what—if you're still digging two hours from now, I'll ski down with some hot cocoa."

Neither of us mentioned last night. She gave me a quick kiss on the cheek as I turned to go, grabbed me by the arm, and said, "I *will* see you again." It was not a question.

"That does seem likely," I agreed.

"Unless you end up dead."

"I'll try to get back up here first."

"I would appreciate it." She suddenly changed her tone into serious. "Be careful. And keep that talisman with you whether you believe in it or not."

It took me an hour and a half to dig the Navigator out. Campbell did show up with cocoa, knocked the snow off the hood of a smaller lump that turned out to be an old Toyota Land Cruiser, and sat there chatting while I took a break. She finally broke down and offered to help dig, but I waved her away. "Man's work," I said grandly, in between wheezing gasps. I hadn't factored in the altitude. Finally I graciously allowed her to assist and she threw shovelfuls of snow aside with a smooth and steady rhythm that made a mockery of my previous flailing attempts. I'd forgotten she was a cross-country skier, probably the most aerobic-intensive activity on earth.

"I'm acclimated to this altitude," she told me, in between swings of the shovel, providing me with a crumb to soothe my ego.

We traded off and finally cleared enough space for me to rock the Navigator back and forth, then gun it backward down onto the main road, almost spinning it out off the other side. I waved my thanks and took off down the hill. Once I got back onto the road it was smooth sailing. The plows had managed to scrape the road into good shape, and when I reached the interstate cars were whizzing by as if there had never been any storm at all. A couple of thousand feet lower, and the only signs of snow were a few lingering patches under the trees by the side of the road. By the time I reached the Bay Bridge, winter was a distant memory. I couldn't wait to get back to my own house and finally relax. Nobody was going to be waiting inside for me this time. Well, I was right. This time, the problem was waiting outside.

ELEVEN

HE WAS STANDING RIGHT BESIDE MY FRONT DOOR. Or maybe I should say *it* was standing there. I momentarily mistook it for a person, and a person who was obviously unwell at that. The face had a sickly, pale yellowish cast as if long devastated by disease, and its body was so bony and cadaverous it seemed improbable it could even stand upright. On second glance, the thing looked diseased but it didn't look weak.

Lost in my thoughts about Christoph, I didn't notice it until I had already closed the door of the van. Louie stiffened immediately but didn't make a sound. He knew there wasn't any need to give a warning, even for someone with senses as dull as mine. There might as well have been a neon sign spelling out "DANGER" around the thing's withered neck. It was wearing a long black Columbine-type goth trenchcoat and a slouch hat pulled down to partially cover its ravaged face. It was the most grotesque figure I had ever seen. It reminded me of the vampire in the silent film *Nosferatu*, none of your suave, elegant Bela Lugosi type vampire, but a creature that looked like a walking corpse. It made me feel a visceral mix of horror, disgust, and fear. I couldn't imagine anything worse. Then it spoke.

"You are Mason, yes?" it rasped. Its voice sounded as if it were passing over old and distant bones. The tone was flat and uninflected, but with a definite undercurrent of cruelty and hunger. I didn't see any advantage in answering it. Besides, I was concentrating on gathering magical energy.

"I am . . . Gaki," it said, shuffling toward me with one long bony hand outstretched in a parody of friendly welcome. I wasn't sure if "Gaki" was a name or a description or an emotional state, but I backpedaled as rapidly as I could, keeping as much distance between us as possible. Lou backed up even faster; whatever this was, he wanted no part of it. It closed the gap between us with a herky-jerky motion that was both clumsy and frightening, moving with blinding, flickering speed. None of that Bela Lugosi slow creep toward his victim. One moment it was across the driveway; the next it was standing close enough for me to smell its rancid breath. I had barely seen it move. Its wasted fingers closed around my arm and I could feel cold seeping in through my shirt. It pulled me close and I could smell the sour odor of putrescence emanating off it in waves. I gestured with my free hand, using its own corruption against it, coupling it with a wilting trellis of ivy that clung discouragedly to one side of my house.

"Dissolve," I breathed.

The fingers which were grasping my arm shimmered for a moment and then solidified as the grip on my arm grew even stronger. This was not how it was supposed to go. Those fingers were supposed to dissolve into flat digits with the consistency of cooked noodles. It smiled and I could see yellow teeth, long and pointed like a shark's.

"No, no," it chuckled, "you cannot affect me." The smile grew. "But *I* can affect *you*."

It pulled me closer. The body might have been skeleton thin, but it was horribly strong. I tried to twist away, but had about as much success as a five-year-old in the grip of a strong man. Louie had circled around behind and was edging closer. His tail was tucked tightly between his legs and he looked terrified, but he lunged forward and sank his teeth into the thing's calf. No snarling and growling this time; he was deadly silent. The creature didn't even flinch. It glanced down at the small figure attached to its leg.

"Ifrit!" it hissed, and without letting go of me reached down toward Lou with its impossibly long free arm.

"Louie!" I yelled. "Back off!" This thing would snap his backbone in a second if it got hold of him. Lou let go and ducked away inches from the grasping fingers.

Once again, the distraction had given me a moment to think. Maybe I couldn't affect this demon, or whatever the hell it was, but I could affect myself. I noted the accumulation of oil in the driveway where my car lived, sucked out its essence and let it flow into my arm, enhancing it with everything I had. I could feel my arm changing, becoming slick and almost boneless, like a Teflon jellyfish. As the thing bore down, my arm squirted out like a watermelon seed and I was suddenly free.

"Clever," it said, mockingly. "Crafty. But no use."

I didn't waste any time in arguing with it. I stepped back and spoke a binding spell, one of the few prepared pieces of magic I know. If it's done right, the spell is guaranteed to stop a charging rhino in its tracks, at least temporarily. Either I hadn't done it right or this thing was truly immune to magic, because it just flashed its horrible grin and continued walking toward me.

The success of my oil slick idea gave me another. If I couldn't affect it directly, at least I could affect what was around it. It was too bad I didn't have enough power to bring a tree down on its skull, or cause the earth to open under its feet, but the principle was the same. I glanced up at the roof, recently tarred against the winter rains, and gathered up what was left of my energy. I pressed my hands together as if I was kneading taffy, threw the energy out and down toward the thing's feet, and made a sort of squishing sound in the back of my throat. It hurt my vocal chords. My voice was going to be hoarse for a couple of days, assuming of course I survived.

The thing took one more step toward me and a puzzled expression appeared on its face. Its foot sank into the suddenly soft pavement halfway to the knee and when it tried to pull out, its other leg sank in nearly as far. The ground beneath its feet had become a sticky morass with a consistency somewhere between warm tar and Turkish taffy. Its strength would now work against it; the more it struggled the further enmeshed it would become, like a mouse in a glue trap. I stepped back to admire my work.

It screeched, making a high-pitched noise that hurt my ears. Out of the corner of my eye I saw Louie flinch. It thrashed for a brief moment, then stopped and remained motionless, not attempting to pull either leg free. Unexpectedly, it sat down, then lay on its back and extended its arms to either side like a man caught in quicksand. Grunting with effort, it managed to pull one leg free. The leg came out with a sucking, slurping sound. I didn't wait around to see what was going to happen next. I jumped back in the van, yelling at Louie to get himself in gear, and backed out onto the street with tires squealing. As I accelerated away down the street I could see in the rearview mirror that the thing had got its other leg free as well. I wished my van was faster; I didn't think there was any way in hell the creature could be fast enough to keep up with a motor vehicle, but I had been wrong before a time or two.

The only place I could think of to go was back to Victor's. I didn't relish having to run to him every time something difficult turned up, but it was preferable to being torn to shreds by an unstoppable demon. Marginally. Besides, if I was lucky, Eli might be there. If anyone could tell me what this thing was, he could. For about the twentieth time I thought, I have *got* to get a cell phone.

When I pulled up in front of the beach house I was greeted by the reassuring sight of Eli's Volvo parked in the driveway. I piled out of the van and sprinted through the front door and up the stairs to the study, Louie close on my heels. Common sense told me that the thing couldn't possibly have followed me so quickly, if it could follow me at all, but that didn't stop me from glancing over my shoulder every few seconds. Victor and Eli were sitting across from each other at the big desk, papers piled up between them. Eli, working on his project again, and at a most inopportune time. They both looked up as I burst through the study door.

"Mason," said Victor. "Come in, won't you?"

"I've got trouble," I said, out of breath.

Victor started shaking his head in mock resignation, but Eli simply asked, "What happened?"

I told them, not leaving anything out, since there wasn't really that much to tell. The whole incident hadn't taken more than five minutes, if that. Even Victor listened intently. When I finished, I turned to Eli and asked him what the thing was, and more importantly, how it could be stopped. He stood up from his chair and stretched. I could hear his back pop from across the room.

"Fascinating," he said. "I've never seen one. I half thought they were only legend."

Victor had moved out from behind his desk and was fiddling with the dial on the safe that stood in the corner of the room.

"Not legend," he said.

I looked at each one in turn. "I'm glad I can provide you both with some interesting research material," I said, "*but what the hell is it?*"

Eli chuckled in a particularly nettlesome fashion. "It told you," he said. "It's a Gaki."

I resisted the impulse to bound across the room and shake him by the lapels of his jacket. It wouldn't speed up his explanation, not to mention that he was quite capable of lifting me off my feet and pinning me against the wall if he cared to. I forced myself to speak calmly.

"And what, may I ask, is a Gaki?"

"Like many things, that is something not entirely clear. They're mostly specific to Japan—you seldom hear of one anywhere else."

"I have," put in Victor, swinging open the huge safe door. "Vile creatures."

Eli looked surprised "When?" he asked.

"When I was younger. Before we met." He paused. "One almost killed me."

It wasn't like Victor to be so informative. That worried me.

"And?" I prompted.

He shrugged. "I'm still here."

Eli gave him another speculative look, then continued. "Well. In any case, the literal translation from the Japanese is 'hungry ghost,' or 'starving ghost.' Supposedly they are spirits of the dead who return to earth, carrying with them an insatiable hunger for the living. Or indeed, for anything, although their preferred sustenance is human beings."

"Sorry," I said. "I don't believe in no ghosts."

"More fool you. But 'ghost' is only a metaphor. What they are, as far as anyone can tell, is a type of entity not fully understood. They may come from somewhere else— another dimension perhaps, or possibly they are simply avatars made corporeal by intense emotion. Who knows? The important thing here is that it's focused on you, and it's quite dangerous. Legend has it they not only kill people, they eat them as well. Every last morsel."

I recalled its hungry look and razor teeth. "I don't think that part is legend," I said. "But why couldn't my talent affect it?"

"Ah. Apparently, since they are not precisely of this world, they cannot be affected by any of our magical energy no matter how powerful."

"Great."

"Oh, it gets better. It is possible, so it's said, to summon one from wherever it resides and compel it to do one's bidding, as long as that bidding has to do with eating a particular person."

"I thought you said they were impervious to magical energy?"

"It is a contradiction, isn't it? Perhaps the summoning

spell incorporates a compulsion, but once the Gaki appears it can no longer be affected."

"Whatever," I said. "I suppose Christoph conjured up this thing and sent it after me."

"It does seem likely. He's probably quite annoyed with you right now, and it would take someone with sufficient power to pull this off. I imagine that a weak practitioner who unwisely summons a Gaki tends to end up as sushi himself."

"This is all very interesting," I said, "but again, how exactly do I deal with this thing?"

Eli looked thoughtful. "It could be difficult," he said. "In addition to being unaffected by magical energies, a Gaki is very fast and very, very, strong."

"I noticed."

"And once it locks onto its particular prey, it can always find it, anywhere on earth, and beyond for all I know. Supposedly, they never give up. Ever."

This was not the most encouraging information I had ever received.

"So I can't fight it and I can't escape it?"

"That does pose a problem. In medieval times Gakis were feared and hated like few other creatures. Perhaps their occasional appearances explains the ubiquity of vampire legends. They are capable of sustaining numerous wounds that would be fatal to an ordinary person without much bother. And since they are not precisely *alive*, they can be quite difficult to kill. One legend tells of a lone Gaki that killed nine armed mercenary knights on horseback who were foolish enough to attack it. But still, things are not hopeless. Their vulnerability is inherent in the fact that they take physical form. Despite their strength they can be hurt and they can be killed."

"Yeah, if you have ten knights helping out," I said.

Victor had been moving stuff around in the safe, and he finally located whatever he had been looking for. He turned his head and addressed me over his shoulder.

"Don't be so melodramatic, Mason. Come, join us in the twenty-first century."

As he spoke, he brought out what looked like an automatic rifle, three or four feet long, then reached back and
came up with two curved magazines. He walked over and
laid the rifle and the clips gently on his desk, being careful
not to mar the finish.

"AK-47," he said, running his hand down the stock.

"Talk about melodramatic," I snorted. "Where did you get
that? Preparing for the fall of Western civilization, are we?"

Victor, as usual, ignored me. Eli bent over to examine
the gun and whistled, obviously impressed.

"The Gaki?" he asked.

Victor nodded. "They're unbelievably tough," he said.
"But nothing is invulnerable. This should do the job quite
handily."

"I don't know how to use one of those," I said.

Victor smiled complacently. "No, but I do. You don't
really think I'd let you handle an automatic rifle anyway, do
you? The civilian casualties alone could be horrendous."

"I appreciate the vote of confidence," I said. "So what
now? You going to follow me around twenty-four seven as
my bodyguard?"

He glanced at his watch. "No need. You've been here
what, half an hour? It ought to be waiting outside for you
by now."

I looked at the study door in sudden apprehension. I
knew I looked foolish, but they hadn't seen it. I had. Victor took some rounds of ammunition from a box and
started loading the clips.

"Each magazine holds thirty rounds," he explained.
"Hopefully, that will be enough."

"Hopefully?" I said. Actually I think I sort of squeaked,
something I'm not proud of.

"Gakis are pretty smart, at least for demons," he said,
tactfully ignoring my squeak. Or at least I think he was
being tactful. Since he pretty much makes it a rule to ignore all my comments anyway, it was hard to tell.

"That's why it's not rushing up here to get you," he continued. "It doesn't know who or what might be inside, so

it's being cautious. It obviously does understand that it's lost the element of surprise, at the least." He finished up the first clip and started on the second. "This time it will probably try to keep concealed and then close with you before you even know it's there."

"It's fast," I said. "You have no idea."

"Oh, but I do. That's why you need to do exactly what I tell you. When you leave the house, stroll casually over toward that van of yours and then stop right by the driver's door. It will see you. Then, when you see it coming, don't run, or fight, or anything. Just drop to the ground and curl up in a little ball. That way you'll be out of the line of fire, and if it does reach you it won't be able to remove anything vital before I can kill it."

"So I'm bait," I said. "How encouraging. And where exactly are you planning to be?"

"In the doorway. As soon as it attacks, I'll step out with the rifle and poof—good-bye Mr. Gaki."

Eli had a dubious look on his face. "I don't know, Victor," he said. "This sounds dangerous."

Victor continued loading the clip. "Of course it is. Gakis are dangerous creatures. But this is as good an opportunity as we're going to get. They learn fast."

I didn't like the sound of any of this, but I liked the thought of meeting up with the thing on my own even less. And if there was one thing I had learned about Victor over the years, it was that he did know what he was doing. He would have made a great mercenary.

I shrugged. "Okay," I said. "Let's do it."

Victor inserted one of the magazines into the rifle, where it slid in with a reassuring thunk. He placed the other in a loose canvas bag with a strap and threw it over his shoulder.

"After you," he said, motioning toward the door

Louie jumped up, but I waved him back. "Stay with Eli," I warned him. The last thing we needed was for Lou to throw himself at the creature and end up riddled with bullets. He hopped up onto a chair where he could see out the window and a second later Maggie, tail twitching, joined him. Things were serious enough for a truce between them, although they were still careful not to touch each other.

I walked down the stairs slowly, Victor at my back. My feet seemed reluctant to carry me. There was something so repellent about the Gaki that it went beyond fear—I wasn't afraid so much that it would kill me as I was that it would touch me again. Still, I affected what I hoped was a non-chalant air. If I didn't, and I survived, Victor would mock me for the next year at least. Pride is a wonderful thing. Here I was, walking toward possible death and certain horror, and the main thing on my mind was to not let Victor get one up on me. I would have whistled cheerily if my mouth hadn't dried up into a wad of cotton.

I paused in the doorway leading outside and looked back at Victor. He nodded and took a firmer grip on the AK-47. If he was nervous, it didn't show. Maybe he was doing the same thing I was, not wanting me to get one up on him. We were like two kids bluffing each other until we both ended up jumping off the high diving board. Of course there was a difference; the kids can turn back and go home. We didn't have that option.

I took a deep breath, stepped out the door, and walked briskly toward my van. My heart was pounding away at about two hundred beats a minute and I expected to feel the Gaki's sharp teeth tearing at my neck at any moment. I paused by the driver's side door of the van and reached in my pocket as if fishing for my car keys. I didn't know how smart the Gaki really was, but I didn't want to give it any indication that a trap was being set. I stood there thrusting my hands into one pocket after another, trying to appear innocent and vulnerable. It was just starting to grow dark, the perfect time for an unseen monster to spring out of nowhere and attach razor-sharp fangs to your throat.

Nothing moved. I realized I had simply taken Victor's word for it that the Gaki would be waiting outside for me. Now that I looked around, it was clear there wasn't enough cover anywhere nearby for a hiding place. Maybe it wasn't that smart after all and was simply hanging around my place waiting for me to return. I started feeling foolish searching one pocket after another, putting on a show for a nonexistent assailant. I had just given up and was turning to walk back to where Victor was waiting when I heard a loud thump on the top of the van. I barely had time to look up as the Gaki bounded over the top of the van, trenchcoat flapping around it like some giant mutant bat. It had concealed itself on the opposite side of the vehicle, then jumped to the top of the van and then straight down toward me. Throwing myself to the ground would have been a great idea if it had been running across the driveway toward me. Now that it was dropping directly on top of me from above—not so great.

Not that I had time to make any decisions. It was on top of me before I could react, driving me flat to the ground with enough force to knock the wind out of me. It flipped me over on my back and pinned both my hands with its own claw-like ones, stretching my arms out to the side and covering my body with the length of its own, forcing my legs wide apart so I couldn't kick at it. It was an obscene parody of the missionary position. I could feel its long, ropy muscles writhing like maggots under its skin and it was grinning its ghastly smile, clearly enjoying not only the imminent meal, but my position as well. Not only was I about to be slaughtered by a ravening ghoul, but apparently by a gay one.

It lowered its head toward mine until its mouth was inches away, and I could smell the fetid odor of its breath. It would have made me sick if my stomach hadn't already tied itself into a tight knot. I wanted to struggle, but the chill seeping out of it was sapping my will as well as my strength. And it was strong, strong. I prayed Victor would open fire. Of course, that would surely kill me as well as killing the Gaki, but anything was preferable to this.

I expected at any moment to feel its teeth sinking into my throat, tearing through soft tissue and releasing the warm salty blood just below the surface. Only a few centimeters of skin and flesh stand between life and death for all of us, and there's nothing like having razor-sharp teeth brushing your neck to really bring that fact home.

For a moment, nothing happened. It pulled back its head a little and stared down at me, relishing the moment, stretching it out in order to appreciate my fear and pain. Whether it was feeding off of psychic pain in some way or whether it was just in its nature to be as cruel as possible wasn't relevant. The net effect was that it waited just a little too long.

I heard heavy footsteps coming up fast, saw two massive black arms grab the thing by its shoulders, and then it was lifted off me and thrown sideways. The Gaki might well possess supernatural strength, but its wiry frame didn't weigh any more than I did, if that. Eli had no miraculous strength himself, but tossing opponents aside came naturally to a two-hundred-sixty-pound lineman, even if he had been off the football field for twenty-five years. I caught a glimpse of Eli's scraggly beard as he flashed by me, and as I started to scramble to my feet, I heard Victor shout, "Stay down!"

The Gaki had grabbed hold of Eli's arm as he threw it aside, and it screeched as it held on. It tightened its grip, and I heard a grunt of pain from Eli, then the dull crunch of bone collapsing. Eli's left arm lost its grip and dangled uselessly in the thing's grasp. With a supreme effort, Eli ignored the obvious pain and used his bulk to momentarily tear the arm loose, stumbling with the effort. He immediately threw himself facedown on the ground, and for just a second the Gaki was standing upright between our two figures groveling on the asphalt of the driveway.

A second was all it took. I heard a quick burst of automatic rifle fire and the Gaki jerked and staggered. There was a longer burst, apparently aimed lower, and its legs went out from under it. It fell to the ground and immediately tried to regain its feet but its legs wouldn't hold it. I rolled over and scurried away out of reach of its grasping arms. Victor was moving toward us, rapidly but not hurriedly, detaching one clip from the rifle and replacing it with the extra clip from his shoulder bag. He walked up to the Gaki, which was still trying to get to its feet, pointed the muzzle of the gun just below its jaw, and let out a sustained burst. It seemed to go on forever, although in reality it couldn't have been more than two or three seconds. The lower part of the Gaki's head flew apart in an explosion of flesh and shards of bone, then the rest of it finally separated from the neck and toppled onto the pavement. The eyes looked up at me, and unbelievably, it was still alive. Then the spark in the eyes dimmed until there was nothing left but a shapeless mass covered with gouts of blood. I shakily climbed to my feet.

"Gosh," I said. "That went well."

I walked over to Eli, who was sitting up holding his left arm. "Thanks," I said, rather inadequately. "You okay?"

"Do I look okay?"

He hoisted his bulk up heavily and stood there swaying for a minute, then walked gingerly over to where the remains of the Gaki lay. Louie had slipped out of the house and was sniffing delicately at a piece of arm that had come detached from the rest of the body. I pushed him away with my foot.

"What are we going to do with this mess?" I asked as Victor joined us. "With all that firepower somebody is bound to have called the police, and unless you've got about twenty spells in reserve they're going to want explanations."

"Not to worry," he said. "Remember, this isn't my first encounter with the dark powers."

Now I knew he'd been shaken. Victor only attempted lame humor when he was totally freaked out. I started to say something further but he held up his hand.

"Wait," he said.

We all stood there silently for a couple of minutes. I was about to ask him exactly what we were waiting for when I was distracted by a growing sound somewhere between a radiator leak and a teakettle. What was left of the Gaki began to hiss and curl like bacon in a frying pan, sending tendrils of foul-smelling smoke into the air. The whole process accelerated until it sounded like a miniature forest fire. Two minutes later, the only sign there had ever been a creature from hell lying there was a slight discoloration on the asphalt driveway. It was just as well, since I could hear the sound of an approaching siren.

"Pick up the brass," Victor ordered, and walked over to my car where he started muttering under his breath and making hand gestures. I picked up all the shell casings I could find, and Louie brought back a few I had missed, spitting them out with obvious distaste. I glanced over at my van and saw that Victor had smoothed over the few wayward bullet holes which had punched through the van door. He'd actually *fixed* them, bless his heart, not just layered them over with illusion.

Victor walked back from the van, glancing up at the study window. Danny's shocked face peered down at us. He had seen it all, and I wondered how Victor was going to explain this one. I didn't think he could. From the look on Danny's face I was guessing we wouldn't be seeing him around much longer. I felt some guilt; if I hadn't come running to Victor for help, he'd still have a boyfriend. Still, something like this was bound to have happened sooner or later. Whenever you get involved with a nonpractitioner, there always comes a day of reckoning. It really narrows down the dating pool.

By this time, Eli was not looking well. His normal skin tone had taken on a dusky grayish hue, and he answered questions with brief monosyllables. Victor employed a deadening spell for the pain and fussed over him for a while until he looked a little better, but it was obvious Eli needed more professional care.

"I'm not good enough for an injury of this extent, and a hospital's no good," said Victor. "His arm's not just broken; the bones are crushed. It would take him months to recover. Besides, the arm would never be the same."

"A specialist, then?"

"Absolutely."

"Campbell?"

"She is the best." He looked suspiciously at me. "You didn't screw things up with her, did you?"

"Quite the opposite," I assured him. "I'll call her."

"I'll do it," he said. He clearly didn't put much stock in my assurances. He pulled out his cell phone and walked away so that I couldn't hear the conversation. After about five minutes, he put the phone away and walked back to where I was standing.

"She's on her way," he said.

BY TWO IN THE MORNING, EVERYTHING HAD BEEN sorted out. Victor had given the police a story about kids with firecrackers and, after a cursory look around the place, they left. I spent an hour going over Christoph's uninvited visit—exactly what he had said and what he had done.

"What I don't understand is how he got past the wards into my house," I said.

Eli gave me an inscrutable look. "I have an idea about that." He shifted position in his chair and drew in a sharp breath as his arm moved. "Later," he said. "We'll talk about that later."

Campbell had showed up about midnight carrying a traveling bag, an assortment of herbs, and a plastic bag full of plaster of paris. She gave me a quick kiss, and Victor gave her a brief but definite hug, something I had never seen him do before with anyone. After he stepped back, he favored me with a cold stare, and I had the good sense to pretend it was a normal and everyday occurrence.

Campbell wasn't real happy about having to work away from her home—she said it limited her abilities—but since broken bones, even crushed ones, are relatively straightforward, she could handle it. It wasn't like what had happened to Louie, where she had needed every possible edge. After she had worked on Eli for a while, she and Victor whipped up a makeshift cast from the plaster of paris. Eli wasn't happy to learn he was going to have to wear it for the next week or so.

"I have my limits," she told him. "You're still going to have to let it heal for a while."

He muttered something about youngsters today and

shoddy workmanship, and then got incredibly embarrassed when he realized she might take him seriously. He started trying to apologize profusely, but Campbell just laughed.

"Glad you're feeling better," she said.

By that time, I was so exhausted I couldn't think straight. I was about to head off home when the sight of Louie curled up in Campbell's lap reminded me it might be polite, to say the least, to offer her the option of staying at my place for the night. I didn't think Christoph would be trying anything else for a while. She considered it for a moment.

"Thanks," she said. "That would be nice."

She left her car at Victor's, and I drove us both in the van. At least my house was relatively clean, which wasn't always the case. When we got there, I wasn't sure if romantic suggestions would be expected or simply boorish. I was bone tired and the encounter with the Gaki had left me feeling filthy inside and out. Sex was about the furthest thing from my mind.

"I need a shower," I said, temporizing.

She settled things by jumping on the bed, peeling off her clothes, and crawling under the covers.

"Don't wake me," she said. "In fact, if you wake me up before noon, you die."

By the time I finished my shower, she was dead to the world. I eased into bed beside her, and Louie wedged himself between us. As I dropped off to sleep, I thought, well this *is* nice.

TWELVE

OF COURSE, AT NINE THAT MORNING THE PHONE rang. Campbell pulled the covers up over her head, making complaining noises. I cursed and dragged myself out of bed and over to the phone. Victor. Naturally.

"Mason. My house. Half an hour," he said, without preamble. He sounded clearheaded and awake. I wondered if he'd gone to sleep at all.

"What, no good morning?" I asked. "No, 'How are you?'"

"How are you?" he said, and continued without waiting for a reply. "Get over here. You've got half an hour."

"I'll be there when I can," I said, glancing at the clock. I wasn't going to let him push me around. At least, not completely. I hung up before he could say anything further. Campbell's head emerged from under the blankets and she fixed me with a malevolent eye.

"Not my fault," I said hastily, remembering her final instructions from last night. "Victor wants me over at his place right away. I'm surprised he didn't call at dawn." The accusing glare did not abate.

"Make some coffee," she ordered, slipped out of bed, and headed for the bathroom. A minute later, I could hear the shower running. Lou was nowhere to be found, which was unusual, but not unheard of. Sometimes he gets up in the middle of the night and takes off on some Ifrit mission I would never understand. He'd turn up when he was finished.

I fired up the coffeemaker and turned on the wall heater to take the chill off the room. I put on jeans and a fresh tee with a flannel shirt over it, and by the time Campbell was out of the shower there was fresh coffee waiting for her.

"Sorry," she apologized, accepting a cup. "I'm really not a morning person, especially on short sleep."

"I didn't get that impression up at your cabin," I said. "Pancakes. Witty repartee. Gifts."

"Ah. Well, I was on my best behavior. First date, you know?" She looked around the tiny kitchen. "What, no pancakes? And where's Lou?"

"He took off. He'll be back when he decides to. And no breakfast, either. Even though his people skills leave a lot to be desired, Victor wouldn't tell me to get my ass over there without a reason. We'd better head out."

I took an extra few minutes to shave and wash up. If this day was going to involve battling evil entities again or casting arcane spells, I at least wanted to look and feel my best.

It was just past ten thirty when we pulled into the driveway at Victor's. I sauntered through the front door without announcing myself, as usual, and climbed the stairs to the study. Sherwood was talking with Eli, who was sitting in one of the deep armchairs by the front window. She and Campbell appraised each other cooly, then both turned their heads in my direction. Talk about uncomfortable. Eli introduced them, which saved me some adolescent stuttering, and after a brief nod of acknowledgment Campbell examined Eli to see how he was coming along. He looked tired, but she pronounced him otherwise well on the road to recovery.

Campbell tactfully made noises about having to get

back home and a few minutes later was gone. Eli settled back in his chair and fixed me with an uncharacteristic glare.

"What?" I asked.

"I'd like to know exactly how Christoph got into your house," he said. "I designed those wardings, remember, and ego as well as common sense tells me that no one could just waltz in past them the way you described. I don't care how powerful they are."

"Well, he did."

"Yes. And how long has it been since you did any maintenance on them?"

I thought back. "I'm not sure," I admitted.

"And how often are you supposed to check on them?"

"Once a month?"

"Correct. At least you can remember that much. And how long has it been?"

It had been at least a year, but I wasn't about to cop to that. "It's been a while, I guess," I said vaguely.

"A while. And what happens when you don't maintain the spells properly?"

I sighed resignedly. "They grow weak." Victor made a tch tch sound with his tongue.

Eli continued glaring at me. His injuries were making him uncharacteristically cranky. "They do not grow weak. If they grew weak, you would notice it. They fray. They *unravel*! Have you ever had one of those CDs covered with shrink wrap that you just can't seem to get open?"

"Of course."

"Now imagine that you can't use your teeth or nails or a knife. Frustrating, no? Now imagine that one corner has split leaving you a nice piece to get hold of. Wonderful! Now you can peel it off like the skin off an onion. That's what happened to the warding on your house."

"Oh."

"Mason, you have got to be more responsible."

"Okay," I said. "I get it."

Sherwood spoke up softly from her chair by the window. "I hope you do, Mason. I know you didn't mean it to, but the consequences of your laziness were almost fatal for Louie."

Ahh, nothing like a good woman to illuminate your personal failings. "I said, I get it."

"Enough," Eli said. "We have more important things to discuss. We've come up with some very interesting information on Christoph, or I should say, Sherwood has."

"What kind of information?" I asked, glancing over at her. She curled up in her chair, tucking one foot underneath her. Victor answered.

"It will be a lot easier if we just show you," he said. "Sherwood?"

She got up and walked over to Victor's desk, where a PC with a twenty-inch LCD monitor was quietly humming. She put her hands on the tower and said something under her breath, spreading her fingers as wide as possible.

"Download," Eli explained. "We'll be able to view what she saw on the monitor. Who says magic and technology aren't compatible?"

We gathered around and the monitor flared to life. It showed what appeared to be a bedroom from a point-of-view perspective. There was a man naked from the waist up sitting on a bed, and as he turned his head I recognized Christoph.

"What exactly—?" I started to ask, but Eli and Victor both shushed me.

"Just pay attention," Victor said.

Christoph was speaking, answering a question put to him by the unseen other party, obviously Sherwood. I wanted to ask her why he had no shirt on, not to mention what the hell she was doing there, but I held my tongue. Then I realized that if Christoph had no clothes, it was highly unlikely that Sherwood was chastely covered.

"What exactly is going on here?" I asked, unable to keep quiet.

"Grow up, Mason," said Victor. "What does it look like?"

Sherwood spoke up, annoyed, but also defensive. "Double standard," she complained. "If you had sex with someone in order to get information, you'd be strutting around like James Bond. When I do it, you're horrified."

"You had sex with him?" I yelped. I hate to admit it, but that's what I did. I yelped.

"So what? It's not like I particularly enjoyed it." A smug expression flitted across her face. "Not that he'll ever know."

"You can't just go to bed with someone like that. You don't even know him, and besides, he's . . . he's . . . What, are you Mata Hari now?"

"Well, I did. Besides, who are you to talk? You had sex last night yourself."

"I did not," I automatically denied. "It was the night before. And that was entirely different. And it's none of your business. And I hate that! I can't ever do anything without you knowing about it the minute you see me. That's why we broke up."

"It was not."

"Well, no, it wasn't, but it could have been."

Eli intervened as usual. "This is not the time," he said. "Watch the monitor, please."

Victor leaned over and touched the screen to replay it from the start. I turned back to the monitor just as Christoph was beginning to speak.

"It's not that way at all," he said. "Power is only the means to an end, and in this case, we're talking about more money than you can imagine."

"I don't see money as the all-important thing," she told him.

"No, of course not. But think of all the good you could do. Foundations. Environment." He smiled winningly. "Baby seals."

"Yeah, right. And where does all this money come from?"

Christoph pulled out the same string of gems that he

had displayed at my flat. Sherwood reached for them, but he pulled them back out of her reach.

"These stones are more valuable than anything you've ever seen. They're almost impossible to obtain."

"So where did you find them?" Sherwood asked. She couldn't take her eyes off them. I could hear real curiosity in her voice, beyond any attempt to merely get information.

"I didn't exactly find them," Christoph said, self-satisfaction evident. "I made them."

"That's impossible. No one could do anything like that."

"Not until now. Of course, I have had to absorb some extra power from other practitioners."

"Isn't that sort of thing . . ."

"What? Unethical? Not allowed? You've been hanging around with Victor and Eli too long. It doesn't hurt anyone, not permanently. Those two just can't stand to see anyone do something they can't."

I shook my head in amazement. Christoph must think Sherwood was a complete idiot. Then I remembered—Sherwood could shield from anyone. He might well think she was nothing more than a marginally talented groupie who had no idea what the true state of affairs was.

"That's amazing," she said, all wide-eyed innocence. "But how do you do it?"

It seemed incredible that Christoph, for all his vaunted potency, didn't seem to realize he was being played. Then again, Sherwood without any clothes might be short-circuiting his thought processes, especially if she was subtly enhancing. She was really good at disguising that particular talent.

A hand appeared on the screen, then disappeared as Christoph covered her mouth. "Shh," he said. "I'm tired of talking." His face spun around until she was staring up at him, and as his face came up to meet the screen. Sherwood reached over and wiped the screen blank.

"I don't think we need to see anything more," she said primly.

"Oh, I don't know," said Victor, almost lewdly. "You never know when some small scrap of information might prove useful."

I wisely kept my mouth shut. I had no desire to view what followed anyway. The whole thing left me feeling uncomfortable. I mean, Christoph, for God's sake. Eli was shaking his head slowly.

"I don't believe it," he said. I couldn't have agreed more.

"I know," I said, looking at Sherwood. "What were you thinking with a stunt like that? Do you know how dangerous that was?"

"No," said Eli. "I mean I don't believe what Christoph was saying."

"You think he's lying about creating the stones?" Victor asked.

"Not exactly. But I don't think he's giving the whole story. He couldn't create something like that, no matter how much power he has. He's just not that good. Remember, Geoffrey thought the same thing. Something else is going on here."

"Like what?" I asked.

Whatever Eli was about to say was interrupted by an angry hissing coming from across the room. Maggie was staring out the open window, fur standing on end. Victor glanced at her, then at the window, then motioned Sherwood to move away from where she was sitting. She eased away from the desk and Victor glided up noiselessly from the other side. Just before he reached the window there was a harsh squawking sound and a black figure dropped off from the eave and flapped away into the cloudy sky.

"What was that?" asked Sherwood.

"A raven," Victor said grimly.

"That's not good. Christoph's Ifrit is a raven."

"Yes, I know," I said.

Sherwood didn't seem overly bothered. "How bad can

that be?" she said. "Christoph's aware I hang out with you guys. I think he even sees it as insurance, a pipeline into this house."

"Ravens overhear. Ravens can speak. Ravens can tell tales."

"Oh. That *is* bad."

"Well, it's not good," said Eli. "Sherwood, you'd better stay here with Victor for a while. Christoph will be furious with you. Nobody likes to be played for a fool, and male ego, if nothing else, will demand revenge. But not even Christoph will be able to break the wards on this place."

"I suppose you're right," Sherwood said. "I don't suppose there's any way I can finesse this."

"No," I told her. "Trust me."

Sherwood shrugged. "Oh, well. I wish I could have found out more, but at least I got something out of him."

"Whatever," I said, still pissed about the whole thing. I cast around for something to change the subject before we got into another fight. "How is that girl we found in the Tenderloin doing?" I asked. "Any problems?"

Sherwood made that back-and-forth hand gesture that means yes and no. "Jenna? No, not really. Turns out she is a Finder after all, along with possessing other talent. And she's a good kid at heart, but she does have issues. Remember, she's been on the street since she was thirteen. No one changes overnight."

"In other words, she's a piece of work."

Sherwood smiled, admitting it. "Well, I prefer to think of her as a work in progress."

WE LEFT IT THERE. I WASN'T CONVINCED WE HAD learned anything important, and I was worried about Sherwood. Christoph had a large ego, and he didn't strike me as the type to let bygones be bygones. If he caught up with her, she'd be in real trouble.

I stopped on my way home for a bagel and some coffee and picked up a ham croissant for Lou. After the stuff he'd been through, he could use a treat. I was surprised to find him still gone when I got home. Maybe he was still recovering in some way that had nothing to do with me. The faintest shadow of worry crept into my mind, but I dismissed it without too much problem. He'd been gone for a day or so before.

By night, the worry was stronger, poking its head from around a corner whenever I looked up, nipping at me with sharp teeth whenever I stopped concentrating on whatever I was doing. I didn't sleep well, waking up whenever I heard a hint of a sound, and when morning arrived, still no Lou. I called Eli, who tried to be reassuring, but I could hear worry in his voice as well.

It wasn't so much that I thought anything had happened to him; Lou could take care of himself, probably better than I could. But at the back of my mind was that same old fear that all practitioners with Ifrits suffer from—that sometimes Ifrits leave. And when an Ifrit leaves, that's it. No one ever sees them again. Ever.

By the second day, I was numb with worry. After a week, I was hanging on to hope by a thread. When I tripped over his water dish and it flipped over, I saw it was dry and empty. That's when it finally became real. Lou had left and he wasn't coming back. It seemed a thousand years ago when I was comforting Sandra at Pascal's North Beach party after Moxie had left her. I had felt sorry for her then. Now I felt sorry for myself.

I didn't leave the house, barely ate, and didn't sleep much. Whenever I'd heard about an Ifrit who disappeared, I'd always assumed there must have been something off about the practitioner. Never in my darkest moments did I dream it could happen to me. Probably a form of denial and self-protection. But maybe I was partly to blame. Maybe there is something not quite right about me. After all, I don't have a lot of friends and haven't had much success at keeping a girlfriend, either.

Eli and Victor spent a day restoring the wards around my flat, making them stronger than ever. If Christoph could break through them now, there wasn't much help for any of us. Even the thought of Victor pulling my chestnuts out of the fire again didn't bother me. That's how low I felt.

I made a few halfhearted attempts to locate Lou, but it was like he had vanished off the face of the earth. Considering that he was an Ifrit, he probably had.

The only person I talked to was Eli, who told me things were on hold. Christoph had gone to ground and hadn't surfaced. Sherwood was a virtual prisoner at Victor's, afraid to even go to the store until Christoph was located. At least Campbell was out of harm's way back home in Soda Springs. Eli and Victor were doing everything they could to track Christoph down, spending every minute on it. They were getting close, Eli said, but so far, no luck. I should have felt guilty that I wasn't doing anything to help, but I didn't. As far as Christoph went, I could care less. I didn't even care about revenge. As long as he left me alone I wasn't interested in his power-and-money drama. Eli didn't push me about it; he tried instead to keep my spirits up.

"Lou will come back," he said. "True, other Ifrits haven't, but they weren't Louie. He's different, even for an Ifrit. I don't know what is going on with him, but he will return. Count on it."

I don't know if he really believed that or if he was just trying to keep me functional until I could deal with the truth. In any case, there wasn't anything I could do about the situation. If Lou was gone, he was gone. I'd just have to live with it. It's not like he owed me anything. And after all, he was just a dog. Sort of.

I couldn't muster enough interest to hustle up the gigs that provide me with a living, although at some point I'd have to. Mostly I worked on guitar stuff, since it was about the only thing I could still manage. I told myself I was woodshedding, sharpening up my chops, but I knew better. When I found myself experimenting with exotic tunings, churning out what could only be described as New Age music, I knew I was in trouble.

When the knock sounded at my front door, I didn't answer. There wasn't anyone I wanted to see, and if it turned out to be yet another earnest young person collecting money to save the trees, I was afraid of what I might do. Unfortunately, whoever it was refused to accept silence as a legitimate response. More knocks, more insistent. More silence. Still more knocks, threatening to turn into pounding. I gave a theatrical sigh, wasted of course since I was alone, dragged myself over, and opened the door.

Campbell.

I gawked. If only I'd been hip enough to come up with a suave and clever greeting, some throwaway line that would show me as the smooth, cool, and self-possessed individual I know myself to be. At least I didn't burst into tears.

"What are you doing here?" I finally managed. She reached out a hand and touched my cheek. The concern on her face embarrassed me.

"Victor called me," she said.

She looked windburned, strong, fit, and disgustingly healthy. She'd cut her hair shorter, but it was still weather-streaked and tangled. All my life I'd been attracted to sensitive, waiflike women, and now that I'd found someone I really liked, she was a goddamned Valkyrie. I stepped aside and she walked past me into the front room, dumping the backpack she was carrying onto the floor. She regarded me critically, reached out, and smoothed away the dark hair hanging over my face.

"You don't look so great," she said.

That's not really what you want to hear from a prospective girlfriend, especially one glowing with health and energy, but I was past caring.

"I know," was all I said. She glanced around the apartment.

"So, what happened to Louie?" she asked, direct as usual.

"Gone."

"Gone? What do you mean, gone?"

I had a moment of déjà vu; it was my exact conversation with Sandra, but now I was on the other end.

"You know, gone. As in not here anymore. He disappeared a week ago. Haven't seen him since."

She looked at me oddly. "Have you looked for him?"

Campbell didn't understand that when an Ifrit decides to leave, there's nothing to be done about it. It's not like Lou was a dog, after all.

"There's not much point," I explained patiently. "Sometimes Ifrits leave, and when they do, they don't come back. If you were a practitioner you'd understand. It's harsh, but sometimes that's the way life is."

"Really."

"Really."

She walked slowly around, peering at the dirty dishes and unmade bed.

"So he just decided to take off, permanently?"

"Apparently."

"How do you know that?"

"Well, he's no longer here, is he?" I said, rather annoyed, not catching her drift. Campbell shook her head impatiently.

"No, I mean, how do you know that it was his decision? What if he couldn't get back to you? What if he's lost? What if he's in trouble?"

I started to explain why that scenario was so unlikely when I realized it was something I'd never considered. Nor had Eli. Even with the whole Christoph situation, we were both so steeped in Ifrit lore, so used to tales where Ifrits inexplicably severed their bond with a practitioner, that it hadn't occurred to either of us there might be another explanation. Campbell was enough of an outsider so that it was the first thing that crossed her mind.

"I never thought of that," I admitted slowly. Campbell looked at me in complete disbelief.

"You never thought of that?"

This reunion wasn't going as well as it might. In less than a minute, I'd shown myself to be either totally uncaring or incredibly stupid, two attributes unlikely to elicit admiration and love. She bored in remorselessly.

"If you failed to come home one day, what do you suppose Louie would have done? Sat around moping? Shrugged his shoulders and thought, 'Oh well'? Or, just maybe, just possibly, gone out looking for you?"

A cold knot started to form in my stomach. What if she were right? Could I have been sitting here feeling sorry for myself while Lou was trapped somewhere, confidently awaiting my help?

"Okay," I said, "I get your point. But it's not that simple." I clung desperately to my belief Lou had left voluntarily. Better to believe that he had abandoned me than that I had abandoned him.

"Ifrits sometimes leave," I continued stubbornly. "It's a fact, and it never occurred to me that this might be anything different. It still seems unlikely. And on top of that, I wouldn't have a clue as to where to start. I'm not real good at tracing things; I relied on Lou for that. And even if I were, finding an Ifrit who doesn't want to be found is close to impossible."

Campbell threw off some of the clothes scattered on the bed and sat down wearily. She unlaced her boots and pulled them off, using the toe of one foot on the heel of the other. Then she tucked her feet beneath her and sat quietly, mulling over what I'd said.

"I don't suppose you have any tea?" she asked suddenly, veering off subject.

"I think I've got some Earl Grey. Just tea bags, though."

At the mention of tea bags, a shadow of disappointment flitted over her face, but she smiled and said, "That would be great."

I busied myself putting a kettle on the stove and searching through the cupboard for the tea I was pretty sure was there. Campbell had dragged her backpack across the floor and started unloading things onto the bed, muttering as she searched for something specific. I glanced over and saw various packets of differing sizes, some made of cloth and tied with twine, some apparently consisting of large leaves folded over and sealed with wax.

I finally found some ancient tea bags, rinsed out a couple of mugs, and poured in boiling water. By the time I'd carried them over to the bed, she had unwrapped a couple of the packages and pulled out some unfamiliar spiky plants and what looked to be a mutant thistle.

"Plants," she explained unnecessarily, taking the proffered cup of tea. She took a small sip and carefully placed the cup on the crowded bedside table. "Have you got any modeling clay around, or Play-Doh, or anything like that?"

"I doubt it. What, are you going to make a voodoo effigy of me? I didn't know you had turned to the dark side." My tone was light, but I was only half-kidding. Campbell gave me an impatient look.

"Don't joke about that. This is closer to dark magic than I'm comfortable with. And yes, I'm going to make an effigy, but not of you, idiot. Of Louie." She glanced around at the clutter in the apartment. "And I'm going to need something of his. Maybe some hair?"

"For the effigy? Why?"

"Why do you think? To locate him, of course." She gestured toward the packets laid out on the bed. "This stuff will do the trick, I think."

"Sorry," I said. "I'm not getting it."

"You said that you're not very good at locating things, remember? Well, I am. With this soil—and don't ask me where it's from—and a couple of these plants, I can whip up something that will show us exactly where he is."

"Great," I said, trying not to sound skeptical. I'd seen her do some impressive healing, of course, but this was a different type of thing, a whole other level. And finding an Ifrit isn't much like finding a person. Ifrits are notoriously hard to get a handle on. They're not exactly immune to magic, but it does seem to slip off of them. Or maybe my skepticism was nothing more than misplaced pride. Since I didn't have the ability myself to find Lou, maybe I didn't think it possible that Campbell could.

"I'll need some kind of clay, or something that I can make a model out of," she continued. "And some pipe cleaners or twigs to make an armature."

"I can't think of anything," I said. A thought struck me. "I've got some cookie dough in the fridge. Would cookie dough work?"

"You eat cookie dough?"

Again, not the suave and manly image you want to project to a potential girlfriend. "Only when I'm depressed," I said defensively.

Not exactly an improvement. Campbell smirked, something I'd never seen her do. Maybe I just hadn't given her sufficient reason before.

"That might work," she said, getting off the bed and opening the refrigerator. "Can you find me something to make a framework with, and some of his hair?"

I went through various bureau drawers until I found a pack of pipe cleaners left over from a long gone and unsuccessful attempt to switch from cigarettes to a pipe before I finally shook the tobacco habit for good. The hair thing was easy, since I hadn't vacuumed the place in a month.

Campbell had found the cookie dough—chocolate chip—and was busy kneading some of it into a gluey ball. She broke off a small piece and popped it into her mouth. Contentment spread over her face.

"Nothing like lab chemicals and artificial flavoring for true gratification," she said, rolling the rest of the dough between her palms. She added some of the dirt from one packet, a spiky leaf from another, and two small purplish leaves from a third. She chose a few wisps of dog hair from what I'd collected and, after mixing everything thoroughly, she set the dough aside and picked up the pipe cleaners, twisting them into a four-legged stick figure. Then she molded the dough around the framework until there was something that might have been a miniature dog, if done by a second-grader with minimal artistic ability. I was not dazzled. Campbell, however, looked well pleased. She cupped her hand over the figurine and intoned:

Lost in distance, lost in sleep
Lost in sorrow, sharp and deep
Seek the way through flesh and bone
Seek the path to hearth and home.

She breathed over her cupped hands and a burst of energy rolled off her and into the little figure. Magical operations are entirely about accessing and manipulating energy, and a reliance on clay, herbs, and second-rate poetry seems feeble. Still, Campbell had healed Lou when I could not, and she had used much the same type of ritual. There was no denying she got results.

I'm not sure what I expected, but the results were disappointing however you looked at it. Campbell uncupped her hands, revealing a lumpy and forlorn figurine of cookie dough that might or might not have represented a dog. She had put little chocolate chips in the head to indicate eyes, but about all that accomplished was to show which end was the head. The energy she'd thrown in was almost unnoticeable, barely glimmering around the edges. I tried to keep a neutral demeanor, but Campbell knew what I was thinking.

"Not very impressive, is it?" she said cheerfully.

I didn't say anything, just made a back-and-forth head-and-shoulder bob that could have meant anything.

"Yeah, I know," she said, "but now it's your turn."

"My turn to . . . ?"

"You're the one who has to animate it. You're the one who's connected to Louie, and besides, I don't have that kind of ability. And you can't just make it move; you have to imbue it with some sort of real life."

"Right. Creation. No problem. And then what?"

She shrugged. "Frankly, I don't know. I know it will work, but I don't know exactly how."

"Oh."

"Or, we could just give up without trying."

"Okay," I said. "I'll see what I can do."

Animating a small manikin—or in this case, a dogikin—

is not an especially difficult task, but infusing it with a life force certainly is. That approaches actual creation, a very different matter than fabricating a simple toy that can move around on its own. In fact, true creation involves powers well beyond most practitioners, and certainly beyond my own.

Even a pale imitation of true life force might be beyond my abilities, but at least I could try. It did help that for once I had the luxury of time for some thought and planning. Most of the time when I have to use my talent I'm in crisis mode and I just wing it the best I can.

I flipped through my CDs looking for something appropriate, something with the energy of heavy metal but with a sweet and spiritual side as well. Not many choices there. I settled on Coltrane's "A Love Supreme" and turned up the volume. As the first strains of the tenor sax floated over McCoy Tyner's piano chords, I opened the back window to let in some air. A slight breeze flowed in, bringing with it a fresh scent from the urban garden that sits right outside the back door. A line of sugar ants streamed unhurriedly through a crack in the corner of a baseboard. I could feel electricity coursing through the ancient wiring of the house. Still not enough.

"I'm going to need to use some of your energy to pull this off," I said apologetically to Campbell. "It might make you slightly tired."

"Be my guest," she invited.

Since Campbell and I had slept together, it was a lot easier for me to access her than it would normally be. I reached into her, finding a life force blazing with enough light to make me feel pale and wan in comparison. I took the small amount I needed, wrapped it up with Coltrane's soaring melodies and the smell of good earth from the garden, added the crackling electricity, and finished it off with the blind survival urge of the mindless sugar ants. Not a bad job, if I do say so myself. I gathered my strength and cast it all into the pathetic cookie dough puppet. Campbell dropped onto the bed, knees suddenly weak.

For half a beat, nothing happened. Then the figure started to glow and, a second later, began to mold itself into a new shape. Slowly, the image of a real dog emerged. Black, with a tan chest patch, tan spots over the eyes, tan paws, and a sharp muzzle. Like a miniature Doberman with uncropped ears and tail. In short, Lou. Of course, although Lou himself is hardly a foot high, this was truly a toy dog. More like two inches. The dog puppet looked around, gave a sharp yelp that sounded more like a mouse's squeak than a dog's bark, and sat up in that familiar begging position Lou uses for all sorts of situations. This tiny imitation Lou was simultaneously heartbreaking and creepy beyond telling. It then wagged its miniature tail and scampered over to the door, scratching to go out.

"Should we let it out?" asked Campbell.

"You tell me. It's your creation."

She nodded. "I think so. I think it wants us to follow it."

I thought about what it would be like following an animated dog puppet the size of a mouse through the city streets. Even in San Francisco, that would make people look twice.

"Look," I said, "even if this is going to work, I doubt that Lou's lolling around somewhere down the block. What if he's hundreds of miles away? Or in another dimension, for that matter? How are we going to follow this thing?"

"I don't know," Campbell said. "Do we have any choice?"

I looked out the front window. It was getting dark, and before long it would be getting cold. I grabbed my leather jacket, which was draped over the back of a wooden chair.

"Well, let's go," I said.

THIRTEEN

AS SOON AS I OPENED THE DOOR, THE DOG RAN down the driveway and stopped in front of the van. Unless Lou was hiding under the backseat, it looked like we were going to be taking a trip. I opened the driver's side door and it launched itself heroically through the air, barely making it onto the floor of the van. It scrambled up the seat like a berserk rodent and then clambered up onto the dashboard. Once there, it sat expectantly and stared out the windshield.

"I take it we're going for a drive," Campbell said.

It wasn't as hard following the silent directions as I thought it would be. The dog sat motionless like a bobble-head doll, nose swiveling in whatever direction it wanted us to go. It was almost like steering to a compass. We sped through city streets, cut through Golden Gate Park, and before I knew it we were crossing the Golden Gate Bridge. I guessed we'd be traveling north up Highway 1 but the dog's head pointed us to the first exit after the bridge. We headed west along the coast, the road twisting and turning. By now it was dusk, and the lights of San Francisco blinked in and out of view like the magical city of Oz as the fog crept in

from the ocean and obscured our view. My interest sharp-
ened as I realized we were traveling the road that ended at
the Point Bonita Lighthouse. I'd actually been out there
once before on a day outing with a woman I'd been dating,
but it wasn't the lighthouse that excited me. The road dead-
ended at Point Bonita, which meant we weren't going to be
traveling hundreds of miles after all. In a short while we
would be at the end of the road, and there wasn't anywhere
else to go after that except to the lighthouse.

Ten minutes later, we pulled up in front of a gate that
blocked the road, the kind with a bar that keeps out cars but
not people. A heavy padlock secured it, and a sign on the
gate, illuminated by my headlights, told us the lighthouse
was closed and would reopen at 11:00 a.m. the next morning. Our dashboard effigy sat motionless, nose pointing
straight ahead toward the closed gate.

"What now?" asked Campbell.

Before I could answer, I saw a figure approaching the car,
looming out of the fog and near-darkness. A quick probe reassured me; no magical residue, no talent, nothing out of the
ordinary. As the figure approached the van, it resolved into a
middle-aged, nondescript Asian man wearing a Windbreaker
over a khaki shirt. There was a blur on his upper left sleeve
that looked like some kind of Park Service patch, but it was
too dark to see it clearly. He peered into the van through
steel-rimmed glasses as I rolled down the side window.

"Hi," he greeted us. "You folks come up to tour the
lighthouse?"

I put a warning hand on Campbell's arm and smiled
blandly.

"Oh, I didn't think the lighthouse would be open this
late," I said, "but I thought we could drive down to where
we could get a good look at it."

The man gave an apologetic smile. "Sorry, folks. We
lock off the access road at five. You'll have to come back
another day."

"No problem," I said. "We wanted to take a scenic drive
anyway."

I gave him another bland smile and rolled up the window. He seemed to want to say something else, then shrugged and walked away. Campbell looked at me with curiosity.

"What?" she asked. "You feel something?"

"No," I said, "but I still don't like it. I didn't catch anything unusual from the guy, no masking energy, nothing to set off alarm bells. But where the hell did he come from? What is he doing here, anyway? There's no other vehicle in sight. It seems unlikely that the Park Service would post someone to hang around after dark at the end of a narrow, windswept road, conveniently available to tell confused tourists that a locked gate means the road is closed. And, right where we're getting close to a missing Ifrit?"

"True enough. So who is he then, and why is he here?"

"I don't know. Christoph may or may not be around; he seems to be fond of using surrogates for his battles. It might be anyone or anything. But we're still going down to the lighthouse." I motioned with my hand. "Come over here for a minute." Campbell slid over next to me and I put my arm around her. "Whatever he is, he's still watching us from out there somewhere. We need to make him think we're perfectly normal."

"I *am* perfectly normal," she said primly. "You, on the other hand . . ."

I pulled her closer, leaned over, and kissed her. She responded without hesitation, clearing up at least one worry. I hadn't been sure exactly where we stood. Reluctantly I broke off the embrace. Much as I would have liked to continue, there was work to do. I took the palpable sexual energy arising between us and cast a minor illusion. I always find sexual energy easy to work with—I'm not sure if that's because it's so primal and strong, or whether it's just me.

I pulled the van away from the gate and parked on a slight incline to one side. Then I leaned across, opened the passenger side door, and motioned for Campbell to get out. I slid across the seat after her, grabbing a flashlight from the glove compartment as I got out. We might need light, and I didn't want to indulge in any more magical tricks than necessary until I figured out what was going on. All kinds of people and things can sense talent being used.

The tiny dog figure hopped down from its perch, bounced off the seat, and jumped out the door onto the asphalt. I almost stepped on it as it skittered away. I wondered if it would crunch like a mouse or squash flat like the cookie dough it was. It trotted self-importantly under the gate, perfectly mimicking the gait of Lou on a mission. I glanced back at the van and saw two blurry figures seated inside, going at it hot and heavy. Not much of an illusion, granted, but enough to fool someone at night thirty feet away.

We followed our dogikin up the dark road, more by sound than sight, since I didn't want to risk the flashlight. The scrabbling of tiny nails on asphalt was perfectly audible even over the sound of wind rushing over rocky crags. A half mile later the road ended at a small parking lot. From there a dirt path led away up a hill. At the end of the path, perched on a rocky crag like a medieval fortress, the Point Bonita Lighthouse squatted. Back when it was a working lighthouse, it would have been shining brightly, a beacon of hope along stormy shores. Now it was dark, grim, and foreboding. The path dropped off sharply on the ocean side, and as we walked, the sound of the surf below crashing against the rocks almost drowned out the sound of our guide. The night fog had thickened and a light rain was starting, giving the entire scene an eerie film noir feeling.

Three quarters up the path, a tunnel hewed straight through solid rock loomed out of the fog. The tunnel mouth transformed the gloom outside into an inky blackness. Our doggie guide plunged in without hesitation, but Campbell and I stopped reflexively at the entrance. As far as I could tell, everything was normal—at least considering the circumstances—but the dark passageway was most uninviting. I didn't want to send out any probing energy that could announce our presence, so I pulled the flashlight out of a jacket pocket and aimed it down the tunnel. The batteries weren't that fresh, and I could only see about twenty feet in. As best I could remember, though, the tunnel was only about a hundred feet long anyway. The rough-hewn sides formed a ragged semicircle, seven feet high at the center, less so on the sides, which meant if I walked right down the middle I wouldn't have to stoop except for low-hanging projections.

"Who dug this, anyway?" Campbell asked. "And how?"

"Chinese laborers. Sometime around the time of the Civil War. No explosives, just pick-and-shovel work."

"It must have taken them years."

"No, I don't think so. I remember a Park Service guide saying it was six months, or nine, or something."

The little dog made its mouse-squeak bark, looking back impatiently over its shoulder.

"I guess we go in," I said.

I kept the light on the dog as we plunged into the darkness of the tunnel. By this time I was sure that our ultimate destination was the lighthouse, although with tourists traipsing through every day it was hard to see how anything could be concealed there. But then, halfway through the tunnel, the dog stopped abruptly, scratched pathetically at the side of the tunnel, gave a tiny exhalation and fell over on its side. When I bent down to see what had happened, our little dog was no more. Instead, the original cookie dough lump lay there, as if it were a carelessly dropped morsel of food. One of the tiny legs was worn almost to a nub from the rough trip along the path.

"I guess we're here," said Campbell

"I guess so. But where is here?"

I looked up and down the tunnel as far as my light would shine. Nothing. I stared at the side of the tunnel where our guide had collapsed, hoping for some clue as to what might lie there. Solid rock. Up toward the roof, several large spiders had spun webs, although I couldn't for the life of me see what they hoped to catch in this cold and dank place. If I'd ever had any doubts, by now I was convinced the little dog had indeed been following Louie's trail. There was definitely something here; I just couldn't find it.

"What now?" Campbell asked.

"I'm not sure," I admitted. "I think I've got to send out

a deep probe. It may bring trouble down on us, if there's anything bad around, but the only other choice is to turn around and go home."

Usually I need a lot of outside stimulus to do anything effective with my talent. It's easiest of course to create spells based on similarities—like using the fluidity of water to morph one thing into another. If I were more talented, or more knowledgeable, I wouldn't need that connection, but I'm not. Put me in an isolation tank and I'd have some trouble getting out. Being in a dark rock tunnel didn't provide the best scope for my abilities.

I did have the cold, though. I had damp. I had darkness. Ahh. I had my flashlight. Light. The thing that didn't fit. Easy. I wrapped them up and sent out a pulse looking for anything else that didn't fit, something askew. The tunnel walls flashed momentarily, almost too quick to register, and what remained was an afterimage of delicately drawn lines, doorway-sized, right in front of where our little dog had reverted back to dough. Okay, there was something behind the wall, and unless I missed my guess, it was Lou. But how to get in? My spell had shown us where to look, but the rock wall was as solid and unyielding as ever.

I felt suddenly exhausted, discouraged, and helpless, in a dank and cold windswept tunnel with flashlight batteries rapidly fading. Lou was counting on me, and not only had I sat around moping for a week, now that I was finally here I'd run out of inspiration. Then Campbell reached over and took the flashlight out of my hand.

"Wait here a second," she said. "I've got an idea."

She walked back toward the tunnel mouth, flashlight bobbing and weaving, leaving me alone in the dark with nothing but spiders on the walls and the sound of wind rushing past rock. Not that standing there alone with God knows what lurking in the darkness bothered me. Not much it didn't. I almost expected Christoph to spring up out of the darkness, large as life and twice as scary, with dripping fangs and glowing eyes. A most unmanly relief washed over me when I saw Campbell returning, flashlight giving off its comforting gleam. She came up to me holding some sort of plant in one hand. Big surprise there.

"Ivy," she said succinctly. "I noticed it growing on the rock face when we came in." She took small bits and started edging them along where the line of the doorway was still glowing. "Can you make this stick to the wall?"

That I could do. Eli keeps telling me I have great potential, and I proved it once again by whipping up a spell to make bits of plant matter adhere to a rock wall. When she was done placing the ivy, she muttered another of her incantations under her breath and stood back. The ivy started to glow, then grow. It wasn't growing into the rock, it was somehow growing into the line of light which outlined the rock doorway. The more the ivy grew, the brighter the line glowed. I looked at Campbell with renewed respect. There were obviously a few things she could teach me. Eventually the entire area around the door was lit up like a Christmas tree, and then, with a soundless crack that I could feel in my bones, the outline of the door separated and fell to the floor of the tunnel, still glowing. In its place, another tunnel led away into the distance, winding its way into the hillside.

"Damn, you're good," I said.

"I know," she said. She gestured toward the opening. "After you, sir."

The tunnel curved and twisted for a couple of hundred feet, then opened up into a large room. Directly across the room was a closed door leading off to somewhere even farther back. I stopped at the entrance and looked around with a combination of interest and horror. The room, a cross between a veterinarian's office and an animal shelter, had cages stacked against every wall, most of them occupied with an assortment of small animals. Empty crates were piled up haphazardly everywhere, and the spiders that filled the tunnels seemed to have proliferated, crowding into every corner. More ominous were the long stainless steel tables like those of an autopsy room. On one table, sharp gleaming instruments had been carefully laid out.

You might expect the usual barking and meowing and

squealing a group of caged animals usually provides, but this place was eerily silent. Because these weren't animals in the cages. They were Ifrits.

"Holy mother of God," I breathed.

Campbell looked around at the cages, but she didn't fully understand the impact it had on me. Practitioners, like anyone else, have disagreements, and those disagreements sometimes turn nasty. Violence is not unknown, and there is even the occasional practitioner who observes no conventions of any sort, like Christoph. But mostly, no matter what the conflict, no matter what the situation, Ifrits are off limits. Even when Christoph had attacked Lou, it was in a fit of anger. This was something very different.

Imagine a Mafia don locked in a turf war with a rival boss. Then imagine his going to that rival's house and murdering the children he finds asleep inside, and you get some inkling of how practitioners feel about those who would target Ifrits. And putting them in captivity? It was as outrageous as coming across a group of four-year-old children sealed up in wooden crates.

Several furry heads snapped around as we entered, but not one of the Ifrits uttered a sound. I'd never seen so many of them gathered in one spot. They must have come from all over California. At least four cats were in cages, as well as a Chihuahua and something odd that looked dapper and ferretlike. Campbell noticed me looking at it.

"Pine marten," she whispered in my ear.

I wasn't paying attention. In the middle of the room, carelessly thrown over the back of a chair, I saw a distinctive gray and black striped wool poncho. The last time I had seen it was at the Challenges in Golden Gate Park, draped over a certain practitioner named Christoph.

"Well, goddamn," I said. I looked around frantically, but no Lou. Then I heard a soft canine muttering, not quite a bark, coming from the back of the room. I took a step sideways to get a look, and there he was, in a cage set on top of two others. He sat there quietly, staring intently at me. No barking. No tail wagging. No frantic pawing at the wire mesh. The cage was secured top and bottom by flat sliding bolts which were protected by a steel plate over the mesh. Even if he managed to chew through the wire mesh, an impossible feat, he still wouldn't be able to reach the bolts.

I quickly started across the room toward his cage, but before I'd taken more than a few steps, the door on the back wall opened. I grabbed at Campbell and ducked down behind a row of unused cages stacked by the tunnel entrance. I stupidly hadn't realized this search for Lou might turn dangerous. I hadn't thought much about it at all.

I was sure it would be Christoph walking through that door, but instead, two men entered. Except, I wasn't so sure they were really men. They both appeared Asian, both youngish, both sporting those same glasses with steel-rimmed frames that the supposed park ranger had been wearing. The one on the left was donning a pair of heavy-duty protective gauntlets, the ones firefighters wear. The other was carrying a pole about three feet long with a ribbed handle and a wire noose at one end, like those used by animal control officers. Without bothering to look around, they headed directly toward Lou's cage.

Lou hunched as far back into the cage as possible, snarling and showing teeth. When the cage door opened, he lunged at the first guy, then swerved at the last second and tried to slip by him to freedom, but there wasn't enough room. The first guy blocked his escape with his gloves and the second deftly slipped the noose over Lou's head. He dragged him out of the cage struggling and kicking, holding him up off the ground at arm's length. Lou was gagging and choking as the weight of his body tightened the noose around his neck. His eyes bulged and his legs bicycled frantically as if he were treading water instead of air.

I found myself across the room before I could form a conscious thought, coming up right behind the one strangling Lou. I slammed my fist against his head, right where the base of the skull meets the neck. You'd think that with my talent, for what it's worth, I could have instead come up with some spell designed to freeze him in his tracks.

But, like Lou, my impulse control isn't the best, and my first reaction is usually to strike out physically. Most unseemly for a practitioner. Sometimes the unexpected outburst saves me, but just as often it just gets me in more trouble.

Instead of crumpling to the ground like I'd hoped, he merely turned around and regarded me with mild surprise. He did drop Lou, but it was more from the surprise than anything else. I probably could have produced the same reaction by jumping out and yelling boo. The man didn't appear hurt at all, but I felt like I'd broken my hand. It was as if I had punched a moss-covered boulder.

As soon as he hit the floor, Lou scurried away out of reach, dragging the pole along with him, still choking. The first guy, the one with the gloves, smoothly glided over in front of the tunnel, blocking any escape. He glittered as he moved, blurring momentarily, losing some of his human aspect and leaving the impression of a crystalline creature, a living faceted gem. Whatever it was, it wasn't human. I should have known. At times like these, I wished I was like Victor, armed with preset power spells that could be triggered by a single word, raining destruction down on my enemies.

Still, I do have skills. I backed up to where Campbell was standing as the first guy moved unhurriedly forward. The essence of this place was that of a trap, a jail, a place of confinement. I reached out and gathered that essence in. I added the prolific spiders, huddling in every corner. And I'm not above using pop icons as a focusing device.

"Don't worry, Mary Jane," I said to Campbell. "They don't know who they're messing with."

I whipped out swirls of energy like spider silk, weaving them into a pattern and looping them around the faux men. Real surprise now registered on the face of the one in front of me, but it didn't last long. In five seconds flat, both of them were trussed up in tight energy cocoons as neatly as a June bug in a web. That should hold them at least a couple of hours, and luckily for them, there was no giant spider awaiting lunchtime.

Unluckily for me, I wasn't as effective as a giant spider. The cocoons I'd fashioned started deteriorating rapidly, huge rents appearing even as I watched. One of the guys already had an arm halfway out, and they'd both be free in seconds.

Campbell had already gone over to where Lou was pawing at the noose. Slipping her fingers under the loop, she worked it over his head. Before I could stop him he bolted, flinging himself at the nearest of his captors. It wasn't going to do him any good; if he tried to bite the thing his teeth would break on its rock-hard flesh.

Wrong again. I've been with Lou for years, but I still sometimes forget he's not a dog. I had bruised my hand on the thing's flesh, but Lou's Ifrit teeth sank into its calf like it was a rare lamb chop. No wonder they'd taken such precautions removing him from the cage. Lou caught him right under the kneecap and began whipping his head side to side as if trying to rip out a chunk of meat. The creature screamed something in a language I didn't recognize, but I had a suspicion it was a bad word. It was still partially tangled up in my web, so all it could do for the moment was to hop up and down and yell.

The other one had already freed itself. It bounded over and grabbed me by the arm. It wasn't as strong as the Gaki, not even close, but it was still stronger than I was. Its mineral-hard flesh as well as its strength gave it an advantage, but that crystalline hardness might also be a weakness. I glanced up and layered the corners of the ceiling with a reflective sheen.

"Scream," I said to Campbell. "As high and as loud as you can."

She didn't ask why, bless her. She opened her mouth and let out a creditable imitation of a woman in a slasher film. I amplified the sound, bounced it off the ceiling, reinforced the harmonics, and directed it through the room. It vibrated strongly, reinforcing itself with every circuit. The sound knifed through my skull and hurt my ears, and Lou, with his more sensitive hearing, flinched and let go of the leg he was chewing.

I was hoping the sound would have an even more profound effect on the crystalline aspects of creatures not entirely flesh and bone. Maybe their heads would explode like a wineglass faced with an opera singer. Nothing that dramatic occurred, but the one holding me did drop my arm and sank to its knees, while the other staggered and put its hands up to its head. Then they both lurched over to the door at the back, staggered through, and slammed it behind them.

As soon as they'd gone, Lou darted to the nearest cage and started trying to get his teeth around the knob of the top bolt, pausing to utter a hoarse bark in my direction.

"Yeah, like I'm just going to leave everyone else here," I muttered.

I moved quickly from cage to cage, sliding back bolts and opening doors. Each time, the Ifrit inside scrambled out, stopped a moment to stare into my eyes as if to fix me in memory, and disappeared through the tunnel which led to freedom.

I kept glancing over at the back door, expecting the imminent return of the captors, this time with help. We couldn't have much time left. I jerked my head toward the front door, telling Lou it was time to get the hell out of here. He ignored me, running to the very back of the room, darting in and out of corners, searching. He stopped in front of a cage in the far corner which had been covered over with a stiff blue tarp, got one corner between his teeth, and started pulling.

I backed him off, untied the rope that was holding the cover in place, and pulled it off. Inside, curled up with her back toward us, was an Ifrit dog I immediately recognized as Moxie. So she hadn't abandoned Sandra after all, any more than Lou had abandoned me. She looked bad. She was horribly thin and her coat was filthy and matted. She whimpered softly as I undid the iron bolts and swung open the cage door.

I reached in and picked her up. As I swung her around to face me, she turned her head to look at me and I nearly dropped her. Instead of the bright and sparkling eyes I remembered, there were only empty and ragged sockets crusted over with dried blood.

FOURTEEN

AT FIRST, WHEN YOU WORRY AT A QUESTION EVERY day, you think about it all the time. Eventually it recedes into your subconscious. And there, deep down in your mind, it lurks. Then, when you least expect it, there comes a blinding and horrific moment of revelation. Everything becomes clear. There is no logic involved, no clever and rational unraveling of mystery. You just *know*, instantly, with the certitude of faith.

Those precious stones, beautiful and mysterious. Sparkling gems of brilliance and light, bright and shining and magical. Like the deep and liquid eyes of an Ifrit.

I don't know how or where Christoph had learned to transform Ifrit eyes into jewels. Maybe from those crystalline creatures guarding the lab. I flashed back to my time in the singularity, where I'd found one of the stones. Bones. Small bones crunching under my feet. Ifrit bones and an Ifrit eye. Maybe it had escaped, slipping through dimensions as Ifrits do, before dying far from home. Maybe the singularity was where Christoph transformed the eyes. Maybe the Ifrits had to be alive for it to work; that's why they were in cages.

It didn't matter. What mattered was the act itself: sick, greedy, dark, and vile beyond comprehension.

And the attacks on me? Of course I had assumed they were about me, but they weren't, not really. Christoph had told me as much at my house, but I hadn't listened. I was just in the way. Once I was gone, whether dead or lost, an unprotected Lou would be vulnerable, another grotesque source of riches for him.

Moxie had been easy pickings. Sandra couldn't protect her; she could barely take care of herself. I was a problem though. Lou was almost always with me, and even if Christoph managed to snatch him up, he'd face me eventually. Sooner or later I'd connect the dots, I'd come after him, and I wouldn't quit until one of us was dead. But that was before. Now he was strong enough that he no longer cared what I did.

Not that I'd done anything. When Lou went missing I moped around the house for a week, oblivious to the real situation. That idiocy had almost cost Lou his eyes. If Victor and Eli hadn't been on Christoph's tail, distracting him by working day and night to find him, I would have got here too late.

At least Campbell was along; in this situation she was going to be more help than I would. I set Moxie down and tried to examine her wounds, but Lou interposed his body and when I reached for Moxie again, he growled and bared his teeth. I was so astonished that I took a backward step. He gave me another warning growl, then turned to her and sniffed over every inch of her body. Finally, he licked her gently on the muzzle. She thumped her tail briefly, then bowed her head in assent. In a flash he seized her by the back of the neck, crunched down with those surprisingly powerful jaws, and twisted sharply. There was an audible cracking and Moxie's legs jerked once, then she went limp. She fell over soundlessly and lay there, splayed out on the floor like a curly brown dog doll. Lou looked up at me with a combination of guilt and defiance as if he'd been caught doing something secret and shameful, something no practitioner should ever see. This was Ifrit business he was telling me, as clearly as if he could speak.

I heard Campbell's sharp intake of breath, but before she could say anything I took her arm and pulled her toward the door. The lab guards could be returning any minute and we needed to get out while we still could. Now was not the proper time to discuss what had just happened. I'm not sure there was ever going to be a proper time.

We headed toward the opening in the wall, Campbell one step ahead, Lou on my heels. Out the door, through the tunnel, back along the path. Partway down, Lou stopped. I peered through the fog and rain and darkness. Farther down, half-hidden by the swirling mist, stood the dim outline of a figure. Lou started up with a hoarse growl—not his warning growl, but the one he uses when he's seriously angry. Campbell grabbed at me.

"What is that?" she asked, nervously. "I can't make it out."

I couldn't either, but clearly Lou could. His eyesight is far better than mine, especially in low light or darkness. Since it's never a great idea to blithely approach something unknown and scary lurking in the dark, I needed to utilize some talent. It would have taken a couple of minutes at least to fashion a vision-enhancing spell, but luckily I didn't need to. One of my occasionally useful skills is the ability to see through Lou's eyes when he's next to me, to see whatever it is that he's seeing. It's not something I attempt often, since whenever I do the resulting dislocation leaves me dizzy and nauseous and produces a splitting headache which lasts for hours. Not an ideal state to be in during a crisis. It's much like viewing on the psychic plane, but even harder on your body and mind.

I gritted my teeth and did the mental leap that puts me behind Lou's eyes. Instantly the dark landscape jumped into focus. It was like wearing infrared night goggles except for the hint of color that remained even in darkness. I staggered, fighting the usual urge to throw up, and tried to concentrate on what he was seeing.

The dim figure resolved itself into our middle-aged

Asian Park Service guy. Except it wasn't. The first time I
had looked at him I hadn't really seen him. I'd seen only a
clever optical illusion, like the goblet that becomes two
faces when you stare at it long enough. Its face was all angles and planes, crystalline, like a multifaceted gemstone.
Like the Ifrit eyes. It glittered as it turned its head to look directly at me. What I had seen before as steel-rimmed glasses
was in truth a shelflike projection over the eyes, maybe for
protection. There was something insectile about it but also
something of the inanimate. Where had Christoph found
these things? It was actually quite beautiful in a weird way.
And dangerous, I was sure. I couldn't believe I'd ever
thought it was human. I couldn't believe it had fooled me so
easily. I was a sorry excuse for a practitioner.

Before I could take note of anything that might prove useful, my vision blurred and I felt the nauseating dislocation
that meant Lou was on the move. I tore my consciousness
back to my own eyes as he took off down the path toward the
motionless figure. He ran forward at top speed, deadly silent,
and I could feel waves of hatred emanating from him.

"Lou! Louie!" I shouted, staggering, trying to regain
my equilibrium. "Get back here!"

No use. I doubt he even heard me. When he was about
twenty feet from the thing, two more figures rose up men-
acingly from where they had been crouching unseen at the
edge of the trail. Lou did a sudden one-eighty, spinning so
quickly he almost lost his balance and tumbled over. Two
seconds later he was sprinting back toward us as fast as he
had been charging away. Out of control he might have been,
but he still retained enough sense to realize the odds had
just shifted dramatically. He scurried up to where we were
standing and ducked behind me, peering around my legs.
Obviously I was supposed to protect him. Wonderful. Who
was going to protect me? The stunt I'd pulled back in the
cage room had taken most of my reserve, and now there
were three of them and this time they would be prepared.

I didn't have much interest in proceeding down the path
toward those three, but I didn't like the thought of retreat-

ing back through that dark passageway behind us, either. That option became moot when I glanced over my shoulder and saw four more figures emerging from the tunnel behind us. It hadn't taken the ones from the lab long to secure help. Excellent. Creatures in front, creatures in back, steep drop-off on one side, steep cliff face on the other. All that was needed to make things perfect would be for Christoph to rise up out of the fog. The figures in front started moving slowly up the path toward us, gliding soundlessly. Campbell instinctively crowded closer.

"I don't like this," she said. "Shouldn't you cast another spell or something?"

I didn't care for it myself. I can handle most things. A bunch of thugs out to cause trouble? Not a problem. Supernatural creatures powerful enough to shield their true natures and kidnap Ifrits? Maybe a touch more difficult. The high-frequency trick wasn't going to work again; without an enclosed area the sound would dissipate up into the night sky.

I bent over and picked up some moist earth from the side of the trail, wove in some fog to give it some substance, drew some sap from a stunted evergreen tree, and cast it down the path toward them. It was a weak spell, a sticky that wouldn't slow anything down for long, but I didn't have energy to waste and I wanted to see what effect it might have. I wasn't too sanguine—my previous experience with the Gaki had shaken my magical confidence and the web spell hadn't held them long. Sure enough, they hesitated, then glided right through more annoyed by it than hindered.

I'd like to think I would have come up with something else, but it might well have been one of those stories that ends ". . . and then the bear ate me." Luckily, the cavalry arrived. As our erstwhile Park Service guy moved forward, one of the freed Ifrits, a large ginger cat, launched itself out of the fog and landed on the back of its neck. I don't know if you've ever been unfortunate enough to have a seriously pissed cat wrap itself around your head, all teeth and claws and feline screams, but it's enough to give anyone pause, even a being of unknown powers. And of course, being an Ifrit, it was able to affect him.

The ginger cat was tearing viciously at him, doing a bang-up job. The guy screamed as loudly as the cat, staggered sideways, and reached up to grab at it. I started running toward them. Once he got his hands on our Ifrit friend, it would be all over. But as he reached up, another cat appeared from the opposite side and leapt up onto his arm, grabbing his attention. Three seconds later I had arrived, running at full speed, and as I came up on the creature both Ifrits jumped off as if they had been scalded by hot water.

I didn't want to close with this guy, or thing, or whatever it was. It was surely stronger than I was, not to mention that it consisted of material impervious to me. My aching hand was a reminder of that. It was, however, standing on the edge of a path with a steep drop-off down to a rock-strewn cove. I put my shoulder down and hit it midway between shoulder and hip. It made a gratifying oof sound and went flying over the edge.

When you see football players on TV it looks easy, but the reality is considerably different. The shock of the hit numbed my entire right side and my momentum almost carried me over the edge after it. Campbell, three steps behind me, reached out and pulled me back to safety. I spun back to face the other two figures but they were already fully occupied. Every Ifrit who had been in a cage was now clawing and snapping at them: the cats, the pine marten, and something else that I couldn't identify. Lou, who now that he had allies was emboldened enough to sink his teeth into any loose appendage he could find, was venting his outrage. The snarling, hissing, and screeching, all muffled by the thickening rain and fog, created a surreal soundtrack to a surreal scene. Then, the faint pounding of approaching feet warned me that the creatures who had been behind us were coming up to join in the fray. I briefly considered the discretion/valor thing.

"Go! Go! Let's go!" I shouted, and took off down the path. The Ifrits got the message and skittered past me, disappearing into the dark.

We were breathing hard, running full speed as we slipped around the gate and approached the safety of the van. The two illusory figures I'd set up were still going at it, but their motions were jerky and disconnected and they were beginning to tile like a television program with a weak digital signal. I flung open the van door, and Campbell let out a high-pitched shriek when she saw who was sitting in the driver's seat. Or maybe that was me who shrieked. It's hard to remember.

Christoph. Who else? I don't expect things to ever be easy, but why do they always have to be so difficult? He didn't have the fangs or glowing eyes, but he was almost frothing at the mouth. He managed to choke out a few strangled words past clenched teeth.

"Do you have any idea what you've done?" he screamed. His psychosis was leaking out before our eyes. "Do you know how long it takes to gather that many Ifrits? I should have killed you when I had the chance."

I started to make a sarcastic comment about that being exactly what he'd been trying to do for quite a while now, but he made a quick gesture and my throat seized up.

"Shut up!" he shouted, beside himself. "Shut up!"

Since I often relied on talking my way out of situations, not being able to speak was a serious drawback. He raised his hand again but before he could act I grabbed at Campbell and took off through the bushes. Lou seemed to have regained his senses, since he was already well out in front of us. Behind us I could hear Christoph scream out some incantation, and a moment later the perpetual drizzle of rain started heating up. It felt like we were now running through a warm shower and I guessed before long the water falling from the sky would be literally boiling. Being scalded to death is not a good way to go. Not that there are too many good ways.

I could only protect us for so long and I didn't have enough power left to reverse Christoph's spell, so instead I enhanced it. I focused twenty feet overhead and poured a small amount of additional energy into the massive power he'd sent surging through the sky. It was just enough to tip the temperature balance. The rain heated up even more and then turned into a supercharged virga, evaporating before it ever reached the ground. I may not be all that bright, but I am clever.

Clever wasn't going to help us much when he found us, though. Even without Lou, I was sure Christoph could see through darkness, or even light up the entire area if he wanted to. I bent down and grabbed Lou by the scruff with one hand and kept hold of Campbell with the other. I formed images of the three of us, but these needed to be a lot more convincing than the blurry figures I'd earlier placed in the van.

"Brace yourself," I said to Campbell. Lou flinched in anticipation. He knew what was coming, but it had to be done if it was going to fool Christoph. I dug a tiny piece of essence out of each of us. It hurt. Lou yelped sharply and Campbell added a couple of choice words. I wove the essence into the duplicates and sent them running back up the hill, crashing noisily through the scrub.

With the last of my reserve, I laid a masking spell over the three of us. It wouldn't fool Christoph if he looked closely, but a rabbit can hide in plain sight if it stays quiet and the focus is elsewhere. By the time I was done, I really was done. I didn't have enough power left to light a kitchen match.

Christoph shouted something inarticulate and took off after the fleeing images. He wasn't that bright, either. He swept by us without a glance, moving fast about two feet off the ground like he was riding a hovercraft. I felt a stab of jealousy. Here I was struggling to maintain a simple illusion while this man had power to burn.

We huddled together, frozen, until he was a good ways off, then made a break for the van. If we could get enough distance between us, even his strength wouldn't be enough to stop us. As we jumped in the van, the ginger cat appeared out of nowhere and scrambled in with us. I jammed the key in the ignition and the engine turned over once, twice, then ground to a halt. I tried it again, frantically, but it was no use. Completely dead.

By this time, Christoph would surely have caught up with the impersonators. Even with his lack of intelligence, he'd be hightailing it back to the van as fast as he could. I summoned up a last effort, trying for enough of a spark to kick over the engine, but I had nothing left. Without a word, Campbell jumped out and ran around to the front of the van, where she put her shoulder into it and pushed with all her strength. Thank God I had parked it on an incline. It rolled ten feet backward with excruciating slowness, barely picking up enough speed for one desperate try. I flung it into reverse, waited half a second, then popped the clutch. The van bucked, hesitated, and then caught, engine blessedly roaring into life. Campbell clambered in just as Christoph came back into view. I tromped on the accelerator, wishing I had Victor's BMW instead. Still, the tires squealed gratifyingly as we roared off down the road leaving an infuriated Christoph standing impotently behind.

My heart was in my mouth for the next two miles and I didn't fully relax until we were back halfway across the bridge. Campbell finally broke the silence.

"I didn't know what I was getting into," she said.

"Sorry," I replied. "I didn't either."

"I don't think I'm cut out for this kind of thing."

"You know," I said, "nobody is, not really." Except, I added mentally, maybe Victor.

Lou sat in the back, communing with the ginger cat in the way Ifrits do. I know they can't talk with each other the way people can, but they do manage to communicate a lot of information to each other.

We were back over the bridge, into the city, and halfway through Golden Gate Park when the ginger cat jumped up onto the back of Campbell's seat and stared out the side window. At the same time, Lou gave a peremptory bark. I pulled over and Campbell opened the van door. Without so much as a backward glance, the cat exited and swiftly disappeared into the underbrush. Cats aren't much for extended farewells, even Ifrit cats.

It would have been nice if it were all over. Lou had been rescued. The mystery behind the gems had been solved. Christoph had been exposed as the villain he was. But nothing had been settled. The hard part was still ahead, and the night was just getting started.

FIFTEEN

AS SOON AS WE GOT HOME, LOU GOBBLED UP SOME stale kibble that had been lying around since before he disappeared, but he didn't act like he was starving. It was still only about nine o'clock. I called Eli, who answered on the first ring.

"I found Lou," I told him.

"Incredible. Where? How?"

"Christoph. He trapped him somehow. But that's not all. I know where the gems come from."

I went into detail, including our narrow escape, and by the time I finished I could feel Eli's fury crackling over the telephone line. When he finally spoke he was calm, though.

"Poor Moxie," he said. "And poor Lou. What a heavy responsibility." He was silent for a few moments. "Okay, we need to do something about Christoph. Now that I know where those gems come from his actions make more sense. The gems are powerful. But there's no way he could use them, considering what they are and how he got them, without severe psychic damage. So he's not only dangerous, not only powerful, but also seriously disturbed." This was not news to me. "And we need to act quickly. For all we know, he could be ripping the eyes out of some other poor Ifrit at this very moment."

"Yeah, but how are we going to find him? I doubt he's still up at Point Bonita," I said.

"What about Lou?" Eli understood Lou's potential.

"Not likely. There's a huge difference between locating a random individual and locating a practitioner who doesn't want to be found."

"True." The fact that Eli hadn't thought of that made me realize how upset he was. "We have another problem," he said.

"Of course."

"There's a message from Sherwood on my voice mail asking me to stop by and see her at Victor's as soon as possible."

"Is she okay?"

"As far as I know. She's not answering the phone. But it sounds like someone else has gone missing."

"Who?"

"She didn't say. But if you're up to it, meet me over there and we'll find out."

I WAS EXHAUSTED. LOU WAS CURLED UP ON THE bed, totally out. I thought of leaving him to sleep; God knows he needed it and Campbell was here to check on him. But I was afraid to let either one of them out of my sight. I shook him gently and he raised his head.

"Sorry," I said. "We've got to go out again."

He yawned, stretched, and looked at me bleary-eyed. With an air of infinite patience and resignation, he stood up ever so slowly and slithered off the bed onto the floor.

"Don't give me that," I said. "I just saved your ass, remember?" He yawned again and turned his back.

Back in the van, back to Victor's. It was worse than being a cabdriver. Eli was already there, and he'd filled

Sherwood in on our adventures in Christoph Land. She greeted Lou enthusiastically and Campbell somewhat less so. As if I didn't have enough trouble. Lou and Maggie had come to a truce of sorts and they ambled off companionably enough into the next room. I looked around for Victor, but he was nowhere to be seen. Nor was Danny, for that matter.

"Where's Victor?" I asked.

"Checking out another Christoph rumor," Sherwood said. "Someone in the East Bay who claims to have seen him."

"Is that likely?"

"No, but that's not why I wanted to talk to you. Jenna's missing."

"Who's Jenna?"

"Jenna from the Tenderloin," Eli reminded me. "That street girl?"

It took me a moment to realize who he was talking about, and when I did, I wasn't very sympathetic. I was tired and I was stressed.

"You get all of us over here because that little street moppet decided to take a hike?" I said. "With everything else that's going on? Jesus, Sherwood, what is wrong with you?"

"Tell you what, Mason. How about for once you just shut up and listen?"

Those words were so unlike Sherwood that it instantly did shut me up. I guess I wasn't the only one experiencing stress. She glared at me.

"Jenna has a lot of issues, but the important thing to remember is what she is. She's a Finder."

"Wait a minute," I said. "You don't mean you sent her . . ."

"No, of course not. Don't be an idiot." Sherwood was on a roll. "Jenna called me a few days ago and offered to find Christoph for us."

"You're joking," Eli said. "How did she even know we were looking for him?"

"Those kids hear everything. With you and Victor scouring the city all week, it wasn't exactly a secret, you know."

"I guess not. So she wanted to help out?"

"No, not exactly. She's still got that street kid mentality. She wanted five hundred dollars to find him."

"Would have been worth it," I muttered.

"I told her to stay away from it. I tried to impress on her just how dangerous Christoph was but I'm not sure I got through. When I hadn't heard from her in a couple of days, I called the Home. Nobody has seen her for the last three days. I'm afraid she might have decided to do it anyway, then demand the money after she found him."

"Not good," said Eli.

"Maybe she's wandering the city, still trying to locate him. Even a Finder would have difficulty locating Christoph," I said.

Campbell gave voice to what we all were thinking. "Or maybe she did find him."

We were interrupted by Victor's return from the East Bay. If he was surprised to see me there he didn't show it, but he couldn't keep his dead-cool demeanor when Lou came trotting back into the room, Maggie trailing behind.

"Congratulations," he said to me. "Although I did lose the bet with Eli. I didn't think we'd ever see him again."

I should have been outraged that he was betting against Lou, but I was too tired. Eli asked if the East Bay trip had panned out.

"Oh, the guy saw Christoph, all right. Only, it was three weeks ago." He looked down at Lou, and the barest of smiles flickered over his face. "When did Lou turn up?"

I related the entire story once again, along with my conclusions. Eli added qualifiers from time to time. Victor's expression never changed, although when I described what had happened to Moxie, his right eye started to twitch. Before he could comment though, Sherwood impatiently jumped in with the news that now Jenna was missing and might have gone looking for Christoph.

"That is a complication," said Victor, "but I don't have time to deal with it right now." He paused, seeming to struggle with a thought. "On the other hand, I suppose we do have an obligation. If we hadn't tracked her down and taken her off the streets in the first place, she wouldn't be the middle of this."

"My thoughts exactly," Sherwood said. "So we're going to look for her, then?"

Victor nodded a reluctant yes.

"But how are we going to find her?"

Eli looked at me, then pointedly at Lou. He knew Lou's capabilities.

"Maybe," I said. "If Lou can remember who she is. But she needs to be relatively nearby for him to locate her. He can't just waltz out the door and find somebody on the other side of town. We'd have to drive all over the city until he picked up the scent."

"Then that's what we'll do," Eli said. You didn't often hear that tone from him, but when you did, there was no point in arguing.

"What, you mean now?" I said, visions of bed and sleep rapidly receding.

Lou was sitting quietly, following the conversation with interest. Or, perhaps, waiting to see if there might be a late dinner in the offing. I'm never sure what goes on with him. Eli leaned over and scratched his ears.

"Where would Lou be now if you'd waited until the next morning to go looking for him?" Trust Eli to zero in on my guilt. He could be as manipulative as Victor when he needed to be.

"Okay," I said. Lou had lost interest in the conversation and it took me a minute to get his attention. I grabbed his muzzle and made him look at me.

"Listen up. Jenna. We need to find Jenna."

Of course, he looked at me blankly. He had no idea who "Jenna" might be.

"Jenna," I repeated. "The girl we followed? Spiky hair?" I put my hands up to my head and wiggled my fingers in imitation. Lou's blank stare turned to one of bafflement. "Remember the street guy?" I squatted down and mimed taking a dump. Lou looked over at Eli and then at Victor. His expression now said, "Hmm, I knew someday he'd lose his mind."

Campbell was trying to keep a straight face. "Sherwood," she said. "Do you have anything that belonged to her? Or something she wore?"

A lot of times I'm guilty of forgetting that Lou isn't really a dog. This time I'd forgotten that in a lot of ways, he really is.

"A bracelet," Sherwood said. "I got her a new backpack, and in appreciation, she gave me a bracelet woven out of hemp that she made. I think I have it here."

She left the room and returned a minute later, holding a woven bracelet. She proffered it to Lou, who gave it a quick sniff and then barked confidently, as if to say, "Oh, *her*. Why didn't you say so?"

Sherwood was adamant that she wanted to come with us, but Eli and Victor both vetoed the idea. "Too dangerous," Eli said. "For all we know, this might be nothing more than a ploy to get you away from the safety of this house."

There wasn't any reason to drag Campbell along either. We could drop her off at my place, start our search in the Mission, and expand out from there. At least it would be easy navigating the city at night when the traffic is light. But it turned out we didn't have to go anywhere. As we walked through the front door, Lou stopped. He turned in a semicircle, nose quivering in the night air. Finally he stood stock still and faced due west, one paw lifted off the ground in his psychic scenting position. There was nothing in that direction but the Great Highway and the Pacific Ocean. And the dark expanse of Ocean Beach at night.

Lou took a couple of slow steps forward, then stopped and looked back over his shoulder at us. We followed automatically. Ocean Beach is no more than a few hundred yards from where we stood, and it's a common meeting

place at night for older teens and young adults. Bonfires
dot the beach, surrounded by party people, marijuana, and
freely flowing beer. It can be dangerous, but it can be a lot
of fun as well. A good place to look for a missing girl.

Before we'd gone more than a few steps, Victor halted.
"Wait here," he said, and ran back into the house. When he
came out he was carrying a heavy flashlight, one of those
halogen Maglites, the ones cops carry that light up the area
like a searchlight.

The Great Highway is two blocks from Victor's house,
and the sparse traffic let us scoot right across and onto the
beach. Lou headed north toward the nearest bonfire, then
swerved and continued past it along the beach. He darted
back and forth with tentative movements, hesitant, unsure.
A quarter mile down the beach, he angled up away from
the surf and abruptly sat down. I had no idea what he was
doing; there wasn't anything in either direction as far as I
could see. I suspected he'd momentarily lost the trail, but
when he continued to sit there, whining softly, I looked all
around.

Victor exhaled sharply and flashed his light on the sand
in front of us. I looked again but still saw nothing. Then it
clicked. I really was seeing nothing. Someone had chosen
an area of sand and layered it over with a concealment. The
spell was hardly noticeable since any one area of beach
sand looks pretty much like any other, but it was obvious
once I noticed it. Victor cleared the spell off with a couple
of words and a gesture as if he were flicking water off his
fingertips. The sand wavered and cleared, but I still
couldn't see anything but sand.

Victor handed me the flashlight, got down on his knees,
and started carefully scooping away sand. For a moment I
was puzzled; then I wasn't. Lou had been asked to find
Jenna. He had led us to this empty dark spot on the beach,
and now Victor was crouched down and digging in the
sand. The implication was not pleasant.

It only took him a minute to uncover the first part of
her body, a small clenched hand. Then, an arm and a

shoulder. The arm was limp, which meant that rigor had
come and gone. She'd probably been dead a couple of
days, then. A faint smell of rotting fish came from the
grave, but it wasn't bad enough yet to send us away retch-
ing and puking.

Victor finally reached her head and brushed away the
covering sand. She'd been buried faceup and her once
spiky hair was now stringy and matted. Hordes of sand
fleas swarmed through it. Half-closed sightless eyes stared
up at the night sky. Campbell made a horrified sound and
crossed herself. Unexpected from a Wiccan and magical
practitioner, but childhood beliefs are seated deeply.

As I played the flashlight beam over Jenna's face, her
eyes caught the light and gleamed with an aliveness so
bright I almost dropped the light. Stories I'd heard of
necromancy came rushing back and I almost turned tail
and ran. Eli's voice snapped me out of it.

"Mason, did you see that? Move the light over her face
again."

I did, and the same gleam sparkled out. Victor reached
out a hand and thumbed one eyelid back. The lid stubbornly stuck fast before finally tearing free. The eye had
been transformed into crystal, like the Ifrit eyes, although
without the same luminous clarity. Instead, it was cloudy
and diffuse. Victor reached out and prodded the eyeball
cautiously as Eli kneeled down next to him.

"Hard as stone," Victor said.

"Or a diamond."

"What's going on?" I asked.

Eli levered his bulk upright with effort. He was still
feeling the effects of the Gaki. "It looks very much like
Christoph is no longer satisfied to use Ifrit eyes. Now he's
trying it on practitioners as well."

"How could that be?" asked Campbell.

"It is hard to believe. Maybe he thought it would work
on her because she was a Finder. Similar to Lou here."

"How awful."

A look of grim satisfaction settled on Eli's face. "Yes, it

is. But it didn't succeed. And Christoph made a huge mistake when he attempted it."

"Why is that?"

"He was only able to transform the eyes partway. And when he failed to complete the transformation, part of his psychic energy got trapped inside. Only a infinitesimal part, but still enough to cement a connection between himself and the eyes. Enough to find him."

I didn't like the sound of that. Using body parts from a dead person, transformed or not, smacked of black magic, and I told him so.

"I would never ask you to do anything like that," he said. "Or Victor. It would be too psychically damaging. But there are others we can call on."

I didn't like the sound of that either, but Eli was no longer paying attention to me. He held out his good hand to Victor. "Your cell phone please."

Victor straightened up and handed it over without a word. Eli walked up the beach a ways, taking Victor with him. They were away for what seemed like a long time. Campbell and I huddled together like children, standing over Jenna's body, trying not to look at it, instead staring out across the dark, chilly beach. Finally, Eli and Victor returned.

"He'll do it," Eli said," but he needs one of the eyes."

Victor nodded briefly and, reaching into his pocket, pulled out a folding knife. Be prepared was his motto. He snapped open the blade and crouched back down next to the body.

"Hold the light steady," he told me.

I was doing the best I could, but my hand wasn't cooperating. I turned my head, unwilling to look, but as soon as I did the light I was holding shifted off her face.

"Damn it, Mason, hold it steady." Stress caused his voice to crack. So he wasn't as cold-blooded as he liked to pretend.

He inserted the tip of the blade into the corner of the eye socket and began sawing around it like he was sectioning a grapefruit. Campbell turned away. It was over quickly, thank God. Victor pried at the eye with the blade, getting the tip into the corner, and with a sucking sound, it popped out into his hand. He handed it to Eli who stuffed it quickly into the pocket of his coat. Victor wiped the blade, put away the knife, and immediately began to pile sand back over Jenna's body.

"You're not going to just leave her here?" said Campbell. If I had asked that question it would have received a biting reply, but Victor was matter-of-fact with her.

"We are. There's nothing we can do for her. I'll restore the concealment spell, and by the time anyone finds her, any traces of our presence will be long gone. The police will consider her just be another unfortunate runaway who came to a bad end. Meanwhile, we've got work to do."

The distance was short, but it was a long walk back up the dark beach. At the house, Eli broke the news to Sherwood. She said nothing, just sat on the couch shaking her head and twisting the woven hemp bracelet with her fingers. Victor immediately assumed his take charge persona.

"We obviously can't meet here," he said to Eli. "And I have a few things to take care of first. Shall I meet you over there?"

"Over where?" I asked. They both ignored me.

"Good idea," Eli said. "Mason, can you give me half an hour, then meet me at my flat?"

I was stunned. I've known Eli for close to twenty years, but I'd never been to his flat. He never invites anyone over, no matter the reason. Even Victor has never been there, and he's known Eli longer than I have. It's a strange quirk of his, but one of such long standing that no one even thinks twice about it anymore. Things were progressing rapidly, but I had no idea in what direction. Enough is enough. I decided I wasn't going anywhere without an explanation.

"Not until you tell me what's happening," I said. "I mean it. What's going on?"

"Mason, we don't have time," Victor said.

I sat down stubbornly on the couch next to Sherwood and crossed my arms. Eli looked exasperated but gave in.

"I've solicited some help. Do you know who Harry Keller is?"

"Oh," I said.

I knew the name, if not the man. It was the nom de guerre of the foremost practitioner of black arts in the Bay Area. Obviously not his true name—it would be like a musician calling himself Count Basie, since the name Harry Keller was that of a respected old-time stage illusionist. Right before Houdini. In fact, Houdini took his first name from Harry Keller, just like he had taken his last name from Jean Robert-Houdin.

And that's why we couldn't meet at Victor's. The wards around his place wouldn't let anyone inside who carried that special taint of darkness a black practitioner carries, and Victor wasn't about to modify them with Christoph still running loose. It also explained who would be using that frightful eye. But still, I found it hard to believe that Eli, the very soul of reason, was turning to a black practitioner for help.

"Dark Arts? Are you serious?"

"Deadly serious. I've already been talking with him, even before this. He can do things we can't."

Like conjuring with parts of dead human beings.

"Or won't," I said. "What makes you think he'll be interested in helping us?"

"Ordinarily, he wouldn't. But this is different, beyond the pale. Even the worst Dark Path practitioner won't countenance what Christoph's been doing." I wasn't so sure.

"But can he really be that much help? Haven't you always said that the whole dark side crap is exactly that?"

"I always believed it was. But lately I've come to suspect I might have been too hasty in dismissing such things. Not that there's an actual Devil, of course, or that one can make a pact with dark forces, but I can't deny there's something to it. I've had to adjust my thinking to take that possibility into account."

"Oh, come on, Eli, black magic? Invocation of evil deities? Pentagrams? What next, the blood of virgins? What does any of that have to do with manipulating magical energy?"

Eli sighed. "I'm not sure anymore. Dark rituals are constructs, of course, but they do come from traditions handed down for centuries. If there wasn't something to them they wouldn't have survived. In any case, belief systems can be powerful, and dark side concepts can be very powerful indeed."

This was disturbing. Eli had always been the voice of moderation, the academic skeptic. If he was now buying into the objective existence of evil, we were all in trouble.

"So, what now?" I asked.

"We need to be proactive. Harry is stopping by my place on his way home. Give me thirty minutes to talk with him alone, if you would, and then come on over. We'll decide how to proceed then and accompany him back to his house."

I told Campbell she should stay at Victor's, but she wasn't interested. "I'll come along," she said. "Maybe I can even be of some help." I thought she also was curious to see what Harry Keller was like.

Campbell and Sherwood spent the next thirty minutes talking together in low tones. I don't know what they said, but Sherwood looked more at ease by the time we left. I fired up the van and we headed over to the Richmond. Lou immediately curled up in the back for a nap. If he had been a person, I'd have said he was in denial about what he'd done to Moxie and was using sleep as a coping mechanism. Lou being an Ifrit, I couldn't say. Maybe he was just tired.

I found a parking spot a couple of blocks away. Eli's place is on the top floor of a two-flat Edwardian, the lower flat being empty courtesy of Victor. Keeping it unoccupied was a necessity considering the experiments Eli conducted. It wouldn't do to have curious downstairs neighbors, and Victor could afford it.

I must admit I was curious to see it. Inside, the decor was all grays and blacks with a few muted earth tones thrown in. A couple of low tables, a huge comfortable reading chair with a lamp alongside, and a hardwood floor. Very minimalist, like a hugely upscale Ikea. Except that every wall was covered floor to ceiling with books: on history, on comparative religion, on magic, on sports, on just about everything. No fiction that I could see. Eli once remarked that the average novel was a long, complicated, and uninteresting set of lies. Myself, I like a good story. Sherlock Holmes. Travis McGee. Even Harry Potter.

Fighting for space with the books, a huge collection of classical music CDs took up one entire wall, along with a McIntosh stereo system that boasted speakers six feet tall and three inches wide. Six thousand dollars if it was a penny. Victor again? Maybe Eli just spent money on what he thought important.

After letting us in, Eli sat down heavily in the comfortable chair. Standing next to a window, casually thumbing through the racks of CDs, was Harry Keller.

I couldn't place the guy for a moment, then I did. The last time I'd seen him he'd been wearing a watch cap and talking up Christoph at The Challenges. African-American, late twenties, dreadlocks and a neatly trimmed beard. It was the dreads that had thrown me. He walked away from the window and sprawled down onto an uncomfortable looking chair, legs outstretched and ankles crossed, giving me a negligent wave and a relaxed smile, very much at ease. He was wearing the standard black leather jacket over a black turtleneck. A diamond stud in his right ear and several plain metal rings on his right hand completed the urban look.

Louie stiffened the moment he saw him but didn't growl. Suspicious, but willing to reserve judgment. Harry stayed in his chair when Eli introduced him.

"Harry Keller," Eli said. "I told him most of your experiences with Christoph and he's agreed to help."

I leaned over and shook hands, but couldn't help remaining skeptical. I'd heard quite a bit about this man over the years and not much of it inspired confidence.

"You know, I'm kind of surprised," I said to him, deliberately rude. "I would have thought you'd be more likely to be getting in line for a few of Christoph's special jewels."

"Well, fuck you, too, Jack," he said, without any particular rancor. "I'm no angel, but that dude Christoph is way out of control." I was subconsciously expecting some sort of lilting Jamaican accent what with the dreads and all, but his speech was pure New York City. "Eli's clued me in on what Christoph's been doing. No way I'd ever have anything to do with that shit. No way in hell. Just because I'm a 'black' practitioner doesn't mean I'm a sicko. Believe it or not, I even possess some ethics."

"Sure," I said. "You're a regular saint."

"Hey man, lighten up, will you. It's all about the most efficient use of power, you know. I don't take any particular pleasure in my methods. If I could get better results by helping widows and orphans, why, I'd be the poster boy for UNICEF."

"I see," I said. "So, you're not a bad person, you just do bad things."

Eli interrupted. "Sorry, Mason, we don't have the luxury of philosophical discussion. Time is not our ally. Remember, Christoph could be operating on some other poor Ifrit right now, as we speak. Or, God forbid, even a practitioner."

I still didn't like it. Then again, who was I to judge? It's not like I was the purest of beings myself. And we could certainly use all the help we could get. Besides the general danger, there was my specific situation. Christoph was not happy with me, and the next thing he sent along to pay a visit might well be worse than a Gaki, although it was hard to imagine how that could be.

"Welcome aboard, Harry," I said, sarcastically. "So, what do you think? Any bright ideas? Any clue where Christoph might be holed up?"

"Well, yes and no," he replied. "No, I don't know where Christoph is hanging out. But I do know a way to find him. Or rather, to summon up something that can find him."

"Of course," I said. "Black arts. Demon summoning. Why didn't I think of that?"

Eli pointed an admonishing finger at me. "Before you get on your skeptical high horse, Mason, you might want to recall something called a Gaki."

"Okay," I conceded. "You do have a point."

Harry Keller whistled. "That's nothing you want to mess with," he said, admiringly. "How did you get away?"

"Not important. Can you do anything like that?"

"Oh, yes. Only nastier. Much nastier. With the . . . uh, object Eli has, I can tie it to Christoph wherever he is."

I had serious doubts about practitioners who believed they could summon demons, but the Gaki had come from somewhere, hadn't it?

"Have you done this before?" I asked, curious.

Harry laughed self-consciously. "To be honest, I've never quite had the nerve. Not with this one. And, I figure it'll take at least three strong practitioners, maybe four, to call it up."

"Victor?" I asked, glancing at Eli.

"He'll be meeting us at Harry's."

Harry tried to reassure me. "Between you, me, Victor, and Eli, it'll be a piece of cake."

"And you can control this thing?" I asked. "Just checking."

"Well, there's always the element of risk. But if it works, it'll be awesome."

That word "if" again. Like "should," and "probably," not one of my favorites. And I still didn't trust him. I flashed him a big, insincere smile.

"But you're willing to take the risk, right? Because you're a good guy and want to help us out?"

Harry dropped his smartass demeanor. "You may not believe this," he said. "But this Ifrit thing is totally over the line, as far as I'm concerned. And now that girl. It's sick, you know?" He hesitated. "And besides, Christoph seems to have it in for me these days. Somehow, he got the idea that I stole one of his gems—before I knew what they were," he added hastily.

I nodded. "I see."

That was better. One of the few things you can always trust in a person, whatever their agenda, is self-interest.

Campbell had been sitting quietly next to Eli, listening, not saying a word, apparently content to be ignored. She broke in suddenly, her voice quiet but easily heard.

"This is a very, very, bad idea," she said, shaking her head.

Harry Keller glanced at her dismissively, but Eli said, "Why so?"

"It just is. This whole approach is . . . misguided. You can fight fire with fire, but you can't fight the Devil with the Devil. I've had dealings with black arts people, probably more often than you. And it's true, they're not all as black as they're painted." Harry inclined his head in mock acknowledgment. "But believe me, it doesn't matter how important the situation is, or how desperate, or even how noble your motives might be. Even if you succeed, it always turns out the same way. Badly."

Eli sat silently, thinking, and finally said. "I tend to agree with you in principle, Campbell, but this time we don't have much choice. Christoph has grown strong, strong enough so that I'm not sure we can handle him now. Somebody else could end up dead. Harry here has his own special way of dealing with threats, and just this once, he may have the right idea."

Campbell said nothing. The expression on her face told me that she wasn't buying it for a moment, but knew nothing she could say was going to change Eli's mind.

"We need to get going," said Eli, getting to his feet. "Victor will be on his way over to Harry's by now.

Campbell walked over to stand beside me. "Can you drop me off back at Victor's?" she asked. "I need to get home and my car is still parked there."

The unspoken subtext was now that Harry was involved, she wasn't going to have anything more to do with us. But I think it was more than just that. She'd finally reached the end of her reserves. Twenty-four hours ago she had been happily ensconced in her cabin in the woods, living a sane and balanced life. Three hours after coming down to help me find Lou, she found herself running for her life, a berserk Christoph in pursuit. Then she watched us dig up the body of a dead teenager and gouge out one of her eyes. Now she was listening to otherwise sane practitioners talking about their plans for summoning demons. She wanted no more of it and I can't say I blamed her. It was ugly and it wasn't her fight in the first place.

"Sure," I said. I looked at Harry. "Where do you live?"

"Up on Potrero Hill."

Lou jumped up and waited by the door. "Okay," I said. "I guess it's time to go."

HARRY, NATURALLY, RODE A MOTORCYCLE. A BLACK Kawasaki Ninja. Eli joined me and Campbell in my van and we dropped off Campbell at Victor's. The BMW was gone, which meant Victor was already on his way. Twenty minutes later, we joined him in front of a surprisingly sedate and mundane house on Potrero Hill. Harry was already there. To my surprise, Maggie had accompanied Victor. Unlike Lou, she seldom left the comforts of home unless she had to.

On the way over I had pumped Eli about Harry Keller and his ilk, and their rather limited views on the working of the craft. The whole black magic thing seemed antithetical to everything Eli had taught me over the years, and now it seemed as if he had done a one-eighty and was swallowing the concept whole without so much as a hiccough.

"I can't believe you're buying into this demon summoning thing," I said. Eli seemed almost embarrassed. "Me neither," he admitted. "But Harry gets results. Honestly, what's the difference whether he believes he is summoning up a demon from another dimension or if he's creating it solely by his own personal energy? It's all semantics. Either way, if whatever he conjures up manages to rip off your arms and legs, the actual mechanism by which it does so is rather a moot point, no? Take the Gaki, for example. Is it actually a creature with an existence of its own? Or did Christoph's sending take that exact form because of the power of myth, the fact that others have used that embodiment before?"

"Inquiring minds want to know," I said.

Eli gave me a weary look. "Sorry, Mason, but you've got one of the least inquiring minds I've ever encountered. Besides, I suspect that the truth of the matter is not an either/or proposition. Questions dealing with the nature of magic and reality seldom are."

"Well, good, at least you've cleared that up," I said. "But here's a far more practical question: can this guy be trusted?"

"I doubt it. But for right now, our interests are identical. He'd rather help us than face an angry Christoph alone. Enemy of my enemy, you know?"

"I guess," I said, and dropped it.

Harry's house sat quietly toward the top of Wisconsin Street. It was a good-sized two-story dwelling with weathered gray shingles and bay windows on the bottom floor. The roof looked as if it could use some attention, and one of the drain spouts had separated away from the building. Either Harry Keller wasn't as successful as reputation had it or he was purposely trying to keep a low profile. Still, I was disappointed, having half expected a massive black Victorian with spirals and turrets and maybe a bat or two. I should learn to lower my expectations.

"I hope we aren't making a huge mistake," I said to Eli. "No matter what his abilities, from everything I've heard, this guy can be seriously unpleasant."

"Yes, I know," he muttered, easing himself out of the van.

Inside, the house was more satisfying. A short hallway led to a living room that held nothing unusual, except for a few unpleasant looking chairs and a tall glass cabinet which housed an immense collection of dolls. The cabinet contained everything from modern-style Barbies to homemade rag dolls a century old. The dolls, which might have seemed charming in some other place, took on decidedly disturbing overtones considering the inclinations of the owner of the house. On the back wall hung a framed movie poster from the forties, proclaiming in German: "Spi-oncentral" starring Conrad Veidt and Vivien Leigh. Conrad stared out at me through steel rimmed glasses under a military cap while Vivien regarded him with either love or horror.

At the rear of the front room a narrow staircase led up to the second floor, and that's where it started looking theatrical. Now, this is more like it, I thought. A series of tiny rooms interconnected by randomly placed doorways filled the upper story, creating a rabbit-warren maze. We passed through several of them, each having a different color scheme, or rather a different hue, since they all were done in shades of gray, brown, and black. Occasionally a deep red leather chair or couch broke the monotony.

Harry led us into a back room, which was larger than the others, and motioned for us to sit. I lowered myself gingerly into one of the red leather chairs with the gut feeling it was not an entirely benign resting place. More like a scarlet mouth just waiting for me to sink back so it could snap shut like a Venus flytrap and suck me dry. Then my withered husk would remain upright as a quaint conversation piece. I'm not usually so fanciful, but Lou must have felt something similar since he refused to come near it.

Harry walked to the back of the room and opened a tall cabinet made of dark wood, carved throughout with vines and flowers. From it he removed a brazier much like the one Campbell had used and set it on a long table, which

had been pushed against the side wall. Next came an assortment of dried herbs and a large crystal that looked like
rose quartz, except that it was a smoky green. Again, very
familiar. I had been expecting something more flamboyant,
but I guess all rituals of evocation are similar at heart, differing only in intent and purpose. Finally he took out an
object wrapped in cloth and placed it next to the crystal. He
uncovered it slowly as if revealing a rare treasure. Inside
was a long double-bladed knife with a black handle, another analogue to a "white magic" tool. But where the
athame, as the Wiccans call it, is used for symbolic or
cleansing purposes, I had a suspicion that this blade's purpose was not so innocent.

"I don't suppose there's any chance that's just a prop?"
I asked. Harry favored me with a humorless smile.

"You can hardly call up a proper demon without blood,
can you now?" he said. "In fact, to do it correctly, what's
really needed is a blood sacrifice." His eyes flicked around
the room. "Any volunteers?"

I was reasonably sure he was joking, but I didn't like the
way his gaze kept coming back to rest on Lou. Maybe he
had been closer to Christoph than he was willing to admit.
Lou didn't care for it, either. He overcame his aversion to
the chair I was in, trotted over, and pressed himself against
my leg. I could feel the vibration of a subvocalized growl.
Maggie had draped herself around Victor's neck, looking
imperturbable as usual. It wasn't at all unusual for Harry
not to have an Ifrit, most practitioners don't, but the way
he kept looking at Lou made me wonder if perhaps there
might be another, less charitable explanation.

Harry set up the brazier on a stubby tripod and put what
looked like a propane torch underneath and lit it with a
kitchen match that he took from his jacket pocket. No little cans of Sterno for this boy. As it was heating, he took a
piece of chalk from the other pocket and drew a five-
pointed star on the floor. It was a rather sloppy star, with
spidery lines and uneven points, but that didn't seem to
bother him. Next came a large can labeled, "Blue Crab Bay

Sea Salt." He poured out a generous portion, creating a circle around the star. So far this was basic "Magic for Dummies" stuff, available at any New Age bookstore or Web site. I was not impressed. Maybe he had something a bit heavier up his sleeve.

A moment later, my hopes were unpleasantly realized when he picked up the knife, held his arm over the cauldron, and sliced a long shallow gash along the inside of his arm. Blood immediately started dripping into the pot, hissing as it hit the heated surface. An unpleasant, cloying, coppery odor started to fill the room. Harry looked at me and gestured me forward with the tip of the knife.

"You must be joking," I said.

"The more blood, the stronger the incantation."

"Try your other arm," I suggested.

He offered another one of his smiles.

"To bind this particular entity I've got to take blood from each person here. In fact, anyone who hasn't mixed their blood for the incantation could find themselves in deep shit. You can't ever be sure of controlling a demon this powerful and raising it without blood protection is just flat-out crazy."

Better and better. We were entering fruitcake city. Victor apparently had no such qualms. He stepped forward and offered his arm, turning his head to regard me over his shoulder.

"If we aren't willing to accept the premise, Mason, then there's not much point in doing it at all," he said.

"Accepting the premise is one thing. Donating my precious blood is another thing entirely. I'm willing to believe that Harry here has found a way to access vast reserves of untapped power, but I don't believe my blood really needs to be part of it."

"You can believe any fucking thing you want," said Harry, "but I can't raise a demon without blood."

He had been holding onto Victor's proffered arm while we were discussing the issue, and suddenly made a quick slash down the forearm, holding the arm over the bowl so that the blood ran down into the bowl and mingled with his own. Victor, being Victor, didn't flinch and managed to look totally disinterested in the process. He stepped back, regarding his arm thoughtfully, and Eli stepped up next. "In for a penny . . ." he said, and held out his good arm for the same procedure. A quick incision, more blood dripping, and then it was my turn. They all looked expectantly at me. I hesitated, then figured what the hell. Far be it from me to spoil the party.

For reasons I don't fully understand, self-healing is incredibly difficult, even for something as simple as a shallow cut. Still, Victor could patch me up later, and even with my limited healing abilities I should be able to return the favor. I didn't think Campbell would be too willing to help, even if she was around. Harry took my arm and cut quickly along the length. I got the impression he sliced just a wee bit deeper than was strictly necessary, but that might have been paranoia talking. It hurt like hell, and after a goodly amount of blood had dripped into the stew I backed off, my arm still bleeding.

"Don't forget Maggie," I said sarcastically, pointing toward Victor. Maggie hissed and showed her fangs.

"Don't need to. The Ifrits won't be affected anyway." At least he had sufficient judgment not to try to take blood from an uncooperative feline.

I watched, still trying to staunch the bleeding, as he gathered up a handful of herbs and threw them into the mix. They were more like noxious weeds than herbs, and dark smoke instantly puffed up, filling the room with a dank and bitter distillation.

"Now the eye," Harry said, holding out his hand. Eli silently handed it over. Harry placed it carefully, almost reverently, into the iron bowl. Next he went to each of us in turn, putting his hands on our shoulders, staring deep into our eyes. His way of gathering magical energies, I guess. I was hoping to see his eyes start to glow, full of power, but they steadfastly remained a light brown. That confirmed for me that he was at least full of something.

He returned to the table, picked up the green crystal, and started a solemn chant. Now, I've got nothing against chanting; I've used it myself more than a few times. But as I've said, for me chanting is about rhythms and patterns, basically a focusing device to channel energy. Harry seemed to be going about it differently, invoking names right out of H. P. Lovecraft. Not only that, he was clearly going to great lengths to pronounce everything just right, as if any of us would have known the difference. We all poured energy into him, using him as a conduit and increasing his power. Hopefully, it would prove enough.

The smoke was becoming chokingly thick. I'd decided I'd had about enough, demon or no demon, when I felt a cold chill enter the room. It's true that in San Francisco there's always a cold chill entering rooms, but this had a psychic component, definitely more of the spirit than the flesh. I began to feel jumpy, nervous, and ill at ease, and the feeling grew stronger as the smoke grew thicker. I glanced over at Eli, who was looking not so comfortable himself. Victor affected his usual nonchalant unconcern.

Harry kept chanting, eyes now closed and face upturned in religious ecstasy. The smoke started swirling around the brazier in a counterclockwise direction, solidifying as it revolved. A figure began to resolve out of the murk, coming clearer with every passing second. It grew in bulk, insubstantial, yet projecting an aura of mass and strength, power and force. It shifted and roiled, flickering through a series of changes as fast as the eye could follow. A horned demon. A bear with a grotesquely deformed head. A giant slug with teeth. Other things I had absolutely no frame of reference for. I had seen things like this before, but this particular apparition presented such an aspect of malevolence and cruelty that it literally took my breath away. Or maybe it was the fact that by now the entire room was filled with thick choking fumes.

There was finally silence as Harry stopped his chanting. The smoke demon, or whatever it was, stopped spinning and regarded us playfully. It looked like it was composed of old melted tires, strong and rubbery, and drippy around the edges. It had no defined head, no features, no eyes, yet still projected a distinct personality, and that personality was not pleasant. I felt my mouth growing dry with an undefined fear. Something about its very presence made me want to stay very still and quiet. I fervently prayed that this thing really was under Harry's control.

"My God!" Eli whispered. "What is it?"

Harry said something under his breath. I couldn't quite catch it, but it sounded uncomfortably like "Uh-oh." He looked at us and smiled, but it wasn't the easy Harry Keller grin that he'd been flashing earlier. It was a nervous, tentative smile, hardly the expression you hope to see on the face of a lion tamer, especially when you're right in the cage along with the big cats.

"I . . . I'm not exactly sure," he stammered. "It's not what I was expecting."

I wanted to snarl out to Eli something like "I told you so," but my throat had closed up. Not from fear, mind you, just from the smoke in the room.

The demon started swirling around the circle, sending wispy tendrils of smoke into every corner, probing every crevice, searching for a weakness. It finally coalesced on the near side of the circle and started exerting pressure. The curtain of air that defined where the circle lay wavered and shimmered like a desert mirage, then started to bulge out like a swollen blister about to pop. I hadn't been enthusiastic about any of this in the first place, and now I got the feeling we were about to be very sorry indeed.

Harry's supposed expertise hadn't impressed me from the start, but now I was earnestly hoping to be proved wrong. I wasn't. Instead of binding the demon with arcane gestures or words of power or whatever it is that dark practitioners do, he started sidling away from the circle, moving toward the door. Before I realized what was happening, Harry was behind me. Now I was situated between him and the malignant spirit in the circle, acting as a convenient human shield. A flicker of remembrance ran through

my mind, me standing in front of the Hall of Justice with
the guy known as Spaceman, iron crosses hanging off his
nose ring, as he intoned his prophetic warning: "The black
man is not your friend!" Well, no shit.

The black man. The African-American? The black ma-
gician? Man dressed in black? Hey, why not all three! The
great thing about warning prophecies is that they are always opaque, always inscrutable, right up until the moment when it's too late. Then it becomes all too clear.

The blister on the side of the circle swelled to the size
of a watermelon, and then, as it broke, so did Harry's
nerve. He bolted for the door and was out of the room before anyone could react, leaving us alone with the thing.
There was a loud rushing sound like air escaping a giant
balloon and the demon squeezed through the break in the
circle, circling around like water swirling through a funnel.
A foul smell comprised of burning rubber, rotting meat,
and even more unpleasant odors permeated the room. It became almost impossible to see through the darkness. I felt
I should do something, but was paralyzed, filled with inco-
herent terror and despair. My last rational thought was,
"Well this is not good at all."

SIXTEEN

I STILL DON'T REMEMBER MANY DETAILS. IN THAT way it was like a dream, though not like any dream you'd ever want to experience.

Three types of dreams bubble out of our subconscious. The first is the garden-variety dream, the movie which unfolds behind closed eyes. With a familiar narrative thread much like our waking life, it can be joyful, grim as death, or as boring and mundane as a bus ride.

The second type is more disjointed. You may find yourself in two places simultaneously, or even *be* two people at once, both actor and observer in a baffling dream scenario.

The third is the bad one, and that's the one I was in. The ego, the very sense of self, had vanished. In dark and formless chaos, synesthesia reigned. Touch became sound; sound, emotion. Emotion metamorphosed into a tactile and plastic rhythm, physically pulling and stretching at the fabric of reality. It was difficult to see, difficult to even imagine what vision might be. Raw emotions permeate this universe, unfiltered by any structure that could give them context. A condition so alien to waking consciousness, a state so primitive and chaotic, that it defies even metaphor.

When I emerged from this dream state it took a few moments to remember not only where I was, but who and what as well. All that remained was that overpowering emotion.

When I finally could see, the first thing I noticed was Eli's flickering image, nearly invisible, black skin merging into smoky haze. He bulked large out of the smoke, swirling in and out of focus. The instant I saw him, long suppressed resentment flared. Eli. The very person who had got me into all this in the first place. The one whose smugly spouted theories were going to get me killed. Who the fuck did he think he was, anyway? Always criticizing. Always superior, always putting on airs, like his shit didn't stink. Well, I finally could see that clearly, and now he was going to learn a painful lesson. I'd put up with his bullshit for way too long.

I started gathering energy for a killing strike. God knows there was enough to work with. Before I could properly focus, though, I found myself gasping for air. The black fumes, still chokingly thick, settled in my throat. Hot tendrils of smoke curled their way into my lungs. Within seconds I was coughing uncontrollably. A heavy weight pressed down on my chest and the dark smoke took on a reddish tinge as oxygen stopped flowing to my brain. I thought the smoke was overcoming me, but it wasn't just the smoke.

From the corner of my eye, I caught a flicker of motion and turned my head just in time to catch sight of Victor. I had been so fixated on Eli that I hadn't remembered Victor was here as well. Not very smart. He was rhythmically squeezing his hands together, as if he were pumping air into something. Or out of something. Like my lungs. I had forgotten what a dangerous little asshole he could be. My arms grew weak and my vision narrowed until his face filled the entire field. He was staring at me with a mixture of hatred, disgust, and contempt, a judgment I returned in spades. Unable to fight back, I sank weakly to my knees.

But as I had forgotten Victor, so had he forgotten Eli. Eli bounded across the room, grabbed him by the throat with one arm, lifted him off his feet, and plastered him against the wall.

"Goddamned little prick," he snarled.

The pressure on my chest eased as Victor's attention was understandably deflected. I was able to breathe again. It gave me a second chance, and this time I had them both in my sights. Eli and Victor were now locked so closely together that I could easily get them both at once. I examined the swirling patterns of the smoke. I pulled the killing sharpness from the knife that was still lying on the table. I keenly felt the currents of hatred coursing like electricity around the room. I took a deep breath, savoring the choking cloud and the foul odor, so perfect for my needs.

I gathered all those things together and fashioned death. Then, right before I unleashed it, I paused. A shift was occurring in the makeup of the murky fog, slight, but still enough to throw me off. The smoke was less dense and the odor subtly different. Under the putrid stench that filled the room was another stink, different, cloying yet also sharply astringent. It was unpleasant and somehow familiar. Pungent. Reeking. Oddly commonplace.

Along with this odor there came a hissing, popping sound, as if cold water had been poured into a hot frying pan. The new odor grew ever more pronounced. It so distracted me that I was unable to complete my attack spell. What was that smell? It was . . . it was . . . I almost had it. It was . . . it was cat piss!

This revelation was immediately confirmed by the sound of Maggie squalling loudly with pain and outrage. The noise knifed through my consciousness and brought me up short. Maggie! And Lou. Where was Lou? I shook my head, trying to clear away the cobwebs, which never works.

Lou's sharp bark cut through the remaining haze, which

was rapidly clearing. The dullness which had been cloud-
ing my mind was lifting as well. Panic overtook me and I
turned back to where Victor and Eli had been struggling,
praying that one or both weren't seriously hurt, or worse,
dead. Eli had set Victor back on the floor and was in the
process of apologizing profusely. Victor, rubbing his throat
gingerly, was waving him away. Harry Keller was nowhere
to be seen. Eli looked over toward me.

"Are you all right, Mason?"

I nodded. "I think so. You?"

He gravely inclined his head. "I believe that I am."

"What the hell just happened?" I asked.

Eli started to raise his hands to his head, forgetting his
bad arm. He flinched and dropped it back to his side. With
his other hand he started rubbing his forehead. Apparently
I was not the only one with a headache.

"The demon," he said. "A most devious entity. It was
never its intention to tear off our heads. It didn't need to. It
just twisted our thoughts and emotions and we did the rest
ourselves."

"Boy, did we ever. But what happened? What made us
stop?"

Victor gave a hoarse croak and gestured toward the
table where the brazier had been burning. I stumbled over
and immediately understood what had happened. At some
point after the smoke had filled the room, Lou and Maggie
had jumped up on the table and relieved themselves of
every drop in their bladders, straight into the container, ex-
tinguishing the smouldering material. Lou had supplied
most of the volume, but Maggie had provided that distinctive cat reek which first caught my attention. She had paid
a price, though. Louie had just lifted his leg and aimed, but
Maggie had needed to squat directly over the flames in
order to douse them. The fur on the back of her haunches
was singed and there were several places where the bare
skin showed through, blistered and red. I hadn't known she
had it in her. She went up several notches in my estimation.

Victor came over, picked her up gently, and looked closely at the burned spots.

"She'll be okay," he wheezed.

Eli walked up to him and started hesitantly to speak, obviously embarrassed. "Victor, about what I called you . . ."

"Prick? Believe me, I've been called worse."

"Still, there's no excuse . . ."

I interrupted. "If you want to apologize, Eli, how about saying you're sorry for trying to kill him? And oh, by the way, he was trying to kill me at the time. And I was trying to kill you. So it all comes out even, really."

"I just . . ."

"And if it makes you feel any better about what you said, you don't want to know what I was thinking about you." I shook my head. "I'm ashamed."

Eli smiled, the first real smile I'd seen from him in days. "Oh, I think I might have some vague idea. Seriously, Mason, none of us are as evolved as we would like to think. Right below the surface lurk primitive emotions carried over from before we were even human. Survival mechanisms. Aggression toward rivals. Distrust of all that is not-me. That entity was created to bring out the fears and prejudices everyone has buried under their civilized veneer. We're not really quite that vicious—those emotions were amplified and distorted in truly malevolent fashion, magnified by the smoke in the room. There's your true black magic. A little magical enhancement, and voila—we're at each others throats." He glanced at Victor. "Literally."

"It didn't take much, did it?" I said, sadly. "By the way, Victor, what exactly was in *your* mind when you were trying to squeeze the life out of me?"

He shook his head and pointed at his throat, miming inability to vocalize. Yeah, sure. I turned my attention back to Eli.

"What about Harry Keller?" I asked.

"Clearly we misjudged him," he said. "I think he summoned up something more than he could handle."

"You think? No, I mean, where is he?"

Eli had started poking around in Harry's cabinet, examining the items inside. "Right now I'm more concerned about where that demon might be," he said, picking up what appeared to be a human skull. "If it dissipated, fine, but if it escaped the room it could cause real havoc on the outside."

I tilted my head to listen. Outside, I thought I could hear the sound of distant voices raised in anger and confusion. Then, quite clearly, the sound of emergency sirens. We stared at each other.

"Not good," I said, fighting the urge to say I told you so.

"This is our fault," said Eli. "We need to do something about it before people get hurt. I don't think the demon will be as potent out in the open air, but the average citizen won't have even as much resistance to it as we did, which wasn't much. It will be capable of some real mischief."

I remembered the aspect of the demon, and shuddered. "And how do we go about that?"

"If we can find Harry Keller, he should be able to help us," Eli said, putting down the skull he'd been examining.

"If we find him, I'll kill him myself," I said. "I'm not so sure he didn't intend this all along."

He hadn't. At the bottom of the stairs he lay curled up quietly, as if asleep, except that his head was tilted at a bad angle. Without the smartass attitude, he looked a lot younger, almost a teenager. Perhaps the demon he'd summoned wasn't restricted to psychic attacks. Or maybe he had fallen down the stairs in his panicked flight and broken his neck. There was no way to know, and I guess it didn't matter to Harry now.

"My apologies," I told him.

Victor bent down to examine him, although there wasn't much doubt. He shook his head. "He's not going to be any help to anyone," he said.

When we walked outside, the sounds of shouting and police sirens were louder. I looked over toward the Mission District where the commotion was coming from. It had started raining lightly again, and it was too far away to see exactly what was happening, but I could just make out a dark, smokey swirl like a giant dust devil hovering over the streets.

We piled into Victor's BMW, a better pursuit car than my rattletrap van, and sped off down the hill. It was easy to follow the trail; on every street corner people were fighting, throwing clumsy punches or wrestling ineffectively on the ground. It could have been much worse—not that many souls wander the streets of upper Potrero Hill at night. Those few who had been out walking were instantly caught up in madness, but the same blind rage that fueled their fights also dulled their intellect, keeping them from coolly considering the best way to kill each other.

Still, by the time we reached the Mission, there were plenty of people out and about, and in the Mission a good many individuals walk around with handguns as a matter of course, everything from Saturday night specials to Tech-nines. Some of them might be clouded enough by rage to forget they were carrying guns, but not all. Already I could hear sporadic gunfire up ahead.

We swung down Valencia, and as we passed by a door-way on Nineteenth Street, a round fired and a neat starred hole appeared in the windshield. Victor cursed and punched the gas, getting out of harm's way. I wasn't sure if he was more upset at getting shot at or at having his beloved Beamer damaged. Everywhere, sirens blared and tires squealed as streams of black-and-whites started arriv-ing. Victor pulled over to the curb to avoid them.

Now we had another problem. The cops were arriving in droves, and they would soon be affected by the demon, too. Cops are no strangers to the emotions of rage and fear—and what they do in those situations is to fall back on their training. And their training focuses on guns. And they all have guns. And the combination of blind rage and firearms is not a good one. Not only that, but if we got too close to the demon ourselves, that same madness would re-infect us and keep us from doing anything effective.

I peered down Valencia to Twenty-fourth Street, where most of the black-and-whites were now clustered. Around them, a miniriot surged. Trash cans hurtled through the air, scraps of lumber rose and fell as people brandished improvised clubs, the sound of angry screams and glass breaking echoed down the street. A mass of late-night commuters from the underground BART station at Twenty-fourth and Mission boiled up and joined in the festivities. Right above the chaos, swirling ominously, was the familiar black cloud. It grew larger and stronger by the second, spinning wildly, feeding off the emotional energy it evoked. The cops seemed oblivious to it, probably because they had more obvious problems right in front of them. Or maybe they couldn't perceive it at all. Several of the cops were opening the trunks of their patrol cars to get at their riot guns and I heard the distinctive sounds of shotgun shells being racked into shotgun breeches. We had maybe a minute before guns started going off and blood started splattering.

I thought frantically. The demon was composed of smoke, so a strong wind might disperse it. I knew practitioners who had some control over weather, but unfortunately I wasn't one of them. Besides, a wind might just drive it to some other part of the city to start all over again. I glanced over at Victor, who was staring intently, but he didn't seem to be having any better luck with ideas than I was. Lou was sitting up, observing with curiously detached interest. Maggie appeared to be taking a nap and Eli was leaning back in his seat with his eyes closed. I hoped he was furiously calculating and hadn't decided it was time for him to take a nap as well. I had just about resigned myself to the coming bloodbath when Eli's eyes flew open.

"It's a small tornado," he said. This was not the brilliant insight I had been hoping for. He rushed on. "A tornado feeds off a rising column of air in the center. As the—"

For once it was Victor who interrupted the lecture on weather dynamics. "Eli!" he almost shouted. "Focus! We have no time."

Eli stopped in midsentence and nodded. "The demon is feeding off energy, not moist air, but since it's taken the form of a tornado it's still dependent on physical laws. Interrupt the energy flow of the central column and it will collapse."

"Then what?" I asked.

"Hopefully it will lose cohesion and dissipate, or at least return to wherever it came from. Mason, can you construct some sort of shield?"

At last, something I was good at. I scrambled out of the car and cast around for something helpful. In winter months, a lot of umbrellas are carried against the ever-present threat of rain, and many of them were now lying scattered on the street where they had been dropped in mad haste. I used them as a strong template, gathered the concept of protection from the innumerable cops running around, and above all, fed off the energy running wild in the street. I threw it with all my force toward the bottom of the swirling black mass, about twenty feet above the street. The only problem was that I didn't think I had the strength to hold it against the ever growing power of the demon. I mean, it was a tornado after all.

Victor, however, had no such doubts about his own ability. He spoke some words, raised his arms with sweeping theatrical gestures, and gathered power. Like I said, Victor presets a lot of his spells; it's a very different way of practicing the art than mine, and a lot less flexible, but for accessing raw power it can't be beat. He flung out his arms in a final grand gesture and power rolled off his fingertips into the shield I'd constructed.

It stopped the demon's energy flow dead, as if a huge cover had capped an out-of-control oil gusher. The demon was too strong for us to contain it for long, but we didn't have to. The instant the energy flow stopped, the tornado form collapsed. The rest of the demon wavered, then simply drifted apart, leaving only small clouds scudding along as if after a violent storm. The smoke drifted down and combined with the rain-slick streets, forming a thick oily sludge.

For a few moments, I thought we'd acted too late. The crowd had taken on a life of its own. People were surging forward, triggered by long standing grievances and frustrations that needed no supernatural influence to keep them alive. The cops still had their shotguns out, and for a tense moment it looked like no demon would be necessary for real disaster.

But for the cops, at least, training prevailed. San Francisco cops have their problems; some are a bit too badge heavy and it's the only large department left in the country which promotes exclusively on seniority, with sometimes disastrous consequences. But the average cop, the cop on the beat, knows how to handle just about anything.

The shotguns went back into the trunks, the batons came out, the crowd control formations materialized out of nowhere. Police lines were formed, but instead of confronting the angry crowd en masse, the cops targeted only the most vocal troublemakers. They formed a solid cordon, shoulder to shoulder, with officers stationed behind it in groups of three. Whenever an angry crowd member got too close, the whole line stepped forward in unison, not attacking, but opening up instead. As soon as the cordon had stepped past the offending individual, it closed ranks again, neatly trapping him behind the line. The waiting groups of officers behind the line then snatched each one up and hustled him away to a waiting police wagon. The less excitable crowd members were easily diverted down side streets where, without any focus for their anger, they began to disperse. As soon as things were somewhat under control Victor motioned for us to get back in the car.

"Come on," he said. "We need to go back to Harry Keller's house."

"What on God's earth for?" I asked, forgetting that my van was still there.

Victor gave me his world-weary, do I have to explain everything look. "Mop up," he said. "Do you really think we can just leave a dead body lying around for the police to find?"

"He fell down the stairs," I protested. "It was an accident."

"And the police will investigate. And they'll talk to the neighbors. And they'll find out there were several people visiting that night, a couple of strange cars, and, if I remember correctly, a lot of cursing and screaming about the time of the 'accident.'"

"I'm afraid he's right," Eli said.

"So we 'mop up'? What does that mean?"

"Don't worry," said Victor. "I'll take care of it. You just follow instructions."

Following instructions isn't my favorite thing, especially when they come from Victor, but this time I was happy to let him take the lead. We traveled the short distance back to Potrero Hill in silence. I gave a huge yawn; the digital clock on the dash read 11:50 p.m., but it felt more like four in the morning. I had the irrational fear that Harry's body would be gone when we got there, either magically revived or spirited away by God knows what. But he was still where we had left him, crumpled at the foot of the stairs.

Lou sniffed at Harry's remains and looked back toward me reproachfully, as if what happened had been my fault. Or maybe I was projecting. Victor bent over the body, but before he could do anything, the sound of the front door opening made us freeze. Hesitant steps echoed from the hallway. The hackles on Lou's neck were raised and Maggie puffed up like a porcupine. I tensed up, but as soon as a figure appeared in the doorway I relaxed. I started breathing again, relieved but embarrassed to realize I had been holding my breath. It was Sherwood.

"Sherwood!" Eli exclaimed. "I was starting to worry about you. How on earth did you find us?"

"You *should* be worried," Sherwood said, and then I was.

The voice was hers, but it wasn't. Totally flat, uninflected, it seemed to come from a great distance. She wore an ordinary expression, but not any that I had ever seen on her face before. She wasn't herself tonight, you might say. A priest would have had no problem understanding the situation. He would instantly denounce her as possessed, and that wouldn't have been far off the mark.

"Well, well," she said. "The triumvirate has gathered."

I was too horrified to utter a word. Victor was surveying her, shaking his head in either disbelief or sorrow. Even Eli seemed fazed.

"Christoph," he said. "It's not possible."

"Oh, but it is. You'd be amazed what's possible to me now."

Sherwood smiled without it changing her face in any way. She walked over toward me, and I scrambled out of the way as if a poisonous snake had just slithered into the room. I didn't want her anywhere near me. In my haste I almost tripped over Lou, who was as eager to get away from her as I was. Then, as if the smile wasn't creepy enough, she laughed, a flat, staccato heh-heh-heh-heh, a perverse parody of the old *Beavis and Butt-head* cartoons. She looked down at Harry's body.

"Hmm," she said. "That didn't go as well as I'd hoped."

"So he *was* working with you," I said, unable to keep quiet.

"Well, he thought he was. But I guess this time he bit off more than he could chew."

She walked into the living room and eased herself into one of the less bloody looking chairs, ignoring the way her skirt rode up almost to her waist. We trailed in after her, not wanting to, but unwilling to let her out of our sight.

"What's the matter, boys?" she asked, humorless smile firmly in place.

Eli answered, which was just as well since I was too creeped out to respond coherently.

"How did you do this? And what have you done to her?" he said.

"Who, Sherwood?" The smile continued. "Nothing much. Just using her for a while." She shook her head sadly. "Poor Sherwood. She really isn't that bright, you know. A minor illusion was all it took." Sherwood's smile took on a mocking cast and she turned her head to address me. "One that even you could have managed, Mason. Your little doggie there, dragging his hind legs down the street and whimpering piteously. She came running out of Victor's oh-so-safe house without a second thought."

"What is it you want?" Eli asked, refusing to get drawn in.

"Want? Why, Mason, of course." Sherwood pointed a slender finger at me and the smile disappeared from her face. "You have been nothing but trouble. You have no idea how much power it takes to fashion those gems. Or what I've had to go through to get them. And freeing those Ifrits—well, that was the last straw. If you'd taken the deal I offered at your house, none of us would have to be here."

"What deal?" I asked. Christoph was making no sense.

"Oh, that's right. Your little Ifrit attacked me before I could get to that part. The jewels. I was going to trade them with you."

"For what?" I was completely lost.

"For him, of course." She pointed at Lou. "You have no idea what you have there, do you? You think the gems I've made so far are impressive? Just wait until you see what I can do with him."

So. Lou really was special, even for an Ifrit. I'd always thought so, but figured it was just personal bias. That's why Christoph had been so single-minded about getting me out of the way. Lou turned his head and glanced in my direction, and despite the awful situation, he still managed to looked smug.

Christoph/Sherwood relaxed again and the creepy smile reappeared. "Anyway, I thought you might like to indulge me in a little game of 'Who's got the power?' since you seem to be so desperate to be rid of me."

I found my voice, though it was a bit unsteady. "Forget it," I said. "Not interested."

"No? You seemed eager enough to fight when I came over for a friendly visit and you attacked me without warning."

There didn't seem much profit in arguing the point, so I didn't. He/she waited until it was clear I wasn't going to say anything, then continued.

"You know, it's interesting. When one's mind is invaded it seems to be a most unpleasant experience. Or so I understand. Now Sherwood is surprisingly strong; I have to expend quite some effort to keep her in check. But the longer I have her, the less of her mind she'll be able to recover when I leave. I would say about two more days and she'll just about retain the capabilities of a four-year-old. One with learning disabilities. But I'm sure with enough time and therapy she'll be able to have an almost normal life. Possibly even manage to live on her own."

"I'll find you and I'll kill you," I said, almost in a whisper.

"Ooh, scary. That won't help Sherwood much though, will it now?"

Eli put up his hand toward me with a gesture that meant, keep quiet.

"Enough," he said, "we get it. What exactly are you looking for?"

"A Challenge. A real one, not the kiddy stuff like the ones in the park. Just myself and Mason. I'll suck him dry, and after he's dead I'll have his power. And then . . ." She turned that fixed smile on Eli. "Now, you're a smart fellow, Professor. I'm sure you know something about quantum physics, yes?" Eli said nothing, just regarded her, stone-faced. She went on. "When I gain Mason's power, it will not only greatly increase my own, but will also jump me up to a whole other level—you know, the whole quantum leap thing? Then I won't have to worry about your interference anymore. Or anyone else's, for that matter. I'll be as far above you as you are to ordinaries." She pointed at Lou again. "And, as the added bonus, I'll finally get little Bright-eyes here."

Lou was trembling with rage, unable to stay still, hopping from one paw to the other, burning with the desire to sink his teeth into the offending Christoph, torn by the knowledge that it was actually Sherwood sitting there and Christoph was out of reach. It was what we all were feeling.

"I told you, I'm not playing," I said. "Pick on somebody else." I glanced pointedly at Victor, just to see his reaction.

"Don't tell me what to do," she said. "Those days are over. Before I had power, you hardly even noticed me, did you? All of you. Strutting around, high-level talents. You make me sick."

So this wasn't totally about power and money after all. It was also about revenge, and a lot about Christoph feeling dissed. How very high school. Then I remembered that feeling dissed was precisely the reason many young men in our fair city gun each other down in the streets.

"Well, if you don't want to play I guess I can't make you," she said, then leaned back in the chair, spread her legs wide, slipped her hand underneath her skirt, and began stroking herself.

"Ahh," she said, in a voice still devoid of feeling. "That's nice. Certainly better than this."

As she spoke, she grabbed the little finger of her right hand with her left hand and bent it back viciously. Before any of us could react there was a muffled crack, and when she let go, the finger remained at an unnatural angle. Victor, who was closest, jumped to her side and clamped his hand around her wrist. She laughed again, that same creepy heh-heh-heh sound.

"Don't worry, I won't do that again. Maybe a seizure, though. A grand mal episode can be very impressive. Sometimes, bones can even break. She can still feel all of it, you know, although I myself can block out the pain. A useful skill, don't you agree?"

"You win," I said. "Where and when?"

"Not so fast," said Eli, lumbering over quickly. "You are the challenged party, Mason. You're the one who gets to pick the time and place."

"Sorry, this isn't open to bargaining," Christoph/Sherwood informed him.

"I'm not bargaining. I'm just reminding you of the rules governing contests. Those rules have come down through the centuries; they're in force for a reason. If you don't want to abide by them, why, I guess you don't have to, but if you ignore them it could affect the power transfer you're hoping for."

Christoph/Sherwood considered that for a while.

"You know," she said, "you might be right. Considering Mason's complete lack of control over his ability, it hardly matters anyway. So sure, whatever you want."

"Tomorrow," said Eli. "Noon. Where doesn't matter; Mason will create his own personal reality space for the contest."

That was news to me. I hoped Eli knew what he was doing. Of course, so far his track record had been spotty at best.

"Mason, do you have a preference as to a place to meet?" Eli continued. I shook my head no. "What about McClaren Park, then? Up by the water tower. Neutral territory. It's out of the way and easy to shield."

"Whatever," I said.

Christoph/Sherwood got out of the chair and stood up. "Until tomorrow, then," she said.

"Hold on," said Eli. "What about Sherwood?"

"Oh, I'll bring her with me. You can have her back then, but I'll keep the psychic connection open until the contest. So if anything unexpected happens before then . . ." She drew a finger across her throat in the classic throat-cutting sign, gave us another bright and horrible smile, and walked out into the night. After she left, we just stood there in silence staring at each other. Eli finally broke the silence.

"I would never have believed it," he said. "Never. No one can possess another person, especially another practitioner. I would have bet my life on it."

"Good thing you didn't," said Victor.

I didn't want to think about it. The invasive nature of a possession was too grotesque to contemplate. Besides, we had pressing business.

"Not to change the subject," I said, "but I have a question. Purely academic. What chance do I have to live through this?"

"Hard to say," said Eli, ever the optimist. "But I do have an idea."

"So do I. Let's show up early and ambush him. Three to one are better odds than this one-on-one battle he wants to set up."

"Won't work," Victor said. "You heard him. He's going to keep an open link with Sherwood. Even if we surprise him, his death while linked will destroy her mind, if not kill her outright. You're just going to have to go through with this duel."

"Well, as long as that's settled." I rubbed my eyes, which felt like there were grains of sand in them. "But how do you expect me to pull this off?" I complained. "Christoph is strong, even stronger than before. My little tricks aren't going to help me much if he can just squash me like a bug. And by the way, Eli, just how do I go about creating this personal reality space you mentioned? You remember the jungle Christoph created in that Challenge we saw? I can't match that. I can't do anything close to that."

"Sure you can," he assured me. "Maybe you can't just whip up any illusion that strikes your fancy, but there is a way you can create a realistic locale, a pocket world, in fact. With my help, of course."

"Of course."

"Don't worry, it won't be that difficult. All you need to do is this: Find in your memory a place you know well, somewhere you've spent a lot of time, somewhere Christoph doesn't know. Maybe a summer vacation spot or something like that."

Like I had a summer vacation spot. Eli rolled on, oblivious to my expression.

"Once you have it clearly fixed, Victor and I will help pull it out of your mind—you won't have to create anything; you'll just be actualizing a memory."

"And then what?"

"Then you'll have the upper hand. Christoph will find

himself in an unfamiliar environment, but you'll know every twist, turn, nook, and cranny."

"You make it sound so cozy. Okay, I see how that would help, but Christoph still has more than enough power to make up for my home court advantage."

"For the hundredth time, stop underestimating your ability. Besides, there's a part two. You know that project I've been working on? The one you always kid me about? Well, I don't quite have it yet, but I'm close."

"How close? And what is it?"

"A few glitches. It's a deadening spell. Thought to be impossible, but it's not. When activated, no talent in the vicinity will operate, yours or anyone else's. That should certainly level the playing field—if it works properly."

"Ahh. That word 'if' again."

"Sorry," said Eli, somewhat miffed. "You want to give me a couple more weeks to fine-tune it?"

"I know, I know," I said. "So how would this work?"

"With Victor's assistance, I'll construct a simple artifact and imbue it with the necessary magical deadening properties. Then, at the optimal time, you simply deploy it."

Whenever Eli starts pontificating in over-the-top academic speak, it means either he's very much at ease or very much worried. I don't think he felt much at ease.

"What about the other thing?" I asked. "You honestly think I can create some memory world?"

"With our help. What you need to do now is to go home, get some sleep, and spend as much time as possible fixing the memory of whatever place you choose firmly in your mind. Not just the visuals, but sounds, smells, emotions—the entire gestalt. The more you can envision it, the more complete it will be."

"Well, that makes sense," I said. "And how long will it last?"

"Until it's served its purpose. Long enough for you to defeat Christoph. When you do, the construct will dissolve and you'll return here."

"And if Christoph comes out on top?" Victor helpfully inquired.

"Well, that won't be so good."

Short and succinct. "What if my memories have grown stale and I can't come up with anything useful?" I asked.

"Then you're liable to end up in a featureless nether-world—with Christoph standing right alongside you and nowhere to hide."

"Point taken. I'll do my homework. One more question—why me? I know he wants Lou, but surely he could get the power he wants from someone else without all this bother.

"Well, I think he really doesn't like you," Eli said. "That has a lot to do with it. But also, it's about your power and your lack of it. Remember how I'm always telling you about your potential?"

"How can I forget?"

"Well, it's real, but you've never bothered to develop it. So you're vulnerable, way out of proportion to the amount of power you possess. When he kills you—"

"When?"

"Speaking hypothetically. *If* he kills you, he'll get the power boost he's looking for. Sadly, if he were to kill me, he wouldn't get a whole lot. Victor would provide him with what he needs, but I don't think he wants to go up against him even with his tremendous power edge. Victor is dangerous."

That gave me a lot of confidence. Now Victor was looking smug.

"I see." There wasn't much else to say. "What time do you want me over at the house?"

"8:00 a.m.," Victor said. "And try for once to be on time. We'll need some extra time to get you ready. I'll take care of the mess here. Just be there by eight."

BY THE TIME I GOT HOME, IT WAS WAY PAST MID-night, and the longest day of my life still wasn't over. I was bone weary, but I brewed some coffee and sat at the table in the kitchen, trying to think. Actually, trying to stay awake. This wasn't going to work; I wasn't that good at remembering things anyway, and being tired made it all the more difficult. I can remember jazz tunes I haven't played in years note for note, but when it came to visualizing past scenes and landscapes I was a bust. I looked over at the bed, which lay there invitingly. Maybe if I could lie down for just a moment and close my eyes. That way, images could flow from my subconscious.

I kicked off my shoes and stretched out full-length. Louie looked dubiously at me, especially when I pulled up a blanket to keep out the chill. Usually he would have quickly dove underneath, but this time he sat staring, as if he understood that my taking a nap right now might not be the best idea. His eyes were deep and concerned, and God knows what thoughts were swirling around behind them. Then he seemed to come to some sort of decision. He cocked his head sideways and opened his mouth. My heartbeat sped up. This was crisis time after all. Now I knew he wasn't just an ordinary Ifrit. Maybe he'd broken through to a new level of consciousness. Maybe, this time, he finally was going to speak.

He sneezed twice, hopped up beside me, turned around twice, wedged himself against my hip, and closed his eyes. Oh well, what did I expect? I mean, he *was* a dog, after all. Sort of.

As soon as I closed my eyes, I knew in my heart I wasn't going to be reflecting or remembering a whole lot. I could feel the weight of my weariness washing over me. Still, I managed to convince myself that I wasn't going to fall asleep, right up to the moment I drifted off. And then I dreamed.

SEVENTEEN

IN MY DREAM, IT WAS DARK AND I WAS LOST. I could barely see, but I could hear Louie barking from somewhere up ahead. I focused on the sound and followed, sometimes losing him but always picking up the sound of his distinctive yelp sooner or later. As I turned and twisted, areas of light started appearing, bright cracks in the dark world. I could hear him just beyond one of the openings and I rushed through. Then, like a movie jump cut, the scene shifted.

I was sitting in a boat, an eight-foot dinghy with a three-power Evinrude engine attached to the stern. It swayed gently, anchored in a flooded salt marsh of reeds and tangled eel grass. The summer sun beat down with stifling power, but it didn't bother me. I was wearing only a pair of shorts and my skin was darkly tanned. Suddenly I understood I was in a dream, so the realization that I was now ten years old wasn't much of a surprise. I was back on the island where my grandparents had lived. A couple of miles from this marsh was the boat dock, and a half mile farther up the road would be their gray-shingled house.

I had never had such a vivid dream. The smell of the marsh filled my nostrils, that fecund mixture of salt, mud, fish, and cloying vegetation. It was strong, but not unpleasant. A reek of primal life, the edge of the sea where water bleeds into land, the zone that is neither and both. Sandy hillocks covered with saw grass poked their way up through the water every few yards. A black-crowned night heron stood motionless fifty yards away, head pointed up, almost invisible in the tall rushes. A black skimmer knifed through the shallows, dragging its bill through the water. Crustaceans no larger than a pencil eraser swirled around the dirty water sloshing in the bottom of the boat. Except for the slap of water against the side of the boat and the sound of the wind blowing through the marsh reeds, it was silent.

An instant later, I had forgotten I was dreaming. I pulled up anchor, coiled the anchor rope in the boat, and started up the outboard motor. I cranked the motor to one side, spun the boat around, and headed back toward the dock. I knew it was vital that I get home, although in the typical fashion of dreams I had no idea why.

When I reached the dock, I bypassed it and steered for the beach, cutting the engine and tilting it up as the water shoaled. I rowed the last ten feet with a pair of battered oars, jumped out of the boat, waded to the shore, and pulled the boat up onto the sand.

Another jump cut. I was passing by the abandoned orchard on the other side of the island. Trees of stunted apples and Seckel pears crowded together. A tangle of raspberry and blackberry bushes loaded with both green and ripe fruit formed a thorny border along one side. I stopped to pick a few, and the more I ate, the hungrier I became. The sweet juice ran down my chin and stained my fingers. Once again I realized I was dreaming, reliving the happiest days of my life.

At ten years old, summer is a timeless season, stretching out endlessly, the old school year nothing more than a distant memory, the year to come impossibly distant. Girls

were vaguely interesting, but certainly of no true impor-
tance. The entire island was mine to explore, days filled
from dawn till dusk. No regrets about yesterday; no worries about tomorrow. My nights were taken up by the dis-
covery of an old Martin guitar which belonged to my
grandfather, but the guitar was not yet the obsession it
would later become. Magic, like sex, would be mostly a
closed book until puberty, but I hung on every word on the
rare occasions when my grandfather told me late-night stories of his earlier life. I didn't realize it until years later, but
he had been a powerful practitioner once, one who retired
to a quiet life filled with birds and fish and plants. He was
in truth very much like Geoffrey, except that instead of
playing evasive word games he fished and grew summer
squash.

Jump cut. Now dusk, standing outside my grandparents' house, once again swept up in the dream, awareness
gone. The stained and weathered shingles spoke of home
as light streamed through the open windows on the ground
floor. The sweet smell of things baking in the oven, bread
or cookies or brownies, stole out into the evening air. I ran
up the three steps to the porch, avoiding the top step which
always sagged as if about to break, reached for the front
door handle and stopped, paralyzed, seized with that unac-
countable dread which so often inhabits the dream world.
I could hear the sound of muffled voices and occasional
laughter, but I could not force myself to turn the door handle. Something started leaking onto my face from the
porch roof, something warm and wet and slightly viscous.
I was afraid to look up, afraid that it might be blood, or
something worse. Panicked, I threw open the door in desperation. The hallway stretched out in front of me, longer
then it should, and then—

My eyes flew open and I was back in my flat, sprawled
facedown on my mattress. Louie was standing next to me,
one paw on my shoulder, licking my face with a wet
tongue. My heart was racing and I had to take several deep
breaths to calm myself. He gave me a sympathetic look.

"You again?" I asked him. "You wouldn't have had anything to do with that dream, would you now?"

He gave me a doggy grin and jumped down off the bed. I glanced at the clock on the bedside table. 6:30 a.m. I'd slept almost five hours. Not nearly enough, but there was no chance of getting any more.

I dragged myself upright, started coffee, turned on the wall heater, and took a long, hot shower. When I got out I poured a cup and looked out the front window at the fog lazily drifting by. A good day to die.

I wondered about my dream. Why so much fear when I was about to enter the house? Maybe the dream world was bound up too closely with reality. It certainly was unlike any other dream I'd ever had. If it was indeed some mysterious blending of dream and reality, then maybe that meant my grandfather could have been a ghost of a sort, and no one, especially a ten-year-old, wants to see a ghost. Or maybe I was the ghost. Maybe I didn't want him to see me. But the dream had given me what I needed, a powerful memory to work with.

At least I had time for a last meal. There was a half a box of Bisquick in the cupboard and real maple syrup in the fridge, so it was pancakes again. Lou approved of the choice. He dogged my steps as I mixed up the batter, almost tripping me a couple of times. He may have been the most useful of Ifrits, but he was definitely lacking in the self-control department.

The pancakes weren't as good as Campbell's, but Lou didn't care. I sopped up the remains of the maple syrup, had a last cup of coffee, and washed up. If everything worked out it would be nice to come back to a clean house. If not, at least I wouldn't be exposed to my friends as the slob I actually am. I took a last look around, locked the door behind me, climbed into my van, and pulled out into the rush hour traffic.

The drive over took longer than usual, with the traffic grinding along. It was a quarter past eight by the time I pulled up in front of Victor's. Inside, he and Eli were still hard at work, poring through a mound of papers scattered over Victor's desk. Most were filled with symbols and equations, like a math professor's textbook. They both looked like they'd been at it all night. Eli gave me a tired smile.

As soon as I came in Eli opened the drawer on Victor's ornate desk and pulled out something that looked like a coconut, only it was the size of a lemon. Victor took it from him and handed it to me.

"Here it is. You can see how tough it is—we had to make the casing extra strength, otherwise it wouldn't be able to contain the spell."

"Lovely," I said, hefting it. It was considerably heavier than it appeared. "How do I make it work?"

Eli produced a jaw-cracking yawn. "As soon as you and Christoph arrive in your memory construct, break it open. That will release the dampening spell, which ought to last an hour at least. Then you'll both be unable to use talent, or at least that's the theory. But this is important: Make sure you break it physically. Smash it against a rock or something hard. Don't use any magical energy to shatter the covering. If you do, the dampening spell will feed back and short-circuit your neural system. At best it won't be pleasant, and it might even drain enough energy to permanently damage you. Or worse."

"Got it," I said, slipping it into my pocket.

Eli stood up from behind the desk and stretched his considerable frame. "And speaking of the memory construct, were you able to come up with anything?"

"Something. But I have no idea how to actualize it."

"Don't worry," he said. "We'll show you."

For the next two hours the three of us worked on an implementation strategy. It was tricky since it was necessary to craft a technique that would enable me to call up the construct without going too far and prematurely kicking it in. The idea was to hold the memory as clearly as possible while we wrapped energy around it. Mostly the power came from myself and Victor, with Eli providing the expertise. At last it was set, like a coiled spring loaded with potential, ready to be released by a simple spell that was hardly more than a few code words.

Technically of course we were cheating; this was supposed to be a one-on-one contest, but this was no game. I would have gladly borrowed one of Victor's guns as an additional edge except guns won't operate in a construct. I wished I'd gotten more sleep. Already I felt drained, and the combat hadn't even started yet. Victor snuck a quick look at his wristwatch. A Rolex, I believe.

"We should get going," he said. "Christoph is bound to be there early, and we don't need to give him time to set up any surprises."

We all squeezed into Victor's BMW. Nothing like traveling to your doom in style. Victor had fixed the bullet hole in the windshield, of course. He was very careful about his car. There was a small rug on the backseat for Lou to sit on, usually reserved for Maggie. Maggie watched us from the upstairs window. She didn't see the need to come with us; if things went wrong it wasn't Victor that was going to end up as the mindless husk. I hadn't expected her to come along. I'm not sure how far out of his way Louie would go to save Victor's ass if the situation were reversed. And besides, she was a cat. Sort of.

There are places in San Francisco where there is no good way to get from here to there. It took us a while to reach McClaren, out in the Excelsior. We parked up at the west end, five minutes from the water tower that stands on the top of a small hill. The tower is a six-sided structure painted a pale sickly blue. Maybe the idea was for it to blend into the color of the sky, but if that was it, it didn't work.

Christoph was nowhere in sight, but atop a utility pole sat a large raven, watching us. Louie spotted it immediately but didn't act worried. As soon as the raven saw us, it flapped down in an ungainly fashion and lit on the ground some distance off. Lou ran up to it, but instead of attacking he stopped next to it and sat quietly. The raven started vocalizing all sorts of squawks, chuckles, and whistles, running through an impressive repertoire. After a minute of this, Lou gave a short bark and ran back to where we were waiting. Ifrits. Maybe they thought they were acting as some sort of seconds to a duel. Just because Christoph and I were trying to kill each other was no reason for them to be uncivil.

At one minute to noon, there was still no sign of Christoph. Maybe he'd thought better of it after all. Maybe pigs were about to sprout wings. At noon we could hear the far-off bells of a church, and as I looked around I saw a shimmering distortion just south of the tower, like heat over asphalt on a hot day. A faint outline flickered in and out of focus and then Christoph popped into solidity. He walked toward us as if he had just stepped off a city bus, brushing nonexistent dust from the shoulders of his jacket. What's more, he had Sherwood with him. She was lethargic and blank-eyed, so he still had a psychic hold on her. He obviously meant this stunt to be impressive and intimidating, since it involved an ability almost unheard of. It must have taken a horrendous amount of energy, which of course was the point. He had power to spare. The raven flapped over and perched on his shoulder, eyeing me with a disconcerting and intelligent stare. I surreptitiously felt in my pocket for the reassuring roundness of the dampening object.

"I want Sherwood," I said. "Right now, or the whole thing's off."

"Not quite yet," Christoph said. "I'll release her as we enter the dueling ground, not before. I don't want you changing your mind at the last second."

There wasn't much I could do. As long as he had Sherwood he had the upper hand and he knew it.

"Let's get this started then," Victor said.

Lou curled himself around my feet. I put myself into what amounted to a mild trance state, trying to recall last night's dream. The feel of the sun on the water. The smell of the tide flats. The sound of gulls mewing in the distance.

My battered and beloved dinghy beached on the shore. The smell of baking from my grandparents' house. I narrowed my attention until the memory was as real as the hill we were standing on, gathered some energy from Victor and Eli, and spoke the few simple words we had agreed on. I felt a rush as the potential was released and the hill around the water tower lost focus, becoming as insubstantial as smoke. The cold San Francisco sky turned a brilliant blue as the sun streamed down and the heat rolled over me like a blessing. The scent of salt air surrounded me. One short step and I would be back on that island, and this time it would be no dream.

Christoph pushed Sherwood away from him. "Here," he said. "Take her." He gestured in the air and spoke several words too low and rapid for me to catch. Sherwood's eyes cleared, and she saw me standing there. She opened her mouth to speak, and then a puzzled expression passed over her face, replaced with one of fear, then horror. Her skin started to glow, first pink, then cherry red, until astonishingly, it burst into flame. Not ordinary flame, but with a magical burst of white and violet, leaping and curling around her. She screamed once and reached a hand out toward me. I saw her lips form the words "Mason, help me," but the sound was lost in the rushing hiss of fire.

Her skin turned black, crisp, then started to melt with bewildering fast-forward speed. One second she was on fire, twisting in agony, the next, all that could be seen was the glowing outline of a skeleton, an X-ray of a human. The bones collapsed in on themselves and what was left of her crumpled to the ground. Three seconds later, all that was left was a scorched mark on the grass.

Before I could react, Christoph seized me by the arm and pulled me into my carefully crafted construct. The raven flapped by my head, and Lou dashed after us. A moment later we were standing on a beach by the edge of the water, under a summer sun.

My initial shock had become rage, and without a word I leapt at him, not thinking, just wanting to get my hands around his throat. Now I knew how Lou operated. Five feet from him I ran into what felt like a brick wall, knocking me off my feet. I lay there on the sand, stunned. Of course. Christoph wasn't about to stand next to me without protection.

He ignored my abortive attack, slowly turning three hundred and sixty degrees, taking it all in. "This is lovely," he said. "I never thought you capable of anything this complex."

He was totally unaffected by what he'd done to Sherwood. Like Eli said, he was psychically damaged. Or evil and twisted. Take your choice. I lay on the sand, pretending to be more hurt than I was. I needed to get control of my emotions. This was going to be a fight to the death, and if I charged ahead in blind rage I was going to lose. I gathered up my despair and rage as if it were magical energy, wound it tight, shoved it deep inside, and covered it over. I would have to pay for that later. If there was a later.

Christoph smiled at me lying on the sand. He didn't seem in any rush to get started on the bloodshed. With all the strength he possessed he had no worries. But he hadn't yet learned that while confidence can carry you a long way, overconfidence has a way of rudely upending you.

I got slowly to my feet and reached in my pocket, feeling the comforting rough surface of my secret weapon. Then I gazed over the expanse of sand and the gentle water. Oops. Talk about overconfidence. A minor glitch reared its inevitable head. Surrounded by soft sand and water, I saw no possibility of breaking that hard shell open and releasing the spell.

Christoph regarded me with mock affection. "I'd love to make this painless," he informed me, "but to get the most out of it I need for you to desperately struggle to the end. So . . ."

He walked to the edge of the water, made a beckoning gesture with his left hand, and barked a command. The water roiled up and at first I thought he meant to drown me, but he had something more unpleasant in mind. A couple of small crabs scurried out of the water and headed up the beach, followed by a couple of larger ones. Followed by more crabs. Followed by even more. Crabs with very large claws, purposeful and aggressive.

Now there's nothing dangerous about a crab or two. They're not even interested in people except as potential threats. Even a hundred or so wouldn't be any problem; maybe freakish and scary, but unless you're lying paralyzed on the sand, there's not much they can do to you. But there were thousands of them making their way out of the water, magically imbued with a very uncrablike aggressiveness, angrily waving their claws as they advanced toward me. If they managed to latch on to me with their sharp pincers it would be like the Chinese death of a thousand cuts.

I automatically turned to head up the beach away from them. I hadn't moved more than three steps when I was brought up short by a barrier, again courtesy of Christoph. Not an aversion spell or energy-draining sinkhole, but a true physical energy screen. It was like a sheet of steel covered with a thin layer of rubber. I expanded my awareness, trying to find a crack or flaw I could exploit, but it was strong and smooth. I didn't have the skill or the capacity to do anything with it.

Lou, who had started backing up the minute the crabs appeared, wasn't faring any better. The barrier stopped him as effectively as it had me. Ifrits are pretty much immune to such things as aversion spells, but this was different. He whined unhappily and looked up at me for reassurance. I didn't have much to give him.

"Problems?" mocked Christoph. He was practically dancing in the sand, unable to contain his glee or remain still. I wouldn't have been surprised if he had started cackling, "I'll get you, my pretty, and your little dog, too!"

I pulled the energy deadener out of my pocket. It looked like I was going to have to use energy to break the casing after all, despite Victor's warning. If it killed me, at least Christoph wouldn't benefit much. The alternative—having

tiny pieces of flesh plucked off by thousands of crabs—
was not an attractive one.

Then, for once in my life, I actually came up with a
good idea. It would take some precious energy, but there
wasn't much point in trying to save it. I spread talent into
the sand, sucked power from the sea, and raised a protective wall of my own between me and the onrushing crabs.
The sand made it strong but brittle, like thick glass. A few
of the crabs had already made it through but the rest were
piled up against the boundary line, vainly trying to force
their way through.

Christoph shook his head contemptuously. He flung out
his hand in one quick motion, sending a pulse of force that
ripped through the barrier I had erected, shattering it with
ease. At the same moment Christoph gestured, I whipped
the dampening object toward the wall like a baseball
pitcher throwing a high hard one. Luckily, Christoph
hadn't been satisfied to just tear down my defensive effort.
Being Christoph, he had to go for overkill. His force tore
through the wall and hit the lemon-sized coconut with the
dampening spell locked inside. It shattered as if it had been
hit with a sledgehammer.

The sharp crack of an explosion almost deafened me,
coupled with a sizzling flash like an exploding power
transformer. Energy surged back into him and Christoph
dropped to the sand like he'd been shot. I could only hope
the power surge had fried every circuit in his brain. The
myriad of crabs, so purposeful only moments ago, milled
around confusedly and scuttled off toward the safety of the
water. Either the dampening spell had been released, snuff-
ing out the motivating magic, or Christoph was unconscious, which would have the same effect. Or both.

I tried a brief power exercise, trying to raise a dirt devil
out of the sand. A whirlwind, not an actual devil. Nothing.
I'd never been so happy in my life to find my power useless. I strode over to where Christoph lay and stared down
at him, anger starting to seep back in. The anger grew. I
didn't need my talent. I could strangle him with my hands.

I bent down and his Ifrit spread its wings protectively over his head and hissed at me like a cat. Christoph's eyes popped open. They were slightly glazed. When he saw me standing over him he paddled his hands around with a circular motion and croaked, "Bind!"

The air thickened around me. I tried to step back out of range but it was like I was standing in quicksand. Something had gone wrong. I had lost my powers but Christoph had not. Another revolting development. Then I mustered all my strength and broke free, something I shouldn't have been able to do.

I couldn't figure it. Maybe what happened was that although the dampening device had worked fine, Christoph possessed too much strength for him to be totally nullified. I had been drained, but he had such a reserve that it only diminished him. If so, he was now a very ordinary practitioner, but I wasn't a practitioner at all.

I needed to put some distance between us, since a weak practitioner wants close proximity to operate effectively. I ran up the beach, urged on by fear, before he could cast anything else. If Victor and Eli had figured correctly, I only had an hour or so before he regained his full powers, and then it was good-bye, Mason. I pushed my fear into the same place I'd hidden my rage. Fear and rage are opposite sides of the same coin, and both would lead me to disaster. I followed Lou to the cover of low-lying scrub brush that paralleled the beach and tried to think of a plan of attack.

Glancing over my shoulder, I saw Christoph sitting up slowly, not yet fully recovered. His Ifrit launched itself into the sky, caught a current of air, and soared overhead. It circled above us, acting as a beacon to let Christoph know exactly where we were. Aerial surveillance. Another thing I hadn't bargained for.

Christoph walked slowly in our direction, still unsteady on his feet. The blowback must have given him quite a jolt. He stood at the edge where the sand met the scrub and began a chant I couldn't quite make out, interspersing the words with jerky little gestures. I couldn't figure out what he thought he was doing since we were too far away to be affected by anything he could throw at us, especially in his weakened state. At least he was expending energy. If he wasn't careful he'd run down his reserve enough so that I could take him out with a well-aimed stone between the eyes.

Then Louie whirled around and I noticed small rustling sounds in the tall dune grass. Great. What now? A small furry shape skittered out from one clump of grass and ducked into another. Louie was after it like a bullet, and I had to yell at him to bring him back. It was a rat, and a big one at that, close to a foot long. More rustling. Little rat heads were peeking out of every available bit of cover. So that's what Christoph had been doing. He might not have much power left, but apparently influence over small creatures was a speciality of his. If slugs and crabs, why not rats?

The rats charged forward, angling off at the last moment before reaching us, edging closer with each sortie. Louie was trembling with eagerness, ready to sink his teeth into one of them. I thought caution the better strategy and started backing up a low rise of sand. One of the rats finally summoned up the courage to launch itself at me, but Lou intercepted it in midleap and crunched down on the base of its skull, whipping it briskly from side to side and quickly snapping its neck. Three more rats took its place, and I kicked at them, wishing I had some sort of stick to beat them off with. The dirt and sand underfoot was another disadvantage; I couldn't get much footing and when I tried to stomp down on them they would squirm out from under my boot as often as not.

The rats learned quickly, some feinting rushes from the front while others slipped in from the rear. Lou kept them at bay although he wasn't much larger than they were, but they kept going for his forelegs. Sooner or later one would manage to cripple him and then it would only be a matter of time. They were smart, and cunning as, well, rats. One of them came up behind me while I was trying to crush an-

other attacking from the front and sank its teeth into the
back of my calf. Lou was on it like a flash, but the damage
was done. Blood stained my pant leg, which whipped the
rest of the rats into a frenzy. They kept coming, always in
increasing numbers. We needed to get out of there. I yelled
for Lou, and ignoring the pain in my calf, sprinted through
some brush, hurdled over a cluster of rats, scrambled over
a small rise, and then stopped dead. On the other side of
the rise were additional hundreds of the sleek brown ro-
dents. The moment they saw us, they started an excited
squealing and swept toward us in a furry wave.

The rats fanned out until we were enclosed in a circle.
From a line of low trees fifty yards away I could see more
reinforcements arriving. I had no idea there could be so
many rats on one small island. Another wave of anger
overtook me as I realized that I might not get out of this
one alive. Lou was panting, sides heaving, and I wasn't a
lot better. I had a pain in my left side and a burning sensa-
tion along my upper thigh. It got worse until I realized
there really was something burning, something in my
pocket. I reached in and pulled out that small token I had
completely forgotten: the wolf totem that Campbell gave
me. It was hot enough to sear my hand, but I kept hold of
it. I had no idea what was causing it to pulse with energy,
but it was no coincidence. Lou stiffened the moment he
saw it, then lifted his muzzle toward the sky and howled
like a banshee. Calling for assistance? I had no magical potency of my own to aid the call, but I clutched the talisman
like a drowning man and prayed for help. If you consider
"For God's sake, get me out of here" to be a valid form of
prayer.

I thought I heard a far-off answering howl, but the next
second I was too busy fighting off rats to listen. Several
more managed to slash my legs and I almost lost my balance and went down. That would not have been a good
thing. I had just about given up hope when I heard the soft
thud of paws striking packed sand. From over the next
ridge three gray shapes ghosted down, sweeping along in

eerie silence. They fell on the horde of rats like destroying angels. I had thought Lou had the rat-killing move down, but the wolves were clearly experts in rodent destruction. Each wolf bent its head down, grabbed a rat by the back of the neck, and simultaneously broke the rat's neck and flung it aside, all in one motion. Without so much as a pause for breath, they moved on to the next. In ten minutes, five hundred rats were dead, and the remaining ones vanished into the undergrowth like a dissolving brown mist. Even Christoph's magical imperative couldn't keep them.

The wolves stood shoulder to shoulder, tongues lolling, muzzles stained with rat blood, and regarded me calmly. The largest of the three had a familiar torn ear and now a muzzle torn by rat bites. Before I could say or do anything, they whirled in unison and loped off over the ridge, disappearing from sight. Not much for leisurely visits or accepting heartfelt thanks. I wished they could have stayed around long enough to tear out Christoph's throat, but I guess it was their way of informing me that Christoph was now my problem. Not that I was complaining, mind you. It's not every day that a totem animal you're not even sure you have shows up to save your rear end.

So I still had Christoph to contend with. My only real chance was to surprise him, to get close enough to take him out before he could use his talent on me. Easier said than done. The merest wisp of an plan started to form in my mind. I jogged across the sand, keeping parallel to the beach, heading up to where the reeds and the mud flats begin to encroach onto the shore.

By the time I reached the flats, I was thoroughly winded. I splashed through brackish water, now almost up to my knees. Lou bounded from high point to high point, staying on the hillocks dotting the landscape. When we reached a point where the water was over his head and the muddy tussocks were too far apart for him to navigate, I had to carry him. Christoph's Ifrit was still soaring above us, uttering hoarse squawks from time to time to guide him. That wasn't altogether a bad thing; I wanted Christoph to be able to follow me, and quickly, since time was running out. Soon, his full power would return. On the other hand, I had to distract the raven somehow or my little ruse wouldn't work. Decisions, decisions.

I finally found the exact place I wanted. I was feeling a bit stronger, which might mean the dampening spell was wearing off. I tried a small illusion spell on Lou, trying to make him look more like the muddy clump of detritus he was standing on. He shimmered a bit, but still looked more like an extremely muddy dog than anything else. It didn't matter, the other Ifrit would see right through my best illusions anyway. But it did indicate that power was returning.

I sloshed over to where Lou was standing on the muddy islet. I needed a few minutes of privacy from prying raven eyes to set up my scheme. I wanted the raven to come closer, but it wasn't cooperating. It circled lazily overhead, well out of range. But just as Louie, Ifrit though he might be, was also very much a dog, so this Ifrit was a raven. And the thing about ravens is that they are obsessively curious. I cupped my hands around nothing, bent over, and showed my imaginary find to Lou.

"Show interest," I told him. "Act excited."

He took to the game with great enthusiasm, pawing at my hands, uttering a short yip of astonishment at what he found there, then barking triumphantly up at the sky where the raven soared. The Ifrit probably knew better, but it couldn't help itself. It just had to see what we had come up with.

It swung down in lazy circles until it was no more than twenty feet overhead. Louie continued his part, now snarling a challenge for it to keep its distance. I gathered all the energy I could muster, focused in on the bright sunlight, used the shiny metal of my belt buckle and the concave shape of my cupped hands, and let loose with a directed blinding flash twice as bright as the sun. With my diminished abilities, this simple parlor trick was as difficult as any spell I had ever thrown, but it worked. The Ifrit squawked in shock, banked sharply, and beat its wings to gain altitude. For the next few minutes, it was effectively blinded.

As soon as it veered away, I tore off my clothes and bunched them, half-submerged, in the muddy water and surrounding reeds. My two boots were jammed in the sand at the end of outstretched pant legs. I piled debris over the clothes as if I was trying to conceal them. It didn't make too convincing a hiding place, but that was exactly the point.

I picked an area ten feet away and poured every bit of talent I had left into the reeds. I wasn't trying to accomplish anything; I just wanted to leave some magical residue. As weak as I was, the effect was barely noticeable, which was perfect. It leaked out exactly as if a practitioner was hiding there trying to shield himself and tiny tendrils of energy were escaping despite his best efforts. Then I plastered mud over my face and head, eased into the tangle of reeds, and slipped naked into the warm water, directly under where my clothes tangled soggily in the mud and rushes. The real me hidden under the fake me. A deep metaphor if ever there was one.

"Guard," I said. "But when Christoph gets here, *don't attack*. Get away. Dive under the water if you have to, but stay away from him. I mean it."

If a dog can shrug, that's what he did. I knew he understood; I just hoped he could contain himself. As was all too clear from his interactions with pancakes and squirrels, self-control is not his strongest attribute.

The water was only eighteen inches deep, but it was so filled with mud and sand that you couldn't see more than an inch under the surface, especially with the reeds and grass scattered throughout. I was effectively invisible, a mask of mud covering my face, only my nose and slitted eyes above water. I lay motionless in the steaming muck, the smell of salt and slime and rotting vegetation overwhelming my senses. A small fish, or at least I hoped it was only a fish, swam into my right ear, examined it for a while, and departed. I could feel things stirring in the mud underneath me. I didn't want to know what they were.

By this time, the raven had recovered and was circling overhead again, but it didn't want to get too close. That was just as well, since a raven's eyesight is a great deal sharper than the average practitioners. I lay there motionless for what seemed like forever. The one thing I hadn't thought through was that my ears were going to be underwater along with the rest of me, muffling all sounds. I could see, but I wouldn't be able to hear Christoph until he was right up on top of me.

In fact, I felt him before I heard him. He was approaching slowly, splashing through the shallow water, and I could feel the current created by his footsteps long before I became aware of any splashing sounds. He was moving cautiously, stopping every few feet to check on his surroundings. He might claim he had no concern about anything I could do, but he was still being careful. Finally he came into view, close enough so that I now could hear faint splashes as he deliberately plodded forward. He stopped ten feet from where I lay hidden, and I could hear Lou snarling ferociously. I cursed silently. He was still too far away.

"Mason, Mason," he said, voice garbled and distorted by the water, which covered my ears. "This is truly pitiful. Is this really the best you can do? What, I'm supposed to be distracted by this poorly hidden collection of rags, fooled into thinking it's you, then you heroically leap out from behind me?"

He had one thing right. Distraction. Hit 'em upside the head with a two-by-four.

He walked up closer, and Lou almost went berserk. If only he would remember to play it safe. Christoph raised his hand, and Lou launched himself, but this time instead of attacking, he dove into the mucky reeds, ducking and scrambling through the muddy water. Good for him. Christoph shrugged and turned slowly around, checking on all sides for danger. Halfway through the turn he stopped, tensed, and then relaxed. He was staring at the area where I had left the dusting of power residue.

"Again, pitiful," he said. "You don't even have enough skill to properly shield your meager talent. I bend over to attack your supposed hiding place, and you strike from behind, from your true place of concealment? Is that how you imagine it? The sneak attack. That does seem to be a hallmark of yours."

Only when I can get away with it, I thought grimly.

"I would like to know how you pulled that stunt with the wolves, though," he continued. "Got to admit, that surprised me." He wasn't the only one.

His back was now turned to where I lay hidden under the clothes. As he spoke, he backed farther away from where the residue lingered, ignoring the supposed phony hiding place he had sussed out so cleverly. Another two feet and he would step right on me. He still wasn't even close to having his full power back, but he had enough left to pull off some mighty impressive shit. He raised both arms to the sun and spoke a phrase in what sounded like Latin. Not a fan of Latin, myself. On his right ring finger he wore a silver band set with a large crystal, something I had never consciously noticed. My lack of attention to detail was going to get me killed someday. But not today.

The ring flashed and the entire area in front of him where I supposedly was hiding erupted in flame, including the water. Neat trick, that. It went up with a loud whoosh, effectively masking the sound I made coming up out of the water behind him. I unlocked the rage I'd bottled up and lunged with a ferocity and speed that would have made any river crocodile proud.

I hit him in the middle of his back, wrapping my arms around him like I was tackling a football dummy, and driving him facedown into the shallow water and mud. It knocked the breath out of him, and when he involuntarily gasped for air, his face was already beneath the water. Immediately he started choking and gagging as the water rushed into his lungs, arching his back in a desperate attempt to reach the now precious air. I shifted my grip to his wrists and pinned him into the mud, jamming my knee between his legs to prevent him from gaining enough footing to throw me off. The water was shallow enough so that I could keep my head above water and still hold him under. He was bucking frantically, desperately, but although his strength as a practitioner was without peer, I was heavier and stronger. In my heart I gloated, remembering Sherwood's plea for help. Talent was no use to him now. He couldn't gesture as long as his arms were pinned and he couldn't speak underwater, especially with lungs filled with water and mud. It was life-and-death as basic as it gets.

A tremendous blow to the head almost knocked me unconscious. His Ifrit had dropped like a stone out of the sky in a kamikaze attack. It dug its talons into my shoulder and started hammering its bill on the back of my head, strong, powerful strikes. The blows rocked me, and I could feel blood starting to flow. There was nothing I could do about it except to hunch my shoulders up and duck my head down. If I let go of Christoph for even a moment, I was dead.

Then I felt a scrabbling on my back as four small paws dug for purchase. Lou scrambled right up my back as if I were a tree and the raven a particularly egregious squirrel. The other Ifrit tried to escape and gain altitude for another attack, but it had only risen a few feet when Lou catapulted off my shoulder and through the air, catching one of the raven's wings. I heard a crunch as he bit down and they both plunged into the water, snarling and squawking.

By this point, Christoph's struggles had grown ever more violent, almost toppling me over. Suddenly, shockingly, the struggles ceased. I knew there was a chance he was playing possum as a desperate last resort. That's what I would have done. But I couldn't help it; I instinctively relaxed, just a fraction, out of reflex. Sure enough, he twisted around, almost breaking my grip, somehow raising his body almost halfway out of the muck. If he'd had a shred of composure left he would have barked out some word of power and this tale would have had a very different ending. But the same mindless survival urge which gave him such ferocious and deadly strength also clouded his thinking. I still had his arms under control so he did the only thing he could, operating in blind desperation. He lunged at my throat with bared teeth. I whipped my head away and he missed his spot, teeth sinking painfully but harmlessly into the side of my neck. I dragged him up until we were both on our feet and then threw myself backward, twisting at the last second so his body fell beneath me again. I was gasping with exhaustion, surging with adrenaline, sobbing for air. But I had some, and Christoph didn't. What little he had managed to suck in while fighting whooshed back out in a rush of bubbles as the muddy water flooded his lungs.

His bucking motion grew weaker, then feeble, then ceased altogether. This time I was taking no chances. I held him under for the longest five minutes of my life and when I finally released my grip he just lay there facedown in the slime and ooze. He wasn't playing possum. He wasn't playing anything at all. He was dead.

I straightened up and rolled over onto my knees. His body didn't bob up to the surface; it just lay there submerged like the dead thing it was. His Ifrit had pulled itself onto one of the patches of mud and plants and was perched there shivering, regarding me with hostile eyes. One of its wings was broken, dragging uselessly in the mud. The sun was blazing, but I was shaking uncontrollably in spite of the warmth. Lou had found another little islet where he hunkered down, muddy and bedraggled as the raven.

I reached under the water and pulled Christoph's head out of the muck. His close-cut hair was matted down on his skull and his mouth was full of mud and sea plants. As I pulled him up, mud dripped out of his open mouth and plopped into the water. His eyes stared sightlessly, nothing behind them. The raven uttered a low liquid whistle, unlike anything I had ever heard from a bird, full of grief and longing. I let Christoph's body drop back in the water and lurched to my feet. I staggered three steps into the tangle of reeds bent over, and vomited. When I thought I was done, I straightened up, took two more steps, and then vomited again. And again.

Finally it was over and I stood there, knee-deep in water, legs trembling. I looked out over the salt marsh, where insects swarmed and red-winged blackbirds were singing their distinctive conk-a-ree. Lou was silent, as subdued as ever I had seen him. The Ifrit raven was still vocalizing, making small human-sounding noises like a sobbing child. Being the winner had turned out to be a lot less satisfying than I had imagined. But as they say, consider the alternative.

As I gazed out over the water, the scene began to lose focus, like a film dissolve. Taking its place, growing more substantial every second, a blue water tower squatted beneath gray skies and green trees swayed in the wind. I was back on a hill in San Francisco. Eli ran toward me and enveloped me in a smothering hug. Victor was leaning against a tree, looking pale, holding his head. When Eli finally let go and stepped back, I shivered in the chill wind. Victor nodded approvingly as I stood there, naked and cold, hair matted and covered in mud and slime, still bleeding from a hole in my neck and the rat bites that stippled my legs.

"Well, okay then," he said, giving me the ghost of a smile. "Just so long as you didn't have any trouble."

EIGHTEEN

IT'S BEEN ALMOST FOUR MONTHS SINCE I CAME back, muddy yet triumphant. But no victory comes without cost, and a malaise has sunk in, gnawing at my heart and infecting my life. Everything is gray. Even music, once my saving grace, fails to please.

Each night, I'm visited by nightmares. Sometimes, it's Christoph who gets the upper hand and holds me down under the muddy water with the sky and the sweet precious air just inches out of reach. Louie sits on a grass hummock, tail wrapped neatly around his feet, sedately watching. Mostly though it's an endless replay: Christoph struggling under my merciless hands, the salt smell of rotting vegetation, me squeezing harder and harder, until I wake up sweating with hands clenched tightly in tangled sheets.

Worse still are the ones of Sherwood. I never dream of that final moment as she held out an imploring hand. Instead, we're together again, sitting at a café, happy, laughing, relieved that her death was only a dream, or just some terrible misunderstanding. Then I wake, and for a moment that feeling of massive relief bleeds over into my waking self. A split second later, I realize it was no dream at all. She really is dead. And each time I relive the sorrow and loss all over again.

Eli dropped by a couple of times but didn't try to lift my mood. He just talked about everyday things, giving me time to pull myself out of my funk in my own way. Grief over Sherwood was a given, but surprisingly I was disturbed by Christoph's death as well. I discovered that killing another human being with your bare hands, even one who so richly deserved it, will eat at you. Eli listened gravely, then simply said, "I'd be worried about you if it didn't."

We spent some time discussing the crystalline creatures I had seen in the makeshift tunnel lab. The day after my duel with Christoph, Eli and Victor had traveled to Point Bonita looking for answers, but there was nothing left there. Some magical residue where the door in the tunnel had been, but that was it.

"How do you suppose Christoph hooked up with those things in the first place?" I asked him.

"I don't know that he did," he said. "Christoph wasn't much of a practitioner, when you come right down to it. He did manage to acquire an impressive amount of power, but like a second-rate athlete pumped up on steroids, when it came to crunch time he didn't quite know what to do with it all."

"Lucky for me."

Eli smiled. "Not all luck, I suspect. Anyway, I think maybe he didn't find them—I think maybe he created them in some way, as helpers. He certainly wouldn't have wanted another practitioner to know what he was up to."

"I don't believe it. He wasn't that good."

"No, but if they weren't truly alive, if they were just constructs, he could have pulled it off with nothing but raw power. I just hope they don't resurface one of these days."

We left it at that. I'm ashamed to say I didn't much care. As long as they were gone, that was fine with me. Left alone is well enough.

Things with Campbell were not going well. I hadn't spoken much to her about the fight with Christoph, but I

know she got the entire story in detail from the ever helpful Victor. She knew all the things Christoph had done. She
had seen poor Moxie firsthand. She knew full well
Christoph had left me no choice. She didn't blame me in
any way for doing what clearly had to be done and was
never anything but supportive.

But still, she looked at me differently. There was a hes-
itancy in her skin whenever I touched her. No matter what
intellect has to say, emotions often speak a different story.
Campbell was a healer. I was a killer. Of course, her feelings about it weren't that simple; feelings never are.
Maybe if we'd had a longer history together I could have
talked to her about it, but we didn't. I've never been good
at opening up to women anyway.

Without really meaning to, we started seeing less of
each other. The reasons weren't clear. Maybe my guilt
about Sherwood's death had something to do with it.
Maybe what I'd done to Christoph had changed me more
than I wanted to admit. Or maybe it was just that I wasn't
the easiest person to be around these days.

Even Lou, usually so constant, was spending more time
away from me. Other than that, he went about life as if
nothing had ever happened. Just like a real dog, he has the
enviable ability to live completely in the present. I wasn't
that lucky—every time he was gone longer than expected, I
worried. I'm not sure if I was worried something else would
happen to him or if I still feared that one day he'd simply
up and leave. But if he left, he left. It's not like I owned him.

I was still playing gigs, but only because I had to. Victor would have lent me enough money to tide me over, but
I'd live out of my van before I put myself in debt to him.

Then, slowly, almost imperceptibly, my mood started to
lift. The weather improved; the winter rains finally ended and
the summer fog hadn't yet started. It even seemed possible I
might someday resume at least the semblance of a life.

On a whim, I decided to drive up to see Campbell.
Maybe it was time to straighten things out, for better or
worse. A surprise visit to a quasi-girlfriend is seldom the

most brilliant of ideas, especially when there's been some relationship trouble. You're liable to find more than you'd bargained for. But occasionally, it's not such a bad idea. At least you find out where you stand.

The trip up to Soda Springs was beautiful, a far cry from the first time I had driven there. Lou stuck his head out the open window despite the chill mountain air of early April. A layer of snow still covered the ground as we neared the summit, but the sky was a sparkling blue and random patches of brown and green peeked out from under slowly melting snowbanks. It was midafternoon before I pulled up the driveway leading to her cabin and saw her Land Cruiser sitting in the driveway. That was a relief—I would have felt foolish if I'd driven all the way up there only to find she was out for the day.

When I knocked on the front door, it opened almost immediately, as if Campbell had been expecting me. Or someone. The welcoming smile never left her face, but it slowly morphed into something subtly different—a fondness mixed with sad resignation. Well, I'd wanted an honest reaction. That's when I finally understood that it was beyond repair. I can't say I was surprised.

We talked for a while over tea, mostly about inconsequential things. Lou curled up in her lap, oblivious. She poked him gently in the ribs.

"He's gained a pound or two," she said.

I looked at him with a critical eye. It was true, but it had happened so gradually that I hadn't noticed.

"Not enough exercise. No more monsters to fight."

"Thank God."

"You mean Goddess, don't you?"

The joke fell flat. It always had. I smiled ruefully and she smiled back, a bit sadly.

"So," she said.

"So," I agreed. We both drank our tea.

Nothing more explicit was ever said; there were no sad good-byes or teary accusations. I think both of us still hung on to a vague "maybe someday" hope, but we knew that for now it was over.

On the way back to the city, Lou curled up on the passenger seat and slept, one paw over his muzzle. By the time I reached the Bay Bridge, it was full dark and the buildings along the San Francisco skyline glowed brightly, etched with glittering lines of twinkling light.

I felt sad, naturally, but not with that sick feeling of devastation I had feared. I still had my music. I still had my friends. I had the city. I glanced down at the small figure blithely dreaming away on the front seat. Campbell might be gone, but I still had Lou. Of course, he's just a dog. Sort of.

ABOUT THE AUTHOR

John Levitt grew up in New York City. After a stint at the University of Chicago, he traveled around the country and ended up running light shows for bands in San Francisco. Eventually, he moved to the Wasatch Mountains and worked at a ski lodge in Alta, Utah. After a number of years as a ski bum, he joined the Salt Lake City Police Department, where for seven years he worked as a patrol officer and later as an investigator. His experiences on the job formed the background for two mystery novels, *Carnivores* and *Ten of Swords*. For the last few years, he has split his time between Alta, where he helps manage the Alta Lodge, and San Francisco. When he's not working or writing, he plays guitar with the SF rock band the Procrastinistas and also plays the occasional jazz gig. He owns one cat and no dogs, although his girlfriend has three.

He is currently at work on the sequel to *Dog Days*.